ON THE T

Again David can ... ing the annoying message he had programm... for just such an occasion:

ACCESS DENIED, STUPID.

Why would such a small company in backwater Maine need all this computer security? Or could it be—remotest of remote possibilities which only the most brazen of the brain cells lining David's vast ego could have dared suggest—that some as yet unidentified bug in his system was causing this? Naw, he thought, canceling the thought before it even fully emerged. His system was bulletproof.

David should have known better than to test karma like that. As soon as he had his arrogant thought, the gods of cyberspace hurled their lightning bolts at him in the form of a message on his screen. It was from his new nemesis, the ghost in the machine, the hacker—and it screamed at him:

WE'LL MEET SOON.

NIGHT CRIES

SIGNET ONYX (0451)

SPELLBINDING PSYCHOLOGICAL SUSPENSE

☐ **THE RED DAYS by Stephen Kimball.** A brilliant mix of high-tech suspense and old-fashioned gut-churning action, this dazzling thriller will keep you riveted until its final provocative twist. "A tense story of eerie terror."—Ronald Munson (176839—$4.99)

☐ **GRACE POINT by Anne D. LeClaire.** When Zoe Barlow moves to the coastal town of Grace Point to make a new start of her marriage, she never dreamed of what was to await her. Her son suddenly disappears, and there is no one to trust as Zoe searches desperately, stumbling through a generation-old legacy. Chilling erotic suspense. . . . "A gripping novel of love, lust, ancient sins and deadly secrets." —Judith Kelman (403959—$5.99)

☐ **NO WAY HOME by Andrew Coburn.** Filled with insight and irony, this electrifying thriller blends roller-coaster action with the sensitive probing of men and women driven by private demons of love and hate, need and desire. "Extremely good . . . vivid . . . one of the best suspense novels."—*Newsweek* (176758—$4.99)

Price slightly higher in Canada

Buy them at your local bookstore or use this convenient coupon for ordering.

PENGUIN USA
P.O. Box 999 – Dept. #17109
Bergenfield, New Jersey 07621

Please send me the books I have checked above.
I am enclosing $__________ (please add $2.00 to cover postage and handling). Send check or money order (no cash or C.O.D.'s) or charge by Mastercard or VISA (with a $15.00 minimum). Prices and numbers are subject to change without notice.

Card #__________ Exp. Date __________
Signature__________
Name__________
Address__________
City __________ State __________ Zip Code __________

For faster service when ordering by credit card call **1-800-253-6476**

Allow a minimum of 4-6 weeks for delivery. This offer is subject to change without notice.

NIGHT CRIES

Stephen Kimball

SIGNET
Published by the Penguin Group
Penguin Books USA Inc., 375 Hudson Street,
New York, New York 10014, U.S.A.
Penguin Books Ltd, 27 Wrights Lane,
London W8 5TZ, England
Penguin Books Australia Ltd, Ringwood,
Victoria, Australia
Penguin Books Canada Ltd, 10 Alcorn Avenue,
Toronto, Ontario, Canada M4V 3B2
Penguin Books (N.Z.) Ltd, 182–190 Wairau Road,
Auckland 10, New Zealand

Penguin Books Ltd, Registered Offices:
Harmondsworth, Middlesex, England

First published by Signet, an imprint of Dutton Signet,
a division of Penguin Books USA Inc.

First Printing, November, 1995
10 9 8 7 6 5 4 3 2 1

Printed in the United States of America

PUBLISHER'S NOTE
This is a work of fiction. Names, characters, places, and incidents either are the product of the author's imagination or are used fictitiously, and any resemblance to actual persons, living or dead, events, or locales is entirely coincidental.

This book is dedicated to
Cindy, Pete, and Michael,
if they want it.

With thanks to Jennifer Enderlin,
Laura Sievert King, Ed Stackler,
Stone Young, and WHFS-FM

Lullaby, baby, what's that in the hay?
The neighbor's kids cry but mine are gay.
The neighbor's kids are dressed in dirt:
Your silks are cut from an angel's skirt.

—Bertolt Brecht,
Mother Courage and Her Children

1

This was always a good time, after a killing. I was calm and wary, satisfied and hungry, all at the same time. It was a fine evening, warm for February in Maine. The feel of the truck bucking under me on the small hole-pocked road was pleasant, stimulating. I listened for the sound of the body bouncing in the back of the truck but I could hear nothing. It was weighted down nicely.

It was always good after a killing. But tonight it was especially good. I could feel it.

I drove at the speed limit out of town for miles, deep into lake country. The night was black and implacable, hiding danger. There were no streetlights out here, no signs to guide one. I sat straight, watchful, as the road rushed up at me like a dagger, ripping at the curtain of fog rising from the thousands of creeks and ponds. Wind whipped through wide-open windows in the truck's cab. Dank, bitter forest smells swirled in my nostrils. My skin vibrated as if electricity were running through my veins.

How much time had gone by since I left town? I'd lost track. I was well into the bog country north of Penobscot Bay. The forest was close, the fog thick and low. It reflected the headlights back at me, encasing me in a cocoon of light. I imagined the truck as a plane flying low through a cloud bank or a ride in an amusement park. The outside world, with all its ugliness, was gone, evaporated. I felt free, lighter than air, detached from the earth. I couldn't remember a more exhilarating sensation.

Despite the fog I knew exactly where I was. I'd passed the turn-off to Ellsworth a while back, a place where ancient

Indian graves had been discovered. The Indians had seen the forest for what it was: a vast place of death. They knew of the violence and decay on which the forest thrived, of the huge rotting logs pocked from the relentless mushrooms, the savage struggle among animals and plants, the large earthworms and tiny nematodes that drilled their way through the fallen animal carcasses melting into the soil. Long ago the Indians discovered that life feeds on death. They celebrated the fact.

Death was very much on my mind right now, had been for months. But tonight was different, special. Up until now the murders had all been done according to plan. I was told to start out with the easy ones—old folks, there were plenty of them around—and the sick, feeble, outcasts, and loners, anyone who wouldn't be missed. Every town had its share of them, especially this one. A lot of them, people would be glad they were gone. Every time it was the same: I would be told who to kill and when.

Lately the stakes had gone up. Now we were getting rid of anyone in the way, including traitors and their families. I would have to make some adjustments in my methods.

My role could be compared to that of a surgeon's, methodically removing dead tissue from a patient's limbs. But I was content with humbler comparisons, like that of a street sweeper or garbage collector. Yes, a garbage collector, removing the trash.

So far the plan was working. Everyone they wanted removed I had done so cleanly, without trouble. We were getting away with murder.

But something was happening to me. The further along I went with the plan, the more I realized its limitations. I'd been given strict orders to collect only those they told me to go after, to follow the plan to the letter. Obey orders like a good soldier, they said, and everything would work out fine. So I listened when they talked, did what I was told to do. I quietly tolerated months of not questioning or being asked my opinion.

I got tired of their plan. I saw it for what it was: puny, slow, and ignorant. Things were going at a snail's pace.

There was no room for creativity or immediate decisive action if an opportunity presented itself to me.

Like tonight. There I was, earlier, on my way home just as Lorton Theroux, a drunkard, was leaving his favorite bar. In a second I knew it was him. He lived alone, no real friends other than other drunks who probably forgot about him the moment he left their company. I'd had my eye on him for quite a while. He was dirty and disgusting, a perfect candidate for removal. I knew what had to be done.

But Theroux was not part of the plan.

Oh, I could've reported back to the timid fools I worked for and they could have taken days, weeks, making up their dim minds to do anything. Meanwhile, an opportunity would have been lost, possibly forever.

At that moment it was clear to me, clearer than anything I'd ever known: to hell with them. The time had come for me to strike out on my own. Destiny was calling. I knew that things would never be the same again. I could never go back to the old way, as a mindless servant of their plan.

I knew where Theroux lived, so I quickly turned my car around and headed home to pick up the truck, specially rigged for such occasions. I went immediately to Theroux's house and scouted the area. He was so drunk he'd probably get lost once or twice before getting there. There'd been several times when I entertained the thought of killing him, but I never actually planned it out as thoroughly as the others I'd done before. I wasn't a spontaneous person.

I knew Theroux's place well, an old lobsterman's house near the center of town. I parked a block over the hill behind an abandoned storage shed and took up position in a grove of young spruces along his front walk. The streetlight nearest Theroux's house was out, had been for months. The only thing it gave off was a buzzing noise that surged and quieted like cicadas as the electricity running through it vibrated the filaments in the dead bulb. Power fluctuations, we were getting a lot of them lately. Theroux's next-door neighbor, an old woman named Grout, had gone to bed hours ago like most people in the town. The darkness was nearly total.

A fog was slipping in off the bay, wrapping itself around

me as I bent down on one knee among the spruces. A light rain had fallen earlier, spawning a garden of yellow mushrooms that leeched over the tree bark. We were having one of those odd warm spells that Maine sometimes gets in February. The smell of decay and wet garbage was heavy in the air, rising from the soil and soul of this rotting little town.

The next stage—the waiting—was the best and worst part. Best in the sense that it was so tremendously exciting, the anticipation of the kill, of taking ultimate power into my hands. Worst in that I had to confront the flood of awful possibilities coming at me from everywhere at once, the many things that could go wrong. What if I failed? What would happen if I was caught? Would I spend my life in prison? My greatest fear was locking up, of getting caught in the middle of such extremes and being unable to act.

So I focused on the mechanics. I looked in my hand at the instrument I held there. The knife, hefty and solid, felt good in my hand. It was a fine specimen, the product of a great deal of searching. I had considered several makes of knives—Henckels, Sabatier, and Wilkinson Sword—before settling on this one. And then there were so many types to choose from: the boning knife, slicer, and utility knife, to name just a few.

My selection was the Wüsthof-Trident chef's knife, an excellent value. It was the top of its class, with a ten-inch blade of hot-drop forged high-carbon chrome molybendum-vanadium stainless steel, edge razor sharp, and polypropylene handles bonded by nickel-silver rivets. The chef's knife was long and heavy enough to completely pierce most body types, even those thick from time or indulgence.

The grip was very important. Most people think the proper way to hold a knife is flat in the palm, with the blade coming out on the thumb side, and to thrust from the chest. But this grip can be easily deflected by the victim and gains nothing from gravity. I held the knife in the power thrust position, with my hand in a fist and the blade extended from the pinky end. From my kneeling position I would bring it down on Theroux like a pitcher throwing a fastball. A single thrust to the kidneys would take him out instantly. A few more thrusts—to the lungs and heart—would finish the job.

I waited silently, feeling the chilly dampness of the earth seeping into my joints. Best not to think about it. Instead I reflected on the milestone that tonight represented. After four months to the day since I had done my first killing—way back last October—I was finally free. That seemed like a lifetime ago, so much had happened in the meantime. But it was strange how vividly I could recall it: the sight of the woman's bare neck, beckoning me, in the dim light of her parlor. The firm, moist sound of the blade piercing muscle, tendons, and, finally, arteries before the last sigh and sag of the body. The delicate taste of the blood spraying lightly over my teeth as I worked the knife in deeper.

They say one's first killing is the most difficult, like a first act of fornication or adultery. It is no small matter—philosophically or technically—to kill another human being. Unless you're born without a conscience, you have to overcome the qualms or misgivings that can haunt you, even cause you to waver and make a mess of it the first few times out. What you have to do is discipline yourself like a soldier who is trained to see his enemy as a threat and an object. I couldn't very well look on an old woman as a threat, but I had no trouble seeing her as an object: garbage to be removed, useless, worthless trash occupying a place better left empty.

I found the technical problems more difficult to overcome. It took me two or three times out before I learned exactly what I had to do. The first one went well enough; I found the carotid artery on the first cut. But the second one was not as precise and clean. I looked everywhere with my knife for those kidneys, searching high and low as the piece of garbage writhed over the floor like a salted slug, screaming and begging for its life. At least we were in a secluded place, with no one there to hear the screams. I was relieved when the whole thing was over.

With time the killings did become easier.

So now, with seven to my credit, I was prepared for Theroux. I could hear the garbage as it shuffled up the street, wheezing and humming under its breath. It came closer, that repulsive wheezing growing louder. I flexed my grip on the knife several times and planted my feet in the soft earth.

I could make out the stooped silhouette through the trees. The garbage cast its shadow over my face. I took one last look up and down the narrow street. Nothing moved except shards of fog around a streetlight, flickering like a dying star two blocks away. I leaned forward and slowly raised the Wüsthof. A light wind rippled through the town, rustling the trees.

Theroux looked up just as I pounced, the blade slicing through what was left of his liver and part of a kidney. I felt every part of myself, each strand and fiber in my body, working in savage unison. And then I saw something I'd never seen before, a picture of myself that had never occurred to me. I actually saw my entire being—my body, my mind—as a knife.

The second and third thrusts followed immediately, hitting him higher in the back, puncturing a lung and then the heart. Theroux's body, riddled now with holes, somehow remained standing for several moments, teetering from side to side.

It sank slowly to its knees and then back into a sitting position. I watched as it sat there for seconds, minutes, its eyes still open, vaguely bewildered. It seemed to have woken up for the first time in years, ironically, seconds before its death. Finally, the garbage collapsed, falling forward in a heap from the weight of its head.

Loading the trash into the truck was not a simple job, but one made easier through experience. Normally I didn't need to clean up after a killing. People hired by the ones I worked for were dispatched to take care of any mess and, of course, the garbage itself. But because I'd taken on this job on my own initiative, I couldn't count on that service and would have to see the whole thing through, mess and all. I quietly brought the truck around and backed it behind the spruces.

In the back of the truck I had rigged a winch with ropes attached to heavy canvas drop cloths. As simple as it was, this setup required considerable work on my part. I had to wrap the garbage in canvas, heaving and pulling the dead weight, lifting it part by part—the midsection hefty from the beer and whiskey—and straining my muscles into all sorts of pulls and spasms. Pure torture.

If that wasn't bad enough, I also had to guide the trash into the truck and arrange it, taking care to cover it entirely under more drop cloths, wrapping it like a mummy. The canvas was lined with plastic to catch the blood that was rapidly leaking from the holes in Theroux's body. While I was there under the spruces, in the darkness with no one around, I took care of a small piece of business: I wrapped athletic weights around his ankles and wrists. Careful not to scratch the truck, I filled Theroux's pockets with solid iron wood-chopping wedges.

I was ready to go, to dump this garbage.

As I drove through the night, I thought of that poem on the Statue of Liberty. I had to memorize it in school. It goes:

> Give me your tired, your poor, your huddled masses yearning to breathe free, The wretched refuse of your teeming shore, Send these, the homeless, tempest-tost to me.

And let me kill them.

I found the small path in the forest I knew so well, just large enough for the truck. I followed it through the fog until the ground began to give way to the marshy bog near Molasses Pond. Branches scraped the sides of the truck.

Suddenly, from nowhere, a powerful bright light seemed to explode in the dark and reach out for me through the window. I heard someone screaming wildly and then realized it was me. I stomped on the brake, and the truck skidded to a stop into a wall of thorns. I could not take my eyes from the light. It glowed hypnotically in the middle of the marsh, twenty or thirty yards away, hovering in the blackness.

What was it? A fire? No, impossible with all this rain. Had someone found me? What would I tell them? Had they found the other garbage I had left here?

I squinted at the light and then realized what it was, nothing more than combusted marsh gas, an ignis fatuus, a will o' the wisp. They were common out here, especially on nights like these. I must have been jumpier than I had realized. I let out a sigh of relief and drove on a bit farther.

The ground was becoming loose and wet and beginning to give under the tires. I knew I had gone far enough. I eased onto the brake and shifted out of gear, leaving the lights on and the motor running. Molasses Pond was near, inches away in the darkness. I could smell the stink of it. Had I driven any farther, I might have ended up in it.

I opened the door and let my legs stretch as I stepped out onto the mushy ground. I threw open the tailgate and inspected the garbage in its canvas and plastic shroud.

"Want some company?" *I asked it.* "There're others waiting for you in the pond."

Not getting a reply, I tried the winch, but the switch failed to turn the engine over. I tried several more times. Damn thing, probably moisture in a circuit.

I knew what had to be done. I unhitched the rope from the winch and then did my best to pull the body to the edge of the tailgate. I climbed back into the cab, and I began "jumping" the truck by quickly accelerating and braking it in an attempt to dislodge the stubborn garbage. But it wouldn't budge. Goddamn it.

Slowly, very carefully, I backed the truck to the edge of the pond. After making sure that the wheels wouldn't roll on me, I hopped out again, spat on the ground, and marched back to the tailgate. I was resigned to disposing of the trash manually. I planted my feet along the rim of the pond, at the edge of the quickmud there, and began pulling steadily on the drop cloth, my face twisted in a grimace, my lungs heaving. I managed to get the body on its side. With a firm tug from me, it began to roll toward the edge of the tailgate.

Suddenly, Theroux's hand shot out from under the drop cloth and grabbed my wrist. I gagged, punching the hand, pushing the body. The grip tightened as the body hung on the edge of the tailgate.

"Get off," *I screamed.* "Let me go."

Theroux's hand held on as he flopped out of the truck, pulling me into the morass around the pond. The body began to slide through the quickmud and into the pond, with me after it. Black mud rose up my legs with a sucking sound. I clawed his hand, beating it, beating his face under the clear blue plastic. Frantically, I tried to break free as Theroux soundlessly pulled me toward death in the still black water.

Fear invaded my brain: Where was my knife? Could I bite his hand off? How long could I hold my breath under water?

Then the grip began to relax. His strength spent, Theroux let go of me and I shoved him into the water. The blue plastic drop cloth came away from him and floated free out onto the pond. I watched the black water boil as it filled his orifices. Slowly he sank, his bearded face the last part of him to go under and his angry eyes riveted on mine until he dipped below the water's surface and disappeared.

2

It was an anything-can-happen day, thought David McAdam as he ladled his fourteenth scoop of coffee grounds into a filter. The signs certainly were there. Saturn was in retrograde. Sunspots had been reported. And the Gulf Stream had pushed closer to the Maine coast, bringing with it a burst of warm, not entirely pleasant, air.

David gazed dreamily out of his kitchen window. The sky was still dark but the stars had disappeared—the first sign of daybreak. He looked east at the birch woods adjoining his wide yard, which sloped down to a pond and the woods beyond. All night long he had been troubled by a sound—was it a dream?—of hysterical laughter or screaming, he wasn't sure which. The sound seemed to come from the woods or somewhere near there. He shrugged and went back to his scooping, certain that it was nothing more than a dream.

David had lost count of the number of scoops he had put into the filter. He always erred on the side of a stronger pot of coffee. To be safe, he topped out the coffee maker with six more scoops. This particular machine was a Krups Ultra-Brew, an industrial-strength office-type model that could fire up a max of twenty-five hearty cups in a single shot. There were days when David drank that many. He wasn't sure yet, but this could be one of them.

David still had the early morning shakes, the last physically telling vestige of his recovery from alcoholism. That and his caffeine jones. The shakes usually went away after his third or fourth cup. After that it was pure indulgence, force of habit, something to do with his hands. If David was deep into a computer project or was on a deadline like he was now, he could streak through the day on a caffeine buzz that rivaled the worst of his old binges. He knew what he had done, trading down on his addictions like a junkie in methadone treatment.

He gazed hungrily into the coffee maker as the water—pumped automatically through a feed on the faucet—trickled through the dark mound of Jamaican Blue Mountain, a rare arabica he had delivered from Kingston to Portland to Sparks twice a month. If he'd had the presence of mind last night, he could have simply loaded the grounds and pushed a key on one of his PCs. David had created what he called the intelligent house. The utilities and every one of the three hundred or so sundry electronic gadgets and appliances in the house, including the sound system, lawn sprinkler, and washer and dryer, were connected to David's computer network. But he still had to load the grounds for the coffee to brew, and so now he had to wait, subjecting himself to an exquisite torture.

David closed his eyes as he drank in the rich, roasty fragrance beginning to waft through the air. It conjured wonderful images of a Viennese coffee house at mid-morning, newspapers draped on stands, and an array of confections—tortes, strudels, tarts—lovingly displayed under glass. Resting on his marble-topped Biedermeier table and presented on fine bone china was that prince of cakes—the Sacher Torte—with its characteristic glaze of bittersweet chocolate over moist cake and marmalade filling, accompanied by a generous dollop of whipped cream.

And, of course, the coffee. So many varieties of it classified with an almost scientific precision. There was the piquant Brauner, the creamy Weisse, and the protean Mélange—espresso blended with milk, the ratio of coffee to milk adjusted to the drinker's taste and coded on a lightness scale of one to ten. No matter which blend one ordered, it was served steaming hot with a European flourish in scrupulously clean Pyrex cups. In the dream, he raised the cup slowly, with appropriate reverence, to his lips, the aroma filling his nostrils, and felt . . .

. . . something licking his feet? David jumped back and looked down in the same motion to find a shaggy face staring up at him with a pleading expression. It was Cupak, one of their stray dogs numbering variously from three to seven, depending on who met whom the previous night. Nara, David's wife, seemed unable to turn anything away that appeared at the door—animal, mineral, or vegetable. Especially animal. Cupak, named after a figure of gluttony in Balinese mythology, had been the first animal to hop on the gravy train, appearing the day after David and Nara moved into the house.

"What do *you* want?" David said before intuiting the answer to the question. "Oh," he said and opened the kitchen door. Seemingly from nowhere a pack of dogs—some of whom David had never seen before—rushed past him in a frenzy, almost knocking him over, and out the door.

Inured to such moments of madness, David said nothing as he watched the dogs furiously wedge their way through the door. Even if he wanted to say or do something, there was no chance to respond. The timer on the microwave was screaming at him. Why? he wondered. What had he done? Then he remembered: the baby bottle.

Nara and David had a child, a hungry one, who coveted his morning bottle almost as much as David did his coffee. The baby's name was Von, a compromise choice between David, who wanted it to be "John" after John von Neumann (considered by many to be the father of modern computers), and Nara, who countered with "Neumann" because "John" seemed too commonplace. David hedged, believing "Neumann" to be perilously close to "Alfred E." So they settled on "Von." It took Nara a while to come to terms with her firstborn's name even though David tried to comfort her by pointing out that Thomas Edison named his first two children "Dash" and "Dot."

David glanced up at the digital clock built into the wall above the sink. It was 6:54. Time to get into position. With bottle in hand, he picked his way through the cavernous living room with its floor-to-ceiling windows, stumbling on dog and baby toys but careful not to step into any of his collection of gadgets—including the computers, monitors, and keyboards lined up and sitting silently in the darkness—plus a recording-studio-quality sound system, lava lights, karaoke system, strobes, several TVs, VCRs, virtual-reality gloves and headsets, and almost every avatar of laptop, palmtop, and other form of micro-equipment. David had also set up around the house a system of motion-activated videocassette recorders to tape Von's every moment. David scowled at one of the cameras mounted on the living room ceiling that squeaked as it swiveled, but only if one was walking toward the rear of the house.

In the dining room at the other end of the house was his favorite spot at this time of the day, front row center before an eight-feet-wide, four-feet-high picture window that looked down over a cluster of homes. From high above the hill on which his house stood, David could observe the comings and goings of the people of Sparks, Maine, most of whom he did not know or intend ever to get to know.

Since assuming his domestic life, David had picked up a number of bad habits, one of which was snooping. His favorite subjects were a family who lived in the house at the bottom of the hill. David called them the Flintstones. They attracted his attention because he hadn't yet figured them out, their odd comings and goings still a mystery to him after months of observation. Despite his eccentricities and counterculture trappings, David still liked a good challenge. And challenging the Flintstones were.

As best as David could tell, the family consisted of a father—Fred—who came and went at strange hours, a mother, and two small children. Every morning David would see Fred leaving early, before daybreak, and returning late in the evening, sometimes after midnight. David noticed light through their window from a computer screen that was usually on an hour or so after Fred got home. But David never had a clear look at the family—he never even saw Wilma, the wife—and found it odd that they never made the usual weekend appearances neighbors make, like raking leaves or shoveling snow.

In his recent memory, spotty as it was, David could not remember living this close to a stranger. Or to anyone else, for that matter. Moving into this house represented no less than complete acquiescence to Nara's insistence on living modestly, despite their wealth, and close to "civilization." According to Nara's logic, this would give their son as normal an upbringing as possible, given who his father was. One of the reasons David had consented to moving to Sparks was because the sleepy, forsaken little hamlet was generally passed over in the Maine summer tourist crunch.

David would have preferred to have stayed on someplace like the island in the middle of Penobscot Bay that Nara, Toshi, her father, and he had retreated to after leaving Florida. It was one of the many remote properties David had acquired around the world back during his days of acute paranoia while he was still at PanTech, the computer hardware company he had created and built into a powerhouse before he was pushed out by the very people he'd made rich. He had even reinforced his anonymity by using Murata, his wife's name, for public consumption.

David's revisionist nuclear family had set up house in a two-room cabin, the only building on the island. He grew stronger from the outdoor work, Nara's Balinese macrobiotics, and freedom from booze. Nara and he even started talking about having kids. Life was good until that bitter November afternoon when David found Toshi sprawled out at the bottom of one of the island's ravines, clutching his chest.

The massive pane of glass in the dining room picture window felt frozen as David pressed his nose to it. With the elbow of his old green Caltech sweatshirt, he wiped away the condensation fogging the glass. He looked at his watch, surprised that it was already seven. Traces of sunlight began to appear on the eastern horizon, silhouetting the top of the birch woods that ran along the yard. A fine mist, the remains of last night's heavy fog, hung in the air. Patches of acid snow (Sounds like a new street drug, David thought), like wet, raw wool and lingering for what seemed like years, harlequined the yard. Observing the scene, he was reminded of New Age CD covers.

David counted only two houses, far away, with lights on. Hands on his hips, his legs flexing restlessly, he grew impatient. Where *are* you? he said to his burgher, Fred Flintstone. He should have been out by now.

Every now and again, during his few introspective moments at the window, David thought about why he snooped. Was it mere curiosity that drove him to it? Did he harbor some primal need to protect his family by keeping track of those bordering his territory? Or was it something else, something more troubling to him? By observing the humdrum lives of others, was he somehow reassured that their lives were as inert and devoid of adventure as his own?

David's head shot up as he heard a sound. He squinted his eyes and peered out the window into the darkness. He didn't see Nara—her long black hair crackling with static electricity in the dry air—sneaking up behind him and digging her fingers into his sides.

"Yeeow!" David screamed before he landed about five feet away from where he had been standing. "God*damn*it, Nara."

Nara looked at him innocently and pressed her finger against her lips. "Von's still asleep," she whispered. "Do you know you're committing a class D offense—violation of civil privacy—that could get you a year in jail and/or a two-thousand-dollar fine in the state of Maine?" Nara was a writer for a magazine called *The Maine Event*, which reported goings-on around Penobscot Bay. The job had made her an authority on local triva.

"Laws are broken all the time," David said with one eye on Nara and the other on the house at the bottom of the hill. "Look at gravity."

Nara stood on her tiptoes and peered over David's shoulder. "Are you ready for a fashion question?" she said.

"Huh?" he said drowsily.

"I have my interview this morning, and I want you to tell me which boot goes best with this outfit."

David, appreciating the importance Nara attached to her request, gave her his full attention. He remembered that she had scheduled an interview with an older resident of Sparks as part of a story she was doing on three generations of women in the town.

Since leaving Florida, Nara hadn't toned down her taste in clothing a bit. Besides her usual array of earrings, bracelets, and necklaces that made her look like a Yemeni bride, she had on a black satin jacket emblazoned on the back in red with THE SCREAMING TREES WORLD TOUR, black skirt, red stockings, and one metallic green cowboy boot and another red one with mother-of-pearl inlay of saguaros and Mexican ladies. What David did not say to her was that Sparks was at best a provincial backwater and that her costume might just overwhelm whoever it was she was interviewing. Instead, he took the coward's way out and mumbled that both boots looked nice.

Nara smiled and thanked him, inexplicably pleased with his reaction. Before leaving the house she ducked into the living room and switched on the digital display signboard—like the kind grocery stores use to advertise specials—mounted on a pole in the floor. She had programmed the display to run continuous messages for David, such as THAW CASSEROLE FOR DINNER and TRASH COLLECTION DAY . . . REMEMBER TO RECYCLE!, knowing he would forget to do everything if not reminded. As Nara set today's message: LAUNDRY DAY. . . DO NARA'S THINGS SEPARATELY, DELICATE WASH . . . REMEMBER TO ADD ANTI-STATIC SHEET IN DRYER, the letters on the display board flickered on and off.

She went back to David, oblivious as he rubbed his chin and stared out the dining room window. She traced the tip of her nose across his cheek. "See you later," she said and then remembered to add, "David, the signboard seems to be on the blink."

"Huh?" he said.

It was usually at this time of the day that David felt a momentary flash of panic at the realization that he was now in charge of a house, a totally dependent child, and four to seven dogs, some of whom might be rabid. The panic lasted only a few moments and was usually mitigated by a mug or two of coffee. But when would it be ready? David was wondering, looking in the general direction of the kitchen.

He turned and spied someone emerging from the house. It was Fred. Well, yabba-dabba-do. And he was lugging two suitcases that he loaded into the trunk of the family station wagon, turning his head back and forth as if expecting someone to appear and catch him in the act, whatever the act was. David checked his watch again: 7:06.

"Highly irregular, Fred," David said to the man who couldn't hear him. "You're almost ten minutes late today. You're never late. And what's with the suitcases? You never travel." David still could not see the man's face. Taking one last look around, Fred climbed in the driver's seat.

David felt a nibbling at his bare feet and looked down, expecting to find Cupak or one of the other dogs. Instead it was Von who, while teething, had developed a fondness for massaging his aching gums on human flesh. Von, like David, has been feeling miserable for weeks, fighting what David called the *paparazzi* virus—one that was as persistent as it was annoying. Forgetting he had left the bottle on the window sill, David scooped Von up and offered him the soft flesh between his thumb and forefinger, which he hungrily chewed.

"Von," David said, bouncing the little tyke in his arms. "Did you break out of Alcatraz again?"

Von cooed happily. When David looked out the window, the station wagon was gone. Drifting up through the darkness was a sound like a loon laughing demonically, coming from the rushes along the pond separating the house from the woods. Was that what he had heard last night? he wondered. If it *was* a loon, what was it doing here this time of year? He heard the front door slam and, carrying Von, he got to the front bay window in time to see Nara climbing into her Land Rover. He noticed that she had followed his advice concerning her boots: she was wearing the green *and* the red one.

From the living room, David could see that the red light was out on the coffee maker's display, telling him that the pot was ready. At last! He ran into the kitchen, Von still chewing on his hand.

The Jamaican Blue Mountain filled the kitchen with its intoxicating aroma. David could almost taste it. He dug greedily through the cupboards for his favorite mug. Where was the damn thing? He looked down and saw the digital display on the coffee maker grow dim and disappear.

Before David could complete his predictable "What the . . . ," the digital numbers reappeared and then the kitchen ceiling lights flickered wildly. He circled around the room and watched as smoke rose from the back of the coffee maker.

"What the hell is going on?" he said out loud. Von stopped chewing David's hand and pointed a tiny finger at the coffee maker, which was hissing and belching smoke. David turned away and, clutching Von close, dived behind the massive butcher block island in the middle of the room a second before the coffee maker exploded, showering the walls and cupboards with scalding hot coffee.

David quickly checked out Von, who was giggling obliviously. Then he looked up at the steaming Jamaican Blue Mountain washing down over the white countertops and collecting on the floor.

Shit, thought David, I really wanted that coffee.

3

"Very weird," David said incisively as he clicked shut the door to the fuse box hammered into the wall next to the basement stairwell. Everything in there checked out fine—no shorts, burn-outs, or mechanical problems. He wrote off the blowup as incompetence on the part of the local electrical utility. A mass culture trivia buff, David knew that a total of 156 episodes of *Twilight Zone* had been made from 1959 through 1964, not counting the thirty rather insipid episodes made in the early 1980s for nostalgic baby boomers. Right now he felt like he was guest starring in episode 157.

He had spent the better part of his morning cleaning up the fallout in the kitchen. Megs of fun *that* was. He had never seen a power surge like that in his thirty-five years of doing electronics, which he had started at age ten. How much electricity would you need to blow up a mid-sized appliance? he wondered. Four hundred watts? Five hundred?

The average house was wired for 120 to 240 volts. But David knew very well that the quality and consistency of most electrical power was no better than that of tap water. That was why his fortune in electronic gadgetry was protected by phalanxes of surge suppressors, redoubts of line conditioners, batteries of noise protectors, and fail-safe microprocessor-controlled continuous sine wave output that constantly reconstructed the dirty power flowing in from the local utility.

Almost every room in the house had at least one computer in it. The big finished basement where David was now loitering was the core of his network, with a mainframe and fourteen computers linked to the twenty-eight upstairs—PC's, laptops, notebooks, and palmtops, and a computer junkie's trove of peripherals. Some of the basement computers were on, as evidenced by the lights twinkling on their keyboards, soaking up data for David's enthusiasms.

David looked down at the floor under his feet. It was littered with clothes he did not immediately recognize. Little clothes—tiny T-shirts and overalls—like outfits for an off-duty GI Joe. A few feet away in a chilly corner was a steaming mound of white cloths. Diapers. Diapers? It was then that David remembered he had a one-year old child who was skimming toward him on his knees across the floor.

"Ack, Von," David shouted, lifting his baby and tossing him in the air. "Want to play with some semiconductors?"

Von's head jerked up and down in lusty affirmation, and David pulled a fistful of green and red semiconductors from his hip pocket, stuffed them into Von's hands, and put him down on the berber carpet. Before settling down to work at his main terminal, David loaded a bundle of clothes into the washing machine.

He always kept four backup coffee makers in the house—not including an espresso machine and a cappuccino maker—and was able to fire up another pot and shoot down five or eight cups this morning before his shakes became unmanageable. Coffee was also brewing in a machine he kept in the basement. He had plenty to do today, so he had to function. It was Monday and that meant he would be spending his morning doing laundry, making dinner, and playing with Von, and the afternoon at the Downeast Mall up in Rockland. David called it his virtual life. His only connection to reality—real reality—was through his computers.

So, with Von relatively safe—playing cars with the semiconductors spread out on the floor—David sat down at the terminal and computer-surfed, flipping among the projects he was involved with right now. One was a program he had designed for Von, featuring the character Little Beebo.

programmed to look and act like Von. David, always willing to attempt complex, technological resolutions to simple human problems, had created a program in which Little Beebo gives up his bottle, willingly undertakes toilet training, and learns to sleep through the night without waking up, all in a series of colorful, animated vignettes accompanied by music and sound effects (such as the tinkling of urine in the toilet bowl) from high-quality CD-Rom. David was having difficulty trying to figure out a way to show Little Beebo coping with teething.

Another project was far more complex. David was trying to work out the algorithms for a fuzzy logic program an old friend from Silicon Valley, Will Karasik, had sent to him over one of the many external networks to which David's computers were connected. Fuzzy logic is an approach to computing that deals with shades of knowledge and ambiguous information, mimicking the functioning of the human mind more closely than the binary logic commonly used for computing. Will, who owned a start-up software company in Palo Alto, was developing the program for a client—an elevator company—that wanted to use it as a controlling system for elevators in high-rise buildings. He was facing an impossible deadline and had asked David for help.

David was at a stage in the development of the program where he had to create numerical values for linguistic concepts. "Fast," "slow," and everything in between were relative terms to which David was assigning numbers that would guide the computer controlling the elevator's speed throughout the day. Right now he was working through algorithms for determining an elevator's speed during peak periods of the day. But the speed of an elevator isn't always constant throughout the ride, nor is the weight of the passenger load the same for each ride, so he was forced to create additional programming for adjusting speed to the length of the ride and weight of the riders. Many other variables also came into play, further complicating the program and his life.

David slurped coffee and stared hard at the columns of

garbled white numbers, letters, and punctuation, the winged and boxed comments, and the other coded runes of C++, the programming language for fuzzy logic. This particular project would keep a team of crack programmers busy full-time for weeks. David, working on it on and off for three days, had completed about half of it. It would have been easier if he'd had the neural network silicon chip he had special-ordered last week. Now that he had laid much of the mathematical foundations for the program, David found it difficult to give up his Boolean, linear approach to problem-solving and move forward into the gray, plastic, unanchored mind-set of fuzzy logic. He told Nara he'd hit a wall and could probably handle it if he knew where the wall was.

Last night Nara had patiently listened to David's convoluted, feverish condemnations of fuzzy logic. What was it good for anyway? he asked. So what if elevators ran more efficiently? They should just make shorter buildings.

Nara quietly observed that the rules governing fuzzy logic reminded her of Zeno's Second Paradox, in which Achilles spots a tortoise ten paces before racing it. According to the paradox, Achilles can never overtake the tortoise because he must pass through an infinite number of points (a half a pace, a half of a half, a half of a half of a half, etc.) before reaching it. David scoffed at the obvious sophism, but a light came on as he realized through the parable that he had a very wide, if not unlimited, range of numerical values between zero and one, indicating the degree to which an element had "membership" in a fuzzy set.

Nara, a recent graduate in physics and philosophy from Bryn Mawr College, suggested a few books and essays for David to read to help him bend his mind out of its logical, rational framework. One was *The Ethics of Ambiguity* by Simone De Beauvoir ("Unfortunately, she's best known as Sartre's wife," Nara lamented, "but I find her philosophy more useful than his.") Another was *Desire and the Figure of Fun* by Giovanni Ferrari. She also promised to dig through her school papers for some Derrida, De Man, and other deconstructionists. She offered to throw in some hermeneutics and try to find a book of koans and haiku poetry she knew was around somewhere.

Bored with the project, David exited from Internet and logged onto Conspiracy, a game he loved (and had helped create), in which one or several users develop theories for famous riddles or possible conspiracies, such as the JFK assassination, Marilyn Monroe's death, UFO cover-ups, and Deep Throat's identity. David had been playing the game for over a year, using vast storehouses of data he and the others on the network could access (legally or otherwise) to prove their theories or disprove those of others. It had taken the five or so players about ten months to agree on the rules, which read like a manual for a Cray supercomputer.

Von cooed merrily on the floor as David called up the game's network over a modem connecting him to Will, Paul Bolger, a computer freak and owner of the local computer store, Leah Todorovski, a computer scientist at Stanford, and a couple of others. No one on the network responded to David's offer to play, so he began alone. He was trying to push the group to pursue a Unified Conspiracy Theory—the Big Bang, he called it—linking all the major conspiracies. For instance, it was relatively easy to posit a connection between JFK's assassination and Marilyn Monroe's death. But it got a bit strained when he tried to link the building of the pyramids with Jimmy Hoffa's disappearance. David dredged out all the big players in most conspiracy theories—the FBI, the Hanseatic guilds, the Vatican, the Mafia, extraterrestrials, the Translateral Commission.

His pet theory right now (in which he only nominally believed) was that extraterrestrials have been breeding humans, or surrogates, for several centuries and placing them in strategic political, cultural, and scientific positions where they can influence the course of history. Actual people have been "replaced" by the surrogates. According to David's elaborate hypothesis, history's famous conspiracies and riddles were the result of mistakes and power struggles among these surrogates. David's many powerful computers had been going nearly full-time for weeks, combing through files, trying to find possible linkages among the conspiratorial people or events identified by the group. The Holy Grail of his search was the files of the legendary MJ-12, the high-level government organization charged with covering up evidence of alien visitors. So far he'd had no success finding them.

David was about to type into the network a description of some new evidence linking the conspiracies when a buzzing sounded in his ears. His head shot up immediately. Were data coming in on another computer? Or was there a problem, a crash? He stood up and surveyed the keyboards littering the basement floor, searching for a flashing alarm light. Nothing. The buzz didn't really sound like a computer alarm. Then he realized what it was: the washing machine.

David groaned. It was bad enough that he had to do the laundry, but his agony was compounded by the fact that the dryer had died, probably at the hands of the infamous power surge. Why hadn't the washing machine crashed instead? David lamented. At least then he'd have had an excuse for not doing laundry at all. Nothing doing. So, for the first time in his life, he had to hang laundry, on the old lines outside he had never taken down since moving in over a year ago. He'd already put up the first load with clothespins Nara had conveniently bought for such a contingency, and he dreaded having to hang another one.

But then he heard another sound, and a smile of salvation spread across his face. The doorbell. He was spared the laundry, if only for a few minutes. He scooped up Von and ran upstairs.

Always reluctant to deal with people other than Nara and Von, David first checked a panel of screens built into the living room wall that showed and recorded activity around the house picked up by hidden video cameras. In one of the screens was Jean Burke, a friend of the family's who came over two or three times a week to baby-sit Von so David could make his pilgrimage to the local mall. David checked the digital clock on the replacement coffee maker: 12:38. How did it get so late? he wondered.

Then something else caught David's eye, a flash of motion in another screen. He watched for a moment and then saw a small animal rooting in the backyard. He looked twice and then once again. If he hadn't known better, he would have sworn it was an armadillo. But that was impossible, wasn't it—an armadillo in Maine?

David raced to the back of the house and peered through his favorite window as the animal scuttled along the split-rail fence near the birch woods. He rubbed his eyes and squinted through the mist. Another thing caught his eye: gaps among the sheets and diapers hanging on the clothesline. Who the hell had stolen his laundry?

He soon got his answer. Coming up behind the armadillo was a small man wearing what appeared to be five or more layers of clothing, including a great coat three sizes too big that dragged on the ground behind him. He was also wearing a canary yellow baseball cap. Almost on top of the armadillo, the man stopped suddenly and, for some reason, looked up at David in the window. Despite the low-lying mist, David got a pretty good look at him. What he saw caused him to gasp out loud.

"Toshi?" David whispered incredulously, seeing the Asian face, with high cheekbones, like Nara's, and the same weathered face and sad, inscrutable eyes. A deep, bittersweet longing gripped David in the chest. A lump of irrational hope lodged in his throat.

"What do you want?" David said to the apparition that couldn't hear him for the distance and windowpane. But it stood still where it had stopped, its eyes locked on David's. "You're supposed to be dead."

Toshi just stood there looking at David, the armadillo escaping into the woods. David felt something pulling at his arm and looked down to see it trembling violently, his nerves in spasm from fear and some kind of alcoholic flashback. He held the arm close to his body and wondered, worried, if he was losing it, if his years of drinking and general dissipation were suddenly catching up with him and he had crossed some invisible line into . . . what? Imagining ghosts and armadillos in his backyard? What was next? Pink elephants and blue dragons?

The sound of an insistent doorbell yanked him away from the window. He scurried to the door where Jean waited, her patience wearing thin.

"Did I get you off the john?" she said sourly before David took her by the hand and pulled her through the house to the back window. "What in the . . ." she managed to say before David threw his hand over her mouth and pointed her at the window.

"Look out there," he whispered, looking at her face. Jean—looking at David looking at her and trying to decide the best way of dealing with a lunatic of his size and weight—gave him an uncomprehending look, her eyes wide and not a little bit fearful. Suddenly realizing the problem, David removed his hand.

"I'm sure the-ah's an explanation for all this." Jean said slowly, a definite edge to her thick Downeast-accented voice.

"Don't you see him?" David asked.

Jean only stared at him. "Who? We-ah?" she said.

David swiveled his head toward the window, banging it on the pane. The sky was a bit lighter than it had been a minute ago, when he last looked. A flock of crows carped at the wind. But there was no armadillo and no Toshi. Where had he gone? Had he ever been there at all?

David felt blood rising up into his face and head. He apologized profusely to Jean, who kept an eye on him even as Von crawled up and planted a gummy kiss on her ankle. David noticed that his hands were shaking uncontrollably, and he thrust them into his pockets.

Jean bent down, smiled, and sang, "The-ah's my little man," as she lifted Von up and carried him into the kitchen. David lingered at the window a bit longer, staring hopefully into the birches. The backyard was emptier than he had ever seen it before.

In the kitchen, Jean put on the teakettle and the *Sid Bromley Show* on cable TV. Bromley, as close to a celebrity as Sparks could produce, hosted a daily program in which he launched kamikaze raids on his guests' egos. Today's topic was couples who could have sex only in unusual places.

"What do you think of him?" Jean said, not taking her eyes off Sid Bromley as he introduced a guest. "You think he's wearing a rug?"

"What I don't understand," David said, pouring coffee and sitting down at the table, "is where they get the people who appear on these shows. I mean, look at them, trotting out their deepest, dirtiest secrets for all the world to see and then taking unholy abuse from this jerk."

Jean shushed David with a wave of her hand, and they watched Sid Bromley for a while as he picked away at a young couple who'd made love in every exhibit at the trolley museum near Kennebunkport. They were absolutely convinced that this was healthy and normal behavior until Sid went to work on them, badgering them, calling them everything from perverts to criminals. Soon Sid was victorious, having completely unnerved them, the wife in tears and the man screaming obscenities at the top of his lungs. The studio audience loved it.

David putzed in the kitchen. Out of the corner of his eye he saw chairs flying across the stage of the *Sid Bromley Show*. He did his best to ignore it. Looking over at Jean holding Von, David saw that she was in her usual flannel shirt that was rolled up, showing forearms twice the size of David's. Jean was proud of her independence—she had put an addition on her house herself and could repair anything. The widow of a lobsterman-turned-lighthouse keeper and a tough fifty-two years old, she now spent her days as curator of the town's tiny Lobster Museum and baby-sitter for Von, whom she loved as if he were her own. David was always happy to see her, since she gave him a chance to get away from the house for a bit and catch up on things that interested him. As she rocked Von in her arms, she complained about the rheumatism in her back, which was flaring up today. Von fell asleep almost immediately.

"You know, David," Jean said softly, her eyes on the TV, "I think you should be on *Sid Bromley*."

"What?" he said, reacting like a deer to the smell of gun metal.

"You'd make a good guest. A househusband, a man who lives off his wife's earnings and takes care of the kid at home. I don't think Sparks has ever seen the likes of it before."

David had to beat down a virulently defensive rise welling up from his guts. Jean, of course, had no idea that David was independently wealthy beyond her wildest imaginings. It had never occurred to her that a journalist, like Nara, working for a small magazine, could never support three people living in a house like theirs with all the *things* they had. He let it pass but felt the need to explain the philosophy of his new lifestyle.

"Remember John Lennon?" David said, absently pouring his twelfth cup of coffee of the day, "how he did the chores and raised Sean in their Dakota apartment while Yoko handled 'the world?' I'm like him. I don't care what the world thinks. I go my own way."

"Mmm," Jean said either diffidently or sarcastically, David wasn't sure which. She rose from her chair, sniffing the air. "What happened, you burn coffee in he-ah?"

"Jean, let me ask you something," David said carefully. "You come from around here. What would you make of a family—neighbors of yours—whose father leaves the house before sunup and doesn't get home until midnight some nights and then stays up all hours, whose kids never play outside in the yard, and whose mother may or may not exist?"

Jean fixed a stern stare at him. "Are these *your* neighbors you're talking about?" she said reproachfully.

David looked away. "Well, yeah," he stammered, wondering what he was stammering about.

The stare turned into a glare. "You should be ashamed of yourself," she began, "poking your nose into other people's business. Think about what you're doing, invading someone's home, stealing their privacy. How would you like it if the telescope was turned around, pointed at you?

People might think *you* were pretty strange, don't you think?"

Telescope, David thought. That sounds interesting.

Jean wasn't quite done. "And another thing. Ever he-ah the story of Peeping Tom? He was caught stealing a look at Lady Godiva when she rode down the street on that horse, and you know what they did to him? I have half a mind to report you to the sheriff."

Without waiting for a reply, she lifted Von from his high chair and carried him upstairs. David headed to the basement to shut down his computers. He switched off the fuzzy logic project and Little Beebo. About to turn off the Conspiracy game, David was surprised to see that someone had responded to his query to play. But something was wrong: whoever had logged on was not one of the regular players.

Is this a joke? he wondered. And then he realized: he'd broken into enough computers in his time to know a hacker when he saw one. And this one was good, very good. David's was a closed network, and the security protecting it was just about impervious to hackers. Or so he thought. David wondered how he got in.

David scanned the many elements of Conspiracy, expecting the hacker to have wiped out the game, but he found nothing wrong. The only anomaly was a single message where David left off inputting the conspiracy evidence he cooked up. The message read:

LOOK NO FURTHER THAN YOUR OWN BACKYARD

"What?" David said out loud. "Look for what?" Just then he heard a child's plaintive crying on the small plastic Fisher Price baby monitor perched atop the Conspiracy CPU. He'd forgotten he left the monitor on.

The child cried out again, louder this time. "Von?" David said. He stumbled to his feet and ran all the way upstairs to Von's room. There, in the center of the crib, cozily tucked in a white blanket, was his son, fast asleep. Like a defused bomb, David thought. Next to the crib sat Jean, watching Von from the rocking chair.

"What's wrong with Von?" David said, out of breath.

Jean looked up slowly, her eyes out of focus and an expression of rapture on her face from watching Von.

"What?" she said drowsily.

"Von. I just heard him crying on the baby monitor."

Jean fixed her hard stare at him again, secretly wondering if she was safe in assuming David was really all right after his erratic display downstairs. "I've been right he-ah since he fell asleep, and I haven't heard a peep out of him," she insisted.

David stood for a moment, nodding dumbly. What was there to say? He shuffled down the stairs, distracted. The sound on the monitor hadn't been static or radio interference. It was definitely a child. But whose child? Where? And how did it get on his monitor?

At the bottom of the stairs he realized: it just might do him some good to get out of the house for a while.

4

The Downeast Mall lay about midway between the towns of Rockland and Camden on U.S. One skirting Penobscot Bay. David usually took Highway 131 north to connect with Route One. But today, on a whim, he went in a different direction to old 73, a small secondary road he'd taken maybe once since moving to Sparks.

As he approached Route One, David marveled at the thought that he used to cross this very highway at its nearly southernmost point in the Florida Keys to get to Toshi's bar from David's island home. Now he was about three hours away from the *northern*most end of Route One at Fort Kent, Maine, on the Canadian border.

Toshi. Damn him, anyway, haunting David like this, refusing to go away, to become simply a memory. David wondered if he'd been working too hard lately, if his three-hours-of-work-a-day schedule was too rigorous.

To get onto Route One, David would have to pass through the town of Sparks, one of a string of tourist traps, forgotten villages, and ragged havens dotting the southern end of Penobscot Bay. Sparks was virtually surrounded by tangled veins of creeks and rivers that fed the countless lakes and ponds and, finally, the ocean. Mysterious proto-Algonquin tribes had begun settling the area around the first century A.D., about the time the Vikings cruised the Maine coast. Centuries later the cold, rocky bay attracted Breton, Basque, and Portuguese fishermen who plied it long before the days of John Cabot, Henry Hudson, and other Age of Exploration luminaries.

Sparks got its name from an obscure incident in 1667—

during the skirmishes preceding the French and Indian Wars—when a ship in the fleet of Sir Edmund Andros, then governor of New York and Massachusetts, on its way to remove the unscrupulous Baron de St. Castin from his Penobscot power base, fired a cannon round at a small French outpost that turned out to be an armory and powder store. It was said that the spectacular fireworks erupting from the explosion—lighting up the pre-dawn sky at the mouth of Penobscot Bay and depositing cascades of sparks hissing over the water's surface—rallied the British crews and carried them to victory over the French irregulars. On his way back from the battle, the triumphant Andros established a town over the still smoldering ashes of the outpost that cartographers later named Sparks.

Never again, it seemed, did Sparks recover the glory of its founding. In the 1990s, it was one of the region's forgotten hardscrabble villages, marginally distinguished by its Lobster Museum, attracting maybe eighty people a year—mostly wayward tourists and local school children on field trips—and its diner known among truck drivers for its "blasberry" pie, a semi-viscous concoction of blueberries, raspberries, and egg custard. Sparks was also the home of the Country Customs Company, a mail-order business specializing in New England crafts.

But other than those mediocre landmarks, Sparks had little to speak of. If you needed to mail a parcel, the nearest post office was down in Tenants Harbor. If you got sick, the closest hospital was the Penobscot Bay Medical Center up in Rockland. If you died, your next of kin, if you had any, would have to ship your remains to the undertaker in Owls Head.

David thought of Sparks as one of thousands of small towns holding on for dear life to the tailcoats of the American Dream. In their mouths was the bitter dust of the cities passing them by as the vanguard of the nation. Sparks was a nervous, fatalistic place, unsure of its past but grudgingly certain of its future as an atavism, a relic, surely going the way of the farms and rural America as nothing more than a backdrop for the cities.

David spun Toshi's black 1966 Ford truck past weatherbeaten lobster shacks huddled along the mouth of the bay and absently turned on the radio. Since Toshi's death David had developed a taste for big band music, Toshi's favorite. Nara, always the insightful one, observed that listening to big band was David's way of keeping Toshi alive. David was still disconcerted by the apparition in his backyard and tried to concentrate on his driving.

The clearest radio reception in Sparks was from a station playing big band at various times throughout the week. The rest of the air time was dedicated to "inspirational programming." David waited out the remaining minutes of an inspirational show in which a young woman from Portland described to an interviewer the relief she'd gotten from painful hemorrhoids since joining The Flow, a movement that promised to "reconstitute the human spirit in unison with the four basic elements: air, fire, earth, and water." Before signing off, the interviewer gave a 900 number to call for more information.

And then came a drum roll followed by the voice of Smilin' Jack, Sparks's "man for all seasons" and host of the big band show. Smilin' Jack kicked off the show with Woody Herman and his Herd doing "Woodchopper's Holiday" just as two massive pylon towers, one red/white and the other black, appeared before David from nowhere on the horizon. Damn things must have been eighty feet tall if they were an inch. From the spreading arms of the towers came forth six high-tension power lines shooting out in all directions. The steel towers were built on a freshly dug berm just inside the Sparks city limits.

Where did these things come from? David wondered. He had never noticed these lines here before, especially so close to Sparks. As he came up along them, the radio crackled and hissed. He tried furiously to spin the tuner, but it was stuck on this station. Even more bizarre, he couldn't turn the radio off. *What the hell is going on?*

As he entered the town, crawling down Main Street with Woody Herman sputtering from the radio, it occurred to David that the city fathers had had the access road to

Route One pass through Sparks to insure at least some visitors to the town. The sidewalks were vacant and the houses shuttered. Most of the storefronts along Main were empty, with the visible exception of the Busy B's Real Estate Company offices, taking up two or three buildings. David thought of visiting Nara at her office somewhere around here, but he remembered she'd be out on assignment right now.

Slow as he was going, David slowed down even more as he came upon the scene near the town harbor at the foot of Main Street. A group of four or five strangers—men in hiking gear—were walking in slow circles, their heads bent down, looking at instruments they held in their hands. Who in the hell were *they*? One of them looked up and smiled as David rolled past in the truck. David couldn't quite make out what they were doing and continued on to the Route One turn-off, the theme music from *Twilight Zone*—tink, tink, tink-tink; tink, tink, tink-tink—floating through his head and with it the image of the smoke from Rod Serling's cigarette drifting up into the sky.

The Downeast Mall consisted of a Sears, eleven smaller shops, three fast-food restaurants, two movie theaters, and a video arcade. Most of the region's consumer action was a few miles south in Freeport, home of the L.L. Bean outlet and dozens of other discount name stores. To David, a trip to Freeport was about as enticing as an afternoon of oral surgery.

He left the truck in the mall's underground parking lot, ran up one flight of stairs, and began his rounds. First, he visited the bookstore, where he picked up something from each of the literature (Dostoyevsky), philosophy (Plato's *Dialogues*), and baby (Brazleton) sections. David, who had studied nothing but computers throughout his educational career, considered himself ignorant of truly important literature and, like many middle-aged computer and engineer types, was hurrying to make up for lost time. He remembered he was down to three backup coffee makers and made a quick detour into Sears and paid cash for three more.

The next stop was the Sam Goody's to see what, if any, new CD's had come in, particularly in the progressive rock and big band departments. Nothing new since last Friday. Then he visited Paul Bolger, the owner of the computer store. Paul was the only person David had met since coming to Sparks with whom he could discuss computers. Unlike everyone else in Sparks, Paul knew David's true identity, as one of the world's top two or three computer demi-gods. But Paul couldn't have cared less who David really was, he was just happy to have found a computer soul mate.

Paul's store—called InCOMParable Products—was like most computer outlets: dingy, overlighted, and devoid of anything resembling sophisticated displays or advertising. Forty-four years old and living alone, nervous-wiry, balding on top with long hair in back, Paul usually wore running shoes and denim shirts to the store. That was how David found him today, sitting on a stool and leaning over the checkout counter, his head appearing detached from the rest of his body.

"My chip come in yet?" David said, ignoring Paul's obvious despondency.

"And how *are* you, Paul?" Paul whined sarcastically. "It was so very *nice* of you to special-order that chip for me. I *know* how much trouble you went to."

David rolled his eyes. "I prepaid for it, didn't I?"

Paul clacked his tongue in disgust and looked away.

"Well, is it here?"

Paul slid off the stool and stalked off.

"Better make sure he gets the right thing," David said to himself, and followed Paul into the stockroom. He found him on a ladder, rummaging through boxes strewn haphazardly on a shelf.

"So, what's going on?" David said, grudgingly showing concern.

"Nothing," Paul said, showing a bit more hostility as he tossed boxes toward the back of the shelf. Sighing heavily, he climbed down, brushed past David, and stomped over to a canvas bin and began fishing around in there.

"C'mon, Paul," David said, giving in a bit. "What's wrong?" Then a thought occurred to him. "Hey, by any chance were you on Conspiracy this morning?"

"You want to know what I've been doing all morning?" he said, flipping through boxes, a little less hostile now.

David, emphatically not a people person, thought: *Do I really want to hear this?* He kept his mouth shut and nodded tersely. Where was the chip?

"Since I got here at seven," Paul said, "I've been filling out *forms,*" as if this were the most horrible fate imaginable. Maybe it was, David considered.

"What it was, three droids from the county building-code office were actually *waiting* for me when I got here this morning, laying some bullshit on me about my electrical wiring, that they had some complaint about it or something. Do you believe that? *My* wiring!"

"You did it yourself?" David said, surprised Paul knew enough about basic electricity, which was, of course, not the same as electronics.

"What really iced it was that there's this humongous power spike that went roaring through the store while they're here. Good thing nothing was on except the lights. So, the droids grok all over themselves at the spike, like it was *my* fault, and whip out a ream of forms, telling me I fill them out or they shut me down. So they sit and watch me fill out their forms until opening time at ten."

"Hey," David said, "times're hard. The suits have to justify their existence. You sell me that chip, we pull out of the recession, and they're out of your face."

Paul didn't crack a smile. "If it only stopped there. I had the health code people in here over the weekend. As if I served *food,* or something."

"Maybe they heard you sold Apples," David offered. "Or that you have menu-driven software."

Paul went on. "Worst of all, the owners of the mall are putting the squeeze on me to give up my store space. My lease is good for another two years, but they're threatening to sue for eviction over some technicality. But no way I'm getting out."

"Hey, Paul," David said, a thought occurring to him. "You have any idea what radio freq a baby monitor operates on?"

Paul looked up from the canvas bag, his eyes not meeting David's, screwed up in concentration. "Let's see," he began, "a baby monitor. It's definitely VHF—Very High Frequency—on band 5 just a few notches below the 88 to 108 freqs on FM radio but higher than shortwave. That would put it on the same frequency range as your car phones, walkie-talkies, and other short-distance radios."

"Is there much interference in this frequency range?"

"Inter*fer*ence? God, it's like a sieve. You get cross talk on 'em all the time."

"Cross talk?"

"You know, somebody talking on a car phone suddenly gets the weather report from a local radio station. Or, you're grating carrots in the kitchen with the baby monitor on and you hear a man's voice over it talking about potholes and it turns out to be a dispatcher for the county talking to a work crew over the Business Radio Service. Pretty spooky, huh? The low end of the VHF range is notoriously porous. Remember what happened to Prince Charles and Camilla?"

David, whose knowledge of popular culture stopped in 1981, did not understand the question. He sat still for a moment, sifting through his thoughts. "Could one baby monitor pick up transmissions from another one?"

Paul's eyebrow's went up. "Sure, easy. In fact, they even warn you not to have two baby monitors going in the same house. You'd go crazy trying to figure out where the crying is coming from. Hey, look!"

Paul reached his hand to the bottom of the canvas bag and pulled up David's neural network chip. "I've never even seen one of these chips before. You want a bag for it?"

"No thanks," David said, deadpan. "I'll eat it here."

Outside the store David noticed Bob Kellum, a retired electrical engineer with whom David sometimes visited while at the mall. Bob was standing with his arms folded, waiting for David to come out. David said his good-byes to Paul and joined Bob, who, as usual, wasted no time with pleasantries and launched into a harangue about some odd activity in the area.

"Tell me about it," David muttered, and Bob led him over to a bench he shared with two other retirees who were in the middle of a heated discussion about the newcomers to Sparks.

One of the retirees, a woman named Clara, was surreptitiously pointing out the newcomers—Asians, Africans, Central Americans, and Eastern Europeans—as they passed the bench, most with children in tow. She railed bitterly against them, saying they should stay in their own countries where they belonged instead of coming here and taking jobs that Americans should have. David, usually oblivious to people, had never noticed the newcomers before. The other retiree, named Lillian, said she didn't mind them so much as long as they pulled their own weight. Maybe they were just tourists, David offered helpfully, but was greeted with a stony stare by the others.

Bob took David by the arm, pulling him aside.

"Look at this," Bob said quietly into the collar of his flannel shirt. He slowly brought out from under his coat an instrument David recognized as a Gauss meter, used to measure electromagnetic fields. David examined it but didn't know how to read it. Bob explained that he'd been getting some improbably high readings lately and wondered whom he should tell. David, only half listening, was gazing at the entrance to the video arcade on the other side of the mall. Ever since he had entered the mall he'd been craving a few games of Double Death, currently his favorite video game. He wondered if anyone was on the game right now. . . .

Before long Bob gave up on the distracted David and joined the debate with Clara and Lillian. David made his escape to the video arcade, where he saw a melange of kids—black leather punks with holes in their jeans, nerdy types (charter members of the pocket-protector set, David observed), and an occasional store clerk on a break. They were crowded around a few choice machines, their faces blank and impassive (the de rigueur look for the truly serious video players, who, by some unwritten law, cannot appear to be having fun while they play).

To David's chagrin, Double Death was occupied and he had to content himself with a somewhat pedestrian game of video golf. He cast longing looks back toward the motley group around Double Death. But they appeared absorbed in their game. The myriad sound effects from the video games—bombs exploding, Ninjas screaming, stock cars zooming—mingled with the rapid-fire pings from the pinball machines to generate enough noise in the tiny arcade to approximate that of a boardwalk amusement park. David teed off on a par three first hole and hooked the shot into the rough. He swore to himself: insult to injury.

As he was about to select a wood from the menu of clubs on a pop-up screen, David felt the skin on his arms tingle and his earlobes grow hot. Someone was watching him, he was sure of it. Pretending to look straight at the club selections, he peered out the corner of his eye. But he could see nothing.

Okay, he thought, we'll just see what we will see.

He spun around quickly, but no one was there. And the kids at Double Death had disappeared.

5

The buzz of the electrical substation was not too bad this time of day, thought Sid Bromley as he rolled his buttocks—numb from sitting so long—over the front seat of his old Pontiac. It was exactly 6:11 P.M., when most business in the area had closed for the day and the demand for electrical power from the substation was low. In a while it would go up again as people turned on their TVs, stereos, and microwave ovens once they got home. But Sid would be gone by then, if the person he came to meet ever got here, for Christ's sake.

Ron Lindblad, Sid's sponsor and boss, told Sid the meeting was for six, and he had broken his ass getting here early. He'd had to rush through a pre-production meeting for his talk show. Damn guests were giving him trouble, making impossible demands. Not that he didn't expect demands from his guests, most of them like children wanting this and that for just a lousy forty-minute appearance on the show. Hell, he was doing them a favor by putting them on, especially the celebrity guests. But lately the demands were getting increasingly out of hand. One of them—a lesbian tennis pro at a local club who allegedly had had an affair with the daughter of a political candidate Sid wanted to smear on Ron's behalf—said she wouldn't go on for less than $50,000. What did they think, that he was made of money?

If Sid had to wait, it was the best that he was doing it in his car. Ever since he was a teenager, he'd liked sitting in his car. He didn't have to be driving it; in fact, that was more of a distraction than anything. He just liked sitting in it, maybe holding the wheel, maybe not. Sitting there, he was safe, the scheming men and cheating women comfortably outside and far away.

He glanced down at the black nylon duffel bag on the floor of the passenger's side and groaned to himself. He had almost forgotten there was still one more stop he had to make after this one, to a playground behind the high school up in Rockland. In less than an hour, Sheriff Lawrence Donner of the Knox County Police Department would be waiting there in his personal car. Sid would see only the beefy face, mustache, and sunglasses that he wore no matter what kind of weather they were having. The sheriff was always early—no matter what time Sid got there—his massive chest and gut wedged behind the steering wheel. Without exchanging so much as a word, Sid would pass him the duffel bag containing what Ron called his "campaign contribution." Only this contribution was never recorded anywhere. It bought compliance, benign indifference, and occasional scraps of information. Sid never knew how much was inside the bag and never asked.

As expected, Sid hadn't seen another car since arriving here at the substation a half hour ago. Almost no one came this way since the coastal road had been fixed up, except maybe an occasional service truck or lost tourist. The substation was tucked in the middle of a depression a mile wide, with the road rising at either end. Running parallel to the road was a line of gleaming new steel towers supporting high-tension power lines brought here by the magic of Ron's influence. The only sound in the area was the bass hum of the power station.

Sid did not look forward to these meetings. In fact, he tried everything he could to get out of them. When he knew one was coming up, he would sneak out of town, refuse telephone calls, and generally avoid everyone he didn't absolutely have to see. But Ron insisted on the meetings to make sure that their projects were on track. And Ron seemed to have a way of knowing Sid's whereabouts at just about any given moment.

Sid was about to meet with his killer. It wasn't so much

his killer—Ron had done all the recruiting and Sid came into the picture later—but Sid had been stuck with the job of front man. The idea of being an assassin's handler was almost as repugnant to Sid as the person of the killer. Sid knew the terrible violence lurking just below the surface of the killer's visage. This person lived in Sparks, the town they were picking apart by murder. How to imagine it? Every day seeing the very people who might one day lie screaming at the sharp end of your knife. The killer's incredible coldness was amazing to Sid. He feared that awful power and stayed as far from it as circumstances would allow.

And Sid disliked what he turned into in the killer's presence—an errand boy, a fool, a cowering, bumbling, begging idiot. Wasn't it enough that Sid was in charge of the crews of people who went in to clean up after the killer struck? Hadn't he paid his dues all these months by hustling off to Mexico or Miami or some shabby border town to take care of problems for Ron? So why did Ron insist on Sid handling the killer? Ron knew how much he loathed the job. Sid deserved more and knew it. But for now there wasn't much he could do about it other than hang in there and make the best of it.

Sid looked out through the windshield as a pair of headlights appeared on the ridge to the north of him. A truck—visible in outline only—gradually came into view. There were no streetlights out here and the moon was not yet out, but he could see something following the truck, right on its tail. As the truck rolled up the access road to the substation, Sid realized that it wasn't something following the truck but attached to it in the back. It was a winch with a hook. What the hell was *that* for? Sid wondered as he rolled down his window. Suddenly the truck's headlights went out.

As the crunch of tires over crushed rock grew louder, Sid began to shake uncontrollably. It started in his legs: an insistent, almost painful shivering that seized his body and was immune to his efforts to control it. The shivering progressed to a full-scale shuddering as the truck, almost upon him, filled up his rearview mirror. His teeth rattled in his head, the skin on his face quivered, and his head trembled on his neck like a wing on a fly. He gripped his hands together in a futile attempt to contain the tremors.

This would be a good time for Sid to hook down some crystal methamphetamine—Power, he affectionately called it—which he kept in the glove compartment. It must have been at least an hour or so since his last hit. He had ducked into his bathroom at the studio for a few lines after that endless meeting he cut short early. That was the last time he'd had any. Hell, that must have been a good hour and fifteen minutes ago. He knew he didn't really need it, but it would help to steady his nerves, calm his jitters. His quivering hand was moving for the glove compartment when a nightmare voice reached out and seized him.

"Cold?" the voice said from inside the dark truck across from Sid, the driver's window rolled down halfway.

Sid forced himself to look but could see only the killer's chin and jawline in the shadows. Sid tried to avoid showing his fear, like a trainer with a wild animal. He took in three quick breaths that helped settle him.

"Y-yeah," he managed to say. He could see the killer's head nodding in the darkness. He held his hands and listened to the hum of the substation.

"You wanted to see me?"

The question jarred Sid back to himself, to the business at hand. He knotted his fingers together on his lap and cleared his throat. "Been a while since our last meeting," Sid said. "What's it been? Four weeks? Five?"

By the lack of response, Sid sensed impatience from the killer. He tried to keep things moving. "Two items. First, I wanted to check up on that assignment we talked over on the phone a couple days ago. We thought it would be done by now."

Still no response.

"M-maybe you don't recall," Sid said, trying a different tack. "The conversation we had on Tuesday. You said you'd get to it right away."

"I remember," the killer finally said, the voice still and passionless.

"Well?" Sid said, betraying his desperation. "There's a certain . . . imperative with this one. The man, Haslem, knows too much—he probably knows everything—and could bolt any time now. We—Ron, this is—trusted him with too much access. I *told* Ron that Haslem couldn't be trusted. I told him that the day Haslem came in for his first interview. But did he listen to me, even for a minute?

"Look where it got us. We have to assume Haslem's wife knows too. They might even have approached the authorities. I have his office and home phones tapped, so I know he hasn't called from there. The local police don't know anything, we're sure of that. But it has to be done right away."

Sid paused. "We're all in jeopardy. So, where are you on it? What's the story?"

"The story," the killer said. "There is no story. I told you it would be taken care of. The less you know about it, the better."

Sid felt sweat at the back of his head. "I appreciate that. But there will be questions. From Ron. This one is important to him. He'll want to know."

The killer sighed softly. "Tomorrow. Or the next day. No later."

Sid bit down, rage building up inside him, competing with the fear for control. "I—Ron," he stammered, "that's not good enough. He'll want to know."

"Tomorrow, then," the killer said, clearly irritated.

"You know their patterns?" Sid said. "Their schedule?"

"Yes."

"Good," Sid said, relieved some progress had been made. "Tomorrow, then." He eased back in his seat, feeling a little better.

"You said you had two things."

Sid straightened up immediately, as if called on in his class. "Er, yeah. There's something, someone else. Turned up a few days ago while Ron was looking over some property deeds in the area."

Without thinking, Sid leaned his head out the window, his face within striking range of the knife that the killer held out of sight. "There's a property just on the edge of Sparks," Sid said, "a house on a hill. A family lives in it. And listen to this. They own the single biggest tract of real estate in the entire township. Even bigger than Ron's.

"Ron thinks they have a couple hundred acres, mostly wooded. You should have seen him last week; he was beside himself over this. What he really likes about the place, besides the size, is that it's at the highest point in the entire Sparks area. You know how worried he is about the water table. He wants to build the Country Customs headquarters—'the capital of my empire,' he called it—right on this site."

"So why doesn't he buy it?" the killer said.

Sid drew his face back into the Pontiac. "You know he's low on cash right now, especially with all the plans he has. Do you have any idea how much up-front capital you need to develop a project of that magnitude? Why do you think he's running triple shifts at the factory?"

The killer shrugged, shoulders rolling in the shadows. "Did you hear about the new property on the market?" The question was posed in their private code and was meant to provoke a reaction.

Sid, distracted by his preoccupation with thoughts of crystal meth had to concentrate for a moment before it registered. "What?" he spat out. "What did you say?"

Another sigh, louder this time. "Another property is on the market."

"Who?" Sid said, that terrible feeling of losing control seeping over him.

"The old drunk. Theroux. Lives over on Newmarket."

"When?" Sid said, still incredulous.

"Last night."

"What did you do with the body? You didn't call Jiffy, did you?"

"No," the killer growled, showing anger for the first time. "I took care of it."

"How? Where?"

"The less you know the better."

Sid tried to process what he was hearing. It didn't sound too bad, the killer whacking an old drunk who lived alone. But this was still disturbing. The killer's complete disregard for the rules of the game had to be contained immediately. Otherwise, it could easily get out of hand.

"We never talked about this," Sid said evenly, moving forward with great caution. "This is totally unauthorized. This—this freewheeling has to stop right now. Do you understand? Everything we do must be coordinated. We have to work as a team."

"A team," the killer said with obvious disdain that Sid overlooked.

He spread his hands open for the killer to see. "That's right. Where would we be without some sense of where we're going? What if Ron and I did things that affected you without your knowing about it?"

"You've said yourself that opportunities have to be seized."

Sid steadied himself on the steering wheel. "Okay," he said, "all right. What's done is done. Let's put it behind us. Only, don't let's start a trend with this. Agreed?"

Silence from the truck. Then the unearthly voice. "So what's the name of the family in this house on the hill?"

Sid groped through his memory for the name. "Some gook family. Never heard of them before. They must keep to themselves."

"Gooks?"

"Yeah. Japs or Chinese or something." He closed his eyes and furrowed his brow. "Murata. That's the name. I can get the address for you."

More silence, longer this time. Sid waited, assuming he would hear protests, demands for more money. Suddenly the engine of the truck kicked over and the killer started toward the access road.

Sid thrust his head out the window. "Keep me posted," he shouted. "Hear?" But the truck was already up the road. He watched as its taillights flared on at the top of the rise and disappeared.

"Fucking animal," he muttered, the feeling of chaos returning, of things unraveling around him. Then he ripped open the glove compartment and fell on the drug like a starving man on a piece of meat.

6

There is a certain part of the day when the usual rules no longer apply, when human perception is at best tenuous, and time, for all practical purposes, is meaningless. It is often a time when aberrant energies are released and is therefore relished by the vandal, criminal, and sociopath who feel free to roam woods and streets, protected as they are by the hallucinatory darkness. This time falls during the waning hours of night, somewhere between two and five, when the prudent are indoors and in deep sleep, blessed by dreams or terrorized by nightmares.

David McAdam could remember back to when this had been his favorite time of the day, when he would work long into the night at the computer. But things were different now, with Von and Nara and something called a schedule—an actual schematic for the day that dictated when and where he would be at just about every moment. The wee hours were now a time for sleeping rather than feverishly creating digital fantasies. Hibernation before cybernation, David observed. Quite a change for him. Quite a change.

It was during this time on this particular night that David, who had just gotten to sleep after getting through the first 187 pages of *Crime and Punishment,* was awakened by a baby's cry. He sat up in bed, alert as a terrier. The cry seemed to come from everywhere and nowhere, as if the darkness itself were sobbing. He slid out of bed and padded into Von's room, finding his son facedown in his crib, sheets of tears covering his cheeks, the result of aching gums and his general malaise. David felt pangs of sympathy for the child. He picked him up and carried him downstairs, through the living room, where he stepped painfully on one of the circuits he had given Von the day before.

In the kitchen, David fixed Von a bottle of milk, which he put into the microwave to warm. The microwave hummed as it irradiated the milk, and for some reason David drew Von close to his own body and stepped back into the living room away from the oven. David knew that microwaves were such wide waves that they could not escape from the oven to harm Von. Still, some protective instinct kept him from staying in the kitchen.

David cradled his son as they waited for milk to heat up, rocking him back and forth. In the dark stillness Von gazed up at David with serene cobalt eyes. As David watched Von watching him, he wondered what his son was thinking, how the neurons were processing the information coming in right now. It was during moments like these that David realized just how protective he'd become of his son, and how having a child has aroused feelings in him he hadn't known he had.

He looked at Von again, completely and utterly vulnerable. David thought: Why shouldn't I be concerned about the microwaves? After all, what are we anyway but a fragile series of electrical and chemical reactions wrapped in high-quality polyvinyl? Who knows what effect a small perturbation in our electrical function would have on us, especially on a child?

David walked Von through a series of rooms until they reached the dining room at the other end of the house. As he turned to go back, David noticed light through the window, coming from the house across the backyard at the bottom of the hill—the same one he watched every morning. The window was a box of light floating in the blackness, a pale yellow rectangular canvas.

David trained his ears and tilted his head toward the window. There was that sound again! The hysterical laughter, the screaming, whatever it was, the only fainter this time, more of a chortle. It was as if the unanimous night was enjoying a joke at his expense. Then the laughter stopped abruptly and David listened carefully, the window-pane as cold as ice on the edge of his earlobe.

He turned his head and peered out the window. "Hmmm," he murmured to himself. Down below, at the foot of the hill, the blue-green of what looked like a computer monitor glowed in the Flintstones' window. But no one was in sight. David squinted; yes, it sure was a computer. Even at this distance there was something familiar about it: the shape of the monitor, the red logo on the CPU. It was an antique, one of the old PanTech 286's David himself had designed three lifetimes ago. Odd. Why hadn't he noticed it before? And what was Fred doing up at this hour, using a computer? What time was it anyway? Suddenly the computer clicked off and the window went dark.

A disturbing feeling of coincidence made its way up David's spine and into his brain. Imagine, the man he'd been covertly watching for months, even to the point of constructing fantastic scenarios about his family and him, owned a computer that David had designed. In an odd and indirect way, part of David was in Fred Flintstone's house right now.

Then David heard a new sound, like someone rhythmically chopping or cutting. Who? Cutting what? The sound was coming from somewhere nearby, but he wasn't sure from which direction. Forgetting the Flintstones momentarily, he raced through the house, thrusting his face into windows and peering out into the darkness.

The process of elimination brought David through the kitchen and to the front door. The sound was closer. He checked through a side window but still could not see anything. He flipped a switch for the front floodlights, drew in a breath, and stepped outside.

Something dark—possibly a wild animal—moved in the balsam trees lining the service road to the house. David could not make out what it was. The chopping sound had stopped. He moved slowly onto the porch and down the front steps.

"What the hell?" he muttered as he saw what the floodlights revealed on the balsam and spruce trees that dotted the front yard. He stepped forward gingerly. The trunks of the trees in the yard—every one of them—had been slashed with what looked like a small ax or meat cleaver. Some of the trees had been cut only once while others had long herringbone gashes that ran up their trunks. Dozens of small branches, each cut clean at the base, were scattered on the ground under the trees. He had no way of assessing the full damage, but was sure that some of the trees would die from the lacerations.

"Who in the hell would do such a thing?" he said to himself. His rising anger was numbed by fear. Questions swarmed at him. What was going on here? Was someone on to his real identity, knew that he lived here? Or was this just random vandalism?

Suddenly David remembered that Von was still in his arms as his son stirred from the night air. "C'mon, Von," David whispered. "let's get you inside."

As he turned toward the house, David's mouth fell open and he felt his blood freeze in his veins. At first he saw only the individual letters, that seemed to shimmer in red on the front of his house. He then put some of the letters together and read "Or Die." He tried unsuccessfully to swallow and could only stare at the message scrawled in red, three-feet high Day-Glo letters over the door and the entire front wall of the house:

GOOKS GET OUT OR DIE

Small streaks of Day-Glo dripped like lava down the wall to the ground. David turned back toward the woods where the dark shape had disappeared. Nothing there, as he expected. he climbed the stairs to the house, the obscene words growing larger with each step. He kicked open the front door, which banged against the wall, waking up Von, who screamed into the night.

7

The next day, David sat listlessly at one of his basement work stations, exhausted at eleven o'clock from a sleepless night. He was trying to finish the laundry (Nara fixed the dryer—David had forgotten to screw in a fuse) and make progress on his fuzzy logic program, failing miserably at both. So far the piles of clothing—mostly Von's—still lay in heaps on the floor where they had been yesterday, and the C++ glyphs on the monitor stared defiantly at him, also unchanged.

He had stayed awake after finding that disgusting message on the wall, partly out of protectiveness for his family and partly out of sheer anger. They say that things always look better in the morning, but *they* never had three-foot high red Day-Glo racist graffiti waiting for them on the front of their house when they woke up. The worst part was telling Nara, showing her the damage to the trees and the house. She took everything in without uttering so much as a word.

They had a quick but decisive discussion about whether or not to call the police. They decided against it. David was a celebrity—a reluctant one, to be sure—but the press hadn't forgotten him since his abrupt departure from Pan-Tech, his company, and society in general about three years ago. David and Nara knew what would happen: they would call the police, an ineffectual report would be filed, a reporter would see the file and run a story, and within hours the house would be invaded by the ravenous media. David and Nara would have to be ready to move even before they called the police.

No, they would grit this one out. It was probably just some local kids who had done this, David said. He agreed to call in house painters and get the mess out of the way before anyone but they saw it.

But the whole thing troubled David: the reference to Nara as a gook, the death threat, and the destruction of their trees. The best thing to do was get back to work. Von was napping upstairs and David was tempted to join him. He was also tempted to check in on the Conspiracy network, especially since receiving that mysterious message yesterday. Earlier he added some security measures to his system that would allow him to trace any further moles. Let 'em try it again.

Exhaustion and anger did not stay David from his appointed rounds at the dining room window this morning. Again, Fred Flintstone was late to appear, by over twenty minutes. And again Fred was carrying luggage, but this time it was a huge steamer trunk that he dragged from the house and loaded into the station wagon, all the time glancing around suspiciously. David watched it all, wondering, imagining. It was getting curiouser and curiouser, as Alice would say.

A couple of hours later, David got an urgent call from Will Karasik, begging him to make some progress in the elevator project or his company would be forced to design video games to make this month's payroll. That would have been about five in the a.m. out in California. David could hear the desperation in poor Will's voice. Just to pull Will's chain a bit, David asked him what was so bad about designing video games, but Will's stony silence was reply enough.

David figured it wouldn't hurt to send Will the programming he had down so far even though it went against his grain, passing off something only partly done. Minutes after the program hit the network, David got a message back on his screen that read:

> 99^{714} thanks, o mighty demigod. May the Great Spirit of the computus mundus smile upon your every hack.
>
> Will, but no way.

David had been dutifully reading his De Beauvoir, but he was getting nowhere with deconstructionism. Worse, the essence of fuzzy logic continued to elude him. For his entire life in computers he had worked from a straight binary system based on absolutes and so-called "crisp" logic, in which the commands AND, OR, and NOT return either a 0 or 1 that drive an application, such as calculating a checking account balance on an ATM machine. Fuzzy logic turned that entire approach on its ear, requiring that all things be thought of in matters of degree somewhere *between* 0 and 1.

But David chipped away at the project, driven by the challenge like any true hacker. The little Fisher-Price baby monitor set on top of the new power booster system next to him was so sensitive that it transmitted Von's every breath, appearing as flickering red dashes on the digital display. David paid the sound no mind, treating it as ambient white noise. Right now he was bearing down, writing a particularly difficult part of the program that required a series of natural language commands. David had never been crazy about natural language programming. He swore to himself when the timer on the dryer went off, breaking his concentration. He got up to remove the load and throw in the last one.

Returning to his computer, David picked up where he left off, trying out some fuzzy rules for handling alternating heavy and light elevator weights. He corrected himself: nothing was heavy or light or fast or slow or good or bad. It was all a matter of degrees.

All of a sudden a tremendous, terrible screaming exploded from the baby monitor, and David's head shot up from the computer screen. He couldn't quite make out what it was—a woman, a child, or several children at once. The wildly oscillating red monitor display mesmerized him like the eyes of a cobra.

It's happening again. David was certain that radio signals from the monitor were bleeding into those of another somewhere. But where was this other monitor? Whose was it? And what was happening to them?

The screaming, now sounding like several screams at once, rose in intensity. David heard someone—an adult woman—shouting "No, no," followed by a long blood-chilling shriek that continued for several seconds, then quickly faded into a whimper and then fell silent. The last one was the most horrible one of all—a thin cry from a tiny voice stifled almost as soon as it began.

David was finally able to move his mouth. "Von?" he whispered, and then raced upstairs as questions, images, flew through his mind. Running in his stocking feet, he slipped on a step and fell heavily on his knee.

"Oh shit," he groaned, rubbing his kneecap. He got up and hobbled into the nursery, where he found Von sleeping peacefully.

His heart hammering in his chest, David fell into the rocking chair. He began to rock nervously, his eyes riveted on Von. He sat for many minutes, afraid to leave his son, his knee beginning to swell up. A film of sweat chilled on his forehead.

Sitting there rocking, David shut his eyes and forced himself to calm down. His breaths grew longer and his thoughts began to drift. Suddenly his eyes snapped open as the memory of the screams came roaring back at him.

It occurred to him to call the police, to have them knock on every door within a mile. But for the same reasons David did not call the police last night, he decided against it now. Besides, he could see the headlines now:

RECLUSE COMPUTER GENIUS TERRORIZED BY THE AIRWAVES

Terrible what modern life is doing to us, David thought. We've all become cowering sheep, fearful of exposing ourselves.

So David stayed put in his chair, guiltily watching his son and rocking furiously.

8

At that moment, on the other side of town, Nara was at the Sparks Diner conducting an interview for the series she was doing on four generations of Sparks women. Her subject was Estelle Grout, a resident of the town for all of her seventy-one years. Nara was trying to get the perspective of both newcomers and long-time residents. But so far only the old-timers would talk to her.

And even Estelle wasn't exactly warming to her. Nara was thinking: Maybe it's my clothes that's putting her off. Or maybe it's because I'm Asian. Maybe Estelle is distrustful, even hostile toward us: Pearl Harbor, Vietnam, unemployment from foreign competition. Just lay it on the Asians. Nara had seen it many times before, and in many forms.

But Nara's pride and hardened self-discipline would not let her give in to such poisonous thoughts. Having been subjected to the role of scapegoat herself, she knew well the danger of self-pity and abnegation of responsibility. *Work harder,* she commanded herself, *concentrate*.

Nara covertly studied Estelle as the older woman picked at her blasberry cobbler, the diner's special. Estelle, in her baby blue suit, faux pearl clip-on earrings, and green silk scarf, had clearly dressed up for the interview. Nara wished she had come more casual. Last week Estelle had been willing, even enthusiastic, when Nara called her to request an interview. What had happened to her between then and now? Why was she so reserved?

Nara did notice that Estelle brightened up every time their waitress, K. K. Thorner, stopped over to fill their coffee cups and kibitz in the conversation. The diner was quiet at this time of the day, so K. K.'s stops were frequent and long. Rather than try to steer K. K. away, Nara got her to talk about herself in the hope that Estelle would do the same.

"Sure," K. K. said in reply to Nara's question, "we get all kinds in here. From the bad to the worse." K. K. waited until she got a smile from Nara and then laughed heartily.

"Tippers, I mean," K. K. said, pouring coffee. "People from Maine are *terrible* tippers. Worst I've ever seen. They must think I'm having such a good time bringing them food and cleaning their tables that I couldn't possibly want a tip. Either that or they hide their loose change in the same place they do their sense of humor."

Nara watched Estelle giggling at K. K., who obviously enjoyed the attention. Are they related? Nara wondered. Why not ask?

Before she could, K. K. disappeared in a flash and returned with a handful of little containers of half-and-half that she threw like dice on the table. Without waiting for an invitation, she sat down at the table, holding onto her coffeepot.

"Now that I think about it," K. K. said, "I've been missing some of my regular customers. A real shame because most of them were good tippers, as they go around here." As she spoke she thrust the coffeepot to emphasize her points.

Nara was amused by K. K. and the expressions on Estelle's face as the coffee in the pot sloshed under her nose.

"There's definitely something in the air," Estelle said gravely, her eyes averted toward the grease-spattered window but not really looking out.

"What do you mean, Mrs. Grout?" Nara said.

"Oh, for heaven's sakes," she said, waving her hand. "Call me Estelle." Nara smiled and looked down, feeling a shot of guilt for doubting Estelle's good nature.

Estelle's eyes drifted back to the window. "It's my friends," she said quietly. "People I've known all my life. Some of them, I don't know, have just up and disappeared.

Like Irene McNamara. One day, about three, four weeks ago, I dropped by her place with some peanut brittle. I must have rapped on her door for five minutes before someone finally came to the door, someone I've never seen before.

"A young woman, about your age," she said looking at Nara, "spoke with an accent. When I asked her about Irene, she just shrugged and said: 'Moved away. California, I think.' Just like that. Now, Irene never so much as uttered a word to me about moving. Next day I waited for the mailman, Norbert Jenkins, and asked him about her. He told me the same thing, that she moved to California. He said he didn't know if she left a forwarding address but he'd find out for me. Haven't heard a thing from him yet."

"Maybe it's true, Estelle," K. K. said gently. "Maybe Irene did go out to California to be with family. Or she had other plans, maybe a boyfriend somewhere she didn't want anyone to know about."

Estelle shook her head and screwed up her mouth. Nara thought she might be fighting back tears. "And then there was Roxy Ward. Last month at church somebody told me she moved to Florida. Now, that's not like Roxy, moving at the drop of a hat like that, especially with the Easter festival coming up in a couple of months. She's the chairman this year."

The three women sat in silence. "What troubles me," Estelle went on, "is that I've known Irene and Roxy for most of my life. What would possess them to move away without so much as a good-bye?"

"I'm sure there's an explanation," Nara said.

"You know," K. K. said, looking up at Estelle, "I think I read something somewhere about those women. There was some . . ." she paused, sloshing coffee to jog her memory, "announcement in a newspaper or flyer. I can't recall what it was."

Estelle sighed and folded her hands, straightening herself up. "Only thing I can think of is that it must be their children, who just go and make decisions for their parents about where to live without even consulting them about it. That's the best I can come up with."

Nara and K. K. nodded and joined Estelle in gazing out the window. K. K. spoke first. "Estelle, would it be okay if I brought Viveca over this afternoon, about two? I have my audition up at the university."

"Why, of course, dear," Estelle said, cheering up immediately. "Bring her over earlier, if you like. I have a lemon meringue pie already made. One of Viv's favorites."

Several thoughts occurred to Nara at once. She saw a possible story here with Estelle, K. K., and her daughter, where the lives of three generations of Sparks women intersected. It also contained elements of the new demographics, a single mother. Nara imagined the photographs that could go with the story: Estelle and the child together, K. K. at the diner. Maybe the diner would put some advertising in *The Maine Event.* The magazine certainly could use some. Nara also wondered what K. K. was auditioning for.

Small, hard flakes of snow began to fall, and all three women groaned as they noticed it through the window.

"Winter never seems to end around here," K. K. said ruefully.

"I just can't understand why they didn't say good-bye," Estelle said.

"Can you give me their names again?" Nara asked, and she began writing in her note pad.

9

Nara came home pensive that afternoon, distracted by the talk at the diner. Estelle and K. K. didn't come across to her as paranoid. Still, what they were suggesting—people disappearing for no good reason—was pretty fantastic, especially in a backwater place like Sparks. So what if a few old folks were moving to the Sun Belt? Who could blame them, even if they forgot to say good-bye? But it wouldn't hurt to look into it, maybe have David do a little checking on his computers.

Leaving her bag next to the front door, she prowled the house in search of her family. She found David in the dining room staring out the back window, his hands pressed against the windowpane, exactly where she had left him this morning. She wondered if he had moved at all today. Slowly she crept up behind him, hands outstretched, and dug her fingertips into his sides. She nearly had to pull him off the ceiling.

"My God, you're jumpy," she said as he gradually caught his breath. Cupak and the other dogs gathered around, yelping wildly.

"Nara," he gasped, "don't—don't ever do that again."

She shrugged off her coat and David winced as she slung it over his disk array file server with three 1.2-gegabyte drives and ethernet adapter, souped up with host adapter, and secondary and external caching on the motherboard. It was one of his prizes—the guts of his system—linking seven of the computers in the living room with fourteen in the basement to search for and store data for Conspiracy. Just getting the file server into the house had been a major undertaking, requiring two big guys laboriously steering the massive piece of hardware around corners and past the furniture.

"David," Nara began, "would your computer system be able to trace real estate transactions?"

"What?" David said, turning from the window. "Listen, I have to tell you. I heard something this morning, it was on the baby monitor. It had to be the most horrible thing I've ever heard. Screams. Lots of them. It wasn't Von, I'm sure of that, but it had to come from fairly close by, from someone with their own baby monitor."

He went quiet for a moment. He looked her in the eye for the first time. "The Flintstones—the people next door—were massacred. I think."

Nara sucked in a breath and pulled away from him, instinctively checking his breath for alcohol. David looked at her sourly.

"You don't believe me," he said accusingly. "You think I'm wrecked, don't you?"

Nara looked down. "I don't know," she said.

David winced at her brutal honesty. "Listen," he said, turning back to the window. "I've been watching their house most of the day—at least since it occurred to me that this was where the screams were coming from—but no one has gone in or out."

Nara looked at David's unshaven face mashed against the windowpane, his breath condensing over the glass. The snow was picking up, sticking to and melting away from the window in the same second. She could almost see the wheels turning in his head.

"Did Fred kill his wife and children and then stuff them in the suitcase, like Raymond Burr did in *Rear Window*?" he said softly, almost to himself. "If so, how did he get home without me seeing him? Could I have missed seeing the station wagon come back? Or did Wilma kill Fred and then the children? Or maybe she killed her children and then herself, or just her children. And what's on that computer?"

Nara didn't even try keeping up with him. "Where's Von?" she said, looking behind the file server.

"I'm going in there," David said tersely.

"Where?" Nara said, looking again at the file server, wondering how he planned to get inside of it.

"There," he said again, pointing at the house. "Cover me."

Nara waved her hand dismissively. "Oh, David, don't be rid—" But he was gone.

Within seconds she saw him appear along the edge of their yard, running in a crouch down the slope toward their neighbors' house. In just his house clothes and moccasins, he slunk through the falling snow along the back wall of the house. Then he slipped around the side of the house and disappeared. Nara watched it all, not believing he could be this stupid.

David, woefully out of shape, sucked in gutfuls of air as he clung to the brick near the side door. He knew that once he went in, nothing would be the same again. He would be breaking the law. And that could be the least of his worries. What if *he* was in there—Fred? Maybe he had seen David coming across the yard and was waiting with a gun. Maybe.

As he stood there against the coarse brick wall, the temperature dropping rapidly, something else—a question—loomed in the dark rafters of David's consciousness, occasionally swooping down and then back up again. It was a simple question, simmering all day in his brain and now boiling over from adrenaline and fear. The question was this: if there had been a murder here, could it have been nothing more than a horrible mistake?

Could the killer really have been after David and his family?

No way to answer that now. Feeling like Grace Kelly invading Raymond Burr's chamber of horrors in *Rear Window,* David inched along the wall toward the door. With one eye he peered inside. Odd. The kitchen was sparkling clean but smelled of cooking dinner. David studied the doorknob, without a clue as to how to break in. So he gingerly tried the door and—wonder of wonders—it opened. It had never been locked.

Once inside he took a deep breath, temporarily freezing at the stark realization that he'd just broken into someone's house, the "someone" showing every indication of being a mass murderer. Suddenly David heard a loud noise—heavy machinery, torrents of water, a test of the emergency broadcast system—he wasn't sure which.

"C'mon, McAdam, hit the Enter key," he told himself, still stuck in his tracks. "You've got to function." Then he recognized the sound as that of his own blood rushing through his temples.

He snapped his eyes and looked around him. For starters he examined the kitchen, amazingly clean, especially for a family with at least two children. The smell he had noticed earlier, cooking oil or burning butter, was overlaid with a tart odor of detergent and antiseptic. If anything had happened in here, it surely had been scrubbed away.

Alfred Hitchcock was very much on David's mind as he began to explore the house. To be specific, he was thinking of the scene from *Psycho* in which the sister of the Janet Leigh character—*who played her, dammit?*—was exploring Norman Bates's house. David peered around corners and snuck up on chairs with their backs to him, half expecting to see the worm-eaten corpse of Norman's mother in one of them. He was surprised at what he found.

The house was not at all as he imagined it would be. It was faultlessly neat, not a speck of dust on anything. Also, there was a lot of red in the decor, formal damask-covered furniture, and scrolls depicting dragons and horses on the living room walls. On the black lacquer end tables were framed photographs of an Asian family, including wedding photos. David checked the closets for the PanTech computer, but he saw no sign of it.

He padded upstairs, poked his head in each of the three bedrooms, and entered the smallest one. He took quick inventory of the furnishings: a twin bed, simple desk and chair, and chest of drawers. The walls had been freshly painted. He looked up and noticed around the top of the walls the painted-over stenciling of flowers and teddy bears, the vestige of a nursery. Whoever had painted the house obviously had done so in a hurry because they hadn't bothered to cover the stenciling with a second coat.

As he was leaving the room, David noticed something on the floor—it looked like part of a toy—protruding from behind the chest of drawers. He crouched down next to it and began pulling out a short rubber antenna, followed by a hand-sized transmitter for a baby monitor. Could this be the one, he thought, the transmitter of death? He studied it, turning it over in his hands as if it were the murder weapon, waiting for an epiphany of some kind—a revelation—that never came.

Meanwhile, Nara kept vigil about two hundred yards away at the dining room window, waiting anxiously for David to come back. Even though she knew he was capable of anything, she still couldn't believe he would actually do something like this, breaking into someone's house. She heard a sound, a car or truck coming, and her eyes widened at the sight of a mini-van pulling into the house's driveway.

"Oh no," she whispered.

She watched helplessly as a family slowly got out, loaded down with a ragtag collection of bags. Nara narrowed her eyes, trying to see the people through the snow. There was something familiar about them, their size and movements. They stood in the driveway for several moments before the driver of the van hopped out and opened the door to the house. The driver got back in the mini-van and drove off. *Why did he do that?*

David, where are you? she screamed inside her head.

At that moment he was in the master bedroom, looking for what he didn't really know. Bloodstains? Bodies piled in the closet? Like the other rooms, this one had an Eastern decor, austere. He took care as he moved from room to room, mindful of the fact that Fred Flintstone, the lunatic husband, could be lurking behind any one of these doors, meat cleaver or Colt Python in hand.

Something else troubled David, his compulsion for trivia grating at his consciousness. The actress's name—the one from *Psycho*—what *was* her name? David's brain—remarkably functional for the epic amounts of abuse heaped on it for so many years—still had a devil of a time recalling small bits of information from his distal memory cells. He knew at least that he associated the actress's name with some unit of measure. Was it "gram"? Siemens? Tesla? Furlong?

Who cared, anyway?

He opened a door and found himself in the garage. This was more like it, he thought to himself, as he surveyed the bundles of newspapers and magazines and bags of garbage. A memory popped in his head of his house in the Florida Keys, in which he had managed to collect considerably more garbage than even that accumulated in this garage. On top of one of the magazine bundles he saw a Country Customs mail-order catalogue with a mailing label on it. He pulled the magazine from under the string binding the pile together, looked at the name on the label, and turned as he heard the sound of a door slamming.

Pacing before the window, Nara rubbed her arms and held her breath as the family tentatively entered the house. *Where is David? Why isn't he back yet?* Would the next sound she'd hear be a gunshot? Seconds ticked by and she thought for a moment and decided to call the police. As she turned toward the kitchen to make the call, she let out a small cry as she nearly ran into David, who was standing there, calmly rocking Von in his arms.

"My God, you're jumpy," he said, a satisfied smirk on his face.

10

Gritty snow was falling on Penobscot Bay, over the roof and boarded windows of the nearby lobster-processing plant, and on my head and shoulders as I strolled along the frozen cranberry bogs on the outskirts of town. As usual it was a quiet day in Sparks, made even quieter by the snow that seized and strangled sounds before they could escape into the air.

From a distance Sparks appeared as it really was: a throw-away place, flotsam collecting on a rocky shore. The gray outline of its huddled buildings looked like roadkill decomposing along the shoulder of a highway. Its twisty, potholed streets were discarded snake skins. Massive basalt boulders rose up out of the gunmetal bay like cracked knuckles threatening the town harbor.

Long ago Sparks had been sucked dry, used up. First, the land had been overplanted by the early settlers, and no one ever gave a thought to protecting the soil against runoff. The granite had been mined out and carted off to build bridges and buildings, like Grand Central Station in New York.

Then the surrounding waters were fished and lobstered out. Finally, the little bit of industry—seafood processing, shipbuilding—was abandoned, left to rust. The tourists, the town's last hope, did their best to avoid the area. No one even ate Maine potatoes anymore. They all preferred those Idaho ones. The place was in the last throes of a long death.

The people of Sparks were equal to their surroundings: contemptible, nothing more than garbage rotting in the stink. Too insignificant to arouse even pity, they gave the appearance of being dumped here: fearful, bewildered, vaguely aware of their predicament. They were human debris drifting in the weather as the seagulls circled overhead. Barnacles needing to be scraped away.

Their faces told the story. They had a haggard, discarded look of those outliving their usefulness generations ago. Now they could only stay here and wait. Wait to die.

People who wanted to make something of themselves went elsewhere or avoided the place altogether. The town defied efforts to renew it. They had even tried to introduce recycling here a couple of years ago, but it never took.

Someone had to take out the garbage here, to sweep the place clean. Sparks needed a trash collector. I was chosen. So be it.

In the two days since taking out Lorton Theroux, everything had changed for me. It was as if I were a prisoner just released from a long sentence, breathing new air. I was alert, watchful, with a newly found purpose in life. My handler's leash around my neck had been cut.

Handlers. Sid Bromley used that word to describe himself. As if he or anyone else could handle me. Bromley was nothing more than an errand boy. Pull a string and see him dance. I could not—would not—let something so insignificant dictate my business to me. I would go along, but only so far. I took care of that one chore for them—painting the message on the Muratas' house. I knew Bromley wanted me to do more, to eliminate the family so that Lindblad could get their property. How much did he want it? I wondered. He was now dealing with a different force when he was dealing with me. He and Bromley would learn to respect me, even fear me.

I had entered a new phase, taking on an entirely different role. I wasn't kidding myself. I was aware of the demands of this role, of the risks of my new freedom. I would have to be crazy not to. When you leave the nest, you're flying on your own. And I was leaving a nest, the security of the organization behind me. The fall was great from here.

And here I stood, alone on a snowy country road, feeling the exhilaration of freedom and fear of total failure.

This was February and the hours of daylight were sup-

posed to be gradually increasing. The nights were far too long as they were. It was during the night when the sights and sounds and smells of my work crowded in, invading my dreams and shredding sleep.

The details were the worst. Shards of memory, intense afterimages of death, infected the darkness: the song Guy Needleman had hummed in his garage just before I struck. The black gaps in Roxy Ward's mouth—without her dentures and partials—as she screamed briefly, the knife going in for the sixth time. Lorton Theroux's searing eyes as he sank helplessly into the marsh near Molasses Pond.

These memories were the bitter harvest of my work. They would linger for a long time, probably forever. The nights would never be the same again.

The nights were also the busiest time for the trash collector. That is, until yesterday when I worked for the first time in the daylight. Despite my decision to act on my own, I still went along when a task was assigned to me. Such as yesterday.

About two hundred yards down the road toward Sparks, someone had begun to chop wood. It reminded me that I needed more wood-chopping wedges to dispose of my next victim. I already knew who it would be.

I could see the man, the woodchopper, appear and disappear in the snow. Then I stood stock still, my eyes closed tight, my eyeballs straining against the lids as the ax fell over and over like snow.

Chop.

Thoughts, flashes of memory, blazed across my mind. The woman whose family I had called on yesterday—Pamela Haslem—was difficult, the hardest one I'd ever done. When I went into the house through the side door, I thought she was upstairs, maybe sleeping while her children napped. Instead she was in the kitchen, sautéing mushrooms over the stove.

Get out now, I thought to myself, this will not work. Pamela will see me and scream. Her children will run, leaking out of the house, away from me.

But it had to be done now. Bromley and Lindblad were

clear on that. Even my own safety was in jeopardy with the Haslems alive.

Just get the woman. Get her now.

Chop.

Each time before, when I collected garbage, I surprised them, catching them completely unaware. I counted on them freezing up, becoming totally helpless. They usually begged and held up a useless hand, all of which I ignored.

But Pamela Haslem somehow had sensed me coming. (She couldn't have heard me: I was as quiet as falling snow.) Like a mother animal protecting her young, she must have picked up my thoughts in the air, felt my vibrations.

She gripped the frying pan, spun around, swinging it at me just as I lunged at her. The hot butter splashed across my arm at the same time as my Wüsthof pierced her stomach.

Chop.

Even through my heavy down parka I felt the burning and backed off, giving her time to stagger out of the kitchen. I followed the trail of blood up the stairs, flexing my burning arm. She had lost a lot of it. She would be weak, maybe dead, by the time I got to her.

From the landing at the top of the stairs, the blood trail hooked right. A hallway. White carpet here, red-splattered now, muffling my footsteps. The trail ended at a door to a room, a nursery.

I entered, the Wüsthof ready, hungry.

Chop.

The next moments were a blur of spasms, bodies in convulsion. I remembered a thrusting knife, twisted faces, arterial spray. And screaming. Small, shrill screams. Then silence. My clothes were soaked with sweat and blood. But the job was done.

As I left the Haslem's house, I looked over the Muratas' place at the top of the hill. It occurred to me that perhaps Lindblad and Bromley saw the Haslems as a trial run before the Muratas. Would it have to be? Would the Muratas heed the message I left them?

They'd better. Or . . .

Chop.

11

Ron Lindblad was still angry. Whenever he was angry his blood pressure rose, his face turned pink, and the muscles around his chin would tighten and begin to jump in an involuntary tic that caused his lips to purse and protrude. Ron was on Atenolol for his blood pressure and had forgotten to take his pill that morning. Norma, his wife, said that Ron's face when he was angry and worked up was the ugliest thing she had ever seen in her life. He breathed heavily through his nose and mouth as he thought about Norma and dredged up his favorite fantasy about her.

In the fantasy, it is a bright, beautiful summer day and Norma is doing her daily laps in their Olympic-size indoor-outdoor swimming pool. Suddenly she gets a bad cramp in her stomach. Of course, she doesn't know that Ron had slipped into her grapefruit juice three hundred mgs. of Amitriptyline—an antidepressant and sleeping pill they kept around—that induced the cramp. Norma, helpless in the middle of the pool, tries to make her way to the side but begins to double up in an even worse cramp.

She calls for Ron, sitting in a chair with his Bloody Mary and *Wall Street Journal*, but he pretends not to hear. He gets up slowly and pushes a button on the wall near the bath house, and the heavy gray nylon pool cover begins to close automatically. It is Sunday when the help is off, and no one is around to hear Norma screaming as the nylon cover begins to close around her. She makes a feeble attempt to make it to the side, but her arms and legs are cramping and she can't hope to fight the slow but inexorable approach of the cover. She casts a desperate glance over at Ron, who is holding his Bloody Mary, rubbing his thumb against the glass as if he were still pushing the button for the pool cover.

"Sauve qui peut," he whispers softly, even though she cannot hear him.

Through lidded eyes Ron watches Norma's face, contorted in fear, for the last time alive. Then she is completely sealed under the cover, and Ron takes quiet pleasure in watching her clumsy efforts to keep the cover up, delaying the inevitable by sucking in the remaining air. In her panic Norma forgets that her screaming and clawing at the cover use up valuable oxygen.

Finally, Norma's muffled cries and the small mounds in the cover made by her punching hands begin to disappear. Ron finishes his drink and then pushes the button again, opening the cover. He then hops in the pool, drags out the body, and leaves it at poolside. He returns to the house with their glasses and, with the most grief-stricken voice he can muster, he calls for an ambulance and waits.

The blare of a truck horn pulled him out of the fantasy, and he snapped the customized Mercedes 300 back into his lane. He had just gotten the Mercedes in a trade-in for his Porsche after getting sick of Norma always calling it his "mid-life crisis car." Ron was on his way back from Freeport, where, as he did at least twice a month, he visited the L.L. Bean outlet store and corporate headquarters. The visit always set him off in the worst way. He punched the button for the intermittent windshield wipers to slap away the snowflakes fluttering in front of his face.

Ron had seen them lining up outside the store early in the bitter-cold morning, the tour buses full of Japanese with the hardest damn currency in the world and ready to buy up everything in sight. That didn't include the Germans, the Scandinavians, and the Australians, not to mention the flocks of Americans from everywhere: the East, West, South. You name it. Imagine, the place was open twenty-four hours a day, three-hundred sixty-five days a year. Worse than a goddamn McDonald's. In the past thirty or so years, the only time it had ever closed was on the days J.F.K. was shot and old man Bean died, in 1967.

Ron had taken his usual spin around the store, pushing through the crush of shoppers. With a jaundiced eye he took in the shelves stocked with blankets, camping gear, and preppie clothes. They even had a children's department. In the middle of the men's section was a pool *stocked with fish.* And not only that, Ron heard a clerk say that Bean's was planning to put its catalogue on *computer,* so people could shop at home directly from their PCs.

But the kicker, the thing that really brought his blood to boil, was outside the store. The town of Freeport itself was one big shopping center, a mecca of outlet stores that sprang up like mushrooms around Bean. Look at them: Cole-Haan, Ralph Lauren, Reebok, Maidenform. The list went on.

Freeport was a tourist center, where people came to do nothing more than spend money. It was Las Vegas without the gambling, New York without the grime. At the center of it all was the L.L. Bean store, as massive and sprawling as an airport. It was one of, if not the biggest, tourist attractions in the state. Money flowed through it like water over Niagara Falls.

And there, where he had always been throughout his life—envying someone else's success—was Ron Lindblad. He felt like a starving man gazing through a restaurant window. Roaming around Freeport, passing the blissful faces of the fools forking over cash in the belief that they were getting a bargain with only a fifty percent mark-up, Ron was haunted by the question that pounded in his head like a mantra, that pricked at the essence of his being: *Why can't I have some of this action?* He felt the nervous tic raging at the right corner of his mouth.

Ron, who looked every bit of his sixty-one years, was doing very well by most standards. He was vice-president and minority shareholder of Country Customs, a moderately successful mail-order company offering New England crafts, such as quilts, decoys, hand-dipped candles, and birdhouses. The factory was in a high-security building just inside the Sparks city limits. For now, anyway. At least, that's what he told the IRS.

Ron had plans for Country Customs, big plans. In fact, his plans extended far beyond the company into an entire theme, a concept. His working name for this concept was Outlet City.

For years Ron had watched Freeport grow into the boom town that it was. He studied every decision the town fathers made, how they positioned the city to command the kind of business it did. The thing that impressed him the most was how Freeport had developed without much planning or infrastructure development. Basically, the town was the same old Freeport it had always been with a slew of stores, a few restaurants, and a sprinkling of hotels.

Why not do it right? Ron thought. Why not *create* a city that was built for nothing but commerce? Ron knew exactly what he would do. First he would trash Sparks as it now stood: the homes, shops, streets, even the underground plumbing. Then he would rebuild it, not with the huge stores you saw in Freeport, but he would start with smaller shops specializing in arts and crafts—paintings, sculpture, handmade furniture, toys. With the connections he'd make as governor, Ron would have the town declared a nonprofit corporation—something like Colonial Williamsburg in Virginia—so that all its profits were tax-exempt.

Having gotten the exemption, he would then swing into phase two, when he would open the city up to major outlets—everything in Freeport and more. He could see it now, all the big names bailing out of Freeport to come to Outlet City. Ron would bring in cable cars, shuttle buses, theme rides, all crisscrossing the city and available free of charge. Hell, make it easy for them to spend their money. He would let the big hotel chains bid for spots in the town, and he would make sure to leave room for bed and breakfasts, honeymoon cottages, and family inns with babysitting. He'd get the state to put in new roads, build an airport, and maybe even get some kind of duty-free status declared for foreigners.

Outlet City. What a concept! With a few well-timed moves and a little luck, it could turn into a monster.

But Ron was hemmed in, for the moment. First, there was Norma. His wife owned controlling interest in Country Customs, inherited from her mother, who had started the company. Norma was adamant about keeping it in Sparks despite Ron's urgings to move elsewhere. Why expand? she would say stupidly. We have everything we could possibly want. Besides, expansion would only make work. Just to get his goat, Norma would talk about selling the company and retiring, threatening to call her lawyer and draw up the papers.

Something else, a problem of a different nature, stood between Ron and his dream. It was water. Bays, lakes, streams, creeks, bogs—water of every kind—surrounded Sparks, making the town's environs inhospitable to immediate expansion and keeping Outlet City nothing more than a dream. Ron might even have been able to talk Norma into opening a bigger factory with an outlet store if there was enough solid ground to build on. He was absolutely sure that the company could take off beyond his wildest dreams if it had room to grow.

Ron had brought in developers, hydraulic engineers, and specialists of every stripe to come up with a plan for him. They all said the same thing: building around Sparks would be risky at best. Most predicted certain disaster: the constant shifting of the soft land would cause significant structural damage, not to mention the effects of repeated flooding on a building. Most of Maine consisted of a thin layer of topsoil over massive granite deposits. Except, to Ron's enormous frustration, for Sparks.

Ron had considered various ways of taking over Country Customs, even by murdering Norma, but so far his plans had gone no further than fantasy. When they had first met, Ron had been the company's assistant vice-president for distribution facilitation, which, as Norma used to say in her usual sarcastic way, meant that he ordered the boxes the merchandise was shipped in. Ron had the perspicacity to see that his way to the top of Country Customs was to marry Norma, who, by virtue of her toxic personality, had managed to drive away every eligible man her mother pushed her way. They were all about what you'd have expected—thin, lifeless-looking boys from the "better" families of Portland.

Ron knew that the way to get to Norma, and the reins to Country Customs, was through Norma's mother, old Mrs. Prescott. So he took up tennis, Mrs. Prescott's only passion, and worked late, making sure that she knew he was there. Mrs. Prescott had him to dinner, and he knew he was in if he could only hang in there with Norma. It turned out to be tougher than he ever expected. But eventually he married Norma and got what he wanted. Not Norma, but the keys to the president's office.

Ron knew he brought strengths to the company it had never had before, such as decisiveness, an oracle's marketing sense, and a keen feel for human nature. Ron could read a person like a sign on the highway. He was especially good for sniffing out losers and people he could use for whatever purpose that was in his, and the company's, best interests.

Norma and her mother made sure she retained controlling interest despite his strenuous efforts to prevent her from doing so. Ron learned a basic lesson: if you marry money, you end up earning it every day. Many were the times when he wished he could have just married the company and left Norma out of it. And then there were the times, more frequent lately, when he simply wished her dead.

Ron was coming up on his place and remembered a call he wanted to make. He snatched up his cellular car phone and said, "Barb Bromley," into it. It was the new Clarion cellular phone, the most advanced of its kind, with voice-activated personal calling that permitted him to call anyone by speaking their names into the phone. The phone was also linked to his CD player; Ron could play any one of five-hundred titles simply by saying the name of the album. He waited as excited air molecules were converted into a series of electronic signals that culminated in a purr in Barb's car phone.

He had added many custom features to the Mercedes. One was an anti-theft device that alerted him if his security has been tripped. If someone broke into the car, Ron would hear an alarm in a remote sensor. With the push of a button he could lock the thief in the car, air-tight with shatter-proof windows, until the police arrived. Ron had tried, unsuccessfully so far, to find a mechanic who would install a system that would also plug up the exhaust, start the ignition, and gas the bastard with carbon monoxide as he was trapped in the car.

Barb was the owner of Busy B's, the largest real estate company in greater Sparks. Ron was a silent partner. The company served many uses for him, not the least of which was leverage for getting Barb in the sack. He hadn't quite managed to pull it off yet—she was a slippery adversary—but he was working on it. It was only a matter of time.

Barb's voice mail answered and he hung up. Too bad, he thought, because he wanted to know if she would be at his party tonight, the big kickoff for his campaign. This time next year Ron expected to be in the governor's mansion in Augusta. There he would have everything he needed to unlock the doors to a major Country Customs expansion. Not only that, he could begin to put the screws to L.L. Bean and its Freeport bonanza.

Ron pulled into the service road that wound through about ten acres of hardwood forest before his house, a twenty-eight-room Georgian mansion, came into view. The house had been built in 1916 as one of several "emergency" houses for John D. Rockefeller, Jr., in case fire or flood threatened his main summer place at Seal Harbor up on Mount Desert Island, or if he had too many guests for the main house to handle. It was far and away the grand home of Sparks, a sprawling estate with riding stables, a deep-water pier in back for yachts, and, of course, the Olympic-size pool.

Ron drove the Mercedes up the tree-lined access road to the garage. The gardeners were out working, no doubt at

Norma's orders. They were planting hardy red and white cabbages along the walk to the house for tonight's party. Sure enough, there was Norma in parka and cords, directing the three men, shivering in the snow and digging holes for the cabbages. Norma was a thin, steely-eyed woman of fifty-seven with short silver hair. Ron hoped to avoid her as he entered.

He parked the car, and as he made his way toward the house, he passed Norma, who called out in a loud voice for the gardeners to hear: "Your face is red as a cherry, Ron. Been up to Bean's again?"

Norma's face exploded in a caustic laugh that burned like acid in Ron's ears. He did not acknowledge her, still laughing, as he strode past her toward the house. He fumbled with his keys and turned the lock.

"Don't forget your pill," she sputtered, "we can't have you going into cardiac arrest before your big party tonight." Ron kept his teeth clenched tight as he slammed the door behind him.

12

That evening, feeling a bit better after his fourth Tanqueray and tonic—TNT's, he called them—Ron looked down from the top of the grand staircase over the crowd milling in the foyer below. The place looked good. High recessed lights caught the glitter of sequins and jewelry on his guests, the cream of the cream from Portland and Augusta—deep pockets and a few political types in gowns and black tie, stuffing their mouths with catered food and knocking back jeroboams of champagne. A couple of carefully chosen reporters mingled among them, but this was not a media event. Those would come later.

Ron had invited people he had plans for—bankers, fund managers, developers, environmental types. Also on hand were the state attorney general and representative of the Federal Communications Commission. Ron circled the top of the staircase. He had not yet seen who he was looking for. A few people had noticed him and were beckoning him down. Ron waved at them but kept circling. Finally Ron saw his man: Al Cheseldine, the executive director of the local electrical utility.

Ron trotted down the stairs and came up behind Cheseldine, who was sliding a shrimp lathered in dill sauce into his mouth. Ron seized Cheseldine's arm, causing him to jump and smear sauce along his upper lip. Cheseldine was always nervous around Ron, precisely to Ron's liking. Ron and Norma were the major shareholders in the utility, and Ron was chairman of the board.

"Let's go back here," Ron said, leading Cheseldine to a dead space behind the staircase. Ron appraised Cheseldine, his rented tux, his scuffed shoes, one with a tassel missing, and the green mustache. Glassy globes of sweat rolled down his temples.

"Nice party, Mr. Lindblad," Cheseldine said, gawking at a tray of mini-quesadillas being passed nearby.

"Glad you're enjoying it," Ron said evenly. "It may be your last one here."

Cheseldine gagged. "Sir?"

"If I see one more fuck-up like the one you had the other day, you'll never find another job in this or any other state. Do I make myself clear?"

"Uh, yes sir, I mean, no. What fu—? What do you mean?"

"That power surge. The big one. It was nearly disastrous. Many homes in this area went without power for nearly twelve hours. Equipment was damaged, including some at my factory. A man was rushed to the hospital when his pacemaker malfunctioned. Fortunately, my people contained the damage and no one outside the immediate area found out about it. But we may not be that lucky again. Understand me, Cheseldine?"

"But, Mr. Lindblad," Cheseldine said quickly, fearing for his job, "that's a highly experimental system we set up out there. I mean, there can't be more than a half-dozen thyristor-controlled distribution stations like that one in operation throughout the entire country. Heh, heh, we've still got a ways to go on the learning curve, if you know what I mean. Especially with those solid-state circuit breakers. Why, the maintenance on those alone would keep us—"

"No more excuses," Ron Lindblad hissed, his mouth beginning to twitch. "One more mistake like that and you're through. Got it?"

Cheseldine could only nod his head lamely. If Cheseldine were just a little bit smart, Ron thought, he would have been able to see right through Ron, who was only bluffing, making him sweat. Ron knew that he had a good thing here, a CEO in his pocket who had obligingly agreed to build a new electrical substation and move power lines closer to Sparks, significantly upping the power supply to the Country Customs plant. All this had been done right under the noses of the town council and the FCC, without their approval.

"Good evening, Mr. Governor."

Ron turned and saw a face he knew very well, one that had been in his thoughts for most of the day. It belonged to Barb Bromley, whose arm was lightly on that of her husband, Sid. Al Cheseldine was relieved to have Ron's attention diverted and beat it out of there fast.

Ron drank in Barb's looks, his eyes moving slowly from her head to her feet. Her carefully colored, highlighted ash-blond hair was heavily sprayed and swept back dramatically off her forehead like Dina Merrill's. Her eyeliner had been permanently applied by a cosmetic surgeon, and she was deeply tanned even in the dead of winter. Her black strapless designer gown showed off her perfect figure, enhanced by daily workouts, liposuction, and a little silicone, judiciously applied. As usual, Ron took in the details; her jewelry, including a diamond ankle bracelet, her fine nails, her white, capped teeth. He wondered how women in real estate managed to get and keep their glamour, that perfect look.

As obviously as he admired Barb, Ron disregarded Sid, who stood off to the side, the proverbial third wheel. But that was fine with all concerned. The dynamics of the relationships among the three were unspoken but well defined.

Ron was clearly the boss, the one who ultimately called the shots. Barb was in the middle while not being a go-between. She couldn't have cared less how well Ron and Sid got along with each other unless her standing in the group was in any way jeopardized. She counted on a certain tension between Ron and Sid; if they ever got too cozy together, it could mean trouble for her, a loss of influence. She played the game as she calculated it should be played by keeping a distance from both men and making Ron believe something could happen between them as long as he treated her well, while making Sid believe that something terrible would happen to him if he didn't.

For his part, Sid understood that he was to be quietly

subservient to Ron at all times, even as now, when his wife was undergoing the kind of inspection typically given a cut of meat by a butcher. After all, wasn't it Ron who had set Sid up with his show and continued to sponsor it with Country Customs advertising money? Nervous, with a surface celebrity charm that hid his essentially mean spirit, Sid was on call for Ron whenever some dirty work needed to be done, which was frequently. He did not know that by accepting Ron's patronage he had given him a direct line to Barb.

Barb fluttered around Ron, her flirtation designed solely to further her interests. She was vaguely aware that she was sexually aroused, not by either man flanking her but by the display of wealth around her. The guests, with their money and influence, did not matter to her as much as the *things* in the Lindblad house. Out of the corner of her eye she considered the Persian carpets, the Waterford crystal chandeliers, and rich Clarence House fabric on the chairs and sofas. The Sherle Wagner custom-designed commode and wash basin in the powder room had not escaped her scrutiny. She even had stolen a look into the master bedroom upstairs, savoring the textures of the Brunschwig and Fils-covered draperies and pillows over the Shaker bed. And was that an *original* Wyeth hanging above the mantel in the living room?

Not oblivious to the attention his wife was showering on another man, Sid considered it all a part of dealing with the sponsor. Secretly he harbored ambitions for taking his show national and was waiting for the right moment to solicit Ron's assistance, possibly as subtle blackmail. Even so, Sid nervously chewed at the membrane wall inside his cheek and thought ahead to when he could casually slip into a bathroom for a couple hits of Power from the vial in his suit pocket.

"So, Ron," Barb said, skimming a perfect fingernail around the rim of her glass. "Is tonight the big night?"

"Big night for what?" Ron said, his voice thick with insinuation.

"For announcing your candidacy for the governorship," Barb said back, smiling. "What else?"

"Couldn't imagine," he said, his eyes fast on her. Sid coughed and pressed the back of his sleeve against his sweaty brow. Ron studied Sid for a moment, taking in the shaky hands, dry lips, and pasty white skin contrasting starkly with his dark brown hairpiece. Then Ron felt a hand on his arm. Oh, great, he thought, Norma was here.

In a way more obvious than he realized, Ron compared Norma to Barb. It was no contest. With her lizard skin, crepe neck, and over-dry salt-and-pepper hair, Norma looked like she could be Barb's mother, or at least an aunt.

Ron felt his anger returning as he compared the two women. Norma was already drunk, he noticed, probably on her fifth or sixth martini. She was imperious and, like most people raised with money, suspicious of the people around her, especially her husband and his friends. Aware of Ron's attraction to Barb, Norma was intimidated by her but not to the point of being afraid of her or Ron. Ron and she were negotiating the terms of their will, and Norma assumed she had Ron around her finger.

"Lovely party, Norma," Barb said, hoping that insincere pleasantries would obviate a scene. Wishful thinking.

"Evening, Barb," Norma said, jiggling the ice in her drink and unable to look her in the eye. "How's your business doing? Let me see, it's real estate, isn't it? Mmmmm, must be difficult putting up those For Sale signs along the road every weekend, especially with the ground so hard this time of year."

Barb smiled, keeping her eyes level with Norma's. "Nice of you to ask, Norma. Actually, a little work never did anyone any harm," taking a broadside at Norma's life of leisure.

It was Norma's turn to look Barb in the eye. "Work?" she said with measured incredulity in her voice. "Funny you should mention that. Just the other day Ron and I were going over Country Customs' budget and noticed how much we spend on advertising through Sid's little show. I suppose that's just good news for your plastic surgeon."

Barb laughed and, with a shade of menace, said, "Haven't gotten any complaints lately." After letting *that* one sink in, Barb offered sweetly, "Perhaps *you'd* like to have the name of my surgeon. He could do wonders for your liver spots, varicose veins, loose skin, and those other little post-menopausal problems.

"Oh, and Norma," Barb continued, smelling blood, "I was going to ask you about those cunning little cabbages you obviously planted for tonight. Are you planning to make a salad with them after the party is over?"

Ron pulled Sid out of the line of fire and over to an alcove where a developer from Portland was going at it with an environmentalist from Augusta. Ron thought they would be safer there.

"We have a problem in Mexico," Ron whispered near Sid's ear. "Lieutenant Diaz wants more than we gave him last time. Word is that his boss, the captain, is demanding more. You have to go down there tomorrow and straighten it out."

Sid's jaw dropped but Ron ignored it. "Give Diaz what he wants but tell him it's a one-time-only deal," Ron instructed. "He'll have to take care of his captain if he wants to see any more from us. Make it clear there are lots of other lieutenants in the Mexican border patrol who are more than willing to talk to us. Understood?"

In his mind Sid had already begun to flip through the scheduling changes he would have to make in his show. In order to stop by Ron's tomorrow morning and pick up the briefcase full of cash and then drive to Portland, fly to Boston and then San Diego, and then rent a car for Tijuana, he would have to do at least two, maybe three, reruns, and reschedule the interviews he had planned for the next three days. Sid could plainly see the kind of mood Ron was in and knew better than to do anything but go along.

Sid figured now was as bad a time as any, so he drew in a breath and said, "I met with our associate yesterday."

Ron's head tilted straight back as he downed his TNT, apparently with little enjoyment. "So, how're we doing?" he asked.

"Well, I'm not sure."

Ron looked at him, his eyes narrowing. "Explain yourself, Sid. I have no time for games."

"We met out at the substation, like you told me to. We talked about the kil—"

"Careful," Ron said quietly, smiling and nodding at passing guests.

". . . kilowatts, the power requirements."

"Go on," Ron whispered after the guests had gone by. "The killings. What's happening with them?"

"Things aren't going . . ." Sid paused, searching for the right words ". . . exactly to plan." He felt moisture seeping down the back of his neck.

Ron shuffled his feet, impatient. Sid began talking fast. "There's been an unauthorized murder. An old drunk named Theroux. We're okay, I checked. Theroux lived alone. No family. The killer was driving through town and, I guess, saw him alone, drunk, and . . . killed him."

"*Killed* him? Why?"

"I—I'm not sure," Sid stammered, sweating openly now. "Maybe as a kind of . . . contribution to our . . . efforts. It means there's a new house for us to work with. I made it clear that this wasn't—was unacceptable. It just couldn't go on."

"Is this the first one like this?"

"Yes. As far as I know."

"As far as you know," Ron said, eyeing Sid.

Ron stood still for nearly a minute, thinking. He knew that every situation offered an upside and a downside. The downside was obvious here: a rogue killer loose in a small town. And not just any killer, but *his* killer. The trail led straight to his doorstep. Even with an ironclad alibi for each killing, Ron stood to lose a great deal if the killer were caught and then talked.

The upside was more difficult to discern. This sudden turn of events suggested to Ron that he needed to move with the situation. Maybe this was an isolated incident. Maybe Sid was right, that the killer was trying to help out Ron's plan in some bizarre way. It was too soon to pu the plug on the killer just yet. Some very important business was left to be done right away. Ron had no one to turn to finish it for him. Certainly not Sid. There had to be some discreet way to handle this.

"Okay," he said, "the first thing I'll do is speak to Barb about having the title of . . . What'd you say his name was?"

"Theroux," Sid said. "Lorton Theroux."

". . . the title of Theroux's property transferred to an estate that we will immediately snap up. Then I'll have her plant another of her little good-bye stories in the magazine, how Theroux went off to . . . let's say, California to live with, er, his son, a construction worker. Something like that."

Sid nodded his head in eager agreement. It had been his suggestion to concoct the good-bye blurbs that appeared in *The Maine Event,* a local magazine, whenever they had someone bumped off. The little notices answered any questions from nosy neighbors about where these people went, and why. Of course, like any good idea Sid had, Ron appropriated it as his own.

"How often do you meet with our associate?" Ron said to Sid.

"Uh, once a month or so. We talk on the phone if something comes up."

"The phone? What about wiretaps?"

"I usually call from pay phones. And we never talk directly, always in code. For example, if the killer just eliminated someone, we say that a house just came on the—"

"I want you to meet more frequently," Ron said, speaking low and furtively. "Once, twice a week. At least twice a week. Tell the killer we're entering a new phase of the operation. Send the message that we need to confer on everything. Unauthorized killings are to stop immediately. But be subtle about it. Offer more money—not much more—but make the point that things are especially delicate now. And keep me posted."

Sid listened, feeling cold gooseflesh spreading over his body. The prospect of spending more time with the killer filled him with intense dread. He needed a good hit of

Power right now. He looked around, spied a bathroom, and was making a move to leave when he was held in his place by the tinkling of spoon against glass.

Calvin Wingate, a Portland business associate of Ron's and early campaign supporter, was clearing his throat and asking for attention.

"Ladies and gentlemen," Wingate said, his voice ringing off the Italian marble floors. "I'd like to propose a toast to our friend, host, and next governor of Maine: Ron Lindblad."

Some guests raised their glasses and cheered, others applauded. Ron allowed a thin smile and nodded at the crowd. His gaze found Barb in the crowd and settled in on her, the perfect first lady, he thought.

Sid, trapped in the crowd and in the early stages of meth withdrawal, was forced to watch his boss leering at his wife. He chewed the inside of his cheek with the intensity of a rodent and tasted blood.

Norma, who was taking in the whole scene, nervously jiggled the ice in her glass.

13

A relentless drizzle mixed with snow glazed the streets of Sparks and smeared the windshield of Nara's Range Rover on her way to work the next day. The gray, waterlogged town gave the appearance of a corpse sucked bloodless by a vampire. Creeping past an abandoned cannery, Nara recalled Swinburne's description of winter as the season of snows and sins. Sparks presented itself not quite as a hell, and certainly not as a heaven, but as a purgatory—where people were sent to be cleansed of their sins.

Nothing felt right to her. The humid air clung to her extremities like plaques of fungus. Every movement she made was an effort. The front seat felt clammy, and the road was slick and treacherous. She fiddled with the heat controls and shifted uneasily in her seat. She'd been edgy for days, ever since that vicious message appeared on the house. Nara didn't kid herself about the message: it had been meant for her.

The word *gook* wasn't new to her, she'd grown up with it. Chink, slope, slant—she'd heard them all, especially at school after the Vietnam War. She remembered men, some claiming to be veterans, harassing her father, a Japanese, at his bar in Florida. But the hassling was mostly tame—all talk—and never threatened death.

How seriously to take this message, she didn't know. Was it mere adolescent aggression or a genuine threat? And then there was the family next door, the people David was sure had been murdered. Ever since breaking into their house, David hadn't said a word as he dug into his computers trying to find out about them. But Nara knew what he was thinking: the murders were really meant for them.

To Nara, the whole thing was so far-fetched. Who, besides David, had heard anything on the baby monitor? No one. And how could some killer just come in, kill off an entirely family, and leave the place spotlessly clean, as David said it was? Were mass murderers carrying Pine-Sol around with them now? Still, it was unsettling, all this talk about killing and disappearances. When Nara was younger she would have shrugged it off and moved on. But now motherhood brought entirely new perspectives and new fears. It was one thing to put herself at risk, but her child . . .

Entering town, Nara spied a group of people she'd never seen before, about six or seven of them, walking in slow circles through the harbor area. Their heads were bent, looking at something in their hands. She downshifted as she passed them, but they didn't notice her, absorbed as they were in whatever they were doing. She shrugged and drove on to the office but made a mental note to take a look later.

One benny of her job was the parking; she always got the same place on the curb right in front of the office. In fact, it was a rare day that Nara saw anyone on the streets of Sparks, which made the appearance of the group at the harbor all the stranger. She entered the office, which she called the Sparks Chamber of Commerce. Posters, menus, and flyers announcing blueberry, lobster, and other festivals of various stripes were plastered over the walls. Nara's "desk" was a sheet of particle board held up by plastic milk cartons and covered over with a swatch of batik.

Liz, the editor and publisher, was deep into a telephone debate on the other side of the room, stabbing her cigarette in the air and constantly crossing and uncrossing her legs. Nara tried not to listen, but it was next to impossible. She had heard this conversation before. Liz was trying to hold on to an advertiser who wanted to pull out on her.

"Have you tried changing the menu?" Liz said into the phone. "Mmm, who knows what tourists want anymore?

Yes sir, I think your prices are fair. That's not why business if off. I'll tell you what it is: the recession. Mmm, yes sir, you do need to think about controlling costs. But this is definitely not the time to stop advertising."

Desperation seeped through the air like a virus. Liz shook her head and stamped out the cigarette. She cradled the receiver in her neck and lit up a new one, listening to her nervous customer.

Nara checked her desk, sifting through the mail and messages. There were the usual flyers on crafts shows and auctions and a slew of press releases from Country Customs announcing its spring line of primitive tin-punched jelly closets. Who did she know actually needed a jelly closet?

Here was something interesting: an invitation to a black-tie party at Ron Lindblad's. Was this the Country Customs Lindblad? she wondered as she read the invitation. She saw the date: the party had been last night. Oh, well. She didn't like going out at night anyway and leaving David with Von, especially since he spent the whole day with him.

Nara opened a folder marked Current, and found a little editing assignment waiting for her. One feature in *The Maine Event* was the Community News column, a mixed bag of birth and wedding announcements, anniversaries, college graduations, and the like. It was a glorified gossip column and everyone around Penobscot Bay read it. Some people phoned their announcements in, and Nara would call them back to work out a little blurb to go into the column. Once in a while someone would send one in all written up and she would only have to edit it.

In the file were four phone messages to return and one written announcement. She read the announcement, recognizing the Courier legal typewriter font and the dippy-cheery writing style from others she had received over the past few months. This one read:

> . . . And our hearts really go out to poor Lorton Theroux, who just last week let us know that he was moving out to California to live with his son, a construction worker. Lorton, a longtime Sparker formerly with the Sparks Sea-

> food Processing Company, will now have to endure those long, hard California winters while the rest of us live it up here on Penobscot Bay. Good luck, Lorton!

Liz hung up the phone and sat quietly for several seconds, smoking down her cigarette and then grinding it into the ashtray on her desk.

"They're dropping like flies," she said, her voice hoarse and raspy.

Nara's head snapped up. "Who?" she said.

"Colonel Harris. He's run a quarter-pager every edition for the past three years. Now he's thinking of dumping us and going to cable TV. Can you believe it?"

Nara now understood that Colonel Harris was the reason why Liz used "yes, sir" in her conversation, something she rarely did. "Did you suggest that he change the name of his restaurant?" Nara said. Colonel Harris, retired career army, named his place The Mess.

Liz grinned at her ashtray. A long silence followed. Liz lit up again and looked at Nara.

"So, are you going to tell me what's been going on these past few days?" she said.

Nara felt her cheeks flush. She didn't know she had been so obvious. Rather than getting into the business about the message on the house, she kept it strictly business.

Nara clicked her tongue. "Oh, just a little run down," she said. "David, Von, and I have been passing around a bug. There's an announcement in the Current file, about the man leaving for California."

Liz had to think a moment. "Oh, yeah, we got a few more things for Community News. Can you get started on them today?"

"Sure. I was just wondering where it came from." She looked at the name in the announcement. "Did Mr. Theroux bring it by?"

Liz chuckled. "Do you know Lorton Theroux? Even if he ever learned how to type, he couldn't see straight enough to write a coherent message."

"He drinks?" Nara said.

"With extreme prejudice," Liz answered. "Now, let's see. Who brought that by? Oh, yeah, it was Barb Bromley. She dropped it off with an ad she wants us to run. A full-pager. Manna from heaven."

"Why would she go to the trouble?"

"Oh, she's like that. You should see her ad trumpeting her full-service real estate system. I guess she considers the announcements part of the job."

"So she sold Mr. Theroux's house for him?"

Liz shrugged. "I guess. Why? What's up?"

Nara went quiet again. She didn't know what to say. It was just a hunch, a possible connection with Estelle Grout and her disappearing friends. "Oh, just curious. Well, I'd better get started."

"I heard about the artwork on your house," Liz said, catching Nara offguard.

Nara looked away from her. "How?"

"I'm a reporter, remember? At least I used to be, before I started selling advertising. Everything okay with you guys?"

"Yes, sure. We have no idea who did it. David said he'd call a painter to come out to cover it up. I wish he'd get to it."

"Call the police?"

"No, we'd rather not bother. What can they do anyway?"

Liz shrugged and lit up another cigarette. "It's your house. In my thirty-four years in Sparks, I've never heard of someone's house getting vandalized like that. Sure, we get graffiti on condemned buildings, but nothing as malicious as what happened to you."

"We'll handle it," Nara said, hoping to politely put a lid on the conversation. She was grateful when Liz stood and ducked into the supply room in the back of the office.

In one of the milk cartons supporting her desk, Nara kept back issues of *The Maine Event*. She pulled out her entire collection and began flipping through it, looking for the Community News columns with the dippy-cheery goodbyes. Here was the one from November—Alan Logue—who "rode off into the sunset to Arizona." What tripe! The next was Irene McNamara, who had retired to California—just like Lorton Theroux, Nara thought. Then came Guy Needleman, who had gone to Georgia, Roxanne Ward, who had retired to Florida, and Gunther Kriebel, who had gone to live with his brother in Wyoming.

Strange that they never say exactly where they're going. And every one was written in the same hokey style by Barb Bromley. Nara tried to remember where she had put that list Estelle Grout had given her of friends who had left Sparks without saying good-bye. She was certain that the names would match some of those showing up in the Community News.

Her thoughts were interrupted by a call from Simon Globus, David's and her lawyer and financial counselor. Simon, based in New York, was David's loyal attorney and investment adviser, even during the dark days when David had been bounced out of PanTech, the company he started. Simon stood by David and kept his whereabouts secret, even when the feds were pounding at his door and serving him a new subpoena every other day.

The conversation started out routinely. Simon was getting used to Nara and the idea that she was now managing David's finances. He first brought her up to date on some investments he'd recently made. Nara had already sent him their tax materials for the past year's filing, and he was calling to verify some information.

"Have you taken a look at your electric bill lately?" Simon asked.

"Yes, I just paid it," Nara said.

"It's outrageous," he said. Nara could hear him shuffling through papers. "Since last October it's increased over a thousand percent. What're you running up there, a Crazy Eddie's?"

"Well, you know how it is. David likes his toys."

Simon just grunted and rattled more papers. "I've never seen the likes of this," he said, his voice beginning to fade as he turned away from his speaker phone. "At least not at a private residence. How many computers do you own, anyway?"

"Thirty or so, maybe more. But that doesn't include a lot of other stuff."

"Stuff? What stuff?"

"David calls them peripherals. You know, modems—lots of modems—file servers, that sort of thing."

"It's costing you a fortune."

"Can we afford it?"

"Of course. That's not the point."

"What *is* the point, Simon?"

"Well, maybe we can economize a little bit. Turn things off when we're not using them."

Nara rolled her eyes. It was "we" now. "I'll mention it to him," she said. Preparing herself for the outburst to follow, Nara went on gamely, "Now, you know what he'll want."

Simon did not suppress his groan. "But, Nara, we've been through this a million times. It doesn't really mean anything. And you have no idea how ephemeral those numbers are. Why, the foreign exchanges alone would take us—"

"So give me the two outside figures. You know he'll want something. And if he doesn't get it, he'll assume something's wrong and be on the phone immediately to you."

"Okay, okay," he relented. "At the low end, your net assets are valued at . . . $704,577,259. Call it seven-oh-five. At the high end, we come out at $781,360,111. Now please, please tell him what's involved in that spread. A lot of his assets—I mean, your assets—are tied up in real estate, much of which is overseas. Putting a cash value on that is like hitting a moving target."

"He'll understand, Simon."

"For instance, that house you're in now, its value is dropping like a bond trader off the World Trade Center."

Nara was surprised. "Why is that?"

"I would think you'd know. The homes in your town are moving like hot dogs and beer on opening day. And prices are sliding just as fast."

Simon always was heavy on the metaphors, Nara thought.

"Can you send me what you have on it?" she said. "I'd be interested."

"Sure," Simon said. "Anything else?"

"No. I may call you again in a few days."

"Fine," he said. "My best to David."

Nara sat back in her chair. How could home values in Sparks have dropped so precipitously? Who was selling them? And why hadn't she seen any For Sale signs?

A noise at the door pulled her from her thoughts. Both Liz and she got up to open it at the same time. Nara got to it first, but no one was there. Liz shrieked and Nara looked down as a small alligator hopped past her through the door.

Nara, who had grown up in the Florida Keys, had seen many strange animals in her time, including her share of alligators. But this was Maine, in February. The alligator decided that *The Maine Event*'s office had nothing to offer, and so it turned around stiffly and went out. Both Liz and Nara craned their necks out the door, watching the alligator stroll away.

"You think it wanted a subscription?" Nara said to Liz, who had not yet closed her mouth.

Stiff and labored as a zombie, the pediatric nurse in a rumpled gray uniform moved to the center of the room, looked down at the chart in her hand, and mumbled a child's name in a tired, defeated voice. All heads in the room went up hopefully, struggling to hear the name. A mother nodded, stood slowly, and packed her child off as the nurse disappeared down a long corridor of examining rooms.

For nearly an hour David had been with Von in the "sick" waiting room at the pediatrician's, jammed with miserable children and even more miserable parents. The "well" room had also been taken over by the ill. Von, like David, had been suffering from a low-grade fever, alternating restlessness and lassitude, and loss of appetite. The children in the room were either sobbing uncontrollably or too sick to cry at all. David noticed the sense of grim urgency in the demeanor of the normally cheerful nurse and secretary. He also noticed that he was the only male in the room above the age of eight.

As he waited, David overhead a conversation between two mothers, one with three small sick children, the other with four. The first mother, a large woman in a sweatshirt printed with I'M WITH STUPID and a finger pointing sideways, explained to the thin, exhausted-looking woman next to her that the cause of all the illness was "the foreigners."

"Think about it," she said in a loud whisper. "The-ah they are in the-ah own countries, walking around in towels and bare feet, picking up all kinds of diseases, eating things you and I would throw down the disposal. Then they get in filthy little boats, where the-ah packed in with other foreigners with other diseases, and sit and fester for months. Then they get he-ah, jump off their boats with their diseases, put their kids in our schools, and suddenly we have an epidemic and everyone's wondering where it came from."

David noticed a young Latino woman with two children sitting impassively in the waiting room, either not understanding or choosing to ignore the woman. He wondered what had brought them to Sparks of all places and, if they had a chance to do it over again, they would still choose to come here. The nurse came out and called them, and they worked their way through the toys and past the glare of the woman in the T-shirt. She also called for Von, and David hustled him through guiltily.

The doctor, usually calm and matronly, appeared addled as she hurriedly checked Von. David asked her what was causing the rash of illness, and she blew a strand of hair out of her face, removed her glasses, and sat back, obviously relieved to be able to pause for a moment.

"In over thirty years of practice, I've never seen the likes of this," she said. "I see children at the medical center up in Rockland, and they're not suffering half of what kids down here are going through. Something seems to be affecting their ability to fight viruses."

A child cried out in a neighboring room as a nurse administered a shot. The doctor's voice went lower. "I hear things," she said. "At the emergency room at the medical center, they say they're seeing more miscarriages, domestic violence, and other stress-related problems from this area than they are from any other. Don't know what to make of it.

"Odd, very odd," she mumbled over and over as she scribbled a prescription for Von and him on a pad, and left without saying a word. On his way out through the waiting room, passing more immigrant families wearing shabby clothes and uncomprehending expressions, David felt something stirring inside him, something he didn't like. Despite being married to Nara, a first-generation Balinese-Japanese, he felt the things the woman in the waiting room had been saying were beginning to infect him like a contagion.

Poisonous questions coated his mind as he held Von close, protecting him. Was his son's illness caused by immigrant viruses? Are we, those who were here before them, as vulnerable to their taint as the Indians were to ours? What do these people really contribute to society anyway? Why do we let so many of them in? David shut off the nasty little voice inside him and took Von home.

But first there was one stop he had to make.

14

With Von in his arms, David raced from the truck up the slope of his front lawn to his house. He reached the front door, his chest heaving and sides aching, and fished for the keys in his coat pocket. It was at moments like these when he realized how out of shape he truly was.

"Man," he choked, still trying to catch his breath and find the damn keys. And then, "Yaaah!" as someone suddenly materialized at his side, causing him to jump and almost drop Von.

It was just Jean, in a black watch cap and peacoat.

"Shit, Jean," he said, trembling. "What the hell are you doing here?"

"Watch your language," she scolded, taking Von from him. "Your son'll sound like a sailor before he's three."

Von smiled a gummy smile at her. "How's my little man?" she purred, pulling his coat closed.

David finally found the keys and opened the door. He was anxious to get back to the dining room window and his new toy. Heading straight for the kitchen, he said, "Want some coffee?" to Jean, hoping she would say yes, giving him an excuse to make a big pot.

"Oh, no, thanks," she said, following him into the kitchen, helping Von off with his coat. "Not staying long. Nara called me from her office, said she'd been trying to reach you he-ah and thought maybe you came by my place. I was in the neighborhood and thought I'd stop in. What's wrong with you, anyway?"

David didn't realize he was still trembling. "Oh, nothing,

a little chilly." He began making coffee anyway and Jean sat down at the table.

"Jean," he said, pouring into a filter some coffee beans he had ground that morning, a hardy robusta from the Ivory Coast he was trying out, "tell me what you think about this. I just spent the past hour up at the Rockland courthouse, going through real estate records for anything I could find on that house behind ours."

Jean, cuddling Von, looked up at David, who was pouring water into the coffee maker. He talked with his back to Jean, making it difficult for her to understand him. "The only thing I could find," he said, "was a new deed to the house registered to the Busy B's Real Estate Company. Ever hear of it?"

"I've seen their signs," she said.

David shook his head. "What's strange is that no other record on the house was on file. I mean, go look at the place. It must be a good forty or fifty years old and had a half-dozen owners. I even asked the clerk at the courthouse, and all he could do was agree that it *was* a bit unusual. The other thing I thought was weird was that the house had been sold just yesterday, and the transaction had already been recorded and filed. The people's name is Haslem, according to the records. Don't you think all this is kinda . . . suspicious?"

David looked at Jean, who put her finger to her lips and pointed at Von, out cold in her arms. She rose and carried him off to his room. David saw this an opportunity to play with his new toy—a telescope trained at the house in the back—and rushed to the dining room.

This was no ordinary telescope. It was a seven-inch Questar Maksutov-Cassegrain with a Nagler eyepiece. ("You could see Beetlegeuse on a cloudy day with this thing," the salesman in Portland had joked as David examined it. "It'll separate double stars and give you astounding detail on Jupiter." When the salesman asked David how he wanted to pay for it, David, who owned no credit cards or even a checkbook, plunked down $16,000 from the $30,000 in cash he was carrying in an old duffel bag. Swallowing hard, the salesman's gulp was audible. "Come again," he said as David left with the telescope in the back of his truck.)

David, now at the dining room window, peered through the eyepiece, frantically adjusting its focus. He had sighted it precisely at the window and was now excited that the blinds were up, affording him a rare view of the living room. He ran his tongue over his front teeth as he studied the room. No one was there, and David could count not only the cat hairs on the sofa but also the number of fabric nubs per inch on the sofa.

"Weird," he said, never one to shirk from overusing a word. "You didn't even *own* a cat a couple days ago."

David had reached the conclusion that this new family was even stranger than the other one, the Flintstones. He found that he couldn't get up early enough to see them leave in the morning. And he never seemed to be able to catch them as they arrived home at night. He had fixed a telescopic lens to a motion-activated video camera, hoping to catch some scenes of the new people, possibly cutting up the remains of the other family. But he had gotten nothing, the blinds usually down.

David suddenly felt a hand on his shoulder and then heard an awful crunch as he bit down on his tongue. He spun around and found Jean standing there, eyeing him balefully.

"Shit, Jean," he said, tasting blood and feeling pain spread across his mouth. "Is *every*body out to scare me to death?"

She spoke slowly, with her big arms folded across her chest and a righteous edge to her voice that was more than her usual grumpiness. "This is wrong, David," she said. "You have no right looking into other people's lives. You could get into serious trouble for this. Have you thought about that? And have you given any thought to what it could mean for your son?"

David looked at her. "Damn, Jean, it's not like I'm robbing them or anything." He found it hard to talk as his tongue throbbed and swelled.

Her blue eyes flickered at him. "You must stop this immediately," she said sternly. "These people are no business of yours. Put your child before yourself for once."

"Jean, listen," David insisted. In a single breath he told her about the house, the screams in the monitor, the new family. He ran down the scenarios he'd imagined of what had happened to the Haslems. He did not reveal his deepest fear, that the family had been killed by mistake, that *his* family was really the intended target.

Jean shook her head as he went through it all, but David sensed something in her, an uneasiness, and he believed the story was getting to her.

"Did you ever know those people," he asked quietly, "the ones who lived there before?"

Jean squinted through the window. "No, but I do know the Mitchells, the people who live in that white house next door to them on Peachtree."

"Hey," David said, excited, "would you mind asking them about that family? Just to find out their full names, or if they saw them move? It doesn't have to be now, but sometime when you're—"

"I'll do it now," Jean said and brushed past him toward the kitchen door. Great, thought David, maybe now we'll get a few answers.

As Jean trudged through the backyard toward the white house, David looked through the telescope again. He trained it on a pile of magazines and books on one of the black lacquer end tables and he read their covers: *TV Guide, English Made Simple, House and Garden.* Suddenly he remembered the Country Customs catalogue he had taken from the house and ran into the kitchen, where he found it under a pile of Von's Barney the dinosaur paraphernalia. He checked the name and address label:

Pamela and Douglas Haslem
84 Peachtree Lane
Sparks, Maine 04842

"That's it," David said, getting an idea. He raced into the living room. "Let's see," he said to the rows of computers lining the walls, "which one of you will be the lucky one?" He selected a souped-up PanTech 586 with an internal modem, switched it on, and entered the Haslems' names into a software program he had created that enabled him to automatically track names stored in just about any computer system in the world.

David could keep several searches going at once on his screen using Windows and hyper-card technology. Rather than do a global database search, he asked the program to run the names through selected national databases for credit history, banking records, telephone status, airline ticketing, moving-company billings, car and U-Haul rentals, and post office files.

Keying in the last of the commands, David shivered as a chill swept over him. He stopped for a moment and reflected on what he was doing. This was no longer semi-harmless mucking around in secured computer files. Each step he took deeper into this mystery brought him closer to its violent core. Was he getting into something here he should just leave alone? Where would it lead him?

He looked up and saw the Fisher-Price baby monitor resting atop his CPU, its red display light stretching the length of Von's every breath. Who put *that* there? he wondered. It must have come on when he switched on the computer. Somehow the little monitor appeared terrifying to him, a messenger of death. He turned it off and went back to the computer screen.

The Haslems' names came up in a bank statement, something about the sale of their house to the Busy B's Real Estate Company, the same one from David's search at the Rockland courthouse. Maybe I'll pay a call on Busy B's, David thought, maybe ask B some questions. But he would need some kind of disguise.

David also found the Haslems' names—Douglas and Pamela—through a Master Card issued by a Boston bank. He discovered that Douglas Haslem had his bachelor's degree in accounting from Harvard in 1979 and an MBA from the Sloan School of Management at MIT. Pamela was a little harder to find, probably because she'd still had her maiden name in college. But there she was, an alumna of Wellesley College, where she had received a bachelor's in political science in 1981, registered then as "O'Keefe" but now as "Haslem" in the college's alumnae affairs' database.

With a little more searching, David found out the name of Douglas Haslem's former employer—Dietrich and Moore—which, as he learned through more checking, was a major accounting firm in Boston. Haslem had had a good salary in Boston but left his job about three months ago, roughly the time David began to notice them next door. David could find nothing else on Pamela Haslem, or anything on their children. Perhaps later he could check hospital records in Boston on the children's birth.

Before searching any further, David began to wonder what a big-time accountant like Haslem would be doing in Sparks. The Haslems apparently had never opened a local bank account, had not changed their address at the post office, nor canceled their telephone service, had not hired a moving company or rented a U-Haul or car, *if* they had moved. And they certainly had not bought an airline ticket. Had they simply dropped off the face of the earth? Or had someone dropped them?

David gazed mindlessly at the digital display board that Nara had set to remind him to pack for their long weekend on Murata Island out in Penobscot Bay. They used to do this once every two or three months, but less since Von was born. David remembered he was supposed to do some grocery shopping for the trip.

His eyes came to rest on the Country Customs catalogue. He wondered: did the Haslems ever order anything from the catalogue? Or maybe, just maybe, the company had a forwarding address for them somewhere in its files. David had no idea if Country Customs even used computers. He began to ask his program to do a search of the company's computers just as Jean burst through the door, ashen-faced and trembling.

David jumped from his computer and went to her. "What is it, Jean?"

"A man," she said, closing the door and bolting it. "Quick, look. Did he follow me?"

David cracked the curtains on the floor-to-ceiling windows. He saw nothing.

"Out back," she whispered. "In the yard. That's whe-ah I saw him."

A thought occurred to David. "Was he Asian?" he asked her, hopeful. "With, like, layers of clothes on and a baseball cap?"

Jean looked at him as if he were nuts, for about the third time that day. "He was big, real big. And dressed all in black. It could have been leather, I don't know. He had one of those haircuts," she said, making a cutting motion over the top of her head.

"You mean a buzz cut?" David said, totally puzzled.

"Yeah. He was sort of . . . lurking near the woods by that house next door. He ran away when he saw me looking at him. I—I really didn't get a good look at him. I ran all the way back he-ah."

With Jean following close behind, David headed for the dining room window and looked out. Threads of smoke twisted from chimneys below. A light wind rattled the pines and spruces. But no one was to be seen.

"He's gone," David said, disappointed. They both looked again. "Find out anything about the family?" he asked.

"I'll have some of that coffee now," Jean said. In the kitchen, sipping the robusta, she seemed to calm down a bit. "I didn't see him as I was coming down the hill," she said. "Dottie Mitchell was home. I hadn't seen her in years. My, she's aged. Anyways, Dottie told me the Haslem family moved in a few months ago. She met Pammy—the wife—but the family mostly kept to themselves. Dottie said they certainly wouldn't have gone anywhere without her knowing about it. I guess you're not the only snoop in the neighborhood."

Jean held up her cup with both hands, signaling for more. "Well, that was it until I spotted that goon over near the woods, watching me."

They drank their coffee in silence. "Did you know,"

David said, trying to break the tension, "that coffee was so important to the Ottoman Turks they actually had a law that a wife could divorce her husband if he failed to keep an adequate supply of it in the house? Grounds for divorce, heh, heh."

"Hmmph," Jean growled. She had knocked back her second cup but was still shaky. "David," she said, sliding forward on her seat toward him, "just suppose something *is* going on around here. Judging from what's been written on the front of your house, I'd say you might be in some kind of danger. Have you given any thought to . . . leaving?"

David sat up straight. "Leaving? Sparks?" he said. "No. Uh-uh."

Jean looked down, shaking her head. "Maybe you should," she said, almost to herself, "for your family's sake."

Then she looked at her watch and stood up. "Gotta get going," she said briskly. "A fourth-grade class from Bath is due at the Lobster Museum at two."

David was mildly surprised when his offer to walk Jean to her car was not refused. Climbing into her old Buick, she said, "Hope that guy didn't get a good look at me. It's not hard to find somebody in a small town like this. See what you've done, gone and gotten me spooked like this."

"I'll call you later," David said, "just to be sure you're all right."

Jean had left the key in the ignition. She smiled wryly as she turned it. "Don't worry about me" she said above the sound of the racing engine. "I still have my husband's twelve-gauge shotgun in the kitchen cabinet, loaded and ready for that guy if he decides to drop by."

The Buick rumbled down the road and David went back inside, looking over his shoulder as he did. A chill swept over him as he stood at the stairs to the porch. Somewhere an owl screeched. He went inside.

He trotted upstairs to check on Von, who was asleep with his eyes partially opened. David always found this disconcerting, but all the baby books that bothered to mention the phenomenon assured him he had nothing to worry about.

Back downstairs, he peered through the telescope again into the house next door, but still saw nothing. Spying the magazines on the end table, he remembered his computer search of Country Customs' files and checked the monitor in the living room.

"I don't believe it," he said out loud. His program for ripping off computer files, probably the most sophisticated of its kind ever made, had slammed into a brick wall in trying to get into Country Customs' files. Absolutely incredible. He had never seen the likes of it. The company clearly used computers or David would have gotten an entirely different response on his monitor.

It was then that he realized something, at least part of the reason why he was so obsessed with what was going on next door. Apart from his curiosity, intellectual vanity, and sense of self-preservation for his family and himself, David felt an obligation toward the Haslems, to finding out what happened to them. After all, if they had been killed as the result of some ghastly mistake and their killer really had meant to get the Muratas, the Haslems had shielded them, if only temporarily.

If someone had done in the Haslems, David swore he would get him.

David's computers apparently did not share his sense of obligation. He was getting nowhere, running the search commands over again.

"Not my day," he sighed and ran a couple of diagnostics that turned up nothing. He even booted up another computer and tried the search again after tweaking the program. But again he came up empty, the screen flashing the annoying message David had programmed for just such an occasion:

ACCESS DENIED, STUPID

He got up and started pacing. Why would such a small company in backwater Maine need all this computer security? Or could it be—remotest of remote possibilities that only the most brazen of the brain cells lining David's vast ego could have dared suggest—that some as yet unidentified bug in his system was causing this? Naw, he thought, canceling the thought before it even fully emerged. His system was bulletproof.

David should have known better than to test karma like that. No sooner did he think his hubristic thought than the gods of cyberspace hurled their lightning bolts at him in the form of a message on his screen—something from his new nemesis, the ghost in the machine, the hacker. The message screamed at him:

WE'LL MEET SOON

15

Carver's Lounge was about forty-five miles down east from Sparks on a seedy strip of Highway One midway between Bucksport and Orland. A fever blister on the northern thumb of Penobscot Bay, the bar's cinder block exterior was a faded mustard yellow, the windows painted green-black, and the bar stools and booth banks were covered in crimson polyvinyl. It was the kind of place frequented by those afflicted with a bad reputation or trying to avoid being seen and getting one.

In the corner booth farthest from the door, Ron Lindblad and Barb Bromley huddled together, discussing their favorite subject—money. His elbows on the table, Ron was pitched like a tent over a double Tanqueray and tonic—his third double TNT this morning—while Barb primly sipped a Manhattan. Ron was feeling big, expansive, as the gin worked its way to the outer reaches of his brain. He was playing hooky from work, and Barb was between visits to home sellers.

"Imagine this," Ron said, his voice low and slurred. "You and me in the back of a chauffeur-driven 1931 Rolls Royce Silver Phantom, pulling up at the Regents Country Club in Portland. Faces appear at the windows of the club: rich, fat faces, envious. We grip the solid silver handles and rise from the doeskin seat, the chauffeur opening the door.

"The help at the club—the waiters and concierge, the golf and tennis pros—fight each other to serve us. Not because we tip them any better than anyone else. Not because they expect any special favors. And certainly not because they like me.

"The reason," Ron said, getting excited, "is the very reason to have money, as much money as one could possibly acquire in one's lifetime. *The reason is that people fear money.* They cringe, grovel, before it.

"And that's precisely what I want," Ron said, making a fist for emphasis. "I want people to fear me. It's the sincerest form of flattery. I want more money than any of them, even the Beans, so I could buy the whole lot of them twice, three times, over."

Unbeknownst to Ron, who was beginning his usual toot over Beans, Barb was having a hard time concentrating on what he was saying. In fact, she was dividing her attention between Ron's fantasy and her husband's show on the TV above the bar. The topic of today's show was people with bizarre extramarital affairs.

Barb watched, fascinated, as Sid questioned a guest who admitted that she'd had affairs with over two hundred homeless men in the past four years. The audience oohed and aahed as the woman described her experiences in flophouses, vacant lots, and even cardboard boxes set up over sidewalk grates in Portland and Boston. The woman wasn't bad-looking, Barb thought, although she could have used a make-over and a new hair color. She did seem a bit strange as well.

At a dramatic moment of the show, Sid asked the woman's husband to come forward. A hush fell over the studio audience as the man walked up on stage toward his wife, both of them with tears streaming down their cheeks. There was a tense pause before he took her in his arms and they kissed. The audience went wild.

Barb was thinking: despite being a complete asshole and a speed freak, Sid could sure put on a show. She tore herself from the TV and turned to Ron, appraising him as she would a house she was contemplating buying. He wasn't at all bad-looking, a bit heavy around the gut but otherwise in reasonably good shape, and always impeccably dressed. And rich. Barb wasn't sure how much Ron was worth, but she knew that through Norma he had a line on two, maybe three, million.

Barb wasn't kidding herself that she was using Ron. By controlling the real estate licenses in the town, Ron had set her up as a monopoly on the home-buying business. It didn't stop there. He even funneled business her way, almost more than she could manage. But Ron was no charity; he took a healthy cut out of every transaction Barb reported to him. Of course, she could sock away more for herself by under-reporting sales and commissions. She understood that she was essentially a front for him and his operations. Sid was in on it as well. Barb never asked what was going on, preferring to stay focused on her business and out of whatever Ron and Sid were up to.

She had her suspicions about them, of course. Knowing Sid, she assumed they were into drugs. But her sense of Ron did not square with drugs. Oh, he was capable of just about anything, especially when it came to money. And yet Ron Lindblad and drug running did not quite fit together in her mind.

For herself, Barb had always believed in the importance of keeping her own nest egg. Her mother, who had raised Barb and her sister alone after their father walked out on them, had drummed independence and self-reliance into her daughters. Never expect a man to take care of you, she taught them. Make sure you always have something socked away.

Sid was Barb's first husband even though she was his third wife. That should have told her something about him, but she decided she would lead her own life. She had met Sid while she was a star real estate agent in Portland, a Top Producer and member of the Ten Million Dollar Circle six years in a row at the Elite Real Estate Company. The gentry on Portland's south coast and around Kennebunkport had been falling all over themselves trying to get her to sell their homes, especially when the bottom dropped out of the market in the late eighties.

At the time, Sid had been a weatherman on a local TV news program, and she always thought he was cute. Mutual friends set them up and they dated for about a year. Then, on a long weekend on Mount Desert Island, they up and got married. Barb found out later about his drug habit.

Barb met Ron through Sid, even though it was never quite clear to her how *they* met. Ron urged her to set up her own real estate business in Sparks, but she didn't have much hope for it. To her surprise, business was great. She knew that Ron was her benefactor without quite knowing how he was doing it and why. Part of her, the vain side, believed it was only to get her in the sack. But another part, the greedy, manipulative side, believed something else was going on here, that Ron had some other purpose that she couldn't quite discern.

She knew better than to ask. It was obvious that Ron was using her to corner the market on real estate in the area for his Outlet City project. He had mentioned once that he used some kind of accounting sleight-of-hand to handle the cash flow required to buy the homes and sell them back to himself at rock-bottom prices. It was all off the books, of course. The people Ron herded into the vacated houses were all Asians and Mexicans—illegals, she assumed—but she never asked about it. The less she knew, the better.

The only thing Barb could not figure out was what was happening to the people whose homes Ron had grabbed. They were all old or infirm, so she just assumed they were packed off to a nursing home somewhere far away, where they were medicated into submission until they kicked off. But Barb sometimes wondered if something else was going on, something too horrible to think about.

Once she had overheard Sid on the phone with a policeman, setting up a meeting somewhere quiet. Sid left with a black duffel bag, but he didn't come back with it. Were Ron and Sid buying off the local police, paying for protection or, at least, silence? Anything was possible with Sid, borderline schizo that he was.

Barb was reasonably certain that she would be safe from the law if Ron's plans came crashing down around him. What had she done, anyway? Handled a few simple real estate transactions. Ran title searches. And those announcements she planted in *The Maine Event*—the ones designed to head off questions from the locals when their neighbors fell off the face of earth—what could possibly be illegal about that?

Whatever Ron's plans, Barb believed she had to string him along by not giving in to his rather obvious advances. She hadn't gone to bed with him yet, but she knew he wanted it and that someday she might have to relent, just to keep the business moving. Deep inside she was deathly afraid of Ron and sex was her only real weapon to use on him.

Barb considered her looks an investment, a part of her business. Curb appeal, she called it. This morning she'd had her hair done, trying a new shade of blonde: Hunt Country Platinum, and her nails done the "French" way, with a pale salmon shade on the nails and a thin white line at the tips. Her makeup was also done in salmon, complementing her silk suit with matching wool challis shawl over the shoulder. She also had a mud treatment and her legs and eyebrows waxed after her step aerobics class, weight work, and massage. She could dead lift 120 pounds even though it was muscle tone, not bulk, she was working on.

While Ron had been talking, a waiter had come and gone, leaving another round for them. Ron was showing the effects of the gin and losing whatever control he had over his already unvarnished come-ons. He was as intoxicated with the thought of being alone with Barb as he was from the gin. As he was going on about Freeport and L.L. Bean's, Barb casually glanced down at his lap and smiled to herself as she saw an erection stirring under his pants.

She took a sip of her new Manhattan, a little less syrupy this time. "I have to tell you something, Ron," she said, cutting him off in the middle of his speech. "I got a call this morning from someone who was interested in making a major investment in a Sparks property."

This news stirred Ron from his drunken haze. "What?" he said. "Who was it?"

"I don't remember his name," Barb said, being careful.

"And I have no idea what he has in mind. I agreed to meet with him in a few days."

Ron looked at her disapprovingly and growled, "Don't I give you enough work? You should be concentrating on the business I throw your way and on nothing else."

It took a bit of concentration, but Barb managed to work up tears in her eyes. "I only did what I thought you'd want me to do," she said, her voice quavering. "I don't expect anything to come of this meeting, and you know I'll tell you everything that goes on in it."

Barb was sorry she had told him anything but figured he'd find out anyway. Ron had eyes in the back of his head, and she had seen what he had done to people he thought were betraying him. She put her hand lightly on his. "You know, Ron," she said, "all this business I'm getting is tremendously exciting for me. We closed the day before yesterday on a place, unloading it even before it hit the computer listings. I don't know if I told you this, but it turns me on to be making more money than Sid."

"Oh, really?" Ron said, liking the sound of what he was hearing. He slid his hand from under Barb's, down to her thigh.

Barb drew in a deep breath, a sound Ron misinterpreted as one of desire. He leaned close to her face and she got a strong burst of gin smell that nearly made her gag.

"I'll help you make more money than you've ever imagined," he whispered, working his fingers into the flesh of her thigh. "I help you," he murmured, "you help me."

"Of course I'll help you, darling," she said, laying it on a bit thick. On the TV, Sid was pitching a new line of Country Customs hummingbird feeders.

"Things would be a whole lot easier if Norma were out of the way," Ron said hoarsely, his fingers freezing in their tracks. "Someday," he whispered, "someday."

Barb studied him, trying to absorb what he was saying. Suddenly a thought flew into her head and she glanced at her Tiffany watch. It was already 2:40 and she had an appointment way down in Sparks at three. She stood up, smoothing out her skirt. "Ron, I really have to run. I have this darn appointment with . . . oh, I can't remember her name, it's in the file in the car. An old woman who's on the fence about selling her house. Have to keep the business moving, you know."

Ron, suddenly realizing he had an erection, didn't stand up to say good-bye. Which was just fine with Barb, who beat it out of the bar as fast as she could and out to her red Jaguar VJ12, the company car she used on business calls. Usually she drove a pickup truck, the most reliable way to get around coastal Maine.

The parking lot was one big puddle of water and Barb was careful not to get her Ferragamo heels wet. She looked up at the low clouds. A cold front was moving in. Barb hated Maine weather, no matter what season it was. She told herself it wouldn't be too long before she would leave it all behind. If she could only hang in there a while longer, enduring Ron and Sid . . .

Drawing her keys from her Gucci bag, she muttered "fuck" under her breath as she snagged and broke one of her perfect nails on the key chain.

16

"What's the name of the town where the movie *The Birds* takes place?" David asked Nara midway up the gradually rising hill in the middle of Murata Island. He felt a pleasant ache in his legs, and his chest was sore from drawing in lungfuls of pure sea air.

They were at the end of a long weekend on their island at the mouth of Penobscot Bay. David had nothing but warm nostalgia for this place where Nara, Toshi, and he had ended up after escaping Florida. Tucked in a grove of oak trees on the southern end of the island was a two-bedroom cabin in which they had lived at the time and where David and his family now stayed while visiting. The cabin looked like a dollhouse miniature from their vantage point on the hill.

It was a singularly dazzling day, the sun high and big in the cloudless sky. To David, the flawless clarity of the air and the intense brilliance of the light combined to create an effect of eerie unreality, as if things were somehow more than real. Normally dull winter colors seemed charged with electricity—the turquoise and crimson of ordinary lichens appeared to explode off rocks and tree bark, spruce needles crackled at the tips with emerald energy, and patches of hardy snow glowed from the folds of the underbrush.

"This must be what the air in heaven is like," David said to Nara as, holding hands, they stepped over a fallen pine.

"Oh, you're just getting over your cabin fever," she said. But she understood him and could feel it too. They all did.

In fact, David had not felt this good in months. Since coming out to the island, his headaches were gone, he slept well, and he and Nara had sex each of the three nights they'd been there (a record for him). The change was even more noticeable in Von, who was now happy and gregarious in his monosyllabic way, eating like a horse and sleeping through the night. David didn't know how to account for these developments other than that they confirmed his deep-seated antipathy for civilization.

And then there was the sea. Even with Sparks three minutes from Penobscot Bay, David missed being right on the ocean, a captive of it as he had been in the Florida Keys. Here, with the sea spread out around him, he remembered how rejuvenating it was, a tonic against the burdens of human noise. The sea had a way of wrapping him in its arms and comforting him, dissolving the pain.

Sparks seemed far away as David watched Von running ahead of them up the slope, falling down every five steps or so but then gamely getting up and running and falling again. At the top of the hill was a bench and a small granite marker with TM carved on the top. According to Toshi's wishes, his remains had been cremated and scattered over the ocean. And even though Toshi asked Nara and David not to do anything special for him after his death, they agreed that Toshi wouldn't have objected to a marker and bench.

David, vividly remembering Toshi's apparition—or whatever it was—couldn't help but feel a bit apprehensive as he approached the marker. He wondered: What if the grave had been dug up? He'd not yet told Nara about the whole thing, although he suspected that Jean might have said something to her, like "Has David been acting odd lately?" to which Nara would probably have responded with "Can you be more specific?"

As they began their walk, David and Nara reflected on the recent mysterious events in Sparks. Nara compared them to the Wayang Kulit, the stylized Balinese shadow theater, and Plato's parable of the cave from *The Republic,* Book VII, in which reality is viewed as nothing more than shadows that play across a cave wall. David nodded, barely comprehending, his mind racing onto something else—an association of some kind—his movie trivia question to her. He asked her about it again.

Nara sighed. "The town in *The Birds,*" she recited, "is Bodega Bay. I think." All the while she kept an eye on Von, who was playing with tufts of reindeer moss wedged in a rock outcropping. David looked at her, wondering how she'd come up with that answer so quickly.

He pulled at a stalk of fireweed, waiting for her to ask him why he had asked. But she didn't, so he said anyway, "Seeing Sparks way over there reminded me of that scene in the movie when you see the town from the seagull's perspective as it circles, waiting for a chance to strike at the townspeople. Remember that one? Something about Sparks reminds me of Bodega Bay. Can't quite put my finger on what it is, exactly. Something dark and claustrophobic."

Nara shrugged her shoulders. "Remember that interview I did the other day, at the diner?" she said. "The woman I talked with, Estelle Grout, was genuinely afraid of something. Friends of hers—people she'd known all her life—were disappearing from town. Even K. K., the waitress, noticed it. I might ask you for some help on your computers in tracking her friends. She'd feel better if she knew what happened to them."

"Sure," David said, his mind associating at the word *computer.* "The thing I can't figure," he said, continuing up the hill, "is why the Haslems had no computer trail after they left Boston. *Everybody* has a computer trail. Even *I* have a computer trail.

"And not only that, I have a hacker in my system. Seems benign so far, but just the thought of him in there, worming around in my files, makes me feel . . . violated."

Nara, who in many ways knew David better than he knew himself, could tell that his intellectual vanity had been affronted with the hacker breaking into his computers. Not only that, David's failure to get into the Country Customs computer files had left him wondering about his own abilities.

"We'll get to the bottom of it," she said, trying to reassure him.

"If it doesn't get us first," he added darkly.

"You know," Nara said, trying to change the subject, "Sparks would have been a perfect location for the movie *Invasion of the Body Snatchers*." Out of the corner of her eye she could see David nodding ferociously in agreement. "I think it's one of the best horror movies I've ever seen, particularly for the details.

"Remember Donald Sutherland's broken windshield that looked like a clutching plant, resonating with the appearance of the alien pods that were devouring and replacing the people of San Francisco? And Leonard Nimoy, Mr. Spock, as the pop psychologist, the guy with about as much emotional content as white bread? What casting! It's like, with humans like him, who needs the pod people?"

"San Francisco?" David said, screwing up his eyes. "No, the location was a small California town. What was its name? Santa something."

"A small town? No way," Nara said, waving her hand dismissively. She put up with a lot from David, but there was no way he was going to make her believe that that movie had been filmed any place other than San Francisco. Neither David nor Nara, even with the vast storehouse of trivia between them, was aware that they were thinking of two versions of the same movie: David the 1956 original version and Nara the 1978 remake.

"Sutherland," David said, "wasn't he the lead in *M*A*S*H*? He *couldn't* have been in *Invasion of the Body Snatchers,* except maybe as a child."

"What?" Nara said again. "What about *M*A*S*H*? Are you talking about Alan Alda?"

"Who?" David said, sinking deeper into confusion as he tried to remember the star's name in the 1956 version. He could see the man's face but the name, the name. What was it?

They reached the bench at the top of the hill, the highest point on the island. It was here where Toshi used to come to sit for hours and gaze at the sea and sky. To the Balinese, the highest ground was the most sacred. Nara called the spot Pura Delem, or temple of death. David was quietly relieved to find that the grave was undisturbed, except for Von, who was triumphantly sitting on the marker. David sat down on the bench and took in the sweeping view of Penobscot Bay below while Nara knelt down and pulled weeds growing over the marker. The smell of balsam and cedar floated in the light breeze.

David sat back and recalled good times with Toshi: driving up from Florida in his 1964 Ford pickup, exploring the island, eating lobster until they were sick of it, and watching Red Sox games on TV. Toshi had tried to talk physics with David, who would turn the conversation toward safer ground: computers. It was Toshi who had indulged David's passions, content with the knowledge that his daughter was happy and soon to have a child who would become a physicist, with any luck.

David remembered the dark November afternoon when he'd found Toshi at the bottom of the hill, barely alive after a massive coronary. He was never sure exactly when Toshi died, but thought it was sometime during the boat trip back to the mainland, as they vainly hurried for Portland. There was too much fog that evening for a helicopter, despite David's offer—announced over his shortwave radio—of a million dollars to anyone who would come in and pick them up.

David also remembered Nara's cremation rituals, which she'd been allowed to perform after David used his high-priced New York lawyers to win a court order allowing a Balinese cremation ceremony under the supervision of a priest from a Hindu ashram in Vermont and a representative of the Maine Department of Public Health. Nara, in her eighth month of pregnancy, had a load of stones shipped in to the island with which she constructed a small tower and then, on top, placed a sarcophagus in the shape of a bull she'd had made in Portland.

The day of the ceremony had been cold and gray. A morning rain had soaked the stone tower, but Nara had covered the sarcophagus with a plastic drop cloth. After the high priest completed his ablutions of Toshi's body, Nara covered it with Susan B. Anthony dollar coins—a ransom to the god of death, she explained. Then, with David's help, the high priest and Nara lit white candles with which they lit the sarcophagus.

David could even recall the dumbstruck expression of the health department official—a heavy, balding man on the cusp of retirement who thought he had seen it all until today—who stood unobtrusively a few yards away from the roaring pyre (and a safe distance from these potentially dangerous cult types), as the big ceramic bull roasted to brown, cracked, and split, spitting sparks over the damp meadow and into the sea.

Nara, finished with her weeding, took a seat next to David on the bench. "Nara?" he said.

"Mmm?"

"In the Balinese religion, do spirits ever come back from the dead and appear to the living? Like, say, Toshi's, for instance?"

Nara shaded her eyes with her hand and looked at him. "That depends on how you define Balinese religion," she said matter-of-factly. "I assume you mean the Siwaistic sect of Agama Hindu, the predominant religion on the island."

Christ, David thought, marry a philosopher and this is what you get. "Yeah," he said, "let's assume that."

"Well," she said slowly, "because my father's body was cremated, he was released from this world, allowing his spirit to join the Supreme Being. So he can't come back, according to this dogma."

But this information was only marginally comforting to David, who vividly remembered the figure he had seen through the back window. He looked down at Von, who was pointing at the water. Cutting across the sparkling bay waters toward Murata Island was the fishing boat to take them back to the mainland.

Nara laughed out loud. "You want to hear something funny? The other day, when I was at my office, I thought my father's spirit was visiting me."

David felt the blood draining from his face. "F-funny?" he stammered.

Nara laughed again and David winced. "Yeah, I imagined I saw him in the form of an alligator."

"A what?" David was about to say when the actress's name from *Psycho,* Janet Leigh's sister, finally unlodged in his head.

"Vera Miles," he announced triumphantly. "I knew her name was a unit of measure."

Nara shook her head. "Let's go pack," she said and picked up Von from Toshi's marker and marched toward the cabin.

17

K. K. Thorner looked down at the cigarette butts ground into the yellowed linoleum floor of the drama department classroom. She tried to imagine different ways of grinding out a cigarette. Women, she noticed, tend to do it discreetly while holding it in their fingers. Men, on the other hand, seemed to want to get rid of the butt as soon as they were done with it and stamp it out on the floor. K. K. had watched as Ray, her boyfriend, ground out cigarettes with the heel of his Frye boot, sliding the heel in a half circle and leaving a black rainbow on the ground. She wouldn't let him smoke in her house, however.

K. K. collected arcane bits of personal style the way other people collected matchbook covers or Elvis mementos. She organized her observations according to categories, such as sex, age, occupation, and body type. Sometimes, when she remembered, she kept notes in a journal. She never knew when the littlest bit of something might come in handy for a role she was playing.

Like the one she was now auditioning for at the University of Maine in Augusta. She was waiting her turn to try out for a role in *Mother Courage*. She sat in a battered desk, one of many that had been shoved aside to make a "stage" for the auditions.

Her attention shifted from ground cigarettes to a string of graffiti carved into the top of the desk. The writers of the graffiti—obviously drama students—seemed to have been communicating for quite some time without knowing each other, starting out with the usual "This class sucks" and "Get me out of here" and progressing to a competition in which each tried to out-pun the other with such wretched takes as "Albee, a monkey's uncle," "Faust is a Goethe word," and "Italian mama asks bambino about torn pants: Euripedes?"

The auditions were free-form tryouts for the three female leads in the play. The actresses—about thirty of them—performed whatever material they brought with them, giving the director a chance to evaluate creativity as well as voice, range, expressiveness, and the other things directors are supposed to be looking for. Like tits and ass, K. K. thought.

She was trying to block out from her consciousness the auditions she had been forced to watch, each one better than the one before it. Like the one going on now. The woman performing in the middle of the room—talented, beautiful, voluptuous, with an incredible voice—was giving an impeccable recitation of one of Lady Macbeth's soliloquies. K. K. imagined the actress with a stage mother who had started her on voice and tap and ballet when she was eight months old, and pushed her all her life.

K. K. wanted the lead part of Anna Vierling—Mother Courage herself. She wanted it bad. But so did everyone else here, she thought sourly. She believed that she might have an edge over the other actresses—all perky twenty-year olds—because she herself was a mother. For weeks she had been putting herself in the role, at first imagining what it might be like to lose Viveca, her daughter, as Mother Courage loses three children by the end of the play. K. K. found it unbearable to imagine such a terrible thing and had to try a new tack.

She keyed into Mother Courage's lusty, ribald, conniving side and was tempted for the audition to recreate a scene from her favorite soap, *All My Children,* taking the role of Erika Kane, the Susan Lucci character. K. K. then got cold feet. The director of the play was known to be something of a highbrow tight ass and might not appreciate a scene from "popular culture." Not only that, Susan Lucci had never won an Emmy for the part even though she had been nominated . . . how many times? One thing K. K. did not need now was bad luck.

Instead, she picked out a few bawdy paragraphs from Molly Bloom's closing soliloquy in *Ulysses*. Even though the soliloquy scene takes place in bed in the novel, K. K. went ahead and wore heels, black fishnet stockings, and a skirt that would ride up her legs as she sat on a stool. All day long she'd been getting discreetly lustful looks from teachers and students on campus. She could endure it if the outfit helped get her the part.

Everyone clapped when Lady Macbeth finished. Suddenly, K. K.'s name was called and she felt her heart tighten in her chest. She closed her eyes for a moment, conjuring the image of Mother Courage she had formed in her mind. At the last minute, completely on a whim, she lit up one of Ray's cigarettes still in her purse, even though she didn't smoke. She stood and moved slowly to the center of the room and carefully began.

"So how did it go?" Ray said, starting up his truck as K. K. slid in the front seat.

She rolled her eyes. "Who knows? It's like a job interview. They smile, tell you, 'Thanks, you were great,' and probably close the door and laugh after you leave."

"Did you screw it up?" Ray asked with a slightly amused nonchalance, sort of an early James Dean. He was just being Ray but laying it on a bit more than usual. His hand dangling casually over the steering wheel, he pulled the truck out of the campus parking lot toward Route 17 south to Sparks.

K. K. shook her head. Ray had more going for him than most guys she met: he had a job, was reasonably clean and good-looking, and didn't mind the fact that she had a kid. At least he didn't let on if he did.

Ray had been a short-order cook at the Sparks Diner ever since getting out of the army, where he had learned cooking in the enlisted men's mess at Maryland's Fort Meade Army Base. Ray was from Maine, farther down east from Sparks, but had no desire to return to his roots. The place he had left behind held nothing for him. Any young people hanging on in the area were either too drunk or stupid to know any better, he would say. What was there for them? The most you could hope for was a job at the post office. Ray wanted no part of it.

Well, good riddance, Ray had thought during the days before and after he decided to enlist. Good riddance to that dark, claustrophobic house that stunk of failure, the cheap, molting furniture, the rust-colored tap water, the cracked windowpanes stapled over with plastic wrap. As soon as he heard the old screen door bang shut behind him, Ray promised himself he would never look back. He had been true to his word.

K. K. had a few misgivings about getting involved with Ray. Her mother used to tell her: don't mix your meat with your potatoes. Well, Ray usually worked days K. K. had off—she considered this an adequate distance between them—so she figured she could balance work and her love life. Besides, she had no plans to make the job or Ray into anything permanent.

"Well, if I don't get the lead I could still be a whore or a mute," she said, looking at Ray out of the side of her eyes, hoping he'd get the joke. He just shook his head and said nothing. Typical.

It was true. The only other female roles in the play were Kattrin, Mother Courage's mute daughter, and Yvette, the camp prostitute. They weren't bad roles. In fact, they were pretty good parts as secondary roles went, but K. K. knew that she could do a great job with Mother Courage. And she had heard that there might be a some scholarship money for the student with the lead role. That sure wouldn't hurt.

Ray was picking up K. K. today because the Pinto she'd had since high school was in the shop. The muffler had a hole in it the size of a quarter, creating a sound Viveca called "the bad dinosaur." K. K. had brought the car from New Hampshire, where she had grown up with her mother, a teacher at a boarding school for problem rich kids. The Pinto had survived two or three fairly significant accidents and the rear license plate—still from New Hampshire because K. K. hadn't gotten around to getting ones for Maine—was bent and scarred and the state motto, "Live Free or Die," now read only "or Die." The garage promised her the car back tomorrow.

New Hampshire seemed a lifetime away. K. K. had come to Maine after getting pregnant and then being dumped by Phil, her boyfriend at the time. She decided that she didn't want to be even in the same *state* as Phil and came back to have her child in an area she considered almost a second home.

K. K., with her mother and father when they were married and things were nice, would come to Penobscot Bay for two weeks every summer. Her father, a writer, would set up a table out on the lawn of the little Cape Cod they rented and work at a typewriter all day while K. K. and her mother took long walks or an occasional ride on a lobster boat. It was her father, Jake—a bohemian holdover from the sixties who pumped gas when he wasn't writing the short stories that were never published—who had given her her name, the one she never used: Ken Kesey.

To make matters worse, Jake would have fun at K. K.'s expense, telling anyone who would listen the story of how she had been conceived, during the great blackout of November '65—affecting some thirty million people over eighty thousand miles—when eight states and parts of Canada were shut down for over thirteen hours. It was the longest blackout suffered in the Western world, forcing people to stop and think about their total dependence on that mysterious but ubiquitous force crackling through the walls of their homes. Jake would throw back his head and laugh when recalling how difficult it had been to get a delivery room at the hospital on that day in August 1966 when K. K. was born. Turned out that a lot of people had used that blackout time much the same way K. K.'s parents had, so maternity wards were dealing with a crunch of deliveries all within about a week of each other.

How Jake talked K. K.'s mother into giving their child that name had never been fully explained, and by the time

K. K. overcame her embarrassment over it she just didn't care enough to ask. She had tried a few versions of the name over the course of her life—Kendra, Kiki, Cassie—but nothing took. The name K. K. was fine with her.

The brittle Maine countryside flew past as K. K. gazed through her window. Yesterday's snow had turned out to be no more than a dusting, a thin white coating over the hardscrabble ground. It seemed to disappear as they entered the Sparks town limits.

"Want to stop over for a few?" Ray said lightly, not looking at her.

She knew what he meant. Actually, sex would have felt good right now, a release from all the tension building up in her for the audition. But the fact that she was already late picking up Viv from the sitter, combined with the thought of getting naked in Ray's cold trailer home with its sorry little wood-burning stove, made her say, "Sounds great, but can I take a rain check?"

As usual, Ray said nothing. K. K. would have liked him to say: How about if I come by after Viveca's asleep? Or *something.* But she had long ago given up expecting men to say the things she wanted them to say. Even so, K. K. had homework to do, lots of it. She was double-majoring in drama and finance, the second semester of her first year, and was finding that either one of those majors would have been more than enough.

She was afraid she might have to drop one of them, and a part of her cringed at the decision the other part would have to make. She knew the drama would have to go. If she had been eighteen again and just starting out, instead of twenty-nine with a two-year-old, she would have dumped the finance in a New York second. But she had no desire to be one of those career waitresses you see all over the place, and she knew that acting could never be her ticket to a better life. She was determined to give Viv some kind of future.

"It's this one here, isn't it?" Ray said, nodding at Estelle Grout's little cottage tucked behind a row of pine trees.

"Yeah. I'll run in. Won't take a minute."

Ray turned the truck into the gravel driveway and kept the motor running as K. K. hopped out and ran to the door. After knocking, she ran her fingers through her hair and smoothed down her skirt, gestures she normally reserved for her mother. Strange, K. K. wondered, how she thought of Estelle as a mother and the closest thing to a grandmother Viveca ever had. Estelle was a godsend, watching Viv three afternoons a week when K. K. had classes in Augusta, and refusing to take anything for her trouble. The rest of the time K. K. left Viv at day-care up in Camden.

Estelle opened the door with Viv in her arms, already dressed in coat, hat, and gloves. "She was such a good girl today," Estelle beamed, waving at Ray in the truck. K. K. stared at him until he waved back.

Estelle, K. K. observed, was a woman without pretense, a good soul, the genuine article. She made cookies for her church socials, called on the sick, and volunteered at the town library, reading to children. K. K. could tell that she really loved Viv. There had been times when K. K. brought Viv home from Estelle's to find new shoes or clothes on her. K. K. tried to pay Estelle but had given up months ago.

"Estelle," K. K. said, "you're . . . I don't what I'd do without you." She leaned over and pressed a kiss on the old woman's cheek. Estelle just laughed and waved K. K. away.

Viveca, sitting straight on her mother's lap, waved to Estelle as the truck backed out the driveway onto the street.

Estelle watched it disappear over a hill. She hugged herself and moved toward the door. Night was falling and the air was already deathly cold.

18

Most people are afraid of the dark. Even if they're not, they would certainly prefer the daylight. They like what is familiar, find comfort in it. For them, darkness is a threat, an echo chamber for fear. Not surprising that most people associate darkness with death.

But not me. I was not one of those people.

To me, darkness was old shoe, a good friend. We went way back together, darkness and I. Even as I sat there in my truck, across the street from my next unscheduled garbage collection, the bruised sky turning black was a reassuring signal of nightfall. Soon I would be in my element, encased in smooth blackness. I would be free.

Soon the house I was watching would be dark. For now I watched as an occasional shadow appeared in the windows. I expected no difficulty getting in there. I fondled the sheathed Wüsthof at my belt in eager anticipation of what would happen once I was inside.

I kept one eye in my rearview mirror, making sure that I wasn't surprised from behind. If anyone passed by, even in a car, I was done for the night. I could not risk being seen here. My other eye kept watch on the house and the street up ahead, as seen through the windshield.

So far no one had passed me. The street was absolutely quiet. Not even a lost seagull had strayed past. So far, so good. All was well. This could be the night.

I knew this street fairly well, having already removed garbage here in the recent past. But that had been just a quick in and out with virtually no planning. Unlike me to be so impulsive. I still didn't know what had possessed me to act as I did. Anything could have happened, but, fortunately for me, nothing had.

Well, it was over now. No use fretting about it. I was enjoying my newly found freedom. Tonight I would enjoy it even more. I had planned this one out carefully. It was important to look to the future.

Or to the more distant past.

As I sat in the truck, having been there over an hour already, my thoughts would drift despite my best efforts to keep them focused on the project at hand. Funny how a few certain recollections can dominate one's entire memory and serve as guideposts to one's life. They might represent special moments of tragedy, pain, or fear—intensive feelings experienced during periods of great change. I had very vivid recollections of this kind. Rather than recall those moments, I would reexperience them—sights, sounds, emotions flooding over me—almost to the point of being overwhelmed by them.

I did not seek out those memories, nor did I welcome them when they came anyway.

My memories were marked by darkness, a profound, unremitting blackness like that in the lowest depths of the ocean. But this darkness was more than the mere absence of light. It was an absence of sound and sensation, a complete eradication of perspective. I could have been sitting on the ceiling in this darkness and not known it. Any sound I made through my mouth was sucked into the black vacuum and disappeared before it reached my ears.

But, more than anything, the darkness had its own sense of time and permitted no other. Seconds became hours, days could be minutes. Once in the dark for what seemed a short while, I could never be sure if it were night or day. Time was as plastic and fluid as the darkness itself. I had no control, no control. I was at the mercy of this unforgiving horseman with a bit in my mouth and a riding crop at my legs. Fighting it was pointless.

From the darkness I had learned to relinquish control, to succumb to its rules and meet it completely on its own terms. There was really no other way. I came to take pleasure in the darkness and its absolute power over me. I was seduced by that power and my subjection to it. I imagined that this was how a country falls under the spell of a dictator and his beguiling promises of perfection.

And then after a while the darkness became trivial, merely there, as darkness inside a coffin. It was around this time that I began to realize that I could inflict pain on others, including those who inflicted it on me.

I was an adopted child in a family of six. We lived in something the maps called an "empty area," a geographic zone sparsely settled, poorly drained, and often lacking basic human amenities. The nearest neighbors were ten heavily wooded miles away. The nearest store almost twenty miles. The nearest school over fifty miles.

My position in the family was particularly awkward because I was the oldest, supposedly the role model. I had been adopted at age eleven. There were already four children in the family and one on the way.

I could remember the December day when I had been picked up at the orphanage by my foster father—a beaten-down backwoods man whose diet of potatoes and Spam gave him the appearance of a lump of chopped meat. We drove for hours in silence until we reached my new house, and a heavy nauseous feeling overcame me as we pulled up in the front yard. I took in the ancient tractor rusting no more than ten feet from the front door, unstuck except for the top hinge. Shingles on the roof were missing, as were bricks in the chimney, and an old vegetable garden was grown over with dead weeds.

As we climbed the wooden steps to the door, I froze in my tracks as I came eye to eye with a rabbit hanging from a rope, blood oozing from its mouth and nervous electricity causing its massive rear legs to twitch.

The Lump gruffly pushed me ahead, and I entered the darkness of my new home.

It wasn't until a couple months later that I learned that the real reason I had been adopted was because my foster parents were given an allowance for taking me in—fifty-four dollars a month—more than the entire family made from other work. At first my new siblings grudgingly withheld tormenting me, something I was sure they did out of fear of punishment from their parents. There were three boys—Randy, Ricky, and Wayne—and a girl, Blanche. But my siblings were only the lesser evil in the house. The real evil was the parents.

Within a week I had seen my first beating. Ricky, the middle boy, had wet his bed, which he shared with Wayne. He tried to hide his accident by drying it with towels the next morning, but his mother caught him and took him outside. I could hear the muffled screams that seemed to go on for a long time. I noticed that Ricky did not come inside with his mother.

I saw him later at bedtime, and caught a glimpse of his buttocks and legs as he was changing. They were deeply purpled and swollen, with fresh cuts crisscrossing old scars. He did not say a word for several days and the other children stayed clear of him, as if associating with him could bring the same fate on them. Later I recalled something I had noted at the time but could not account for: the lighthearted cheeriness, almost rapture, of my foster mother. Later I came to realize that whenever she punished one of us she would lapse into this state of near ecstasy, having exorcised her demons for the time being.

Up until this time neither she nor her husband had so much as uttered a cross word to me. There were many other punishments given to the other children. I felt as if I were walking on a frozen pond in March, not knowing when I would misstep and break through into the abyss of my family's anger. My exemption from punishment did not escape the notice of my siblings. They did their level best to provoke me into a fight. I was a head taller than any one of them, so they were reluctant to push me into a fistfight.

They started with small things. The family owned a dog named Lucifer—a vicious mutt the size of a terrier—that had taken an immediate dislike to me the first day I arrived. He would growl at me for no reason and would nip at my ankles whenever I had to pass by him leashed outside. Ricky would sneak Lucifer into the house at night and put him in my bed. They knew I couldn't stand being near the animal, he sensed my fear, so I would end up sleeping on the cold linoleum floor. Lucifer would always be gone when I woke up in the morning.

I would never tell my foster parents, fearing I would get it from both ends. And I never cried, no matter what they did. They kept at me, hiding the toilet paper before I went into the outhouse and throwing open the door while I sat on the toilet. Unable to provoke me, they upped the pressure. Randy, the oldest boy, had a BB gun and took to shooting it at me whenever I'd go outside. I would run but he followed, pumping shots at me.

"Run, pig," *Randy would say as he fired the shots.* "Try and hide."

The shots hailed over my shoulders and legs and back as I desperately tried to cover my head and eyes. The BBs peppered my skin, stinging me savagely, raising welts that wept blood.

"No," *I cried,* "leave me be." *I would fall over, weak from pain and fear, to the sound of frenzied laughter in the background as Randy emptied his rifle at me.*

But I still would not cave in, that is, until that day when Blanche found me alone in my favorite place—a moth-eaten old chair facing a window in the parlor. She stood there for a moment looking at me, four years old and wide-eyed, a slip of a thing. Then she did something none of the children had ever done. She smiled kindly at me. I was delighted, overwhelmed, as if a ray of light had peeked through the darkness. It had been so long since someone had treated me with kindness. I smiled back and Blanche took my hand, helped me from the chair, and led me upstairs. I followed, still elated.

The house was quiet except for the creaking of the steps as we made our way upstairs. My foster mother was out running errands, and my foster father was off somewhere hauling junk for pennies. I didn't know where the other children were, and didn't care.

Once upstairs, she pushed open the door to our room and raised her finger to her lips. What surprise did she have waiting for me? Would we become friends, allies against the others?

I entered the room and suddenly her hand left mine and everything went black. I heard muffled voices and then my feet went out from under me. Someone was rolling me over the floor. I screamed once and tried to pull off whatever it was covering me. Then I heard a door slam and, when I finally managed to get the blanket off, I realized that I had been locked in a closet.

The darkness rolled over me like a boulder. Something seemed to be sucking the air from the closet. I felt myself suffocating and labored hard for air. The malignant blackness gnawed at my skin, probing and puncturing me. Sweat broke out on my face at the same time that a horrible shivering cold gripped me. I banged on the door, kicked it, and scraped it with my fingernails.

I heard Blanche giggling softly on the other side of the door before I filled my lungs with the last remaining air and began to howl.

I don't know how long I had been screaming, but I stopped when the door opened. Not knowing what to expect, I curled up in a ball and hid in a corner of the closet.

"Get up," *someone said. My ears were ringing from my own screaming, and it took me a moment to recognize the voice. It was my foster mother's.* "Come out of there," *she said.*

I uncurled myself and crawled out. The light on the ceiling hurt my eyes. When I focused them, I saw my foster mother's face looking at me with an expression I couldn't discern. At first I interpreted it as one of amusement or intrigue, but then it appeared . . . triumphant. She led me downstairs and to the parlor window, the one I liked.

"Did you do this?" *she said. I looked up and saw that the windowpane was shattered, as if it had been punched in. I shook my head slowly.*

"Come with me," *she said, and guided me by the shoulders to a storage room.*

Next to a shelf of canned goods was a narrow door behind

which were steps leading down into a root cellar. I had never been in the root cellar before, fearing it as a place of dark menace and unclean pests. She said quietly, "Get in there, liar. Get in there until you can tell me the truth."

I looked in past the door but could see nothing but total blackness. "Mind the step," *she said, and pushed me in. I stumbled on the step and fell down the stairs, slamming my head and seeing lights exploding around me. When I awoke I was in a darkness that had never seen light, the cold, obsidian black that everyone sees when they close their eyes for the last time.*

I was still in the root cellar. It took my eyes what seemed like hours to adjust to the dark. I sat very still and quiet. Shapes formed slowly and shadows loomed over me. Angry, frightening shapes with sharp edges and burning eyes. Hungry shapes moving closer, crowding around me, deciding what do with me.

I felt warm wetness heating my legs. But I sat still, perfectly straight, even as the wetness turned cold.

They let me out for dinner, which I barely touched. When everyone was done, my foster father asked me if I had broken the window in the parlor. The table was quiet, all eyes on me. I looked at each of their faces, trying to come up with the right answer.

"No," *I finally said,* "Randy did it." *Then I closed my eyes.*

"No," *I heard Randy say, panic-stricken.* "It wasn't—" *Next I heard a chair scraping the floor and Randy's screams as his father seized him by the hair and dragged him to the back of the house. I did not allow myself a smile as Randy's wails filled the night.*

But this was not the last of the root cellar. My new parents had finally discovered my weakness and threw me in there at the slightest provocation. As before, the darkness and the shapes would conspire against me, but less and less each time. Oh, I played it smart, kicking and screaming each time they brought me to that green door and swung it open. I did not struggle on the steps out of fear of falling again. I walked compliantly down the steps and into the arms of the dark shapes.

What I learned was that the shapes and the darkness were not as terrible as what awaited me on the other side of the door. It took many painful trips to the root cellar before I came to this realization. I made my peace with the darkness. It hid me, sheltering me from those who would hurt me.

My days in the darkness strengthened me for my time in the light. After two years with my new family, I knew it was time to put up a wall between them and me. It was time to give back some of the pain they had given me.

I began to watch carefully, observing the things that were important to them. I discovered that Randy and Blanche had a special fondness for Lucifer, who always perked up when either of them came near. I watched them closely from my window. They always had a treat—a piece of meat or half a biscuit—which they would surreptitiously feed the dog. Lucifer would lick their hands and face, and they would enjoy the few moments of pleasure their meager lives offered them.

I took to squirreling away food during lunch—the one meal my foster father was away and only two eyes, instead of four, were watching us. I also began to notice Randy and Blanche as they hid something they didn't care for. At first Lucifer was suspicious of me when I came toward him, so I just threw the scraps to him and he devoured them immediately. It wasn't long before he associated me with Randy and Blanche, and let me come to him and feed him from my hand. I did not like him licking my face, but I put up with it.

I even saved Sunday dessert for Lucifer, the only time during the week when anything remotely sweet was offered to us. When it was cake or cookies, I would slip it into my napkin and then a pocket. I didn't bother with pie. Saving desserts was riskier than lunch food, but I knew that passing sweets on to the dog would endear me to him more than the others.

I was right. Anytime I came near Lucifer, his tail would wag and he would pant heavily. He dutifully crawled to my feet when the boys slipped him into my bed at night.

One day, as Randy spent the afternoon in the shed with the wounds from his latest beating and the others were off playing, I went to Lucifer with a fistful of angel food cake. As he chomped away at it, I untied him from his tree and nonchalantly worked the long rope around his neck and tied it into a strong knot. I began to walk him, keeping the leash short. I talked quietly to him, reassuring him that all was well.

We walked for hours, off the paths, deep into the woods. After a while the terrain began to change. The ground began to slope, steeply in places, and deep ravines cut into the forest floor. We were into bog country, a place we were strictly forbidden to enter. I had been there many times.

I led Lucifer to a place I had found months ago, where the ground seemed to drop out from underneath you as you walked. The trees—mostly spruce and pine—grew closely together. I began to let out the rope, letting Lucifer get ahead of me a bit. I also began tying a fist-sized knot at the end of the rope. I watched Lucifer, steering him toward a particularly steep drop I knew of. But almost anywhere around here would have been fine for my purposes.

I began to run. I kept my head down, protected from the low branches. Lucifer turned to look at me and I shouted, "Run, Lucifer." *He seemed to smile at me and then picked up his pace. He could run faster than me, being a dog and not having to dodge sharp branches. I kept my eye on where we were going, where the dog was going. Up ahead was the drop, about twenty yards in front of us.*

I let out the rope as far as I could without losing my grip on the knot. Lucifer took this as a signal to run even faster, so he burst ahead, oblivious of the danger. He reached full speed just as the ravine came up, and he put on the brakes about a second too late. I watched his short legs churning as he tried to stop and then, losing his traction on the leaves, he yelped and began to slide down the gully.

Moving swiftly, I wedged the big knot between a forked branch to look as if it had been caught there behind a runaway dog. Then I jumped in front of the branch and held the rope in both hands. It snapped taut as Lucifer tumbled into the ravine, tightening around his neck.

I stood there for several seconds, making sure the rope would hold. Then I made my way to the edge of the ravine. Looking down, I saw Lucifer's face looking up at me, his tongue dangling limply over his eyes.

It took Randy and his father weeks of searching before they found Lucifer. From then on, things changed in the house. The children—Randy and Blanche especially—kept to themselves, not bothering to raise a fuss with each other. The house became very quiet. Sometimes I would catch Randy looking at me, studying me, wondering if I had anything to do with Lucifer's death.

I never let on to anyone what I had done. And never again was I sent to the root cellar, but I would spend every possible minute down there, enjoying the darkness.

19

Estelle Grout had trouble sleeping that night. She tried to read and watch TV, which wasn't the same for her since Johnny Carson left. She just couldn't get used to Jay Leno, especially his political humor and that big chin of his. So she paced her room and decided to fix herself a cup of camomile tea.

As Estelle descended the steps in her old house, the heater kicked on, hissing through the walls. She thought of getting a new heater but joked to herself that the race was on: either she or the heater would die first. This time last year Estelle had resolved that it would be her last winter in the house and in Sparks.

For years her sister had been after her to move to Florida and share her Fort Myers condominium ever since her husband had dropped dead, just seven months after they moved down there. And Estelle hadn't been feeling well lately, sick all the time, getting headaches for the first time in her life. Maybe Florida would be the best thing for her.

So she answered one of the flyers left in her mailbox by a real estate company—Busy B's in Sparks. She even met with an agent—a pretty woman named Barb Bromley—who at first was very sweet, listening to Estelle and seeming to understand about the hard Maine winters. Estelle even told her how she had been thinking about moving down to Florida to be with her sister. Barb worked up a listing for her and said she would have a buyer in no time. Estelle began packing some things and cleaning out the attic.

Yet something held her back. Maybe she couldn't let go just yet. Maybe she needed some time to adjust to the idea.

Maybe Florida wasn't everything it was cracked up to be, all those hurricanes.

At the last minute she decided to hold off a while longer. Estelle could tell that Barb Bromley was not happy when she had asked her this afternoon to take the house off the market. She made such a to-do about it, telling Estelle that she'd be sorry, that she'll never get a chance like this again. When Estelle asked her why this particular time would be different than any other for selling her house, Barb gave her some mumbo-jumbo about market cycles or some such thing. Estelle didn't buy it.

Estelle puttered around the kitchen, trying to remember where she had put the tea. She had left her glasses upstairs. So it didn't matter much if the light was on, she couldn't see any better anyway. Then she remembered she'd had it out this morning when Viveca Thorner was here. Ever since she had started baby-sitting Viveca, Estelle, who had no grandchildren, had a new lease on life. She found that her weeks revolved around the days when Viveca would come. Maybe that child had had something to do with Estelle's decision to stay in Sparks.

Estelle had been reading to the girl about Peter Rabbit, whose mother gave him camomile as medicine after almost catching his death in Mr. MacGregor's watering can. Reading about the tea had given her a yen for some. She had left the can out on the pantry counter and was now groping for it in the darkness.

As the old woman fumbled for her tea, I waited patiently in the pantry, hidden by the shadows, with the Wüsthof cook's knife in hand, its blade freshly sharpened. Even if the woman had had her glasses on, she wouldn't have seen the cut—in the shape of a small arc like a rainbow—in one of the door's windowpanes, through which I had unlocked the door.

Sometimes killing can be extremely unpleasant for the killer. I tried not to think about the cramping in my legs as I squatted in this corner. My bladder was filling, and the heat was blasting at me from the radiator less than a foot away. The hot air was too much, especially in my down parka and ski mask. I took a calculated risk and removed my ski mask.

Practical questions flooded my mind: Given the woman's thick girth, how many cuts would it take to kill her? Would she scream? Would it be possible to get to her throat first? Where would the blood go?

This time I had to clean up the mess myself. As with Lorton Theroux, I was flying alone on this one. In fact, it had been after killing Theroux that this one occurred to me. She lived right next door to him. The audacity of the act appealed to me. It was like playing Monopoly and acquiring an entire block of property.

And then, right after this one, I had another visit to make. Somewhat different in style, but similar in spirit. No rest for the weary.

It helped for me to think of these as simple garbage collections. I imagined the woman—Grout was her name—as an old appliance or mattress left on the curb. Here I was, happy to oblige.

Estelle finally found the tin of camomile and drew a tea filter from a hook on the pantry wall above the electric can opener. She decided to turn on the light and reached for the chain dangling from the bare bulb on the ceiling. At that moment the killer raised the cook's knife, but the light came on first. Estelle looked up quickly and, blinking hard, spied the killer emerging from the corner of her pantry.

"You?" she sputtered before the massive blade came down heavily on her heart.

20

"Yes, yes, I *know* it's difficult," Will Karasik said over the cellular phone to David McAdam, who was pacing the living room with a screaming Von. "Why do you think I needed your help? Hell, we've got about a hundred guys on the payroll, all freshly minted from places like MIT and Caltech, and they don't know shit about anything.

"Our clients are nipping at our heels, David. I couldn't hold them back anymore. I promised them I'd deliver some product today. You're the man, David. I need that old magic."

It was the next morning and David's first day back from the island. He wished he had stayed there. His headaches had returned and Von was back to his irritable ways. Even Nara was getting into the act, snapping at David over the least little thing, like his leaving a disassembled computer motherboard on the kitchen table and counter this morning.

David was having trouble focusing on Will's fuzzy logic project. Who could worry about something as prosaic as elevator protocols when a mass murderer was on the loose, as close as next door? Even worse was the possibility, growing larger by the minute in his mind, that the murderer was really after him. He still hadn't gotten around to calling someone to paint over that disgusting message scrawled on the house. Then there were the people at the Sparks harbor, the hacker invading his system, and the unsettling apparition of Toshi's ghost.

It was tempting for David to just keep his family on the island, a course of action he had considered seriously as

Nara and he were packing. But he knew that she was anxious to get back home and poke around a bit into the disappearance of those townspeople. David knew that he wouldn't be content to sit out there on the island and wait until . . . when? And, Nara reminded him, they had left Cupak and his dog friends only enough food to last three days. All of it was probably gone the first day, David said.

Where was Cupak, anyway? David wondered. He hadn't seen him all morning.

No, David had to get back to Sparks. He had been thinking through all the craziness and had decided on a plan, or, more exactly, a pretty wild first step.

"Willie, let me ask you something," David said, bouncing Von.

"What?"

"What's the name of the town where *Invasion of the Body Snatchers* takes place?"

"What?"

"You remember. It was a small town somewhere in—"

"Hold on." Will went off the line and David could hear him speaking with someone.

"It's an army base," Will said, back on the line, "in Alabama somewhere."

"*Army* base? In *Alabama*? That can't be right."

"It *is* right. Vincent, one of my programmers here who goes to see everything, said he saw it last weekend. Says the movie sucks, but Gabrielle Anwar looks hot in an adolescent kind of way."

"Gabrielle who?"

"Now," Will said, returning to business, "just give me what you have at this moment. You've already made a lot of progress on things we haven't touched. If you send it on the network this morning, I'll have it to our clients this—"

"Can't do it," David said. Von reached for the phone and hit the redial button.

"What was that?" Will said.

"Beeep," David said, pulling Will's chain a bit.

"No, what you said."

"I said it's gonna have to wait. I have a couple things to do first."

David could hear the massive release of air from Will's lungs. "When, then?" Will said.

"This afternoon. First thing."

Will relented, mostly because he had no choice. David was doing this as a favor, and Will knew better than to press his luck.

After Will hung up, David touched a button and was connected to Simon Globus's private line. David was Simon's wealthiest non-institutional client. David was aware of this and tried to be careful not to throw his weight around when he dealt with him. But even so, whenever David called he noticed that the investment lawyer grew quiet and cautious, as if David was going to tell him he wanted to withdraw fifty million or something.

After they exchanged pleasantries, Simon said, "What can I do for you?" with strained offhandedness.

"I want to withdraw fifty million," David said.

Long silence on the other end. Then a sigh. "Fifty million," Simon said. "May I ask the purpose?"

"I want to set up an account in Portland. Something like an escrow. Only it has to be under your name and I have to have access to it."

"Mmmm," Simon hummed, trying to parse through the absurdities of David's request. "Are you in any kind of trouble?"

"Not at all. One other thing."

"Yes?"

"I want you to take next Friday off."

"Huh?"

"Tell your office you're making a business call in Maine—be specific that it's Sparks—and then take a long, quiet weekend in the Hamptons. Don't got out anywhere, like a restaurant. Okay?"

"You must tell me what's going on. You're about to make a killing?"

"What?"

"It's a deal, right?"

"A deal. Yes."

"So what is it?"

"We have to keep a low profile right now. I won't even touch the money. It just has to be there. Will you trust me on this one?"

Another long silence. "Next Friday," Simon said. "Okay. Fine. But you don't want to move fifty million just like that, especially into a bank. We'd have to notify the Fed and you wouldn't be FDIC insured."

"Oh, right," David said, feeling naive and stupid.

"What we'll do is set up a line of credit. If it comes from us, it's even better than cash. You'll have full access. How's that?"

"Perfect. Thanks, Simon," David said and turned off the phone. It occurred to him that he'd talked more this morning than he normally would in a week.

While on the island, something Nara had said to David made him realize that one of his closed-circuit mini-cams set up outside around the house might have recorded any strange doings at the Haslems' last week. David gave Von a water-filled pacifier he'd heated in the microwave, put him in the playpen, and went out the basement door to the rear of the house. He found the stepladder on the ground, underneath the dining room window, and stood it up against the wall.

The camera was hidden inside a converted Country Customs wren house David hung on fishing line from the eves of the house. He had to be careful, he was so shaky, having had only six cups of coffee so far this morning. Slowly, he withdrew the tape from the camera. He paused for a moment to look at the Haslems' window, its shades drawn.

Inside, David rushed to one of his six VCRs and rewound the tape. He tried to remember the last time he replaced it. It was a motion-activated recorder, so it did not have to be replaced very often.

The tape stopped rewinding. David started it up, waiting anxiously for something to appear. The camera was trained toward the ground so that the motion of high clouds, birds, and airplanes wouldn't set the tape rolling. Snow appeared on the screen and David wondered why there would be static and he quickly tried to adjust the tracking controls. The snow stopped and started again and he realized that it was real snow, from the snowfall of a few days ago. He fast-forwarded the tape, past scenes of Von and David in the yard, Nara taking a walk, the dogs playing. David hoped to see the Haslems going in and out of the house at morning or night, but it was always too dark.

Suddenly, Toshi's ghost—or whatever it was—appeared, following the armadillo along the back fence near the woods. David's heart almost stopped. The ghost's face was hard to see, his head bent down and covered with a baseball cap. He was layered with strange clothing, just as David remembered. The tape was dark and in and out of focus, like a recording of a bank robbery. In a moment Toshi's ghost was gone and David sat back, breathing deeply.

So he *had* seen someone. Or some*thing*. The tape played on, but the ghost never appeared again. Von cooed in the playpen. David had an urge to call Nara at the magazine, but then sat up straight as he saw someone in a large parka entering the Haslem house through the same door David had used to get in there. Immediately after entering, the intruder came out again since nothing moved in the camera's field in the meantime.

Who could this be? David wondered. The killer? He immediately thought of the large man in black leather Jean had seen last week. David had attributed that to an overactive imagination. But perhaps she had seen something.

On the screen the intruder's face was hidden under the hood of the parka. The figure slunk around to the front of the house and was gone. David wondered if, through image enhancement, he could get a face to appear from inside the parka. Too bad he hadn't put light intensifiers or infrared into the cameras; otherwise he could have seen whoever spray-painted his house in the dark. He made a mental note to pick up some light intensifiers in addition to the image-enhancement equipment.

In the next animated scene, appearing shortly after the

previous one, a white van with JIFFY CLEANING SERVICE painted on the side rolled into the Haslems' driveway. A platoon of people in white overalls jumped out and went inside, wheeling in heavy-duty cleaning equipment. David could not make out their faces. A procession followed, with the cleaning people lugging out bag after bag of garbage, returning for several trips, and then loading up their equipment and driving off.

The screen sputtered with electronic snow and suddenly went black. Show over. Sometimes David could think better with loud, raucous music on, so he sat through a couple of tracks by Nine-Inch Nails. A disturbing thought entered his mind: what if the person in the parka had come to David's house checking it out for entry points? How could he find out? He had another mini-cam hidden on the east exposure of the house, the side facing the woods. That might have something on it.

David went out the front door and picked his way through the evergreens that grew thick on this side of the house. He was looking for another wren house, this one hung from a spruce tree. He wouldn't need the ladder to get at this one. A distant sense of foreboding tugged at him, a feeling that the Haslems' killer was somewhere near, watching him. As he pulled back a pine branch to get by, he heard a noise behind him and turned. A frightened crow took wing from the top of a dead pine, cawing in protest over the intrusion.

David turned back, and suddenly something furry and wet jumped out at him from behind a tree, clinging to his face, smothering him.

"Yaaah," he shouted, tearing away at the thing, but it flew back at him, crashing into him, filling his mouth with an awful wetness.

David spat fiercely and pushed the furry thing away. His foot caught a root and he fell to the ground. Looking up, he tried to make out what the thing was. It was still close to his face, hanging from a low branch in the same maple tree as the wren house.

Finally the taste in his mouth came through to him. It

was blood. First he saw the legs, then the tail and limp head. Severe nausea began to well up from his stomach and into his mouth when he saw the face with its tongue hanging loose from its mouth.

It was Cupak, hanging by a rope, his throat pierced by a knife.

21

Ron Lindblad uncrossed his legs and propped a Gucci-clad foot up on the red leather ottoman in his study. He glanced at the Portland newspaper reporter who was interviewing him as part of a series on his gubernatorial campaign. Young and eager to make a good impression, she lobbed easy questions at him. Ron felt like he was on a roll, coming off as the elder statesman—sage, self-effacing, and charming. He was relaxed and in command and wanted to show it.

Ron's study dripped of power. Lining its rosewood-paneled walls were framed first-edition lithographs of French monarchs from a nineteenth-century folio. Framed photos of Ron shaking George Bush's hand at a Country Customs shop in Kennebunkport, receiving civic awards, and hobnobbing at the Regents Country Club littered a Louis XIV mahogany table. A few of Ron's many trophies and testimonials were discretely displayed on the bookshelves among the complete collection of leather-bound classics that had never been opened.

The reporter flipped through her notepad, found what she was looking for, and leaned toward Ron. "In a speech last month at the Rockland Rotary Club," she said, reading from the pad, "you went on the record as advocating tougher sentencing for repeat offenders. What particular kinds of crime would you go after as governor?"

Before he spoke, Ron ran his tongue across his front teeth and consulted the lines he had rehearsed. "One of the saddest commentaries on the present administration in Portland," he began, sounding like a winner, "is its soft stand on crime. Why, here we have a governor who is doing his best to keep business out of the state, but rolls out the red carpet to the hardened criminal."

Ron laughed lightly. "Sorry about that, Denise," he said to the reporter, trying his best to sound sheepish. "I have some pretty strong personal feelings about this issue."

Denise smiled and waved her pencil at him. He went on. "It's well known throughout New England that Maine has no death penalty. Criminals of every variety are flocking here, ripping off tourists and residents alike. Last year we had three times the number of violent crimes since four years ago and twice the number of murders."

Ron's voice went softer, his eyes narrow and focused. "I will go on record right here and now as supporting maximum penalties for any repeat offender. And I would vigorously pursue legislation for the death penalty. As I've always believed," he intoned, offering up what he was sure was a good quote for a front-page call-out, "crime prevention begins with the electric chair."

Denise scribbled furiously in her pad and Ron sat back, quietly pleased. Then his pulse jumped as Norma entered the room. He squirmed in his leather armchair, sending out noxious sounds, and shot Norma a look that said: Get out, you're not wanted here. Norma, understanding Ron's look but sensing an opportunity here, smiled wickedly. Ron braced himself for what was to come.

"Excuse me, dear," Norma said sweetly. "But you really should be getting on your way to Dr. Bennett's. Remember your appointment."

Denise's head shot up and said, "The doctor? Oh, do you mind my asking if you have any health problems?"

Ron felt the blood simmering below his skin. He was about to speak when Norma jumped in helpfully. "Oh, no," she said in her most insincere voice. "Ron's visit to the cardiologist is merely *routine*. Ever since his . . . well, problem, he sees Dr. Bennett regularly. But just as a *precaution*, you understand."

"Thank you, Norma," Ron choked, a smile pasted on his crimson face. "Perhaps Denise would like a drink," he added, hoping to get his wife out of there so he could smooth this over.

Without looking up, Denise said, "No, thank you," as she scribbled in her notebook. "That was Dr. *Bennett*, wasn't it?" she asked.

But Norma had left, knowing she had done all the damage she needed to do. Ron was speechless. "Well," Denise said, closing her pad and standing up, "I think I have enough for now. We'll be in touch about the next installment, Mr. Lindblad."

Denise began to leave as Ron sat there with his mouth open, momentarily confused, wondering, on the one hand, if he should follow the reporter out while, on the other, fighting the impulse to go after Norma and throttle her. But Denise was gone and Ron began to search the huge house for Norma, his fury growing with each step he took. He finally found her in a changing room in the bathhouse. He tried the door, but it was locked.

"Do you have any idea what you just did?" Ron said slowly to the door, trying to contain his profound anger. "That was the coarsest, most inexplicably inane display I've ever witnessed, even from you. I—I just don't know how to describe it. 'Idiotic' would be too simple. And 'obscene' doesn't capture the vindictiveness. I think the best description is 'grotesque,' like some medieval gargoyle with stone for brains and its mouth wide open, a drain for the dirty water collecting on the cathedral roof."

Ron paused a moment to catch his breath. Sweat trickled over his nose and he felt his blood pressure zooming. "Norma," he pleaded, "can you explain what was going through your mind as you were very possibly derailing my chances for the governorship?"

"Oh, Ron," Norma finally said, still inside the changing room. "I did nothing of the kind. You're overreacting as you always do. If you want to know, that's the reason you have a heart condition and an ulcer."

"No, Norma," Ron corrected her, "the cause of my problems is you."

Suddenly the door swung open, almost in Ron's fac

Norma, adjusting her swimming cap, casually strolled past him toward the heated pool. Ron stood motionless, watching her walk away. He was tempted to follow her, but decided to leave, to get in his car and go.

Passing through the dining room, Ron heard a splash as Norma dived in and then he noticed something on the table, a legal-size document he hadn't seen there before. Momentarily forgetting his anger, Ron read the document. It was Norma's will, revised just days ago. What did it say?

Ron riffled through the first dozen or so pages of legalese before he got to the terms of the will. He shook his head in total disbelief as he read, the muscles and tendons of his chin spasming. *Norma had just about written him out of the will.* Except for agreeing to maintain Ron's minority share in Country Customs, which wasn't hers to give him anyway, she was leaving everything else—the majority share of the company, the house, her jewelry, and miscellaneous stocks and bonds—to a second cousin she hadn't spoken to in years and didn't even like.

"The bitch," Ron muttered. "The ungrateful, unprincipled bitch."

Ron stomped back to the pool, but Norma was already in, doing her laps. He followed her along the side of the pool as she swam free-style, shouting at her, making damn sure she'd hear him this time.

"Just what the hell is going on, Norma?" Ron said. "What kind of stunt is this? Where do you get off just writing me out of your will? After all I've done, all I've given back to you and the company."

Norma kept on swimming, ignoring him, enraging him. "You'd better listen to me, Norma," he screamed. "I'm not some lowlife gardener or caterer you can just order around, treat like dirt."

Suddenly she looked at him and stopped swimming. She stood on the floor of the pool and unscrewed rubber plugs from her ears. "What is it now?" she said evenly.

It was everything Ron could do to keep from jumping in right there and holding her head under until . . . He checked the thought. "I want to know what's going on with the will," he said, restraining the anger, "why you're writing me out."

Norma curled up her lips in mild disgust. "It's just something Neal drew up last week." Neal Sullivan, her sleazy lawyer. No surprise to Ron that *he* was involved in this. "And I haven't written you out. You'd get what you have now, your interest in Country Customs."

Instead of swimming free-style, Norma did a crawl, permitting her to talk with Ron. She pushed off the end and kept going as he followed after her. "So tell me this," Ron continued, "why did you designate Sylvia as the executor and primary beneficiary?"

Norma jutted her chin up, putting her mouth above the water line. "Funny you should mention Sylvia," she said. "I called her the other day, just after the will came back. She was absolutely delighted to hear from me, even said she'd been thinking about *me* lately. Can you imagine?"

She pushed off the other end and Ron stayed with her. "She even became a bit morose when I told her I was considering her in the will. The dear. I can't believe it, but maybe I've been misjudging her all these years. There may be a heart underneath that Boston snobbery after all."

Ron listened carefully, trying to hear between the lines. Was Norma bluffing, stringing him along about the will? Was she just getting even for whatever she thought was going on between Barb Bromley and him? Or had she had the damn will executed already? He couldn't be sure. If she had executed the will, he would do his level best to have it withdrawn, even if he had to go to court. But there was nothing he could do right now except to wait, to devise a plan.

"Just tell me one thing, Norma," Ron said. "Why?"

"Why what?" she said, a bit winded now after her tenth or so lap.

"Why did you write me out of your will?"

"Oh, Ron," she said, "you look so ugly with your face red like that."

Ron watched her push off again and crawl toward the other end of the pool. He looked down at her glass of grapefruit juice on the patio table, then at the switch for the pool cover, and stalked out.

22

The Country Customs factory had a hushed, reverential feel to it in the middle of the night. Ron prowled the corridors, slipping into assembly and paint rooms, observing his workers, jotting down a note or two if something caught his eye. He liked to come in at odd hours to check on things, to keep everyone on their toes. If something was wrong, he would talk to the lineman or foreman, never to a worker. Most of them couldn't understand him anyway.

The third shift was on, manning the assembly lines with quiet intensity. The shift had a quota to fill and hell to pay if it didn't meet it. At this moment four factories in and around Sparks were going at full capacity, churning out furniture, dried-flower wreaths, birdhouses, and other authentic New England crafts. Ron watched as stone pottery coffee mugs clattered down a conveyor belt toward painters who each had four seconds to slap the semblance of a flower on each one. They never missed one in the ten minutes he stood and watched.

Ron kept a careful eye on the electrical power in the factory. It'd been acting up again today, that damn Cheseldine still unable to get it under control. Ron counted up twenty four minutes of downtime because of the power fluctuations, as the assembly lines and machinery had to be stopped and retimed. He had a good mind to send Cheseldine a bill for the losses.

Watching the assembly line, Ron's thoughts began to drift toward Barb, as they had been doing all day. Some-times he imagined her naked, stretched out on the bear r on the floor of his study. Other times he pictured her on his desk, her head hanging over the side.

Barb needed a nudge, a little scare, for Ron to be able to nail her. What would be appropriate? All he had to do was turn up the pressure a bit in the right direction. The way to get to her, he concluded, was to give her some competition for her real estate business. Yes, that might do the trick. Besides, it was the American way.

A few days ago Barb had told him about a call she'd received from a big New York investor who was interested in putting money in Sparks—for tourism, Ron guessed, because he couldn't imagine any other reason. Ron had no intention just yet of letting go of his plans for Country Customs, but he did have a plan to use this guy to get Barb into bed and collect a little nest egg for himself. What was that guy's name? Had Barb even mentioned it? Ron would not only ask her the name, he would let her think he was giving the guy some of her real estate action. That would show her he meant business.

Before leaving the factory, Ron stopped by his office for his keys and coat. He fixed a TNT—most of it gin—in a thirty-two-ounce 7-Eleven Big Gulp cup with a picture on it of Shaquille O'Neal slam-dunking a basketball. He wanted to drink and drive but not to attract the attention of the state police by swigging from his flask. How would it look if the future governor of the state were picked up DUI?

As he stirred the drink, Ron gazed at the chart on his wall of the local power grid. At the core of the grid was Ron's substation. He bit the rim of the cup as he sipped down on his drink. Shrugging on his coat, he decided to make a stop on his way home.

The music of Wagner crashed out of Ron's car and into the still Maine night. Through his cellular phone he had ordered one of his favorite CDs—selections from *Songs of the Niebelungen* by the Boston Pops, particularly the opera *Twilight of the Gods.* Right now he was enjoying one of

Brunhilde's arias, a particularly piercing one that caused the windows to vibrate.

Ron thought the Wagner music particularly appropriate because all around him were images of intense power. Towering above him were silhouettes of power lines suspended by red and black pylons, massive iron giants lined up like sentinels along the highway. He felt a surge of power, knowing he alone was responsible for moving them here. A word from him could put them back where they had been, five miles outside of town in a long wash where the FCC had recommended they be built.

About ten yards down a slight slope was the power station, partially hidden behind a border of white pines. Ron knew it well. Klieg lights blazed around the station, sparking flashes of light on its surrounding chain-link fence and its inner workings. He had bitten into the cup where he had been drinking, leaving a crescent-shaped gash around Shaquille O'Neal's neck. His brain felt bruised from the gin, and he tried to deflect the pain by thinking about Barb, her perfect looks, her body. He opened the door and got out.

The air was sharply cold, but it felt good to Ron, who had been sitting in recirculated conditioned air all day. The power station was the nerve center of one of the most important facets of his operations. He had been deeply involved in its design, virtually dictating its power specifications to Al Cheseldine. Cheseldine, that simpy slob, had whined and fought him through the whole thing, but Ron got his way in the end.

Singlehandedly, Ron had managed to upgrade the old distribution substation—one that had been receiving a small-time 69,000 volts and squirting out a mere 34,500—to a larger intermediate station that took in 139,000 volts directly from the power plant and transformed it down to 69,000 volts for lesser distribution substations elsewhere—34,500 for industrial purposes, and 12,500 for residential use. In residential areas, the 12,500 volts were fed into single or three-phase transformers—the kind you see on tel phone poles—and into homes or offices using 120 to 240 volts.

This dazzlingly powerful substation played into his plans in a lot of ways. First, it allowed him to ratchet up production at Country Customs so that he could bring down prices and increase volume. It was beginning to work. One thing Ron needed to turn Outlet City into reality was cash. Lots of it. The up-front capital for a project of this magnitude required as much cash as he could lay his hands on. With the beefed-up power and a larger work force, Ron was churning out six times the number of Country Customs products he had been this time last year, and starting to rake it in.

The power from the substation would also allow Outlet City to hit the ground running. Ron knew that as soon as word got out about his plans, the Freeport crowd would be all over him, trying to cut him off at every turn. One sure thing they would do would be to use political muscle to make it hard for him to get building permits, build roads, and increase the electrical and other power. Well, between this substation and his winning the governorship, no one could stop him.

There was an unintended benefit of the substation: it made people sick. At least Ron thought it did. Sid told him that the increased electromagnetic field might somehow be to blame for the high rates of illness in the area. It was all gravy, as far as Ron was concerned. If people got sick, maybe some would leave the area. That was fine by him.

And if the substation wasn't enough, Ron had insurance—a fail-safe—one person who could do the job of three substations in clearing the deadwood out of Sparks. That person was probably working at this very moment, moving through the town like Death, cutting down anything in Ron's way. But Ron was still careful, more so than ever since his killer had begun going off halfcocked and whacking people without his permission.

Ron walked what seemed like a long way to the front gate of the substation. Spewing plumes of dragon breath into the night air, he was greeted by the four-by-six-foot sign bolted to the fence screaming HIGH VOLTAGE—EXTREMELY DANGEROUS—ABSOLUTELY NO ENTRY. He paused to think for a moment and then opened the cover to a digital combination lock, and punched in EB42WAT—the entry code. The gate opened and he entered the power station.

Like a father admiring his child, Ron took in the station's awesome size, complexity, and potency. First he listened for the unmistakable hum of power emanating from the massive coils, pylons, and switching boxes. Looming in the background were the giant transmission pylon towers with copper-clad steel wires feeding into the substation. Ron gazed fondly at the transformers, crackling as they transformed alternating currents, and the stepdown transformers that lowered the voltage. Disconnect switches linked up with the circuit breakers, close to the ground, that served as on- and off-switches in the event of current overload into the substation. Ron was especially proud of these circuit breakers, digitally managed by computers installed in adjacent steel-reinforced cabinets and representing the latest in substation technology.

But above all, Ron drank in the sight of the condensers that stored the vast electrical current flowing through the station and emanated waves of electromagnetic radiation over the entire area. He closed his eyes and could feel the power dancing over the skin of his face, seeping through his pores, and igniting the marrow of his bones. Power stirred in his pants, the electricity rising below his belt. Out of nowhere Ron heard something strange in the night, a sound that caused him to open his eyes. Was it a laugh?

He turned for the Mercedes, his legs heavy as he walked through the substation. Inside the car, he picked up his cellular phone and spoke the name on his mind all afternoon. One ring, two, three. Where the hell was she? Then Barb picked up and he could relax.

"Where *are* you?" Barb said, obviously pleased by his call.

"I'm in the dark, at the power station."

"The power station?"

"Off Route 73."

She giggled. "Well, are you feeling powerful?"

"Very. What are you doing?"

"I just got out of the shower. You wouldn't believe what kind of day it's been."

Ron grunted. "What are you wearing?"

Pause. Giggle. "Not much."

"Tell me."

"A T-shirt and . . . panties. Why do you ask?"

"What color is the T-shirt?"

"White. Actually, it's a tank top. Sleeveless."

"Do you have a bra on?"

Giggle. "No."

"What kind of panties?"

No giggle. "A silk thong."

"What color?"

"Taupe."

"Take off the shirt."

"Okay."

"Is it off?"

"Yes."

"Now the panties."

Pause. "Okay. They're off."

"Barb."

"Yes."

"Touch yourself."

"Ron!"

"Do it."

"No."

"I want you, Barb. You know it, don't you?"

"Ron, go home. Are you drinking?"

"No."

"How about lunch tomorrow? I have to tell you all about—"

"No. I want you and I'm going to have you."

"Oh, Ron, you know I'm attracted to you. But we—"

"It's not enough. I want more."

"So do I, Ron. But let's give it time."

"When?"

"What?"

"What time? When?"

"I don't know. Soon. Ron?"

"What?"

"Sid asked me to tell you something, before he left for Mexico. He said that he was worried that your associate would try something again in the next couple of days."

Ron was quiet for a moment, trying to interpret the message. Then it hit him. The "associate" was the killer whom Sid must have called to warn about the unauthorized murders. Sid was saying that another such killing might take place anytime.

"Ron? Are you there?"

"I don't believe it. He *told* you all this? Did he say anything else?"

"No, I don't know. That's all I know."

"Sid back tomorrow?"

"Yes. His plane gets in at—"

"Have him call me. I'll call you tomorrow."

Ron hung up. As electricity crackled around the powerhouse, he slid back in his leather seat, his mind working, plotting how he would nail Barb and get that bothersome killer back in line.

23

Not far away, K. K. Thorner was in bed, barely awake, in her tiny four-room converted lobster house built on stilt pilings over an inlet of Penobscot Bay. Ebb tide waters lapped gently against the pilings as she drifted in and out of sleep. Lying next to her in bed, dead to the world, was Ray. They had been making love ever since Ray dropped by unexpectedly, after K. K. had put her daughter to bed.

From experience, K. K. knew that men don't like to talk or cuddle or do much of anything after sex, except maybe eat. But nothing in her experience had prepared her for Ray, who, right after finishing, went from mute to comatose in forty-five seconds. Tonight K. K. didn't feel like raising it again with him and said nothing. She simply rolled over and nodded off.

While she succumbed to sleep, a blurry image of Mother Courage formed in her mind. It was a composite of several Mother Courages—played by Judi Dench, Glenda Jackson, and Pat Carroll—with herself woven in as well. And then something strange: Estelle Grout's face mixed in among them. When preparing for a role, K. K. could usually conjure up a living, breathing picture of the character she wanted to portray. But this time it was different.

The more she read the play, the harder it was for K. K. to get a bead on Mother Courage, to find pieces of herself that would fit the character and enable her to do the role. There was a brutality to Mother Courage that K. K. had trouble relating to, a greedy, parasitic side that would sacrifice her own child for some measly pocket change.

K. K. was thinking in particular of the scene in which

Swiss Cheese, one of Mother Courage's three children, is wrongfully arrested as a thief by a military spy during the Thirty Years' War. The spy is willing to cut a deal with Mother Courage if the price is right. Yvette, the prostitute, acts as intermediary between the spy and Mother Courage, who haggles over the price of her son's life even as the possibility of his execution grows with each unresolved minute. Finally, Swiss Cheese is killed and Mother Courage—not shedding as much as one tear for the son whose execution she is responsible for—hitches up her wagon and heads for the next battleground where she can hawk her brandy.

K. K. wondered how she would handle this scene as Mother Courage. Would she emphasize Mother Courage's stoic peasant nature, and march her unflinchingly through the scene? Or would she just make Mother Courage look bad, as the small-minded, money-grubbing witch she could so easily become. Or might she reveal a sympathetic side—perhaps through a sob only the audience hears—that hints how Mother Courage is another victim of war and really torn up inside by her son's death?

K. K. had no idea how she would play it. She let go of the blurry image and allowed herself to float into the fog of sleep. Then she heard something, someone, a voice in the dark shrouded in static, that yanked her from the fog.

"What are you wearing?"

"Huh?" K. K. said, fighting the serotonin that smothered her synapses.

"What color is the T-shirt?"

T-shirt? she wondered.

"Do you have a bra on?"

"Ray"? K. K. whispered. She was awake now, listening to Ray, who was snoring loudly. Was he talking in his sleep? she wondered.

"What kind of panties?"

"What color?"

Who *is* that? K. K. almost said aloud.

"Take off the shirt."

K. K. snapped on a reading light. Sure enough, Ray was out cold. She looked around the room. No one was there.

"Is it off?"

How weird, K. K. thought. The voice, she realized, was coming from her clock radio.

"Now the panties."

Uh-oh, K. K. thought, getting kinky here. Was this one of those call-in radio programs or some creep on a 900 number? Or a joke? Could Ray have hidden a tape recorder in here?

"Barb."

"Touch yourself."

Whoa! K. K. thought and sat up in bed, straining her ear toward the radio to hear what Barb did.

"Do it." A glob of static spurted through the radio.

"I want you, Barb. You know it, don't you?"

He sounds pissed, K. K. thought. Barb didn't do it. *Way to go, Barb!*

"No."

Hang in there, Barb, K. K. cheered silently.

"No. I want you and I'm going to have you."

C'mon, Barb, dump him. He's a creep. There're plenty of fish in the ocean.

"It's not enough. I want more."

See? I was right? Where's your self-esteem, girl?

"When?"

Pushy bastard. Tell him to go . . .

"What time? When?"

Good God. Back off, already.

"What?"

Hey, let's go, Barb. Pack him off. Long, staticky buzz. A long pause.

"I don't believe it. He *told* you all this? Did he say anything else?"

The voice drowned in radio noise and then disappeared.

K. K. sat up in the dim light of her bedroom. The impact of the experience began to set in. She felt cold, clammy, and deeply anxious, and she drew the blankets up to her shoulders.

Who is this sick bastard and what the hell is he doing in my radio? K. K. thought.

The ebb tide was picking up, slapping the pilings. The voice lingered in the room, clinging to K. K.'s skin like mildew. She recalled nights as a child when she was ill with a fever and the air in her room quivered with a threatening texture and everything seemed unhealthy, tainted. Tonight was such a night.

K. K. felt somehow violated by the intrusion. She wasn't sure where the voice came from, but she had heard of this before, of people hearing voices on their radios or stereos from cellular phones and walkie-talkies. Whatever the source of the voice, she had a profound sense of apocalypse, as if other worlds were colliding into her own. Privacy, if it ever existed, was no more than a tattered vestige. That, or she was going crazy.

She slid down in the bed, pulling the blankets up to her chin. She looked over at Ray, his back to her, snoring obliviously. She took in a deep breath and closed her eyes. For the first time in years, she slept with the light on.

24

When K. K. woke up the next morning, Ray was gone, as usual. She didn't bother to look for a note. She was running late and would have to hurry to make her nine o'clock marketing class at the university. She dressed quickly and groaned when she saw herself in the mirror: she looked as if she had spent the night in jail.

The day care in Camden would be closed today, and K. K. had arranged with Estelle to take Viveca. K. K. gently, reluctantly, tried to wake her daughter. The poor thing didn't want to get up. K. K. had been worried about Viveca, noticing that she seemed to be sleeping a lot more than usual. Waking her in the mornings had been difficult. Viveca was still asleep as K. K. dressed her, bundled her up, and buckled her into the car seat.

Viveca woke up and began to cry when the Pinto hit a pothole. K. K., driving the car, was ready with a bottle, but Viveca pushed it away and wailed louder.

"What's wrong, sweetheart?" K. K. said into the rear-view mirror.

Viveca answered with screams. Her crying made it harder for K. K. to do what she usually did while driving in the morning—sorting through the things she needed to do today. She knew she'd be getting a quiz in her marketing class, probably something about pricing. But she was ready, having read through the three chapters of her textbook during her breaks yesterday at the diner. After the test she would drop by the drama department, where she'd check the bulletin board for the list of names for call-backs for

Mother Courage. She'd prepared herself for the bad news, already believing there was no way she'd be on the list.

In the afternoon K. K. had her usual noon to six shift at the diner. Nothing new there. Then, pick up Viveca at Estelle's, read or play with her for an hour before bed, and then hit the books again. K. K. knew she wouldn't be hearing from Ray for at least three days, normal after-sex behavior for him. Viveca was still crying and K. K. turned on a local radio station that played big band music. It was the only station she liked. Oh, great, she thought, a Billie Holiday song was on—"God Bless the Child"—and K. K. sang along with it. She was anxious to get moving and became irritated at a stoplight when the guy in front of her—in some old black relic of a truck—just sat there after the light had changed. He waved when K. K. tooted at him and he moved on.

At Estelle's house, K. K. helped Viveca out of the Pinto. Odd, K. K. thought, Estelle was always out here by now, helping her with Viveca. Whenever K. K. brought Viveca to Estelle's, she imagined the dear woman waiting by the window, watching for their arrival. There had been times when K. K. was late and Estelle had been out on her doorstep, wringing her hands, imagining the worst. K. K. always made a special effort to get to Estelle's on time.

Even stranger, Estelle didn't answer her door when K. K. rang the bell. K. K. waited and rang it again, longer this time. Still nothing. She muttered under her breath, ducked under a juniper tree, and followed the path under the widow's walk around to the back door. She pecked on the door and peered through the window. No sign of Estelle. The kitchen looked different somehow, as if the furniture and the things on the wall had been rearranged.

K. K. looked down and noticed white flakes scattered over the doorstep. She bent down on one knee and picked up a couple of pieces on her finger. Was it . . . putty?

Viveca started to cry again, and K. K. stood up and bounced her in her arms. She tried to concentrate on what she should do next. Maybe Estelle was in there, hurt or worse. K. K. should call someone, but who? The closest police station was in Rockland. She could call the volunteer fire department; she knew all the guys from the diner.

Estelle's neighbor was Lorton Theroux, an old drunk whom K. K. knew that Estelle didn't much like. It was improbable that Theroux knew where Estelle could be and even more unlikely that Estelle would be there. Still, K. K. marched over and tapped on Theroux's door. No answer. He's probably sleeping it off somewhere, K. K. said to an uncomprehending Viveca.

K. K. decided to go home and call Mr. De Vries, the mayor and justice of the peace, the only local authority. So much for the marketing quiz and finding out if she had made call-backs. Oh, well. K. K. was worried about Estelle and had to do something.

Heading back to the Pinto, Viveca in her arms, K. K. spied something in the shaggy grass along the widow's walk. She buckled Viveca in her car seat and returned to examine the object. It was hard, frozen to the touch. She recognized it as an iron wood-chopping wedge. Even if Estelle had a wood-burning fireplace, she was too old to be chopping wood.

"Strange," K. K. said to no one. "What would Estelle be doing with this?"

25

That day David McAdam was home with Von, feeling the walls of the house closing in around him. It was hard to tell who was more miserable—David, peripatetic from caffeine, roiling fear, and sheer restlessness—or Von, who had to put up with David. So David called Jean and asked her, *begged* her, to come over for a while to stay with Von, but she turned him down, telling him she couldn't do it today. With more than a tinge of sarcasm in her voice she suggested he take Von with him; the fresh air would do them both good. David reluctantly agreed to try it.

David loaded stroller, diaper bag, toys, books, and Von into the truck, and they took off for the mall. Rolling up the service road, he studied the house in the rearview mirror. Earlier this morning a crew of painters—David had agreed to pay triple overtime to get them to come immediately—put on a fresh coat of white latex enamel. Just before they left, they put on a second coat over the red scrawl, which was now barely visible. They would come back tomorrow to finish the job.

David looked at his hands on the steering wheel. Even though he had scrubbed them close to a half hour after burying Cupak yesterday, there was still some dirt under his fingernails. It had been a sad ritual—cutting the dog down, covering him up and loading him into the wheelbarrow, and searching out a burial ground—all taking far longer than David wanted because he had to wait for Von, who was tarrying behind.

David found a clearing in the woods and dug for a long time, making sure the hole was deep enough so that nothing would dig up the body and drag it back to the house. He didn't want Nara to know. Should she ask, he had rehearsed a story that Cupak ran away or was hit by a car. It would be the first time he ever held something back from her.

Anger was growing in him like a malignant tumor. It was the worst kind of anger—rage at his own helplessness. He wanted to scream, to punch at something. But he kept it all in, fearful that Nara would notice. Finally, yesterday afternoon she asked him what was wrong, and he caved in and told her. She showed no emotion, but she was unnervingly quiet the rest of the evening.

Instead of sleeping, they stayed up and vacillated through the night on whether or not to call the police. At first Nara was the pro-police advocate, arguing that the harassment wasn't going away, just getting worse. David's first reaction was to keep the police out of it and avoid any snooping by the press. But then he came around to her way of thinking just as she was softening her position, wondering what the police could do for them anyway, especially Lawrence Donner, the sheriff, whom she knew and had never trusted. And on and on. They finally fell asleep around five, about a half hour before Von woke them up.

Passing through Sparks and heading north to the highway, David tried to get his mind off his problems by taking in the scenery. But it was no help: dreary and mundane. For reasons he couldn't fathom, he was acutely aware of the nondescript electrical utility devices he barely ever noticed along the roads: transformers, switching and control boxes, and maintenance cabinets. Ever since the truck radio had gone kaput near the high-tension wires, it had been stuck on the local big band station and he couldn't turn it off.

Waiting for a traffic light to change, he noticed in his rearview mirror the driver of the battered little car behind him—an attractive young woman—singing along to the same Billie Holiday song he was listening to. David watched her intently; she knew all the words. He was unaware that the light had changed, and the woman tapped on her horn. He gave her a little wave and pushed off.

At the Downeast Mall, David made his rounds, this time in reverse: video arcade first while Von was still asleep from the car ride. Maybe this time he would have a shot at Double Death. Heading into the arcade and the cacophony of electronic *pings* and *bleeps,* David spotted a new, interesting-looking machine surrounded by punk-looking types he'd seen here before. They periodically burst out with invectives or encomiums for the person at the controls. David heard many different accents among them.

Was it his imagination or did the arcade suddenly get a lot quieter when he passed through? Von slept in his stroller as David played through a couple of uninspired games of Double Death and left.

Out in the middle of the mall, he noticed a group of six or seven men walking, as if in slow motion, their heads bent down, staring intently at something in their hands. They almost seemed to be dancing to the synthetic waltz being pumped into the stores. He was certain he had seen these people before, but where he couldn't quite recall.

What the hell, he thought, and he pushed Von right up to them and bluntly asked them what they were doing.

From the rear of the group, a short, plump man with white hair, goatee, and overalls perked up and stepped forward. "You're the first person in this town to ask us that question," he said. "I find that somewhat remarkable."

"We're from The Flow," he went on, expecting David to recognize the name as if it were as well-known as the Rockettes or U.S. Marines. Actually, David did recognize the name, but from where?

"I give up," David said. "What is The Flow?"

"That depends on the context of your question," the man said.

David was beginning to get annoyed. "Suppose we start from *your* context."

The man looked at the others in the group, and they all smiled in unison. "The Flow," the man said, "is a movement to reconstitute the human spirit in unison with the four basic elements: air, fire, earth, and—"

"Water," David finished for him. "I've heard your ads on the radio. What're those things you're carrying around?"

Another man stepped forward from the group, extremely tall, thin, and wearing a wide-brimmed straw hat. "The elements tend to exist in disparate states," he said. "Rarely do you get a convergence of them. Until, perhaps, now. That is to say, here."

"Here?" David repeated. He noticed that Von had woken up.

"Yes, here," said the plump man. "Sparks. We've been getting unusually high energy readings for some weeks now at our headquarters over in Andover."

"Andover?" David said, thinking. "Isn't that where the . . ."

The plump man smiled. "The Comsat transmission center is, yes, precisely. The hub of all transatlantic satellite traffic. It's an area remarkably free of frequency noise, if you're sufficiently shielded from the Comsat traffic."

"But boring as hell," said the tall man.

"Oh, don't mind Nelson," the plump man said aside to David. "He hasn't found his inner child yet.

"We've been monitoring frequencies and power surges throughout the region for some time in anticipation of a great elemental convergence," the man went on. "We believe you are on the verge of experiencing one here on south Penobscot Bay. Why, the very air is alive—"

"With the sound of music," David finished dryly. He eyed the plump man suspiciously. "Hey, don't I know your voice? Sure, you're Smilin' Jack, aren't you? The host of the big band program."

The man nodded briefly, a curt acknowledgment. He kept talking where he had left off. "We believe we are almost upon the epicenter of the convergence. It can't be more than a mile from here."

"I have a suggestion for you," David said quietly. The group moved in closer toward him.

"Take Route One north until you're about to enter the

Sparks town limits. You'll come upon some power lines—the big, high-tension kind—along the road. Stop and take a few readings. I think you might find your convergence there."

The group got very excited, thanked him profusely, and trundled off with their equipment. David was glad to be rid of them.

He searched around the mall for Bob Kellum, his engineer friend, but couldn't find him. He spotted Clara, another mall habitué, on a bench and stopped by to chat. After she finished fawning over Von, David asked her about Bob.

Clara looked down at her K-Mart running shoes and shook her head. "I haven't seen Bob or Lillian for days," she whispered. "I even called them at home, but no one answered. It's the foreigners," she said, looking around for one lurking nearby, "they're moving in, taking over."

David listened politely, nodding his head and grunting in polite intervals, but he got away at the first opportunity. As he scooted a restless Von toward Paul's computer shop, David tried to shake off an unnerving sense of being followed. But the more he thought about it, the more he wondered: Who the hell would be following him here? Or anywhere else, for that matter? Unless it was the press, those tireless protectors of the public interest, who would have liked nothing better than to sell a few papers by plastering his face over the covers of their rags.

Or unless it was the killer.

David made tracks to Paul's and ducked in. Actually, he had an ulterior motive for dropping by. For days David's suspicions had been growing that Paul was the one who had hacked into his computer system. (Who else in Sparks knew enough about computers to even begin to get past David's major-league security?) David was going to do a little fishing.

Paul was with customers when David entered the store. David killed time while he waited for Paul, trying to interest Von in video games. Every so often he would peer out into the mall to see if anyone was lurking out there. Just as he was about to finish a game, helping the Mario Brothers prevent total destruction of the solar system, Paul appeared at his side.

"Aren't we off schedule today?" Paul said, rubbing Von on the head and getting a growl from him. "I mean, you're usually not here until Friday, isn't that right?"

"Usually," David said. "Say, Paul, I've been meaning to ask you something. The other day a message came up on Conspiracy. Seemed to have been put there by—"

The telephone at the front counter trilled lightly, and Paul held up a hand and went to answer it. David sighed and jiggled the handles to the stroller to settle a whining Von. Come on, Paul, David thought. But Paul was having problems of his own. David could hear some of his conversation.

"I told you yesterday," Paul said, his voice rising an octave or two, "I'm not interested. Don't you people *listen*?" He paused a moment and began ferociously scratching his cheek. It looked painful to David. "No, absolutely not," Paul went on, his irritation turning to fury, "I'm good here for another two years. I've got a lease. This is harassment and I'm getting a lawyer. That's right, asshole, see you in court."

Paul slammed the phone down and stomped over to David, one side of his face streaked red, his breathing labored. "Fucking bastards," he grumbled. David grimaced and looked sharply at Paul and then down at Von, who was taking it all in. Paul didn't get the hint.

"What chutzpah," he said. "I'm getting a restraining order on those pricks. They've been in here three times this week, squeezing me like a dishrag. Who do they think they're dealing with?"

"Just keep your head about it," David said, realizing this was not a good time to be quizzing Paul about the hacker. Besides, David was now sure that Paul wasn't the one.

"Gotta get going," he said, turning the stroller toward the door. As he wheeled Von into the mall, David glanced over his shoulder at Paul standing in the doorway, staring out into space and clawing at his cheek.

David had little enthusiasm left to do much else, so he headed for the elevators to the garage. Passing the bookstore, he felt a chill crawl down his back. He felt unseen eyes like lasers raking his back. Someone was following them! He was positive this time. He spun the stroller into the bookstore and ducked behind the New Arrivals shelf.

In a few seconds David noticed a dark-skinned, doe-eyed woman dressed in black stirrup pants and a black nylon jacket, her head down, picking over a bin of marked-down remainders near the front door. He looked closer and saw that her head was shaved except for a knot of tight corn rows braided in the back. She looked up at him staring at her, then giggled and disappeared. David ran to follow her, but she was gone by the time he managed to get the stroller outside into the mall. He pushed Von into the shops on either side of the bookstore, but there was no sign of her. Shaking his head all the way, he took the elevator down to the second parking level.

The parking garage was deserted except for David's truck and a few scattered cars. An inexplicable tingling rose from the nape of his neck. Someone else was down here. He couldn't see anyone, but he was as certain as he ever been about anything.

Sweat began to seep through David's pores, greasing his palms as he briskly pushed the stroller down the handicap ramp, over the curb, and toward the truck. From somewhere deep in the garage came the bone-grating sound of a loose muffler being dragged over cold pavement. David tried to think, to push out the terrible thoughts crowding in on him. Where could someone be hiding? How close was an exit if he needed to run? Was Von strapped in his seat? Yes, god*damn* it, David would have to carry Von and the stroller if they had to run. Was there anything heavy in the back of the truck, something he could use to defend himself? Where were his keys?

David felt his heart stop as Von and he were suddenly surrounded by the punks from the video arcade. They seemed to come from everywhere, slowly forming a half circle around them, trapping them against a wall. David counted about seven or eight punks, all young and grinning at him, dressed mostly in black with heavy boots, jarring haircuts, and jewelry in improbable places on their faces. In the middle of them stood a strapping monster—at least six five and two hundred twenty-five pounds—with a buzz cut and all in black, like Death itself.

Then David realized: the prowler at the Haslems! The one Jean had seen. Maybe there wasn't just one killer but many. And here they were!

Despite the profound threat facing him, David felt remarkably lucid. From somewhere in his consciousness he recalled an idea from Arthur Koestler's book *The Arrow in the Blue*—Ahor, short for Archaic Horror—describing the raw, primal fear that lurks at the bottom of our deepest fears. For David, who, as a kid—a fairly geeky "good student" who loved mathematics and calculators and went out of his way to avoid encounters like this—being encircled by a gang of black-leather punks in a dark, lonely garage was truly Ahor. His heart was thumping like the bit of a pneumatic drill against concrete.

He looked down at Von, who was staring wide-eyed but fearlessly at the punks. David's greatest worry was for Von, sitting vulnerably in front of him in the stroller. He tried his best to hide his fear even though his teeth were chattering. Then he began to notice things. Like how young these kids were. And the black pocket calculator fastened to the big guy's hip. And the girl from the bookstore, who looked small, fragile.

Groping for something to say, something really tough and masterful, David stammered: "Why—why aren't you kids in school?"

The punks looked momentarily stunned and then they all began to laugh hysterically. David thought this might be a good time to pick up the stroller and make a run for it, but from the middle of the group stepped a small, dark-skinned, geeky-looking kid with a maroon turban on his head and shirt pocket protector festooned with pens and markers.

"Mr. McAdam?" he said in a clipped British accent. Now

David was *really* worried, hearing his real name for the first time in two years. "Allow me to introduce myself. I am Mohan Singh," he said, bowing slightly and taking David's moist hand. "But please call me Moe."

David gingerly took his hand and kept an eye on the others behind him. "It is a great honor to meet you," Moe said. "I am deeply sorry that we had to meet in such an unpleasant place. Let me introduce you to my friends."

Moe introduced David to each of the punks, a blur of Lithuanian, Khmer, Honduran, Hmong, and Croatian names. Shyly, each one came forward, bowed, and shook his hand. The young woman from the bookstore, who Moe introduced as Pia, curtsied.

"We only realized perhaps three weeks ago that you lived here in Sparks," Moe said. "It was truly an exceptional moment when we discovered that David McAdam—PanTech employee number one, virtually the inventor of the personal computer—was here among us all this time.

"I hope I will not be embarrassing you by revealing that you are our greatest hero. We would consider it a truly unusual privilege if you gave us a brief talk about parallel processing or some other topic of mutual interest. At your convenience, of course."

David, who had not yet said anything to them, was about to ask, "All *what* time?" and who "we" were. Then he understood: these were cyberpunks—hitchhikers on the information superhighway, whiz kids who eat, sleep, and breathe computers with the same kind of fanaticism kids used to reserve for sex, drugs, and rock 'n' roll. They were the closest thing to a fan club David ever had.

David felt a tremendous sense of relief flooding over him. "What the hell," he said. He pointed at the truck and said, "Jump in."

26

K. K. Thorner, wearing mittens and a heavy Norwegian sweater, stomped her feet from the cold and waited impatiently in front of Estelle Grout's house. It was about four-thirty in the afternoon, already dark. She had been here since before four, the time when Dwight De Vries—the mayor of Sparks, justice of the peace, and only local authority she knew of—was supposed to meet her. To be able to be here, K. K. had switched shifts with another waitress who owed her a few favors. Viveca was asleep in the Pinto, as she had been most of the day. K. K. didn't know what to do about her.

Before long, K. K. spotted De Vries's tan Taurus coming up the street. She'd seen the car before, many times, in fact, at the diner. De Vries, with a wife and six children, was seeing Camilla, one of the night waitresses, on the sly. This was K. K.'s only leverage, to get De Vries to come out here today without his blowing her off. When she'd called him, she'd made a point to do so at his home. Before explaining the situation, she casually let it drop that he might remember her from the diner. He told her he'd meet her at Estelle's right away.

De Vries pulled up, his wheels scraping the curb. It took him three tries to extricate himself from his seat, his gut wedged against the steering wheel. Obviously displeased about this perturbation in his schedule, he shot a nasty look at K. K. and headed straight for the house. After banging on the door a few times he turned toward her and spread out his hands as if to say, "I've done everything. What else can I do?"

"I've been knocking all day, Mr. De Vries," K. K. said. "I think we should just go in."

De Vries screwed up his face and looked at her skeptically. "On what authority?" he said.

K. K. shrugged. "Yours, I guess."

"You guess?" he blurted, the loose skin on his neck quivering. "Now let me tell you something, young lady."

Young lady? Christ!

"I don't make a habit out of knocking down people's doors and I certainly don't—" His mouth snapped shut as a car—a shiny red Jaguar—slowed to a stop in front of them. It pulled into Estelle's driveway behind K. K.'s Pinto, as if her car didn't look bad enough all by itself, she thought.

Emerging from the car was a woman K. K. had never seen before, not that someone driving a 1995 Jaguar would be seen in any place *she'd* frequent. The woman was dressed to kill—in a full-length sable coat, a suit underneath K. K. guessed was Yves Saint Laurent, Hermes scarf, Ferragamo shoes, impeccable hair, nails, and makeup. Obviously an out-of-towner.

But De Vries knew her.

"Hello, Dwight," the woman said, flashing perfect teeth.

"Mrs. Bromley, how nice to see you," he said, looking puzzled and vaguely apprehensive.

Mrs. Bromley sized K. K. up and down in a way K. K. didn't like. What, K. K. thought, you don't care for my outfit, pieced together from some of the better outlet stores in Freeport? She brushed past K. K. and joined De Vries at the door.

"What brings you here?" he said.

"I happened to be driving by and saw you," she said, not sounding very convincing, K. K. thought. "I just sold this house and thought you might need a hand."

"Excuse me," K. K. said, stepping forward. "You couldn't have sold this house."

Mrs. Bromley did not acknowledge K. K. "Dwight, who is this?"

"Uh, a young woman who called me just an hour or so ago. Claims to know the person who lived here."

"*Lived* here? Listen, I'm K. K. Thorner and I know Estelle Grout. I just saw her a couple days ago. She baby-sits my daughter. She wouldn't have moved without telling me."

"Are you a relative, dear?" Mrs. Bromley asked.

"No," K. K. said, stung by the question. "Something is wrong here. I think we should break a pane of glass and go inside to look around. Estelle could be—"

"You'll do nothing of the sort," Mrs. Bromley said, getting tough. "This house was sold by Mrs. Grout two days ago."

"Sold to whom?" K. K. asked.

"To me," Mrs. Bromley answered coldly, "not that it's any of your business."

K. K. wanted to punch Mrs. Bromley in her perfect nose. "Prove it," K. K. said.

"Now, Mrs. Bromley," De Vries said, "you don't have to prove anything. We're just getting ready to go."

"It's all right," Mrs. Bromley said, walking toward her car. She pulled something from a briefcase on the front seat and came back.

"This is the deed," she said, holding it out to K. K. "Signed by Mrs. Grout. I appreciate your concern, but Mrs. Grout approached me many months ago about selling. She wanted to join her sister in Florida."

"Bullshit," K. K. said, really steamed now. "I don't buy any of this. Estelle is not the kind of woman to just up and leave like that. I'm going in there, whether you approve or not."

"Now hold on there, young lady," De Vries again.

"No, you hold on, old man." Calm down, K. K. told herself. "Something is wrong. And I intend to find out what it is."

"You go in there and you'll spend the night in jail," said De Vries. "And you won't see your child for quite a while either."

"Hold on," Mrs. Bromley said, stepping between K. K.

and De Vries. She rang the doorbell three times in rapid succession, and within moments a face appeared at the door, an Asian face.

"It's okay, Mrs. Kwun," she said. "There's been a misunderstanding. This woman knew the lady who lived here before. She just didn't know she had moved."

Mrs. Kwun, fear on her face, nodded and disappeared. Like the Cheshire cat, K. K. thought.

K. K. shook her head. This was getting her nowhere. She turned to leave and, as she headed for the car, she noticed that the wood-chopping wedge she had seen earlier along the walk was gone. She sprayed the Jaguar with gravel as she roared around it and out of the driveway.

27

Late evening at David's, the cyberpunks were out of junk food and down to the last of the soft drinks. They resorted to invading Von's supply of rice cakes and Zwieback. Stretched out on the floor of the living room, crumbs all over the place, David was showing off to an appreciative audience.

He had already shown them Little Beebo and a few other games he'd invented over the years, and had even gotten some good ideas from them on the fuzzy logic program. But his deepest satisfaction came from showing off his gadgets, especially to Moe, who really appreciated them. David was showing them the 3DO player on top of one of the many TV sets in the living room. The 3DO—a small black box with a controller on top—could play a CD or video game, connect to a network or on-line database, or project simulations—like taking off in the space shuttle—onto the TV.

"But isn't the 3DO still in prototype?" Moe asked, awestruck.

"Yep," David answered, proud as a papa.

"How did you get it?" Moe wanted to know.

"Friends in the Valley," David said casually. Actually, it was Will Karasik who had gotten it for him, the only payment David wanted in return for doing the fuzzy logic program.

"Wow," Moe said.

David thought he had the cyberpunks all sorted out now. Their leader was Moe Singh, a Sikh from New Delhi, from which he'd emigrated with his parents, an industrial engineer and network consultant. Moe's hobby was mathematics, with calculus his favorite branch of the discipline. Mostly low-key and inscrutable, he lit up when he described proofs he'd done of the theorems of Ramanujan, the mysterious Indian mathematics genius who had died at age thirty-three. His pet hobby was encryption, a man after David's own heart.

Moe reminded David of a miniature version of Punjab from the Little Orphan Annie comic strip. When David asked Moe if he'd ever read Little Orphan Annie, Moe, in a clipped British accent, responded with "Pudden?"

The woman from the bookstore, with shaved head, multiple corn rows braided in the back (a *Kuncha* do, she explained), and nose pins, was Pia Meharatab, an Eritrean from Addis Ababa. After Eritrea had voted for independence, she had escaped with her mother and father, both journalists, from Ethiopia to England, where she had taken every course on computer science she could sneak into at the University of London, before coming to the U.S. The software expert among the group, she played dinosaurs with Von on the living room floor.

The big cyberpunk was Laszlo Graubakus, sporting a buzz cut, a black, worm-holed leather ensemble that David guessed he slept in every night, and, yes, a calculator on his hip. Laszlo, from Vilnius, seemed to know almost as much about David's career as Moe. David was profoundly impressed with Laszlo's knowledge of systems engineering but still a bit leery of him and the others. Laszlo, half listening to David and Moe, was at a computer doing a Veronica search of God-knows-what on the Internet.

"And to think I was scared of you guys," David said, still looking at Laszlo.

"Scared?" Moe said. "Of him? Laszlo would be the one wearing a helmet in a mosh pit."

The kids laughed. Others in the group included Shiao-ping Min, a Hmong refugee from a village in the Chinese Himalayas, and Jun-Ying, her friend; Ysidro from Montevideo, Uruguay; and Derya, a Palestinian from the West Bank. David kept their names straight by associating them with the music they liked. Moe had a passion for industrial,

Pia was a big Sinead fan but also liked rave, Laszlo was into grunge, and so on.

The kids enthusiastically tried on David's virtual-reality goggles and glove, did some impromptu programming on his laptops, and fought over which CDs to play from the thousands in his collection. The conversation never got personal, partly because David lacked the presence of mind to ask the kids much about themselves—such as where they lived—and also because they didn't volunteer much information. But David trusted them enough to speak of what had so far been unspeakable. And, who knows, maybe they knew something.

"I wonder," he began carefully, turning a Sony Handycam—a video camcorder no bigger than a 35mm camera—in his hands, "if you guys have noticed anything . . . funny going on around here lately."

The kids grew quiet, and David could feel the tension rising. "Funny?" Moe chirped. "What do you mean, David?"

"Oh, just a few things, maybe nothing special. Like abnormal power fluctuations, weird animals showing up around town, and the family next door disappearing.

"It's like Sparks is an image of a Mandelbrot fractal: the closer you look, the more chaotic it gets. Somehow I sense that this chaos in Sparks is just the manifestation of some central mystery, some core evil."

Moe screwed up his face, Laszlo chuckled nervously, and Pia put on a cryptic Mona Lisa smile. David trained his eyes at the cyberpunks, but not one would meet his gaze. Hmm, he thought. What do they know? What are they hiding?

"I wonder something else," he said, and each of the kids looked at him. "What do you know about the Country Customs Company?"

Strong outputs here. Stony silence. Withdrawal. Palpable fear.

David waited quietly, patiently, until the phone rang, and he trotted off to answer it. In the Murata household, answering the phone was a deceptively complex undertaking.

David had twenty six telephone lines running into the house, most of which he used for data transmission. Five of them served purely as telephone connections. With the alarms on the forty-two computers in the house sounding like telephones, and the five telephone signals, he got confused easily when the phone rang.

Finally, after picking up the receivers on three phones, he found the right one in the kitchen.

It was his answering service in Portland. A woman named Della told him a message had been left for him.

David had to think a moment. He had just ordered the service yesterday.

"You received a call at 7:34 this evening from Mrs. Barbara Bromley of the Busy B's Real Estate Agency," said Della. "She was calling to confirm a meeting in her office this Friday at nine A.M."

"Oh, yeah," David said, "good."

"Mr. Murata?" she said.

"Yes?"

"*I* took that message, and it was, well, a little strange."

"Strange?"

"Well, garbled or something. The caller—Mrs. Bromley—asked for a Mr. Simon Globus. I just do my job, you know what I mean? Like, I don't ask questions. But I don't have anything in my log book or notes about any Mr. Simon Globus."

David assured her that he was taking Mr. Globus's calls as well. Just as he hung up, Nara came through the door with obvious surprise, if not shock, registering on her face as she took in the cyberpunks—stretched out on her floor with her child—but no sign of her husband. K. K. Thorner, holding a sleeping Viveca, followed Nara in.

David shuffled in from the kitchen. "Hey, Nara," he said casually. "Has everyone met?"

He introduced the cyberpunks and shook hands with K. K. "Haven't we met somewhere?" he asked her, trying to place her from the stoplight earlier that day.

"K. K. has to go on her shift at the diner in about a half

hour," Nara explained, "and desperately needs a babysitter."

"Fine," David laughed, "you have about ten here to choose from."

K. K. looked at Laszlo—in black leather and drop earrings playing Little Beebo with Von on a PC—and rolled her eyes.

Sitting on the sofa, checking out Nara's clothes, Pia smiled and said quietly to her, "You know, something's wrong with your jacket." It was the black nylon one with SCREAMING TREES WORLD TOUR emblazoned in red on the back.

Suddenly self-conscious, Nara checked quickly for snags and holes. "What's wrong with it?" she said.

Pia smiled again and said earnestly, "To my knowledge, the Screaming Trees never did a world tour."

28

The next morning, sweat rolling down her face and shoulders, Barb Bromley slipped into one of her favorite fantasies: what she'd do with all the money she'd ever want. The fantasy took on different forms from one time to the next. Sometimes she'd focus on jewelry, other times clothes or art. This time she dreamed about having her own place in the Caribbean—maybe St. Bart's. The house would not be on the beach but up in the hills, commanding the most magnificent view on the island.

And it would not be just a house but a palace, with clean white marble and tiles and open, sweeping spaces enveloped by palm trees and the most beautiful tropical flowers. The air would be clear and the sun warm and bright year 'round. In the fantasy she is seated on the open terrace, fragrances drifting on the morning breeze, and a tall, dark man with an athlete's build prepares to dive into the pool.

"Mrs. Bromley!"

She snapped her eyes open and saw Stacy, an aerobics instructor at the Ship Shape Spa, shouting something at her. Barb was working out on a running machine, doing program 12—a nine-mile run that threw three major obstacles at you per mile. She had been into the second obstacle of the seventh mile and was starting to feel it, the blood rushing through her head, when Stacy called.

Annoyed at the interruption, Barb eased down and could hear again. She had already been through an aerobics class and two circuits on the Nautilus machines. Before hitting the road, she'd catch a sauna and a massage. Stacy was still shouting her name.

Barb stopped, hanging onto the bars of the machine, trying to catch her breath so she could tell Stacy off.

"Telephone, Miss Bromley," Stacy said. "He says it's urgent." Stacy gave Barb a little smart-ass smile and pranced off before Barb could say anything to her.

Barb took the call at the front desk. It was Ron. She wiped herself down and held the phone away from her ear, the interference was so bad.

"Good news," Ron said, his voice sounding tinny from the car phone. "We have another couple of properties coming on the market. Could be as soon as tomorrow."

He broke into my workout for *this*? Barb thought. But she played along, saying, "How exciting, Ron. You *know* how news like that gets me all worked up."

Then, in a low, insinuating voice, Ron said, "I want us to meet before the houses go on the market."

Barb's antennae went up immediately. Ron had never asked to see her before a house had gone on the market. Actually, the houses he gave her never actually went on the market. Not that it mattered. Ron wanted something and Barb was reasonably sure she knew what it is. How would she handle him? The best way would be to avoid the situation entirely, to put him off at the last minute. But what if he really did hold up the listings on her if she didn't put out for him? What then, Barb? she asked herself.

Before she could answer, Ron said, "One other thing. Give me again the name of your visitor, the investor from New York coming up tomorrow morning."

Shit, Barb thought, so this was why he had called. She hadn't even thought he would remember about Simon Globus. She wanted to keep that to herself.

In her sweetest voice—the one she always saved for the husband while his wife was inspecting the kitchen of a house she was selling, and she had him to herself for one minute—Barb said, "Oh, Ron, I can't remember the name offhand like this. It's at the office. I'll stop by on the way home and call you from there."

"Don't bother," Ron said, his voice fading in and out. "I have to be in town for something else and I can stop by and check with Rowena."

Like hell you will, Barb thought.

"One other thing," Ron said. "I think we should have this meeting at Country Customs. Might be a little more comfortable, don't you think?"

Barb tried to make light of the whole thing by changing the subject. "Ron," she said quietly, looking around but seeing no one within earshot, "there's something you should know about. Yesterday I got a call from Mrs. Kwun. She's occupying the Grout house in town. She said someone was at the house, pounding on the door for a long time, looking for the old woman.

"I stopped by and found Dwight De Vries there with a woman who was looking for Grout, a friend of hers. She was very upset and seemed certain something had happened to the old woman. I showed her the deed and even had Mrs. Kwun come to the door. But I don't think she was satisfied at all. She looks like trouble. I think we're going to hear more from her."

Ron was quiet for several moments. Barb could hear the roar of a truck he was passing. "What's the woman's name?" he said finally.

"K. K. Thorner. I checked on her. She works at the Sparks Diner, takes courses at the university in Augusta, and lives alone with her two-year-old daughter out near the old packing plant, down on the bay."

"Mmmm," Ron said. "I'll see to it . . ." he began and his voice faded out, ". . . no more trouble."

Then he said what Barb had been dreading all along. "After the meeting tomorrow, we can go in my car up to Sedgwick, the old Acadia Motel. We'll need a little R&R by then." He chortled obscenely.

Barb knew the place, a flea-bitten dump on the other side of Penobscot Bay. She groaned and said quickly, "That sounds *lovely*. I'd love to do it. But Sid comes in tonight and I have *scads* of appointments tomorrow afternoon. Let's see how it goes, okay?"

"Just plan on it," he said and hung up.

Barb's mind raced, shuffling through plans, options. First thing, she had to do what she could to keep Simon Globus to herself. Immediately she called her office. Rowena, her secretary, picked up the phone.

"Rowena, I want you to go home now."

"You want me to go *home*?" Rowena said.

"That's right," Barb said, "just lock up and take the rest of the day off. Only do it now. This minute."

Rowena laughed lightly, unsure what was going on here. She had seen lots of strange things since starting at Busy B's, so this wasn't too out of character for the place. Still, Mrs. Bromley was not the type just to spring for a day off out of the goodness of her heart. "Well, Mrs. Bromley," Rowena said. "if that's what you want . . ."

"Yes," Barb said, "that's what I want. I'll see you tomorrow." And then hung up.

Rowena held the phone for a few seconds, thinking this through. She had gotten all her work done—just a few contracts that needed typing—and the usual filing. Now she was printing up her daughter's wedding announcements on the nice italics fonts of her word processor. Mrs. Bromley wasn't around, so Rowena decided to do a few more before she'd go.

Ten minutes later, with the announcements safely stowed in the canvas bag she carried, Rowena turned everything off in the office and stepped outside to lock the door. Just as she found the keys in her purse, Ron Lindblad pulled up in his Mercedes 300. He stepped out, saw Rowena quickly locking up, and chuckled to himself.

That Barb, he thought.

29

Country Customs resembled a fortress to David as he pulled up at a guard station in his rented Cadillac. A grim-faced rent-a-cop stepped out of the station and asked him his business. David noticed he was carrying a large gun or small cannon—possibly a .44 Magnum—in a hip holster. After David mumbled something about meeting with Ms. Bromley, the guard backed into the station without taking his eyes off him.

David peered through the windshield at the high fences surrounding the Country Customs compound. Double rolls of barbed wire encircled the top of the fence, which, due to the small boxes attached to poles every twenty yards or so along the fence, he concluded was electrified. Closed-circuit cameras built into the side of the building slowly scanned the perimeter around the fence. He assumed that there were sensors—motion, heat, or pressure-sensitive—implanted in the ground.

Strange, David thought, how he had lived in Sparks for two years now and never knew this place was here. No less strange was *why* he was here; he really didn't know other than that someone claiming to be from Barb Bromley's office had told him over the phone yesterday that "other interested parties" wanted to meet him. David only wanted to visit the real estate company and talk to Bromley one on one, perhaps get some answers to his many questions concerning the Haslem family. But the caller, a wheezing late-middle-aged man, insisted—a bit stridently, David noticed—that the meeting site be moved to the Country Customs Company. David relented and decided to make the most of his visit.

"Go on to the front door," the guard ordered. "Stay on the road."

On the way, David wondered if other mail-order companies were this paranoid. He wouldn't be surprised, judging from the impersonal nature of mail-order shopping. Imagine, an industry that existed on the premise that people don't need or want to interact with another human being, other than a disembodied, infinitely patient voice on the telephone.

The cameras followed David's every movement as he parked the big Cadillac and headed toward the front door with the black briefcase he had bought just for the occasion tucked under his arm and aimed up at the security. He left his overcoat in the car. The air was unseasonably warm, which was not uncommon for a Maine February. Enormous dark clouds began to mass overhead and the air grew still, portentous.

A young man in a suit as nondescript as David's who reminded David of Eddie Haskell from *Leave It to Beaver* was waiting for him just inside the door. "Mr. Globus," he said, extending a hand toward David. "I'm John, and I'll be your escort to Mr. Lindblad's office."

"Mr. Lindblad?" David asked, originally expecting to hear Barb Bromley's name. John nodded tersely and led David past a console of closed-circuit screens manned by a guard in a suit, and toward a bank of elevators. David decided it best not to pursue his question and followed along, briefcase still tucked under his arm.

John slid a key attached to a chain into the elevator panel and pushed six. He stared at the tops of his shiny black wingtips as the elevator glided to the top floor of the building. The doors opened into a suite of oak-paneled offices decorated in Louis XIVth: antique furniture, tapestries, heavy felt curtains.

"This way, please," John said, extending his hand toward a pair of medieval-looking doors at the end of a hall. He opened the door and, stepping in, David could tell that this was someone's office only by the placement of the telephone, lamps, and computer on a marble-topped credenza. But what an office! It was more of a throne room. With thirty-foot ceilings, a massive oak table and chairs carved with intricate hunting patterns, tapestries, Persian rugs over thick wall-to-wall carpeting, and dominated by an enormous oil painting of two people—a florid-looking, middle-aged man and stern, gray-eyed woman—the room was obviously designed to project power and wealth. To David, it was utterly distasteful.

His attention was immediately drawn to the computer on the credenza. He couldn't determine the make, probably custom-built. What did they need *that* for? One thing caught his eye, something totally anomalous to the sumptuousness of the room: on the wall over the credenza was a chart that David recognized as a power grid. What would that be doing here?

At the head of the table, three people were huddled together: two men and a woman. David recognized one of the men as a somewhat older version of the man in the painting, obviously Mr. Lindblad. The other man looked vaguely familiar, and David quickly tried to place him. The woman was not the one in the portrait. Was this Barb Bromley?

John cleared his throat and all three turned at once. The one David assumed was Mr. Lindblad rushed over to him, a big, heavy hand thrust out, fingers extended.

"Ron Lindblad," he said too loudly. "Welcome to Sparks."

David recoiled from a nasty electrical shock from Lindblad as they made contact. "Thanks," David said, rubbing his hand. "I feel like I've already been here for years."

"Yes, I understand completely," Ron said. He waved the other two people closer, giving David a chance to size him up. Ron looked to be in his late sixties, thin white hair, sharp gray eyes, his gut straining against his pink polo shirt. Around his nostrils and mouth, hundreds of tiny red filaments of blood vessels and capillaries wormed to the skin's surface and then disappeared into the red-pink flesh.

"I want you to meet my associates," Ron said. "I believe you know Barb Bromley."

Barb was exactly as David had pictured her: a real estate princess. She didn't bother to shake hands and kept her arms crossed. The other man was her husband, Sid. David suddenly recognized him as the host of the talk show Jean watched, "The Sid Bromley Show." Barb Bromley. Sid Bromley. Why hadn't David made the connection?

Ron invited David to sit at the imperial table. Ron took his place at the head, and Barb and Sid sat across from David. An awkward silence descended on the table, and David, sensing it was some cheap ploy to unsettle him—like car salesmen disappearing to "talk with the manager" during sales negotiations—had no intention of breaking it.

Ron finally spoke up: "Well, Mr. Globus, this your meeting. What can we do for you?"

David pulled at his collar and cleared his throat. "I, that is, we at Globus International, have been following recent . . . financial activity up in this area. The communities around Sparks have seen significant growth over the past three or four decades—shopping, hotels, small concessions—all connected to the tourist trade.

"We believe Sparks and its environs may be poised for similar growth, and we want to be, ah, in ahead of the curve, so to speak. I have investors who are ready to commit resources to the area. Substantial resources."

Ron Lindblad slid forward on his huge oak armchair. "How substantial, Mr. Globus?"

David cleared his throat again. "Well, the answer to that depends entirely on the level of local interest and—and, of course, the opportunities available."

Ron's eyes narrowed and he scratched an invisible mark on the shiny tabletop. "Let me ask you something, Mr. Globus. Do you mind if I call you Simon?"

"Please do." What would the real Simon have said? David wondered. He looked up at the power-grid chart hanging on the wall. At the top was written Substation Number 2, Knox County. David recognized the power station as the one out near Route One, just beneath the power lines there. Why was Ron Lindblad so interested in it?

"How much . . . research have you and your people done on Sparks?" Ron asked.

"Research? What do you mean?"

Ron tilted his head, his right ear almost touching his shoulder. "Oh, the kinds of things you Wall Street fellas usually do. Demographics, feasibility studies, geographic surveys, that sort of thing."

"Oh, that's all been done."

"Ah, good. I'd be interested in your assessment of the potential of this area."

"Potential?" David said.

"For growth, profit. What are your projections?"

"Good," David said resolutely. "The projections look good."

"Mmmm. I doubt you'd come all this way from New York if they weren't. Unless you were looking to make a killing."

David sat up straight. "A what?"

Ron smiled broadly. "Just a joke, Simon. We're Down-east country people up here. No match for you Wall Street types. Now, what level of investment were you considering here? Ballpark it for me."

David's internal debate lasted picoseconds: give them a figure now and risk their disbelief in him as a high roller or go for the reaction? No question: go for the reaction.

"I have an amount more than ten but less than a hundred million dollars deposited in a Portland bank," he said blankly, watching their faces. Barb drew in a breath and touched her throat lightly. Sid wiped his forehead with his hand. Ron didn't blink.

"It's my working capital," he went on. "I can use all or part of it to invest in this area. At this point the only holdings that would require any significant portion of it are the Country Customs Company and Busy B's Real Estate, both of which are represented here at this table, am I not correct?"

"Correct," Barb said, eyeing David suspiciously. Does she, could she, recognize me? David wondered.

"I understand you have a very active real estate market here right now," David said, fishing. "How do you account for that in a recession?"

Ron frowned broadly, raising his open hands. "News to me," he said. "We have a very stable population here in Sparks. People just don't want to leave. Isn't that right, Barb?"

Barb pressed her silicone-inflated lips tightly together and said brightly, "That's right, Ron. Sparks is such a great place to live, nobody wants to leave."

David nodded and restrained himself from asking if anyone had ever been *forced* to leave, like in a body bag.

Another awkward silence followed, broken by Ron hawking phlegm from deep in his throat. "Let me ask an obvious question," he said, trying to figure out what to do with the phlegm, now in his mouth. "Your working capital," he said, "where is it from?"

"Investors," David said. "Individuals, institutions. Why?"

"Just wondering," Ron said, smiling and swallowing hard, vessels and capillaries about to burst through his face. He slapped his thighs and stood, his crotch level with David's face.

"Well, you've given us a lot to think about, Simon," Ron said, looking off through the window. David wasn't sure, but it *appeared* from the bulge in the middle of Ron's crotch that he was sporting a significant hard-on. "Anything else we can do for you?" he said.

"Uh, mind if I take a look around?"

"Look?" Ron said, not understanding. "Around?"

"Country Customs, the plant. I thought I'd just wander around. But I don't want to get in anyone's way."

Ron's eyes went in and out of focus. "Er, there's really nothing much of interest here. I can get you a catalogue." He moved to buzz his secretary.

"Already have one, thanks," David said. "No, all I wanted to do was to see the setup. The workshops, the facility. You know."

"Mmmm," Ron said, gears turning in his head. "I don't suppose it could do any harm." His face brightened. "Why, sure. Sid here would be happy to show you around. Sid?"

"Right you are, Ron," Sid said eagerly. "Happy to."

Ron went straight to Sid, put his arm around his shoulder, and whispered in his ear. Barb suddenly appeared at David's side, thrusting a business card into his hand.

"Call me," she whispered fiercely before Sid touched her lightly on the shoulder.

"Ron wants you, dear," Sid said to Barb and then turned back to David, pointing toward the medieval doors. "This way, Mr. Globus."

"Please call me Simon, Sid."

"Of course. First, let me show you our computer facility, then an assembly room or two, just to give you a feel for the operation."

"That'd be great," David said. Actually, just the computer facility would be fine.

David turned to say good-bye to Ron and Barb, but all he saw was their backs as they exited through a side door he hadn't realized was there. Sid led David to the elevators and pressed the button. The elevator arrived, and Sid waited until David was inside and then stepped in, produced a small key on a chain just like John's, and slid it into the panel and pushed B for basement. David held his briefcase under his arm, at precisely the level of the panel.

Sid smiled and dropped the key and chain into his right hip pocket. He rocked back and forth on the balls of his feet, wiping perspiration from his forehead about every ten seconds. A Benzedrine head, David thought. Or crystal meth. It really didn't matter which. David had seen lots of speed freaks when he worked in Silicon Valley years ago. And Sid was certainly one.

The elevator dropped two and a half floors before suddenly grinding to a halt, the lights flickering out.

"What the—?" Sid said in the darkness.

"Appears to be a power outage," David said. "You get many of them here?"

"Not at all," Sid said in the dark. "Never."

A minute crawled by and nothing happened. David could hear Sid breathing heavily. "You have a backup system?" David asked.

"Yeah, sure," Sid growled. "It'll take a while before it kicks on in this sector." And then, in a much softer voice, he muttered. "That asshole."

I wonder which asshole he means, David thought. There seem to be so many here to choose from.

30

Ron Lindblad could barely steady his hand to get the key to his cabin door into its hole. In his other hand he held a brown paper bag in which a steel thermos full of icy Tanqueray and tonic sweated wet rings into the paper. He laughed self-consciously as he tried to find the hole in the darkness at 3:00 P.M. A storm was moving in fast and the air was moist, restless, and eerily warm. Thunder rumbled in the distance.

"Are you okay, Ron?" Barb said, trying to peer over his shoulder to find out what was taking him so long to get the damn door open. Fat drops of rain spattered her head and bare forearms. She looked around the Acadia Motel grounds, hoping she wouldn't see anyone watching them out here like this. The nearest cabin was about fifty yards away through the spruce and white pine. She felt completely alone with Ron and wasn't sure it was a good feeling.

"Yeah," he said under his breath and leaning into the door. "Damn light, where'd it go? There, almost got it. Just another—"

Leaning into the door, Ron and Barb nearly fell forward as the key jumped into the hole and flung open the door. Barb helped steady Ron and she was suddenly conscious of his closeness, his hand on her arm. Then they were both aware that they were finally, utterly alone in the musty cabin, their other world miles away.

Barb could hear Ron stumbling in the dark of the room. Something crashed to the floor. Then the light came on.

Ron was on his hands and knees, desperately trying to save the last of his TNT spreading over the floor.

"Fuck it, fuck it, fuck it," he chanted as he scooped ice cubes and clear liquid into the thermos cup.

Barb stepped over him and toward the bathroom. She passed furniture anomalously contemporary in the rustic setting, two oil paintings of poodles—picked up by the motel's owner in lots of thirty at a hotel auction in Portland—and orange chintz curtains covering the streaked windows. Normally Barb would never go to the bathroom in a place as public as this, having had to do it for so many years as an itinerant real estate agent traveling to the most godforsaken places. But now she had to pee real bad, having already put away half a thermos of gin and tonic on the way up here.

After unrolling toilet paper on the seat and sitting down, Barb kept her eyes closed so she didn't have to look at the insect carcasses littering the floor or the brown mildew stains overtaking the walls. She concentrated her thoughts on the meeting with Simon Globus, or more precisely, on the big figures he had tossed off like tips at the hairdressers. The floor, the *minimum*, he had talked about was ten million. If she saw only a third of that, she'd have as much as she ever wanted to set her for life. Imagine, she could dump this two-by-four town and begin looking for her palace in the Caribbean.

And, if she played her cards right and got a little lucky, she could walk away with some really big money and could buy and sell the likes of Ron and Norma Lindblad on the open market. It was all so amazingly close, so real.

The thought of big money—of such wonderful wealth, power, and freedom—was something Barb could almost taste in her mouth and deep in her throat. It washed over her like a drug, making her chest warm and fingertips tingle. She felt flushed in the neck and in the insides of her thighs.

The sharp crack of thunder shook the thin walls of the cabin and yanked Barb from her dream. She stood up from the toilet and pulled up her panties. Then she thought, what the hell, and kicked them off. That cozy feeling lingered in her thighs. She felt good, strong. She was even ready to face Ron.

Barb slowly pushed open the bathroom door and stepped into the darkness. Rain clattered over the cabin's corrugated tin roof. From somewhere on the other side of the room, she could hear Ron's labored breathing. She guessed he was on the bed.

All around the cabin the storm raged like a war zone. Rain wind whipped the flimsy pine walls. Lightning swept past in bolts and sheets, exploding over treetops. The thunder was deafening.

A bolt of lightning shot like a flare through the room, followed closely by the boom of thunder. Afterimages—transparent worms squirming over blackness and dots like falling snow—registered across Barb's field of vision. She steadied herself on the back of a chair. Another lightning flash lit up the room, and Barb could see the outline of Ron's body beneath the sheets. A thunderclap fell on the cabin like a bomb.

"Come here," Ron said matter-of-factly.

Barb moved mindlessly toward him like matter pulled into a black hole. The floorboards were rough under foot. Wind murmured through the pine wall slats. An errant piece of light—from where?—glinted off something on the nightstand next to the bed. She squinted at it, trying to make out what it was.

Ron's car keys. Barb could snatch them up now, bolt through the door, and drive away. It would take him hours of trouble, not to mention the explaining, to get out of this one. She was tempted to just go, to leave him here to himself. He would deserve it.

But she did not run. She stood over the keys nestled on the nightstand and looked at Ron, tried to see his face in the blackness but thought better of it. Lightning uncoiled and snapped directly over him, and he looked at her, trying to find her eyes, which she kept fastened on the windowpane, streaked with running water. She watched the lightning leaping past the window like a wild animal.

"Well?" Ron said.

"I was just remembering the day when my mother died," Barb said, standing over the bed, her eyes still on the window. "I was seventeen, just graduated from high school. It was a Sunday afternoon. I had a friend over, Catherine Woodburn, and we were listening to records upstairs when I heard my mother moaning down in the kitchen.

"I found her on the floor and called the ambulance. The paramedics seemed to be there, working on her, even before I put down the phone. I remember one of them telling the other to get the power to three hundred fifty joules to shock her heart back into beating. I thought he said 'jewels,' like 'jewelry.' And I remember wondering: How were they going to use jewels to bring my mother back? Funny, isn't it? They never did bring her back."

"Are you coming in or what?" Ron said, annoyed.

Suddenly Barb felt as if she could kill him right then and there. It would be so easy: just pick up the cast iron lamp from the nightstand and bring it down over his head, splintering his skull into a million pieces. So easy.

Instead, she shrugged off her blouse and undid her skirt in a single motion. She had nothing on underneath. She slid into the sheets and suddenly lost her breath as his massive body rolled over on top of her. For one terrible moment she felt as if she were being buried alive, the weight of him was so great, his flesh clingy and porous like loose dirt. She struggled to breathe.

Even though Ron was bigger, Barb was stronger. With a single bench-press motion she shoved him off her, and he rolled with a grunt to the other side of the bed. She came up on his side as lightning flickered across his grinning face, creating the effect of a ghoulish mask.

Gritting her teeth, Barb locked one leg over Ron's meaty hip and, quick and fluid as mercury, she mounted him. She smiled at his gasp of surprise as she straightened up astride over him, connecting like an electrical plug in a socket. He moved his hands toward her breasts, but she rose up out of reach and fell *smack* on his stomach, hoping to hurt him. But Ron just hummed in pleasure, his mouth twitching uncontrollably.

The bed rocked like a dinghy in high seas, their bodies heaving out of synch. The electrical storm was reaching its frenzied peak, lightning flashing through the window every few seconds, followed by shattering thunder. In the wildly kinetic light they looked like cannibals tearing away and devouring pieces of each other.

Barb looked down briefly as she bounced over Ron, who was strangely passive. The bedsprings groaned wearily beneath them. She cut her thoughts free of the moment and let them drift. She felt sun on her face and bare chest, heard the sound of gentle waves, and watched Caribbean light playing over translucent water. She imagined the sensations, the associations, of wealth: chinchilla softness, the glow of twenty-four-carat gold, the gleam of Italian marble, the scent of leather in a chauffeur-driven car.

Below her, Ron's body was slick with sweat-matted hair. The wind shrieked in trees that sighed from the battering they were taking. She felt Ron's body tense, as if in rigor mortis, as he prepared to come.

Barb watched, amused, as Ron's eyes rolled in their sockets and bulged. Charged electrical particles seemed to emanate from his pores and crackle in the heavy humid air. His mouth was open, teeth radiating light. A Kirlian photograph would have revealed the jagged aura surrounding his body.

As he came, a low, rattling noise issued from deep in his larynx. His body began to relax, went slack, and then he began to gulp down air with labored wheezes. Barb was still breathing evenly and had barely broken a sweat. She had never felt as much as a scintilla of pleasure from the entire experience.

Ron couldn't have cared less about Barb's feelings. Instead, he leaned back, gruffly content and pleased that he had been able to pull it off. He felt masterful, triumphant. The storm was passing and the light rain in the high evergreens sounded like applause to him.

They sat silently on the bed passing back and forth the stainless steel thermos cap of watery gin and tonic. A cold front was heading in as the storm moved out. Barb, feeling more self-conscious than cold, wrapped herself in the sheets. She tried to sort through her feelings for Ron. Did she feel contempt for him, envy? Was she here simply for the money? Or was there some deeper, more primitive attraction toward a male image of power and status? Whatever the reason and despite herself, she wanted to talk to him, hear his voice.

"Tell me something," she said, taking the thermos from him. "Do you think Simon Globus is on the level?"

Ron watched her drink the TNT, careful that she didn't take more than her share. "Why?" he said, holding out his hand for the cup.

Barb ignored him and took another sip, knowing he was watching her, wanting it back. "Didn't he seem a little strange to you?"

"Strange?" he said, seizing the cup from her and draining it in one gulp. Some of the liquid slid down his windpipe and he coughed violently.

"He didn't strike me as a . . . well, a financier, a Wall Street type."

"Oh, really?" Ron said, still gagging and debating in his mind whether he should get up out of the warm bed and get a drink in the bathroom or just stay here and ride out the irritation.

"He just didn't come across," Barb said.

"Come across," Ron said finally, his cough under control.

Barb looked at him. "I've had lots of dealings with big-money types. Mostly from selling them summer homes on the southern Maine coast. Globus isn't like them at all. The way he acts, the way he dresses. He just doesn't fit."

"Well," Ron said again, "it's certainly hard for me to refute such scientific observations. But in case you're interested, I looked into this Mr. Globus.

"First, I checked out all the Portland banks and found that Mr. Simon Globus had established a line of credit for fifty million in the Key Bank there. Second, I called someone I know in New York and asked him about Globus, his integrity, his financial status. My friend said Globus is solid gold, sitting on top of billions in smart money, and considered one of a handful of boutique financial gurus, guys who are beyond reproach.

"And third, the real kicker. My friend called a friend of his who *works* for Globus and found out that he took today off to travel. After a little more digging, the friend found out the place Globus traveled to. Are you ready?"

Barb shrugged her shoulders, resigned. She knew him well enough to know when he knew the answers.

"Sparks, Maine," he said, triumphant again. "That information cost me ten thousand dollars."

Barb burrowed deeper in the covers. "What's our next move?" she said.

Ron laughed his horrid laugh. "Our next move is precisely this: nothing. Separating Mr. Globus from his fifty million will be like taking candy from a baby. Even though it will be important to keep the ball rolling with him, the worst thing we can do is appear too eager. We will wait for Mr. Globus to come back to us."

"You think he'll turn over the full fifty million to us?" Barb said, trying to sound more disbelieving than interested.

"Of course," Ron said. "Fifty million dollars, which you and I will split down the middle."

What about Sid? she almost asked but had the good sense not to. Instead, she raised another matter. "What did you do about K. K. Thorner?"

Ron was quiet for a moment, trying to connect the name through his TNT and post-coital fog. Finally it registered. "The trouble-maker. We have a couple of them to deal with right now. There's the Thorner woman and a couple of others. They'll all be taken care of."

"What do you mean, 'taken care of'?"

"Ah, don't worry your pretty head about it," Ron said in his patronizing way. "Keep your eyes on the prize. Imagine, twenty-five million dollars. What would you do with *that*?"

This set off Barb and her associations again. Sumptuous images flooded her head. She felt an old itch between her legs.

Ron watched her, knowing the reaction he was causir

in her. "Once we have that money," he said, making the effort to prop up on one elbow, "we won't need anything or anyone but each other. Norma will finally be out of the way. Imagine, being rid of her once and for all. And you can throw away Sid and that real estate business. We could live anywhere. Hell, we could have a dozen places all over the world."

Barb edged over toward Ron and threw her leg around him, locking him under her. He couldn't budge. The bed jumped with a loud crack.

"What's 'at?" Ron said, his mouth beginning to twitch.

"The box springs," Barb said, settling in on him and plugging him in again, "they broke."

Ron grunted and shut his eyes.

"Don't knock real estate," she said, bearing down now. "You know what they say."

"Who? What?" Ron muttered, his eyes rolling in his head.

"Real estate is just like sex."

"How's that?" he managed to say.

Barb began to rock back and forth and sang, "Location, location, location."

31

As Barb and Ron finished off the last of their bedsprings, K. K. was on the pay phone at the Sparks Diner with Fort Myers directory assistance. The dinner peak was just starting, and she struggled to hear the woman's voice over the clatter of plates, sizzle of fried food, and buzz of conversation punctuated with loud laughter.

Since yesterday's debacle at Estelle Grout's house, K. K. had been on the phone to the sheriff's office in Rockland, the county records office, and now Fort Myers directory assistance, trying to track down Estelle. She was getting nowhere with directory assistance, having been handed around to probably every supervisor in the office. It didn't help that she didn't know the name of Estelle's sister, the only person K. K. could imagine who might have any idea where Estelle was.

"Well, can you check middle names?" K. K. shouted into the phone. "Grout. G-R-O-U-T. Yeah, like tile grout. I'm not sure of the town.

"She mentioned someplace once, Bonita something. Could be. Can you check it? Yes, an emergency. Of course I'm in the family."

Not only did she have to contend with this phone witch with an attitude, K. K. was getting dirty looks from the new waitress from Owls Head, whom K. K. had taken a dislike to the minute she met her. K. K. was sure she wasn't coming clean with all her tips. Directory assistance came back on the line and reported that no one with Grout in their name was listed in the entire Fort Myers-Cape Coral calling area. K. K. desperately asked if there was anyone else there she could talk to, anything else she could try. She gave a cold thank-you to the woman for her suggestion to contact Fort Myers police, and hung up.

What could she do now? K. K. wondered. She'd tried everything, short of calling the FBI. Maybe she should; that might shake things up around here. She decided then and there to go back to Estelle's house after her shift and before picking Viveca up from day-care in Camden. Having watched Mrs. Bromley ring the bell three times in a row—obviously a signal of some kind—K. K. would try it herself and see what happened.

Ray, cooking today for Jerry, who was off with the flu, waved K. K. over and handed her two platters, one an artery-busting deep-fried chicken steak with side orders of onion rings and corn on the cob dripping with butter, the other a cheeseburger rare drooling with blood, boardwalk fries, and gravy.

"Table six," Ray said quickly and began carving off a piece of meat loaf, the blue plate special, for the next order. K. K. served the platters to an elderly couple who bared their dentures in a smile as their food arrived.

The door to the diner opened and in walked one of the strangest-looking groups K. K. had ever seen in there. They were all men, seven of them, ages forty-five to sixty. The first one, apparently the leader, was a short, dumpy-looking guy with a goatee and in overalls, followed by a tall one, must have been at least six five, with a broad-rim straw hat. K. K. noticed that they all were wearing the same dumb smile and carrying small boxes—Geiger counters or something—strapped over their shoulders. She guessed they were aging Boy Scouts or one of those men's groups that get together and bang drums on the weekend. They sat in a row at the counter.

Right after them, Nara came in, carrying Von, and waved to K. K. Nara's hair was done in a long braid and she had on a yellow Nehru jacket—K. K. hadn't seen one of those in years—and a big pendant that Von was chewing on. She was also wearing baggy bright green I-Dream-of-Jeannie pants over red high-top Converse All-Stars. The whole restaurant stopped to watch her as she trooped through to the last table in the back.

K. K. let the waitress from Owls Head deliver the meat loaf and joined Nara.

"I love your outfit," she said. "I don't know how you get away with your clothes in this town."

Nara shrugged and said, "Thanks. Believe it or not, these are the only clean things I own right now. David's really gotten behind on his chores, especially the laundry, since getting wrapped up in all the intrigue around here."

K. K. slowly shook her head. "Intrigue," she repeated, "there's definitely intrigue, but what's really going on? Does David have any clues?"

Nara opened a panel in her jacket and began nursing Von. "The clues, if you can call them that, seem to revolve around the Country Customs Company." She moved in closer to K. K. and said quietly, "Can you keep a secret?"

"Are you kidding?" K. K. said, her eyes growing bigger. "Sure."

"David went over there today in disguise, to Country Customs, to check them out."

"For real?" K. K. said, laughing, imagining Nara's husband in drag. "What kind of disguise?"

"A businessman," she said, "a real tough role for him."

"What'd he find?"

"Don't know yet. He hadn't gotten home by the time I left. Say, have you heard anything about Estelle?"

The smile left K. K.'s face and she looked at her hands. "No, nothing yet. But I'm still working on it. They can't put *me* off so easily.

"Listen, Nara, I don't know about you, but I've been feeling pretty uneasy about things lately. I mean, Sparks is so small and everywhere I look, I imagine I see something . . . evil. Somehow I feel like it's getting closer, that any minute something's going to happen to Viv or me."

Nara touched her hand. "I know. David and I feel it too. There's something in the air. But we'll just have to look out for one another.

"Oh, I wanted to tell you," Nara went on, moving Von

to her other breast. "I've been looking into the disappearance of those people Estelle told us about. One of them—Gladys Kolbeins—turned up okay. She was just sick in bed with the flu. I visited her at home just to be sure.

"But two others—Roxanne Ward and Irene McNamara—are nowhere to be found. Their phones have been disconnected with no forwarding numbers. And no one answered their doors when I stopped by. It's strange, just like with Estelle. I've started calling them *los desaparecidos.* I'm even thinking of doing something about them in the magazine, an investigative kind of piece."

But K. K. wasn't listening. She was thinking about Estelle, remembering her innumerable favors, the uncompensated generosity. K. K. could feel her optimism for seeing Estelle again slipping away.

Somebody's going to pay for this, K. K. thought. Even if I have to ring every bell in Sparks and sit in jail for my trouble.

"Oh," Nara said, "speaking of *The Maine Event,* I found a strange series of announcements in the Community News section placed there over the past six months or so. These were all good-byes to old folks from Sparks who were supposedly leaving for places like Florida and California. But one odd thing was that some of these people were Estelle's friends—the same ones she thought their children had taken them. Another strange thing is that the announcements were written, rather poorly I might add, by the same person—Barbara Bromley."

K. K.'s head shot up on hearing the name. The real estate witch. "You know what you might try," she said.

"What?" said Nara.

"Go to those houses and ring the bells three times in a row, and then wait. I'm going over to Estelle's after work and trying it."

"Why?" Nara said.

Before K. K. could answer, she heard Ray's voice. He was standing up front, hand impatiently on one hip and the other holding up the telephone. On her way to him,

K. K. passed the new waitress, whose face was pinched in a reproachful frown.

"Be careful or you'll get more wrinkles," K. K. said without looking back for the reaction.

The call was from Greta, a friend of hers in the drama department who breathlessly explained to K. K. that she'd been calling her at home but had gotten no answer. Greta, a coat checker at an Augusta roller skating rink, was at work and eating something crunchy, obviously out of a machine.

"Where've you been, girl?" Greta said, her jaws grinding a Frito, pork rind, or some such thing. "The postings for call-backs have been up for two days and no one's heard from you."

"So what?" K. K. said, nodding her head to Ray, who was pointing at two plates of blasberry pie.

"So what, because you're on the short list for call-backs," Greta said. "You have a shot. You could get Mother Courage."

K. K. felt her knees grow wobbly.

"Final auditions are tonight at seven. You better be there."

K. K. was stunned. She thanked Greta, hung up the phone, and looked over at Ray, who was ignoring her now. "One minute," she said to him, and rushed back to Nara.

"I got a call-back," K. K. said excitedly to an uncomprehending Nara. "For the part I tried out for. But I have to be on campus tonight."

"That's great," Nara said. "Why don't you bring Viveca over and pick her up tomorrow morning? She'll be fine with us."

"Thanks," K. K. said absently as she tried to figure out how to make her audition and still get to Estelle's house.

What's really going on?

K. K.'s question flew around inside Nara's head like an annoying fly as she drove home. As simple as it was, it raised more questions, disturbing questions.

What was happening to these old people? Where did

they go and who was moving into their homes? And what really had happened to the family next door?

Nara had had the front seat of her Range Rover custom-built so that she could see over the wheel. Even with that adjustment and her bright lights blazing, she had trouble seeing the road, dark and unmarked. More questions crowded in on her, such as: Who painted that awful message on their house, slashed their trees, killed their dog, and made each day a terror, each face a threat? What did they want? What were they still capable of doing? The whole thing was snowballing, picking up a terrible momentum of its own.

Another side of Nara, the mercenary part, smelled a story here. She could imagine following these threads, weaving them into an investigative piece, even having fun with it. But these events were too close, too real. She now appreciated the fact that fear can be relished only when it comes at someone else's expense.

She checked in the rearview mirror and saw Von, his mouth open and eyes closed. In the other car seat, Viveca stared solemnly out the window at the darkness. Nara offered to take her home for the night while K. K. went up to Augusta for her audition. Stoic and reserved, Viveca went along obediently. Nara would do something fun for her for breakfast, maybe make Mickey Mouse pancakes.

Nara decided that tomorrow she would do what K. K. suggested and ring the bells at Irene McNamara's and Roxanne Ward's homes. She would have a photographer there with her and maybe someone with a minicam. Maybe, if she played her cards right, she could get a TV station in Portland to pick up the story. Now, that would stir things up around here, force some people to show their hands.

Nara almost missed the hidden entrance to the dirt road leading to their house. Along the road, the spruce trees rushed at her, the splayed ends of their moss-covered branches seemed to grasp at the windows. With the bright beams on, the road looked like a dark tunnel draining down into more blackness. She bucked through the potholes and slowed to a crawl, hoping to keep Von from waking.

"Look!" Viveca said, pointing at the message still burning red through the white coats of paint. At least David had made some progress on it. Nara did her best to ignore the vandalism as she rolled past and parked. She turned around to face Viveca.

"Viv, sweetie, I'm going to take Von in first and put him to bed. Can you be a big girl and wait here in the truck until I come back for you?"

Viveca nodded her head and sat back in her seat. Nara smiled at her, unbuckled Von, and slid him slowly out of the seat. "Be right back," she whispered.

Nara had forgotten about the locks David had put in the front door. Usually they kept the house open. Those days were gone, she thought sadly. She fished around in her pocket for the keys and found them. First the dead bolt, then a latch at the foot of the door, and finally the doorknob.

Nara picked her way around the computer equipment strewn over the living room floor. She did not turn on the lights. As she carried Von up the steps, she felt his warm breath on her neck in soft intervals. She was pleased he had managed to stay asleep this long, being the hair-trigger light sleeper that he was. She lay him down in his bed and gently took off his coat and shoes. He sighed and rolled over. Anxious that he might wake up, she held her breath until she heard his regular breathing again, a labored, congested wheezing.

Nara padded down the stairs. She tried to think what she could feed Viveca, wondering what four-year-olds liked. She had some spaghetti in the refrigerator, if David hadn't eaten it today. Maybe they would just have something light, this close to bedtime.

She stopped in her tracks as she reached the foot of the stairs. The door was closed. She was sure she hadn't shut it. Nor had she heard it slam from the wind.

"Viveca—" she tried to say but was cut off by two strong arms wrapping around her face, stifling her breath. Her body stiffened, her eyes snapped open wide, and she kicked and tore at the heavy gloved hands. Nara was strong but had no leverage. She was out of position to fight. She grabbed at the air, for anything, and grunted as she kicked with her heels.

Go for his crotch, she thought. But she couldn't connect with her heels, and then, snorting for air, she felt an arm moving from her face toward her neck.

A knife was suddenly at her throat, the blade light against the soft skin below her chin. The other hand was still on her mouth. Nara tried to relax, to think. She was sure she was going to be killed. What should she do? What *could* she do? She couldn't fight a knife at her throat.

If I get the chance, I'll give him elbows and go for his eyes. Maybe I can save the children. Give me a chance. Just one.

She held her body still, collecting herself, gathering her strength for one big lunge. She felt movement behind her, and the hand on her mouth slowly moved away. Then the pressure of the knife on her throat relaxed. The knife drew away.

This is it. She paused one heartbeat, two, then lifted her legs and arms and, with all her might, pumped her elbows and tried to tear free by going under her attacker. But the attacker's hand, quick as a ferret, came back under her chin and seized her before she could release her full weight. Then a flash of whiteness appeared at the corner of her eye.

Nara closed her eyes, desperately thrusting elbows, feet. When she opened them, the whiteness was on her face, covering her nose and mouth. Heavy chloroform smell welled up in her sinuses. She tried to keep from breathing but could not stop herself. Her lips and tongue grew numb and tasted like peppermint. Her legs and arms seemed to inflate and float into the air. She heard muffled cries and then realized they were coming from deep in her diaphragm.

Her last thought was of Von—asleep in his crib, helpless—before her head filled up with air and drifted away.

32

David, his suit jacket and tie lying in a heap in the back of the pickup's cab, exited Route One and headed home from the rental lot where he had dropped off the Cadillac. He was glad to be rid of it. What an afternoon, spending most of it trapped in an elevator with that meth head, Sid Bromley. Country Customs' electrical backup system never had come on, forcing them to wait through the brownout until a maintenance crew could make its way down the shaft and pull them through the top of the elevator.

David had had about all he could stand of Sid Bromley, especially after he used up the crystal meth in his pocket ("It's for my asthma," Sid said.) and started pounding on and clawing the walls of the elevator. David was tempted to try to get Bromley to talk about Ron Lindblad and Country Customs, but chose instead to leave the man alone with his problems and stay out of his line of attention.

Still, it wasn't an unproductive visit. With the microcamera hidden inside his briefcase, David was sure he had gotten some good shots of the company's security system. He would develop them as soon as he got home and use them to figure out a way to get inside the plant and *really* look around.

David looped around the long country lane that took him to the service road to his house. The last moments of twilight clung to the damp air, the temperature falling quickly. He peered through the trees lining the road and spied the Haslems' place, light on upstairs. He wondered if his luck would hold and he'd have some videotape of the new family in his other hidden camera.

As the truck approached the house, crunching over gravel, David felt the blood rising up his carotid artery. The "Gooks Get Out or Die" message remained—at bit dimmer from the paint—but still a glaring reminder of his own impotence in dealing with whoever had put it there. Nara's Range Rover was parked near the front walk, but there was something . . . different about it. David's carotid was now throbbing as he drew closer to the wagon. What was it? He leaned forward as close as he could to the windshield, peering out. Three feet away he let out a breath of relief when he saw that it was nothing more than an open door on the passenger's side.

"Get a grip, McAdam," he mumbled.

He killed the engine of his truck, hopped out, and moved slowly toward the open door. He checked the front seat: no one there. But in the back seat . . . what was this? A little girl—David did not recognize her—was sprawled over the seat. He stood still, watching her, wondering what to do, hoping that she wasn't . . . Her hand twitched and she rolled to the side, snoring lightly. She was asleep. Poor thing, whoever she was. David took off his jacket, covered her with it, and gently closed the door.

But where was Von? And Nara?

He carefully entered the house, stopping in the center of the living room, straining his ears to the darkness. At first there was nothing. Then he heard something, a faint whistling sound upstairs. He raced up the steps, not knowing what to expect when he got to the top.

The whistling was coming from around a blind corner. David crouched down and ducked behind a laundry hamper inside the room. The sound was nearby, coming from somewhere higher than him. He slowly rose, coming up even with the sound and the face of Von, asleep in his crib, his breathing constricted by the congestion in his chest. Otherwise he was fine.

But still no Nara.

David scoured the house, checking every room, every closet. He went through the basement, laundry room, turning on lights and whisper-shouting Nara's name. Nothing.

Upstairs, an ominous sign: Nara's purse and keys lying on the living room floor.

From a kitchen cupboard he took a storm flashlight, checked it, and hit the floodlights surrounding the house. He poked and thrashed his way through the trees and shrubs outside, trying vainly to convince himself that she might have stumbled and hit her head while bringing in the kids. Still no sign of her.

He circled the house twice, looking farther out onto their property. Finally—down by the pond in the shadows beyond the reach of the floodlights—David saw the figure sitting on the ground, slumping forward away from a sapling.

Nara?

David felt his legs sag and breath leave him. His body seemed heavy as if it were filled with wet sand, and he staggered toward her, the flashlight beam jumping wildly before him.

"Oh, no, no," he said weakly, reaching her.

Her arms were wrapped around the trunk to her back and bound at the wrists. Her head was bent forward, covered by volumes of black hair. The flashlight still jumped in his trembling hand. He knelt down and gently pulled her back by the forehead. Her mouth fell open, drooling saliva. Then her head rolled back, giving David a clear view of the long, thin slit across her throat.

"Nara!" he moaned. He held her head in his hands and felt for a pulse on her neck.

"Come on," he said, groping for the pulse. "Where is it?" And there it was! Weak but definitely there. She was alive.

David suddenly had the presence of mind to check Nara's wound. It spanned the width of her throat, at least six inches, but the bleeding had long since stopped. The cut—horrible-looking as it was—had barely broken the skin. With his thumb he lifted her right eyelid. A bloodshot eye looked squarely at him, trying to focus.

"You're going to be okay," he said to her. He bega

loosening the cord binding her wrists. He smelled the chloroform on her face and blouse.

It was then that David understood the full meaning of this attack: this was their third and final warning.

"My best advice to you is to leave," Sheriff Lawrence Donner said solemnly to David. They were huddled over the kitchen table, mugs of coffee in front of them. David had hardly spoken a word since the rescue squad left nearly an hour ago. The paramedics had checked Nara thoroughly but she needed treatment only for the superficial wounds on her throat and wrists. She was now upstairs in bed, sleeping off the chloroform.

"I've seen this kind of thing before," Donner said, sipping his coffee loudly. David noticed that Donner's eyes never met his as they talked. "About four, five years ago, a family lived off Route 73 began finding mounds of sh—uh, defecation, on their property. At first they thought it was an animal, but it kept reappearing, getting closer to the house. Pretty soon they figured out it was human, not animal. Other things were happening—kids' toys turned up missing, tires on the car deflated—and they called us in.

"We staked the place out for a few nights. This was back when I had a deputy and could spare the manpower. Sure enough, the deputy caught someone roaming around the property, looking in windows. He caught the guy trying to crawl through a window in the garage. And get this: he was buck naked."

"Who was he?" David said.

Donner shook his head. "Drifter. Lived in a little lean-to he built in the woods. Scavenged for food. Turned out he'd escaped from a halfway house in Portland and somehow made his way to Sparks. He just got it in his head to bother these people. Would've kept at it if we hadn't gotten him."

"Where is he now?"

"Jail, in South Windham."

"Could he have gotten out?" David said, straightening up. "Come back here?"

Donner looked at the floor. "Not likely. But I'll check it out. What's happening, Mr. Murata, is that somebody's got it in their head to harass you, and they're keeping it up. Kids, probably. You should have reported those other incidents, got us on the case sooner."

David tried to catch Donner's eye but couldn't. "Can you stake out our place? Like you did for that other family?"

Donner grimaced, his concern unconvincing. "Best I can do is pass through here on my patrol. At least we'd establish a police presence, get the perpetrators to think about it, maybe move on. Who knows, maybe we'll catch them."

David nodded his head. He briefly considered the possibility of hiring private guards who could patrol the place twenty-four hours a day. But the thought of being a prisoner in his own house with strangers prowling around at all hours appealed to him about as much as that of Sheriff Donner parked outside, watching David's every move.

No, the thing to do was to get out. Had things been different, if David hadn't had Von and Nara, he would have stayed. But their well-being came first. It seemed no one, including this shifty-eyed sheriff, wanted them around here.

Fine, David thought, let's accommodate them.

Donner seemed to be reading his mind. "Meanwhile," he said, "is there anyplace you can go until this blows over? Some relatives somewhere?"

David looked down at his coffee and saw his own reflection, distorted and flickering on the black surface. "Not really," he said laconically.

True, David and Nara had no relatives in the area. But they did have a place to go. Many places, in fact. There was the island cabin on Penobscot Bay and another one hundred or so estates, ranches, and haciendas around the world, all under his name. He had at least a half-dozen places in Canada.

Canada sounded good to him right now. From what he knew about it, it hadn't gone off the deep end like the U.S. The place was still under the control of sane, civilized people, not the homicidal, gun-loving maniacs who made the rules in this country. And it wasn't far away. He could drive there. All he had to do was call Simon Globus, who would get the place ready, have it stocked with food, diapers, coffee, anything David wanted.

So Canada it would be.

The chair legs squealed under Sheriff Donner as he rose to leave. David expected the man to rub his belly and burp. "Well, Mr. Murata, let me know if there's anything else that comes to mind. And call me immediately if you see anything suspicious."

David looked at Donner. *I see something suspicious right now.* But he didn't say it. Instead, he followed Donner out the door and watched as the taillights of the police car disappeared up the service road. Suddenly he felt very alone. The encircling darkness smirked at him, licked its lips in anticipation of his vulnerability.

David closed the door and locked and chained it. He began turning out lights before going to bed and then thought better of it and left them on. He was starting up the steps when he heard a light tapping on the kitchen door. Passing through the kitchen, he drew a long carving knife from the butcher block knife stand.

He peered through the door window into the night and saw the outline of a figure, thin and narrow-shouldered. He put the chain on the door and then slowly opened it. The figure stepped closer and David raised the knife.

"David, it's me," a voice whispered. It took a moment before David recognized the British accent and the turban. Moe's face came forward, out of the darkness.

"What're you doing?" he said, looking at the knife in David's hand.

"Making coffee," David said. "Want some?"

33

Sid Bromley sat still in his study, at the burned-out end of a disastrous day. The house was silent, a morgue, but he welcomed the quiet after his harrowing afternoon in the elevator with Simon Globus. It was horrible, the whole thing, being stuck in that dark little box with a stranger who could have done anything to him. Sid had run out of Power within the first twenty minutes or so of being trapped and had to ride out the next two hours on his own. Still, he thought he'd handled it pretty well, letting Globus think he was suffering from asthma and gritting it out until the rescue crew got through the top of the elevator cabin.

Even so, Sid couldn't recall a worse day, at least not since he was a patient in the psychiatric ward at the Maine Medical Center. That was three years ago, just after his second divorce and before he met Barb. Things had been going great for him. He was a local celebrity, having landed a cake job as weatherman for a Portland TV station. But little things began to nag at him, like he couldn't get a decent night's sleep and he'd keep screwing up his lines while doing the show. They were just little things. So what if he had trouble getting things done and taken to sitting in his car for hours at a time? He liked his car. Besides, people were becoming a tremendous pain in the ass to him.

One in particular, that prick of a makeup artist at the TV station where Sid worked, always making cracks about Sid's hairline and suggesting that Sid go see his brother-in-law who had a hair-weave business in town. He didn't have much to say after Sid fractured his jaw in two places and broke a couple of his ribs one night after a bad show. Only problem was that the stunt cost Sid his job and got him thrown in jail, that is, until his brilliant lawyer got him off in return for a psychiatric evaluation.

Some deal that turned out to be. Sid ended up spending seven months in the psychiatric ward, being forced to write with crayons, take up volleyball, and listen to one asshole after another spill his guts in group. He was never sure what he was supposed to have had, every goddamn doctor calling it something different: paranoia, affective disorder, involutional psychotic reaction. Even though Sid was pretty heavily medicated through the whole thing, he got bored and restless.

"Jesus," he'd tell the doctors, "just give me some Prozac and let me the hell out of here."

But they didn't give him Prozac or anything else he'd heard of. The involutional psychotic crowd won out and they gave him a choice: another six months to a year of conventional therapy, or electroshock. To Sid, it was no contest.

It wasn't until after the electroshock that Sid understood what it was. In most people's homes, the lights and appliances run on 120 or so volts of electricity supplied by the power company. What Sid got was *150 volts* pumped straight into his skull for a full half second, three times a day. The electricity didn't really do anything for him; it was the convulsions it induced that were supposed to straighten him out. The doctors offered to put Sid out for the whole thing, but he said, Uh-uh, no way I'm gonna let you knock me out while you jerk around with my brain.

So he got to watch, a ringside seat. They'd give him a couple of shots before each treatment, slowing him down a little. But he saw them, all right, as they washed his head and slapped on jelly and stuck on the electrodes. Then the boys—six of them every time—would gather around and pin down his arms, legs, and hips. By this time Sid had the guard in his mouth so he wouldn't bite his tongue—he wondered if they washed it off between treatments.

Then someone would pull the switch and *Whoooooaaaaa,* felt like a whip had been cracked across his scalp. Images would swarm all around him—fractured, violent ones—as real as the pain and the men holding him down. The next thing he'd know he'd be waking up, surrounded by pillows and one of the six guys, the biggest one, standing over him. It always took him awhile afterward to remember who he was, where he was, and what the hell was going on. Remembering was no great comfort.

They let him out of the hospital within six weeks. He was happy to leave and they were glad to be rid of him. Sid felt good, better than he had in a long time, even though he had trouble remembering some things. No one in broadcasting would touch him now. He had no idea what he'd do or where he'd go, until he met Ron Lindblad at a bar in Rockland—Ron remembering Sid from his weatherman days—talking with him and inviting him to dinner.

They palled around for a while and Sid thought maybe Ron was queer or something until Ron finally asked him if he'd like to work for him. Ron was offering Sid his own talk show. It would have to be on cable, but that was all right. Sid knew he had to start somewhere, and Ron said he could plan most of the shows on his own.

It was too good to be true, and it was.

Ron just about fronted the show through Country Customs' advertising budget until Sid could scrounge a few other sponsors. But Ron made sure that Sid never had *too* many, keeping the leash short and tight. It wasn't long before Ron started asking Sid to do small things, such as taking trips to places like Seattle, Miami, and San Diego—always with a briefcase Sid was forbidden to open—to be delivered to some nameless, faceless person. Sid would sweat bullets the entire trip, certain that the FBI, ATF, and every other cop in the world was on to him. Ron expanded Sid's duties, making him set up a cleaning service—Jiffy, they named it—and take care of the mean-looking Asian and Mexican guys who were its foremen. It wasn't until later that Sid understood Jiffy's true purpose.

Sid saw what was happening—getting roped into Ron's scams—but he could do nothing to stop it. Ron played hir perfectly, giving him a lot of freedom with the show a all the trappings that went with it. Sid married Barb, who was obviously accustomed to the good life that he had to keep up. And Sid knew he was in deep, probably guilty of dozens of crimes. If he ever tried to pull out, Ron could just jerk the leash.

Then came the biggest thing of all—the killings. Sid could remember Ron telling him that the operation had moved into a new phase. Before Sid could ask, "What operation?" Ron told him what it was he had to do and who was going to do it. Sid went along, pulled by the gold ring in his nose. There were times when he had to just stop and pinch himself to believe it was real. The money could be big, tremendous even, but the risks were even greater, especially taking into account what Sid had to work with, the instability of the people involved.

Suddenly the phone rang, snapping Sid back into the moment. It was Al Cheseldine at the electrical utility, whom Sid had ordered to do a complete sweep of the power grid after today's blackout. The jerks had gone through every inch: the electrical plant, power lines, and transformers until finally Cheseldine could call to say:

"We found it," he proclaimed, breathless and happy, "the cause of the blackout."

Sid waited. "Well?" he said.

"An animal."

"A what?"

"In the substation. We found an animal. Damned thing somehow got through under the fence, burrowed right on under there, and got caught in a circuit breaker. That was one crispy critter we found there.

"You can tell Mr. Lindblad that everything's under control. You do that, Mr. Bromley."

Sid could almost hear the sweat dripping from Cheseldine's face. Ron had done a number on him. "So what was it?" Sid said.

"What was what?"

Sid groaned. "The animal. Ron'll want to know."

"You're not going to believe this."

"I'll believe anything right now," Sid said.

"An armadillo. It looked like an armadillo."

"A what?"

And so on, until Sid got fed up with the sheer stupidity of the conversation and hung up. He looked around his office, done in high-tech minimalism with black leather Italian furniture, chrome and glass bookshelves, and recessed lighting. On his desk—a square glass table with black iron legs—were three telephones and a computer, custom-made and presented to him courtesy of Country Customs. It gave him a direct line into the company's computer system. Soft George Winston piano tinkled in the background. Sid could not stand listening to anything but instrumental music.

Now, prowling around the office, Sid felt fatigued and edgy, almost to the point of being violent. With his toupee—the Derek model—on its stand in his bedroom, he had an uncomfortable sense of being exposed, vulnerable. Nursing a vodka rocks, he went over to the wall, pressed a hidden panel, and a small door snapped open. Inside was a box in which he kept his largest stash of crystal meth, his Power.

Sid always kept a supply to last him four months of gradually increased dosage. He knew he didn't really need it, only when things got crazy at the studio or if Ron had a rash of chores for him to do on top of everything else. He snorted back six hefty spoonfuls and chased them with vodka to even out the high.

He settled back in his chair, letting the drug work its way from his liver through his intestinal tract and over his body. He felt pumped, recharged, as if he had put his finger into an electrical socket and let the current flow through every cell. Sid knew at this point he could do anything. The rest of the world was moving in slow motion, almost backward. He alone had the power to push events forward on the strength of his will. He was omnipotent.

Sid was planning his shows for the rest of the month. He was now waiting on calls from his assistant producers, who begged, bribed, cajoled, and threatened people into bein
guests on the show. His top priority right now was to
up the show at which Ron Lindblad would officially

nounce his candidacy for the governorship. Sid knew that he had to deliver on this one, that Ron would settle for nothing less than a grand slam.

The problem was that Sid and his assistant producers couldn't find enough credible people to speak on Ron's behalf. Some of the people they'd called claimed to be out of town on the day of taping, others said they had conflicts in their schedules. Sid was angry and ordered his people to pull out all the stops, promise the moon, but just get enough guests in to make Ron look good.

At the same time, Sid was helping Ron in another way, by doing a special series investigating the finances of the current governor and the sexual preferences of his daughter. Sid was trying to get the daughter on the show, or at least the female tennis instructor with whom she was purported to have had an affair. The instructor said she'd do the show for fifty thousand dollars and Sid—knowing he couldn't come up with that kind of money—tried to bargain, offering her twenty-five thousand dollars and a spot on an upcoming tennis special he planned to do. The instructor hadn't called him back yet with an answer.

Meanwhile, Sid had to think about other shows, his bread and butter. If he could make bail for someone awaiting trial in Bangor, he'd have what he called a quorum—a minimum of three guests on a particular topic—for one of his upcoming shows. The topic for the show was husbands who have killed unfaithful wives. The guest Sid wanted to get had been charged with second-degree murder in the nail-gun death of his wife. Sid was promised color photos of the crime scene and corpse if he could put up bail and another five thousand dollars.

Other problems bedeviled him, such as a salary increase demanded by his studio audience, who were threatening to join a union. He thought about replacing the whole lot of them, but they might picket him and cause unfavorable publicity that Ron wouldn't like. Sid pressed a button on his dicta-telephone and dictated a memo for the audience, advising them that free lunches would no longer be served [illegible] the studio. That should show them he meant business.

A phone rang and Sid picked it up quickly, hoping it was Buzz Thayer, one of his assistant producers, with word on guests for Ron's special. Instead it was Lawrence Donner, Knox County Sheriff.

"What are you doing calling me here?" Sid demanded.

Donner snorted and fell quiet for several moments. "You got a problem," he said flatly.

"What?"

"Something just happened you should know about. The-ah was an incident tonight, involved the family living up on top of Drury Hill just outside Sparks. The wife was attacked tonight. Someone entered the house and held a knife to her throat just before knocking her out with chloroform. Her husband found her tied up outside under a tree."

"That's terrible," Sid said. "What'd you say the name was?"

"I didn't. Murata. Japanese name. Curious thing, though, the husband's not Japanese, not even Oriental."

"So why are you telling me this?" Sid thought he should say.

"Just a warning, Mr. Bromley. This incident was very sloppy. Good thing the woman wasn't hurt worse or killed. I'm going to file this as a simple breaking and entering, but a paramedic crew from Rockland was out the-ah. I was on the scene before them and smoothed things over a bit, told them it was a domestic accident. But word could get around about this."

"Well," Sid said, chewing on the raw membrane inside his cheeks, "you sure are handling your job well. Sounds like this Murata family might be well advised to move on somewhere else."

"That's exactly what I said. Guy seemed to be thinking about it. But you never know. Some folks can be really stubborn."

"Yeah, well," Sid said, tired of dealing with incompetents and not wanting to talk anymore.

"I hope we don't need to have this conversation aga

Donner said in his cop voice. "Things could turn out different. Get me?"

"Absolutely, Officer," Sid said, mocking him.

"One more thing," Donner said. "I've been getting calls from someone named K. K. Thorner. She says a friend of hers has disappeared, an old woman named Estelle Grout. You wouldn't know anything about that, would you?"

"Why should I?" Sid said.

Donner snorted. "I strongly advise you to take care of this situation immediately. This Thorner is a troublemaker and she's not going to go away."

"Well, Officer, sometimes people step out of your way just when you need them to."

"You better be right," he said and hung up.

Sid sat still, gripping the phone tightly, his eyes closed, riding out the wave of anger and a Methedrine rush. A terrible sense of unraveling—the same feeling he had just before his big breakdown a few years ago—slid through his head like a snake. It seemed the more effort he expended to keep things on an even keel, the worse they got.

He slammed the phone back down on the receiver, took a pencil and pad of paper from the bookshelf, and began to write down all the things going wrong. He wanted to see them in front of him, line them up, and maybe he could deal with them that way. He wrote:

1. Special on Ron is fucking up, no one wants to go on record supporting him—HE'S GOING TO SHIT MISSILES WHEN HE FINDS OUT!!!
2. Tennis instructor who could put the governor away wants 50 g's to appear—WHERE DO I GET THAT KIND OF MONEY???
3. Women-behind-bars show is in serious trouble—TRIPLE SHIT!!!
4. Guy at the mall—computer store owner—refuses my best offer for a sell-out—BAD IDEA!

   Murata situation a total screw-up—CALL THE KILLER TO SET UP A MEET

6. K. K. Thorner is raising trouble—WHAT'S BEEN DONE ABOUT HER?

Sid sat for several minutes looking at the blue lines on the white paper. He held the pencil between his thumb and index finger, twisting it almost to the point of breaking it. He drained the last of his vodka before he wrote:

7. Barb and Ron

He thought awhile about going for another hit of crystal. But first he snatched up the phone and punched in one of the pre-programmed numbers. He remembered Ron's warning about wiretaps, but he didn't care. Damned if he'd go out at this hour looking for a pay phone.

One ring, two; it always took two. Then the voice came on: brittle, hollow, sinister. Sid began the conversation slowly, not jumping into anything heavy just yet.

"How've you been?" he said.

"Oh, fine," the voice said without interest.

"Have your payments been in order?"

"Oh, yes. That's never a problem."

Sid paused, trying to gather his thoughts with the crystal meth swirling in his head. "I just got a call, an official one. It was about your . . . activities this evening, concerning a certain party we've discussed."

Silence on the other end. Talking to the killer was always difficult for Sid, but tonight it was especially so. He had to walk a very fine line here between getting the killer back on track and not making a volatile situation worse.

"Do you follow me?" Sid said evenly. "We've got a problem here. This is just the latest one in a series."

Another long pause. "I'm doing what must be done," the killer said. "It's not a simple thing. You've given me no flexibility."

"Flexibility?" he said.

"These things take time. Sometimes the lighter the hand the better the results."

"Lighter hand?" Sid blurted out. "This isn't brain s

gery we're talking about. You knew what was expected of you."

"Don't tell me my business. Find yourself someone else if you don't like my methods."

"All right, all right," Sid said, feeling like he had trod into the danger zone. "Listen. We need to meet." He looked at his watch, the numbers swimming in the digital display. "How about an hour from now? At the factory."

"The factory."

"See you there," Sid said, and hung up. He took in a deep breath. He relished the prospect of meeting with the killer about as much that of calling Ron. But he needed to hear what was going on, not that he would like it.

Something else occurred to Sid, something that had been in the back of his thoughts for some time. Maybe now was the time to get out, to get away from Sparks, away from Ron. Everything was coming apart at the seams here. Why should he stay to take the fall? Sid knew his way around Mexico, even had some friends down there who would take care of him. He could make some quick transfers from his bank accounts and pull out as much cash as he would need for a while.

Yes, that's what he would do. It was time to think about himself for a change. First thing tomorrow he would make a couple calls to Mexico City, book a flight, and take care of his finances. Then he would be ready.

Sid was about to push the button for Ron's number when the jangle of keys in the front door made him jump from his chair. He rushed into the living room, professionally decorated in shades of white: stark Navajo white walls, pearl-wash paintings, ivory flokati rugs. Sid always hated this room and its pristine preciousness. He reached the door as Barb came through it, carrying the shoulder bag she always took to the spa, shrugging off her coat and hanging it in the closet. She wore a cream-colored silk suit that looked badly rumpled and her ash blond hair was abnormally askew.

"Been working out?" Sid said, his hands shaking in his pockets.

Barb looked at him once, quickly, and then strode silently past him to the stairs. He watched her cream and ash blond back as she climbed the long white-carpeted staircase, melted into the whiteness toward the top, and vanished.

34

Sid Bromley was driving in complete darkness, winding up the long single-lane road that snaked through the trees four miles north of the Sparks city limits. He kept his headlights off and his foot lightly on the accelerator. The only sound he heard was that of wet gravel crunching softly under his tires. Even though Sid was going uphill, he felt he was heading in a downward spiral.

At the end of the road was a massive black shape outlined in the moonless sky: a reconstructed barn. Sid left his car behind a clump of bay trees and made his way toward the building. At the end of a dirt path about fifty yards from the barn was a group of four converted chicken houses. Coming up on the barn, Sid could hear the faint snores and wheezes issuing from inside them.

From among the many keys on his key ring, Sid slid one into the outsized padlock on the barn door. The padlock sprang open and he pushed the big door into the vast room. Sid clapped his hands and light from three hundred fifty-watt bulbs blazed on overhead. This had been an abandoned nineteenth-century barn, with high beamed ceilings and hardwood floors. After Barb had screwed a family desperate to sell out of the property, Sid had fixed it up into a serviceable factory and training facility.

He passed through the training room, clapped his hands again, and the lights in the first room went out. He was in the dark again, in the tin-punching room. All along the wall were stations at which lamp bases, switchplates, and the front panels for pie safes and jelly cupboards were made by punching sheets of tin. Primitive designs were now the fashion. Ron had his people cranking them out, increasing his production so he could lower prices and undercut his competition. It was a hard way to make money, but Ron wasn't really doing the work. He was just taking a risk.

Inside, Sid tried to get his bearings in the deep darkness. As he walked slowly through the big room, his shoulders shuddered involuntarily and he tried to control them. What was it? he wondered. What was making him twitch like this? His ears listened in the darkness. What was that faint noise coming from the corner?

Sid clapped his hands again, activating the light. Cold hands gripped his heart. In the far corner of the room—sitting quietly on a Shaker stool among a line of rustic bird feeders—was the killer.

"Well, hello?" Sid said casually, careful not to incite hostility in this most volatile of personalities. "How did you get in here?"

"You trained me well. I came in through a back window."

Sid forced himself to smile. Go slowly, he told himself. Proceed with great caution.

"I'm glad to see you can handle yourself so well," he said. "Is that how you got into the Murata house tonight, through the window?"

The killer smiled like a cobra. "Didn't have to. The front door was open."

"Why didn't you kill them? You had the chance."

The smile went away. "The husband wasn't there. Besides, I only wanted to scare them."

Sid looked up at the ceiling, as if praying for restraint. "I don't understand this," he said. "You kill people you're *not* supposed to kill and don't kill people you *are* supposed to kill."

"There was no reason to kill the Muratas," the killer shot back angrily. "They're leaving. I frightened them off. You'll get your property."

"Listen," Sid said, speaking as if he were dealing with an unruly guest on his show. "We all have our roles to play in the plan. I have mine and you have yours. If you want to change your role a little bit, let's talk about it. But let's not go off halfcocked, just ignoring the—"

"I want out," the killer said abruptly. "I'm done."

Alarms went off in Sid's head. What's going on here? he thought. "Ha ha, that's good. You just can't do that. You're an important part of this project."

"Find someone else."

Sid tried to think quickly, to avert the disaster forming before him now. "But why?" he said, spreading out his hands. "Why do you want out?"

"I'm tired. I've had enough."

Why me? Sid thought. What have I done to deserve this? "Don't we pay you enough?" he said, seizing an obvious ploy.

"That's not the reason," the killer said quickly. "You've paid me well and I've delivered for you. That makes us even."

Sid fought an urge to rub his eyes and curse. This couldn't be happening. Not now, of all times. Gears turned in his head.

"Look, I know how you feel. This is dirty work, thankless work. I realize it must be tiresome for you. But, believe me, the end is in sight. We're seeing the light at the end of the—"

"No, I've decided. I'm out as of now."

Heat rose at the base of Sid's neck, up through his face and prickling his skin. He fidgeted and scratched furiously under his chin, craving a hit of Power.

"But this," he said, trying to collect his thoughts, "this just can't be—"

"Is there a problem?" said a voice behind Sid. He spun around to find Ron hovering in the doorway, a hand in one pocket and the other holding a briefcase. Ron strolled in, casual as you please, surveying the room. He placed the briefcase on the floor and picked up an unpainted two-bird house in the shape of a barn.

He held the birdhouse, turning it in his hands. "When I started at Country Customs twenty-two years ago," he said, quietly, calmly, "birdhouses were our most popular items.

They got us through some tough times, the recessions of the seventies, eighties. They're still our best-sellers."

Where is he going with this? Sid wondered. Did he know who, what, he was dealing with?

"Some things," Ron said in that even voice and looking directly at the killer for the first time, "are indispensable. No matter what the circumstances, even in the worst or best of times, you just keep with them, knowing you'll always need them. Follow me?"

The killer said nothing at first, watching him intently, shark's eyes unblinking. "I've done my share, Mr. Lindblad. I've done everything asked of me."

"Unquestionably," Ron said, even smiling a little. "Mr. Bromley was quite right when he told you that we were approaching the end of this phase of the operation. The next one will not involve you at all unless you want it to."

He placed the birdhouse back on the shelf. "But until that time, we need you. Like Mr. Bromley and me, you are indispensable. Each of us three knows a lot about the others' roles in this. We've formed something of a balance of terror among ourselves. It's not such a simple thing for any one of us to simply walk away. Do we understand each other?"

The killer sat quietly, gazing at Ron with those steady shark eyes. The tension in the room was so thick, Sid thought, he could have cut it with a knife.

"Now," Ron said, reaching into the inside pocket of his Ralph Lauren safari jacket and drawing out a brown envelope. "Here is payment for two more assignments. I've added a bonus, as good faith." He set the envelope atop the birdhouse. "Mr. Bromley, have you briefed our friend on these assignments?"

"We've talked about it, yes," Sid said quickly.

"These will be your biggest challenges yet," Ron said, sounding to Sid like a football coach at halftime. "The risks are great as are the added . . . complications. For these reasons I've brought you something."

Ron bent over, picked up the briefcase, and brought it over to a Shaker stool near the killer. He placed the briefcase on the stool. It sprang open as Ron pressed hidden panels on the sides. Inside was a gun, a Walther PPK, broken down into parts that were stored in compartments within the felt-lined interior.

Sid watched the killer, whose eyelids snapped at the sight of the gun. Then, out of curiosity, he leaned over and looked inside the briefcase himself.

"Is that a silencer?" he asked.

Ron grimaced and cradled out a long cylinder from one of the compartments. "This," he said, holding it up, "is known as a suppressor. It is easily attached to the barrel, here, which has been professionally lengthened and threaded to accommodate the suppressor. Upon firing there will be a sound, but a very contained one, as the gas in the gun's action is released far more slowly than usual. You should be able to operate in a populated area without detection.

"The gun is a semi-automatic, each magazine clip holding eight rounds. I would seriously doubt that you would need that many to do either job. I will give you ammunition that has been especially tailored for this gun to minimize sound."

"But I don't use a gun," the killer said. "It's been years since I've even handled one."

"Sid here knows a lot about guns," Ron said, momentarily forgetting the formal "Mr. Bromley." "He will give you as much help as you need to master the basics, starting tomorrow. Time is of the essence. Right, Sid?"

"But I have to show a tape tomorrow," Sid protested lamely.

Ron smiled at him. "You'll just have to work around it, won't you?" he said softly.

Suddenly a noise, a signal of some kind, seemed to sweep in out of the air. Sid looked around nervously, his junkie instincts taking over, expecting police to come pouring through the windows. Instead, Ron scowled, drew back his jacket at the hip, and pressed a button on his beeper.

"Gotta go for a minute," he said gruffly, and disappeared through the back door and out to his car.

Sid shared an awkward silence with the killer, the gun a silent, potent presence between them. In a few long minutes, Ron returned, his face the color of rare beef.

"Everything all right?" Sid said.

"Fucking Norma," he hissed. "She just called from Portland, where she'd been with her goddamn lawyer all day. She's coming back tomorrow and expects me to sign a new will she's had executed. Do you believe that bitch?"

Sid kept an eye on the killer, who was observing Ron's outburst expressionlessly.

Ron stood over the felt-lined case. "What I wouldn't give to put this gun in her big goddamn mouth and pull the trigger. Just to see her begging for mercy and then not to give it. Just to see her crawl."

Sid watched the killer, who was watching Ron, eyes narrow now, engrossed in his words. What is going on behind that inscrutable mask of a face? Sid wondered. Where is all the violence stored and how close is it to the surface?

And, most important, could it ever turn on him?

"Okay, I think that covers it," Ron said, turning toward the door. "Now tend to your business."

35

Late into the night, staring numbly at a computer monitor, David felt anger and self-loathing burning over him like lava. An irrational guilt raked him, guilt that he had let his family down by allowing the events of the past few days to occur. Over and over he relived the horror of finding Nara tied to the tree, the skin on her throat slit, and those agonizing moments before finding her pulse, imagining the unthinkable.

And now Moe was over, sitting with David on the floor of his living room, surrounded by computers. It hadn't taken much prodding for him to get David to tell him about what had happened to Nara. David had even got into the stuff about Cupak. Moe could see what David was going through and tried to lighten things up, but it seemed that each time he raised a new topic for conversation, David would dump gloom and sarcasm all over it. Moe even put on a Glenn Miller CD—something he would never have dreamed of doing willingly—in an effort to cheer David up.

But Moe plugged on. "Hey," he said brightly, "want me to show you a Multi-User Dungeon I've been into for the past few months? It's called Agua Caliente, in which the marginalized patrons of a bar—Agua Caliente—at the headwaters of the Amazon plot and intrigue among themselves for control of a large contraband organization. In it, I am Enriqueta, a coquettish but dangerous Bolivian gun runner with a weakness for cigars and men with tatoos."

David knew about MUDs, sort of long-running, often byzantine, cyber-theater in which members of a group assume personas within an invented location and milieu, playing out their roles, making and breaking alliances, falling in and out of love, sometimes killing each other's alter egos, without ever revealing their true identities. Gender bending was common. David even had played through a couple MUDs for a while but had grown bored with them.

"It's way past cool," Moe said, getting excited. "I invented it. I'll even let you be Queta."

"No, thanks," David said, not even looking at Moe. He was entering commands to download into his system yet another computer code-breaking program from a secret network used mostly by corporate espionage types. His target was the seemingly impenetrable Country Customs computer system. He was sure the key to the mysteries swirling around Sparks was to be found in that system.

After a few minutes, he sat back and slurped coffee from an old PanTech mug, the kind given away at trade fairs. He rubbed his eyes with his free hand and stretched his legs.

"What it's all coming down to," he said slowly, wearily, "the question that preys on the mind of the average American is not: When will we achieve social justice? Or: What must be done to restore the national economy? It's more like: Will I be in firing range when the maniac—the guy everybody later says was such a quiet neighbor—climbs the water tower with his assault rifle? Will my back be to the guy they just let go from the office when he returns with a sawed-off shotgun?"

David set his mug down on the floor. "It's come down to this basic level—self-preservation. People feel surrounded, under siege. We know the madness is beyond our control. Our lines of defense are either thin or nonexistent. I don't know where it's going, but it won't be pleasant."

"Mmm," Moe said, gravely nodding his head.

David stood up and stretched. "Well, we're not sticking around to see it."

"Huh?"

"Day after tomorrow, we're outta here."

"What? Where?"

"Canada. I've a place up in New Brunswick, an old island spa on Grand Lake. It'll be ready for us in two days. If w don't like it there, we can move farther west, to British Columbia. I actually own a town there, on the Strait of Georgia, north of Vancouver."

Moe looked at his hands. "Will you come back?"

"Who knows?" David said. "We'll see what kind of coffee they have." He looked at Moe, still staring down, and brought up a new project he'd been working on up on the screen. "Ever seen one of these before?"

Moe slid over next to him. "That's a fuzzy logic program, isn't it?" he said, recognizing some of the algorithms he had seen when hacking into David's system.

"That's right," David said, surprised. "Have you worked on one before?"

"No, no," Moe said, not quite ready to tell David that it was he who had kibitzed on his Conspiracy game and left the messages.

David shook his head. "They give me fits. Nara's been stuffing books down my throat to get me to make my brain double-jointed enough to handle them."

"What's this one for?" Moe said, moving closer.

A shadow of anger passed over David's face. "I want answers, straight answers, to some rather convoluted questions. Such as: What is happening to old people in Sparks, people who live alone? What is behind these wild power fluctuations we're seeing? How do you explain the sudden appearance of bizarre animals—like alligators and armadillos—in Maine? Maybe fuzzy logic can do what regular logic can't."

"What are you getting?" Moe asked, fascinated but not ready to ask too much.

David pushed back from the computer, crossed his arms, and scowled. He spoke softly, almost to himself. "So far, not much. But there's one piece of the puzzle still missing. I really haven't devoted the time to getting at it."

"What is it?" Moe asked but was sorry he had as soon as David answered slowly, solemnly:

"Country Customs."

"What, how is that important?" Moe said, trying to cover up his nervousness.

David looked at him. "That's just it. I don't know. But some significant lines in this mystery seem to intersect there. For one, a high-priced Boston accountant and his family who had been in Sparks for a few months up and disappear like that," he said, snapping a finger.

"What would he be doing in Sparks? Hell, it's a nice place, I live here, but what would have brought him? Who around here would he be working for? The Lobster Museum?"

David waited for Moe to answer, but the cyberpunk was silent. David plowed on, unfazed. "Then, the real estate agent who is reaping a windfall from all these disappearances made me meet her at Country Customs, where she's with a group of the sleaziest people you'd ever want to meet in most places outside of New York and L.A."

David's voice was almost a whisper when he said, "And then, the strangest thing of all. On two occasions I tried to break into County Customs' secure computer files. I used my standard programs and they're very good, good enough to get through the security of ninety-eight percent of all American companies. But I came up zippo, *nada*."

"Kuchh nahin," Moe said, lapsing into Hindi.

"Yeah," David said. "This place is strange. Take a look at these pictures I took when I was there."

Moe politely examined the photos, turning each one around a couple of times to figure out what he was looking at. What he saw were shots of remote cams mounted on the side of a building, a fence that he assumed was electrified, interior shots of a man at a console, and something that looked like an elevator panel.

"A lot of security," he said, not sure what else to say.

"Yeah, all electronic. That fact might come in handy sometime. But for now, the problem is getting into that mainframe."

"You're sure they use big iron?" Moe asked.

"Don't see how it could be anything but. A distributed-architecture environment wouldn't have the kind of power it takes to resist my probes."

"They're doing a lot with distributed LAN security the

days," Moe said, forgetting his modesty and showing off a bit. "Like virtual machine monitoring, information labeling, and, one of my favorites, breaking down the power of a UNIX root and organizing it in an inverted-tree format. Only a privileged few in the host organization have access to the root directory."

"A privileged few," David said, chewing on that for a few moments.

They were quiet for a while, pondering the magnitude of their challenge. Moe was the first to speak.

"Even if it is mainframe secured, a lot of them have trapdoors, backdoors, and vulnerable access points. Have you tried for Internet and Bitnet connections? AT&T?"

David nodded his head ruefully. "Who knows? Maybe I missed something. I get surprised all the time. But I can't believe that it isn't a mainframe. Hell, this is backwater Maine, not Silicon Valley or even Route 128. Anybody paranoid enough to put in that level of security would not likely trust his employees to the point of giving them discrete PCs, even networked ones. No, the pattern here is one of control."

Moe looked around the room. "You've a lot of power here. Ever think of linking it up?"

David's eyes narrowed. "You mean, I should LAN my house?"

"How many computers have you?"

"Forty, at least. And a mainframe in the basement, in a cool place. What d'ya have in mind?"

"Well . . ." Moe said and began to describe, timidly at first, a way of linking David's computers into a single system—a local area network—that could run millions, billions, of decryption combinations simultaneously. With David's knowledge of systems and general decryption techniques, and Moe's of exotic, cutting-edge algorithms, they just might be able to break the back of Country Customs' security.

They got to work, unplugging and plugging in cables, refitting jacks, and wiring systems together. While he worked, David hummed "Iron Man" by Black Sabbath and

Moe joined in. Pretty soon they were singing it. Moe, more than half David's age, had trouble with the second and third verses, but that was okay. He sang the guitar part, really getting into it.

They were almost done with the upstairs computers when Nara, awakened by their noise, came down in her black Korean robe with dragons embroidered on the sleeves and back. Still shaky from the chloroform, she watched David and Moe for a moment as they went on working, oblivious to her presence, and then yawned, shook her head, and went back to bed.

David plugged in the jack that finally connected the upstairs computers. "Now the basement," he said.

Down in the sound-proofed basement, Moe smiled when David put on "Temple of Dreams" by Messiah, one of Moe's all-time favorite industrial CDs. How did he know? Moe wondered.

The basement computers were more complex than the upstairs ones, even though there were fewer of them. "Temple of Dreams" in all its various avatars—the long and short versions, and the rave, hardcore, and destroyer mixes—played through about three dozen times before they were done. David gave Moe the honor of plugging in the last jack.

"Now, let's cook," David said, and they each sat down at their own computers. Through their modems Moe and David each called a different phone number at Country Customs. David also called Ron Lindblad's home number, which he had pilfered through the directory-assistance database. Then they began to program.

Moe was as quick as lightning, and after a while David stopped and moved over next to him, awestruck by his technique, occasionally whispering, "Shit" or "I didn't know you could do that."

"If this doesn't work," Moe said, writing a trapdoor program for the Diffie-Hellman key exchange, something he'd always wanted to try, "we can hack into a supercomputer somewhere and see if that can handle these algorithms. Maybe a couple or three."

And then it hit David. "Hey," he said, "by any chance are you the guy who's been hacking into my system?"

Moe stopped, his blood running cold. "We're done," he managed to say, his throat tight.

"It *was* you, wasn't it? And all this time I thought it was Paul Bolger. Hell, he couldn't program his way out of a wet paper bag."

David took Moe by his narrow shoulders. "Moe, man, hey, it's all right. I don't care. I'm glad it was you and not some stranger."

Then David looked closely at him. "Moe, you've been acting weird all night. What's wrong?"

Moe, still avoiding David's gaze, gently shrugged David's hands off his shoulders. "Nothing. We'd better check the system upstairs."

36

At first glance, Moe would have generously described David's living room as chaotic. A few dozen computers lined the wall, clumped together without any apparent purpose. Myriad other equipment—some David admitted to having used only once—cluttered whatever space was not taken up by computers, like a remainder sale at an electronics outlet. And the cables, miles of them—coaxials, twinaxials, extendas, gender-changer connectors—stretched and coiled over the room and behind hardware, almost taking on a life of their own, reminding Moe of the snake-infested tomb floor in *Raiders of the Lost Ark*.

But on closer examination Moe quickly discerned the precision and purpose of David's setup. David had created almost from scratch his own high-powered network. It was quite a feat. Each component, each connection, was carefully thought through and elegantly adapted to David's obviously high standards.

Now every computer in the house was wired together in a single objective: to figure a way of getting into Country Customs. Moe surveyed the living room computers, humming along, the programs they wrote burning through their routines, accelerated many times over by the linked network. Now came then hardest part, the waiting.

Moe knew that David was watching him, puzzling over his solemn silence. In the short time he had known David, Moe had come to like and trust the man immeasurably. His hero was everything he thought he'd be, and more. But Moe still wasn't sure how far he could go in trusting David, how much he could reveal about himself. It wasn't so much

Moe protecting himself, but the others, his family and friends. What would David do if he knew everything? Where might he go with it? Moe just couldn't be certain, and his doubts spawned the confusion and guilt that kept him taciturn, sullen.

"This is reverse synergy," David said, now the one making conversation. "The whole is greater than the sum of its parts. You do any work on Buckminster Fuller?"

Moe shook his head and frowned inscrutably. He sat quietly on the couch, reading the latest edition of *Wired* as David putzed around the room, turning this, tweaking that. Nearly an hour went by, and Moe rose to check a computer monitor.

"Oh, bloody hell," he said.

"What?" David asked, joining him at the screen.

"It's into a loop, going through the routine again. It didn't work the first time."

"Are you sure?"

"Are you sure they have computers at Country Customs?" Moe snapped back, frustrated.

"Yeah, I saw them," David said, either missing Moe's rhetorical sarcasm or choosing to ignore it. "I don't know what kind they were. They looked custom-built to me."

"What do we do now?" Moe said, suddenly feeling tired, the adrenaline fading from his blood.

David held his chin in his hand, rubbing the scar there. What did he still have on this investigation? What was still alive?

"Something you said before," he said, "about that inverted tree security protocol."

"Oh, you mean breaking down the Unix root and providing access only—"

"Yeah, to the privileged few. I've been thinking about that. Who are the 'privileged few' at Country Customs?"

"Well, there's Ron Lindblad," Moe said. "But we tried his number. And his wife we know is the president of the company. Are you thinking that she might have her own number?"

"No," David said, settling down at the keyboard. "Someone else. Someone who might, just might, be a little less careful than Ron."

David quickly typed in a series of commands that put him in the middle of New England Bell's database. A few more commands and he had Sid and Barb Bromley's unlisted home number up on his screen.

"Okay, Sid baby," David said, "here we come." Within seconds, David unleashed the power of his system at Sid's computer. The poor unprotected thing didn't stand a chance. David was right: Sid's computer was hard-wired into the Country Customs system.

"Hot damn!" David shouted as Country Customs' computer files tumbled down his screen. Moe and he high-fived each other and generally whooped it up before they settled down to pump the Country Customs database.

"What are we looking for?" Moe asked, out of his element now that the decryption had been done.

"Dunno," David said. "Let's try to figure out how this database is set up." Just to be on the safe side, he downloaded a copy of the database onto his computer and then made ten more copies of it, which he squirreled away into various parts of his system.

It didn't take them long to figure out that each of the database codes represented a part of the business: production, payroll, finance, personnel, distribution. To get things rolling, David typed in a command to search for the name Haslem throughout the database. But nothing came up.

"No surprise there," he mumbled. "Let's look at, oh, distribution."

Expecting a somewhat brief, innocuous entry, David was shocked to find it took up over half of the database. Over two hundred trucks were listed, each described in exquisite detail: make, age, size, cost, mileage, miles per gallon, and number of trips taken. And boats, there must have been fifty or sixty of them as well: tugboats, launches, fishing boats.

"Trips where?" David wondered out loud. He turned to Moe, noticing his tired, bloodshot eyes for the first time. His turban was askew on his head, cocked like a sailor's hat. "This is a mail-order company. They ship their merchandise out UPS or FedEx, depending on how much you want to pay. What do they need all these goddamn trucks and boats for?

"And just look at the trucks. Moving vans, refrigerator trucks, vans outfitted with tons of carpet-cleaning equipment. What the hell are *they* for?"

Moe shrugged his shoulders.

"Okay," David said, "let's try 'personnel.' "

Here, David found the reverse of Distribution. Country Customs listed exactly twelve employees: nine telephone operators, John Purves—the guy David first had met at Country Customs—and then Ron and Norma Lindblad. Purves was described as "security director," but no other security people were listed, not one of the many guards David had seen the day of his visit. David queried the computer on the Lindblads and—how nice—a copy of their tax return from last year came up on the screen.

"They wouldn't trust an accounting firm to do their taxes," David said, scrolling through the complex document. "I'd say they were underreporting income big-time," he said. "Hey, get a load of this. They reported a loss last year and took a deduction. Another deduction, over here: Ron gave $35,000 to the Lobster Museum. Wow. And, hello? Ron picked up a little pocket money from serving on the board of the local utility authority, as chairman, even."

The combination of Ron Lindblad and the power company set off a distant alarm in David's mind, some association from somewhere. David thought hard but couldn't salvage it. He was off on another search for any reference in the database to Sid or Barb Bromley, but could find none.

"This is nothing more than a skeleton staff," David said, perplexed. "Who does all the real work?"

"Bastards," Moe muttered out of David's earshot.

David called up the Finance directory and found budgets for the various departments, as well as insurance and investment files. "Sonuvabitch," he said. "I've seen cooked books before, but these take the cake. Country Customs owns property all around Penobscot Bay, and up and down the Maine coast. And would you look at that? They even own the Downeast Mall. I had no idea. What're they up to?"

"Expanding?" Moe said.

"Apparently. Look here," David said, scrolling down through various files, "the company's balance sheet, in Lotus. It even gives last year's actuals. Wow, look: production's more than doubled since last year. That's a lot of quilts to be pushing out with no employees."

David moved through the spread sheet. "But look down here: net profits are flat from last year. All that real estate they're buying is eating into them.

"Let's see," he said, bored with finance, "what haven't we tried yet? Hey, how about physical plant?"

David keyed in the code "pp" and the architectural plans for the entire County Customs plant began to appear on the monitor: floor plans and detailed schematics for the plumbing, heating, and electrical systems.

"Hmmm," David hummed, sitting back with his arms folded.

"What do we have?" Moe said, feeling he'd asked that question about twenty times now.

"Well," David said, rubbing his eyes and laughing. "Everything and nothing. We have just about everything on Country Customs we'd ever hope to get, but not a shred of evidence or so much as a clue to clear up these mysteries. Like I said, everything and nothing.

"Hey, ever read Borges?" David said, his mind jumping to something else. "He has this neat little parable in his *Labyrinths* collection that—"

Moe was too tired to listen. He stood up and stretched. Dirty light was beginning to filter in through the windows on the eastern side of the house. He dragged himself to the back of the house, peered through the rear picture window, and almost gagged.

"Hey, I'm putting on some coffee," David said, coming up behind him. "How do you take it?"

"Uh, er, black's fine," Moe stammered, backing off from the window. "Coffee. Sounds good."

"What's the matter, Moe? What's going on outside?" David tried to look past him, but Moe stood purposely in the way. But David, half a foot taller, merely looked over him and there—trudging through the cattails and bamboo grass down along the edge of the pond, unearthly and nearly obscured by the early morning mist—was Toshi's ghost, or whatever it was.

"Hey, look," David said, excited. "Do you see that?"

"No, I don't see anything," Moe said.

"What?" David said, incredulous. Out on the marshy border of the pond, the figure was stooped over, picking bamboo shoots.

Moe stood on his tiptoes and looked over David's shoulder. "Tsk, tsk," he said under his breath.

"Moe, this is great," David said, excited. "You see it, don't you? Don't you? Listen, I know who he is."

"You do?"

The ghost looked up, seemingly aware someone was looking at him, and darted toward the woods. "C'mon, Moe, let's see where he goes," David said, breaking for the door.

"No, that's okay," Moe said, heading toward the other side of the house. "How about that coffee?"

David was already into his coat and boots. "Ah, forget it for a minute. Let's go." He burst out the door and into the woods, hot on the ghost's trail.

"Oh, bloody hell," Moe said, and grabbed his jacket and lit off after David.

37

Like many hackers, Moe was in terrible physical condition. The cold air bit into his skin and chilled his heaving lungs as he tried to keep up with David and his "ghost." Bay branches whipped his cheeks, burrs grabbed his clothes. Then it occurred to Moe that he didn't need to run. He knew exactly where they were going. He slowed down, tried to catch his breath, and walked, hands on his waist.

Deeper in the woods, David would intermittently gain and lose sight of the ghost, who moved deftly through the heavy underbrush. The spruce and maple grew close here, grudgingly allowing shafts of light to pierce the dark forest. David had lost his bearings and realized he might not even be able to find his way back home. He stopped for a moment in the silent forest and sniffed the air. Was that smoke he smelled? Or coffee? He realized his caffeine jones was bigger than he ever imagined. Then a light wind carried a sound to him, a shred of a sound, something totally improbable: big band music.

"Toshi?" he whispered.

David shook his head and staggered through the rooty forest in the direction he last had seen the ghost headed. His lack of sleep, food, and caffeine began to conspire against him, and he felt heavy-legged, dopey. He crashed through the woods, slipping on logs rotted through with yellow fungus and falling into blackberry brambles. His face burned and he found blood welling up from the scrapes on his hands and wrists.

Tired and out of breath, David sat down on the damp forest floor. He felt something incongruously hard and rubbery under his ass. He groped around with his hand and found a heavy coaxial cable that disappeared in the undergrowth. What the hell is *that* for? he wondered.

Up ahead was a thick screen of spruces and oaks stretching as far as David could see in either direction, reinforced by rows of waist-high fern. He fought his way through the screen, his hair catching in wire-brush branches. Finally breaking through, cursing and picking burrs and needles from his hair, he stopped in his tracks at the incredible sight waiting for him on the other side.

Sloping down away from him into a meadow of emerald heather and moss, and protected like a harbor on every side by heavy undergrowth, was a sprawling, primitive village of canvas tents, lean-tos, and small makeshift A-frames. There must have been sixty or seventy of them. Wisps of smoke curled up through tin and plywood roofs. The unmistakable smell of burning dung hung in the air, trapped by the canopy of trees. David blinked, trying to assimilate the unbelievable. And then he heard it, for the second time, he realized: Duke Ellington's "Take the 'A' Train."

In the early morning light, David spied people in the village, some moving through the narrow streets that wound through the shantytown. He watched a woman, her head covered with a bandanna, heading away from a stream. Carrying a pole with buckets balanced on both sides, she turned up a narrow path before disappearing into a hut packed with earth. A pair of small children scampered through tiny backyards planted with mushrooms and vegetables and scrambled up an embankment into a patch of fern. A dog was barking, and from somewhere at the edge of the village David could hear the bleating of goats.

Though a window of a nearby lean-to, David could see an old man reading a yellowed newspaper by candlelight. This was Duke Ellington's house, he realized, and he walked sideways down the steep slope and into a single-lane street. A strong aroma of coffee billowed out from one of the houses. David had forgotten about Toshi's ghost, his mind focused on one thing: coffee.

In search of the coffee, he cracked open the door to one

of the better-constructed A-frames and found himself in something out of the bazaar scene in the movie *Blade Runner*—high technology in a low-rent Third World setting—when the old Chinese woman in her battered little stand puts what Harrison Ford thinks is a fish scale under her electron microscope. "Not fish," she cackles to him. "Snake."

The first thing to catch David's eye in the A-frame was the high-end, late-model PanTech computer with modem on a makeshift desk in the corner. The walls of the hut—covered with military green canvas—were brightened with pictures taken from magazines. David spotted a couple of Mr. Spock, a few of rock stars he didn't recognize, and then several of him—David McAdam—clustered around the computer.

He stepped closer, feeling very strange about this. These were old photos of him when he had been with PanTech, one a cover of *Time* magazine when he had sold his millionth PanTech computer. Where the hell did they come from? he wondered.

He left the A-frame and searched out the coffee. Before the door of the old man's house, he drew in a breath and knocked on the two-by-four supporting the green canvas door. He heard shuffling around from inside, and the man poked his head from behind the canvas.

"Evet?" the man said. He had short white hair and big, friendly features.

Evet? David thought. He hadn't heard *that* before. "Coffee," he said, feeling stupid and small.

The man smiled and pulled back the canvas door. *"Gel,"* he said, *"hosh geldiniz."*

"Yeah," David said and stooped to enter the house. The smell of coffee was overwhelming, intoxicating. The man led him to a tiny table next to a space heater, sat him down, and disappeared behind a piece of rose-colored chintz hanging over a doorway. On a table covered with green felt was an old RCA radio tuned to the big band station in Sparks, playing Glen Miller doing "Begin the Beguine."

David glanced at the newspaper, written in a languag

he didn't recognize. The banner read *Millyet,* whatever that meant. The date on the paper was April of last year. A question surfaced in David's mind: Where did this guy get the power way back here in the woods to run a radio and a space heater?

The man reappeared with a small cup of coffee, which he placed before David, and then sat down on a cot in the corner to watch him drink it. David looked at the coffee—thick, rich, heavenly—and took a sip. He concluded at once that this was the absolutely finest thing he had ever tasted in his life.

"Türk Kahve," the man said, still smiling. *"Istiyormüsünüz?"*

"Good," David said, taking another hot, wonderful gulp.

The old man smiled again. "Good," he said. "That good."

David smiled and finished it off, sucking up the sweet molten grounds at the bottom of the cup. The man seized the cup and trotted off behind the chintz to get David another. Just then a face appeared through the canvas door: dark, bleary-eyed, and topped off with a purple turban spotted with green burrs.

"So," Moe said sardonically, "you finally got your coffee."

38

The dumpster at the Downeast Mall was overflowing after a weekend of the last of the post-holiday clearance sales. It was nearly covered by the stacks of discarded winter catalogues and cardboard boxes that leaned into it from all four sides and rose up to a peak, like one of the pyramids at Giza. In the mid-morning wind, signs, banners, and popped balloons blew freely away from the pyramid and across the parking lot.

Donnie Popham was a little late getting started on his Monday route for the KAT Solid Waste Removal Company. He had already made the rounds at the Rockland restaurants and picked up loads at the Penobscot School and Winter Terrace apartment complex in Owls Head. He had stopped by the landfill near Thomaston and disgorged the compacted garbage before coming down toward Sparks. He wasn't even half of the way toward reaching his capacity of twenty thousand pounds, but he figured since he was already there at the landfill, why not get rid of it?

Donnie would need to go no farther south than the mall; there was nothing to pick up in Sparks. To his knowledge, there wasn't a single dumpster in the entire town, even with that Country Customs Company operating there. For all he knew, they handled their own garbage.

Since the truck could get no better than forty-five miles an hour, Donnie stayed off the main roads and tried to time his runs for the quietest times of the day. He also did his best to time them so that he could refill his tank before it got too low. Donnie's truck—a five-gear hydraulic model—got about eight miles to the gallon.

The mall stores were just opening up as he pulled into the parking lot. The dumpster was right in the middle of the lot, near the mall, giving every store about equal access to it. Donnie clicked his tongue as he saw the garbage rising around the dumpster. His union said he didn't have to pick up uncontained garbage, but he always did it anyway. Good for business, he figured.

Donnie came up on the dumpster at a crawl, maneuvering the truck precisely so that the forks at the front of the truck slid right into the handles of the dumpster. The dumpster shuddered as the heavy iron prongs locked into place. Donnie hit the brakes, setting off the beeping reverse signal, and pulled the lever over on the shotgun side that engaged the hydraulic lifter. His field of vision went black as the pyramid of garbage crumbled away and the dumpster swung up over the top of the truck and dumped its load into the compactor, the guts of the truck.

Donnie could hear the garbage—slowly at first—begin to drop in dull thuds into the compactor. Then the trash began to loosen up and slide wholesale into the truck. He waited a moment and then worked the lever to begin the compactor and return the dumpster to its place on the ground. The compactor began with a chorus of squeals, followed by a deep crunching sound. Donnie would pick up the loose stuff after he was through with the big load.

It always took a couple minutes for the compactor to digest a load, especially one this size. From the glove compartment he took out a bag of trail mix—his breakfast—and shook a handful into his mouth. He chewed heartily, enjoying the cashews and sunflower seeds the most.

"Aw, hell," Donnie groaned as he heard the signal going off, telling him of a problem in the compactor. It could have been anything: a loss of hydraulic fluid, material stuck in the compactor blade, or even something as bad as a fire in the compactor. About this time last year he had picked up a load at the apartment complex, unaware that one of the tenants had thrown in hot ashes that set off a combustible—a can of hair spray or something—in the middle of the load. Donnie had a full-scale fire in the compactor that was on its way to spreading to the cab before he dumped the whole load in the middle of a softball field and called the fire department.

Donnie didn't think he had a fire or anything too serious here. Probably some clown had thrown a mattress or drywall in there, maybe even some stubborn cinder blocks. He had seen it all.

From deep in the compactor, he could hear the blades grinding and hydraulic system squealing from the strain. Something was definitely lodged in there. He would take a quick look before calling the dispatcher to send a mechanic. With a sigh he put on his emergency brake, threw open the door, and jumped down from the cab.

Donnie was a Department of Transportation-certified driver, but company and union rules prohibited him from touching the compactor in the event of a malfunction or jam. Still, he figured he could save himself and somebody else a lot of trouble by taking care of this alone. And, as Donnie was the first to admit, he was downright hard-headed about doing most things himself.

He took a look around to see if anyone was watching and then scrambled up the side of the truck, his steel-toed safety boots clanging on the heavy walls of the compactor. He was extra careful as he approached the top. One slip and he could be down in the jaws of the compactor before he knew what was happening. Donnie knew of at least two guys who had tried to unjam compactor blades themselves, only to lose fingers in the process. Fearful of losing their union cards, they never revealed how they lost their fingers, passing up insurance benefits to keep their cards.

Donnie was at the edge of the compactor's mouth, just about to peer over into the mess, when something gave inside, the hydraulic system eased, and the compactor blades thrashed freely again. Whatever it was, was gone now, the compactor chewing it away. Out of curiosity, he looked inside the compactor—something he never liked to do—but saw nothing more than the usual shapeless mass of congealing rags, spongy pressboard, and fetid refuse from the mall restaurants being churned by the blades

Thick steam rose from the leachate—the liquid ooze from the compacted garbage—and infiltrated Donnie's nostrils. After taking in enough of the stench, he jumped down.

If Donnie had stayed up two seconds longer, he would have seen the head of Paul Bolger pop out from the blades to the top of the pile, only to be sucked back in the compactor with the rest of the garbage.

39

The beach was empty, as I knew it would be. From where I stood at the edge of a bluff high above a narrow cove, the shoreline below was a thin, pale strip—scar tissue over an old wound. Behind the beach a hard crust of snow sealed in the rocks and soil, and ice coated the rocky slopes rising up to the bluff. A bitter, briny wind whistled in my ears. The bay out beyond the breakers was rough, water sluicing over the stooped granite in a rage of sea and rock spray.

Seagulls nesting in the breakers escaped the tidal blasts only to do battle with the violent wind. They wheeled and dived at lights flashing off the water's surface but came up empty. Seagulls.

Before starting down to the beach, I scanned the dunes behind me—bleached white in the winter sun and stretching a mile to a green line of balsam trees. No one in sight. But I really needn't have worried; nobody came to this place anymore. I tapped the brown bag I had brought with me and tucked it under my arm. I needed both hands to make my way down the steep, slippery path.

There had been steps here long ago, when people used to come to this beach. An ancient snow fence, mangled by the elements, alternately rose and disappeared in the frozen hawkweed like the spine of a sea monster sighted in a lake. I took to walking sideways to get better purchase on the icy rock. I paused a moment to adjust the Walther in my belt, its silencer beginning to dig into my hip.

There, that was better. I carried on, moving carefully.

Gusts of wind howled and ricocheted off the smooth cliffs stained orange from oxidation. They boomed through the cove and slammed into me, causing me to slip and stumble several times. I dropped the bag and its contents jumped out—kitchen scraps, old bread—and a soot-colored gull swooped down and tried to carry off a piece. I shooed it away and smiled.

"You'll get it soon," *I said to the bird.*

Last night, after Ron Lindblad had left the factory, Sid Bromley took me inside. Poor man was anxious about his TV show and needed time to tape it despite Lindblad's orders to give me shooting lessons. I could tell Bromley was uncomfortable around me. He was sweaty and nervous—a human wreck—so I told him I could get the target practice in on my own. I said I could get my aim back in no time, even with the silencer.

He seemed truly relieved when I said this. Before he left, he reminded me that the silencer was illegal and to keep it out of sight. I told him not to worry. I knew how to keep a secret. He knew what I meant.

Once I'd had time to digest the idea of using a gun, the prospect didn't seem so bad. The gun offered more speed and efficiency, things you should never take for granted in my line of work. In fact, there might even come a time when I couldn't go back to the knife. If that were so, then this morning—behind a computer shop in the Downeast Mall parking lot—would mark the last time I would use the Wüsthof.

Lindblad and Bromley wouldn't care. Actually, the less time I spent with them, the better. They had no idea how my plans were evolving, how my role as a custodian—a sanitation specialist, they call themselves now—was crystallizing, taking shape. I was emerging as a force to be reckoned with. All the skills I was developing now—the ability to move in and out of a place undetected, proficiency with the knife, the gun—were preparation for greater contributions.

Even now, as I was striking out more and more on my own, I could spread my wings only so much. My few incred-ible forays into complete freedom were short-lived, limited. was like a surgeon trained to do the most sophisticated gery but relegated to stitching superficial wounds.

I could even foresee a time when I would work independently of them, free of the shackles of schedules and others' expectations. Better to stay away from them than to give them, however innocently, the slightest clue as to what I was doing.

And perhaps most exciting of all, my plans were not limited to this two-by-four town. Garbage could be found anywhere, but nowhere in greater quantities than in big cities. What challenges waited for me! The sheer amount of the garbage combined with the anonymity of the cities made for excellent prospects. Imagine, places like Portland, Burlington, Boston, even New York. The possibilities were limitless.

I could remove garbage with tremendous force and speed in one place—perhaps eliminating ten, twenty, thirty pieces in a few nights' time—and then move on to the next city before the police could pick up my trail. I could go after the truly marginal trash—the homeless, the indigent, the prostitutes. Maybe after a while, just for fun, I could double back to a place I had just been and collect some more garbage. Who knows, maybe they would welcome me, grateful that someone was doing the important, dirty work no one else wants to do.

But for now Sparks would have to do. It was a place distinguished only by the high concentration of garbage within such a small area. I was outgrowing it, perhaps had outgrown it long ago. Just two more authorized garbage collections—two commitments to complete—and I would be done with this place. That didn't count any collections I made on my own.

Imagine: authorized collections. Who were they to tell me what and when to collect? They were nothing more than dispatchers, mere administrators. Their small-mindedness and complete lack of vision were incredible, frustrating.

I could hardly wait to be done here. Patience was not my strongest attribute. But I would have to wait at least until tonight to strike again, to make another pickup. Or perhaps two, one scheduled and the other unscheduled, done on my own initiative. A nice balance. Something Ron Lindblad h said last night, a small but telling remark, had given me the idea for the unscheduled pickup. I was happy to oblige.

I was about three-quarters of the way down the slope when I spied a fishing boat out on Penobscot Bay. I froze in my tracks. What was it doing out there now? Waves slapped it and the wind pushed it off course. I stood still and watched until it was out of sight. I wanted complete privacy for what I was about to do.

In a rush I made it to the bottom, slipping and sliding all the way. I gingerly stepped over the clotted, ice-covered seaweed and rocks treacherous with barnacles. It was a relief to reach the sand—crunchy and sure underfoot. The beach was at its widest in the middle of the cove—no more than six feet or so—and that was where I took my place.

I stood for a moment and took the wind's measure. It was high, coming in at thirty or so knots an hour. A herring gull scuttled past me on the beach, scrounging for grass shrimp, mollusks, anything, and leaving light webbed footprints on the sand behind it. The constantly shifting wind would alternately blow back and pin down its feathers.

I watched the gull as it pecked the ground and then began watching me out of the corner of its eye. For weeks the snow and ice had covered the ground and access to its natural food. The gull was hungry, waiting for me perhaps to toss something aside for it to snatch.

Not yet, not yet.

Herring gulls are notorious scavengers, scrounging waste from ships and litter on beaches. Many of them, particularly those nesting near the resorts, live off garbage and frequently harass bathers and picnickers by stealing food. I knew that gulls eat not only small prey and garbage, but also the eggs and young of other birds. Sometimes they eat their own young. I wondered if the one foraging on the beach in front of me had resorted to cannibalism, had become so desperate that it attacked its own.

Why not? I thought. Anyone is capable of anything if driven to that point. Some might resist longer, but they'll give in eventually. Extreme conditions call for extreme measures.

Another gull landed on the beach, the first one snapping

at it but too engrossed in watching me to care very much. Soon another one joined us, then another. I moved a hand toward the bag and began to draw back the opening. The gulls stood still, their eyes—tiny and black, like beads of buckshot—were locked on my hands.

With one finger I drew out a soggy potato skin and flipped it into the air. In a great flurry of beating wings and jabbing beaks, the gulls attacked the scrap, which was ripped apart several times and devoured before any of it could touch the ground. I moved another finger into the bag and, with my other hand, gripped the Walther still hidden under my coat. It was loaded with the maximum eight rounds. The gulls were circling me, more and more of them, eager for the next scrap.

In a single swift motion I threw a scrap of bread into the air with one hand and with the other drew the Walther and fired at a swooping gull. The first shot, muffled by the silencer, missed, so I snapped off another that hit its mark, the gull exploding in a burst of blood and feathers. The other birds pulled away, screaming and chattering. I noticed that a gull, a large white one, had captured the piece of bread.

The flock sensed danger, but their fear competed with their ravenous hunger. I threw up another scrap and the hunger won out, two dozen seagulls diving toward me. I laughed and took aim at a brown and white gull off to the side of the flock. The shot sawed off one of the bird's wings, sending it tumbling end over end into the sea.

I scattered a handful of garbage over the beach, but the gulls hovered overhead, cautiously waiting and dipping into the fierce wind. Finally one of the more daring ones dived for the treasure, and I peeled off several shots, hitting it twice, three times, before its remains splattered on the beach. With a quick stab, another gull seized one of the dismembered gull's webbed feet rolling on the sand and gobbled it down.

I knew I had two more shots before the clip was empty. I looked around for that large white gull, the biggest in the flock. There it was, hovering about ten yards out over the water. Between the gale-force wind and the silencer that weakened the power of the gun, I knew I would have to draw the gull in closer to get a good shot. But the gulls were now reluctant to come closer, circling the shore, confused by the death of their kind all around them and their ferocious hunger.

I reached in the sack and grabbed a handful of the garbage and then slung it out along the shoreline. The gulls started forward, but I was watching for that big white one. I saw it hanging back as the other gulls plundered the shore, its pure, brilliant white feathers shining in the sun, its massive wings riding out the wind. I wanted it. I wanted it dead.

I held the Walther loose by my side and waited. I knew I could get it, even on the fly. I had learned to shoot at a young age, first using the gun I forced away from my stepbrother. Rifle, pistol, I had used them all. I was ready.

In a blur of pounding wings the white gull rushed toward the beach, diving at the few scraps left.

“Careful,” *I told myself,* “careful. Wait.”

There. Now.

I bent my knees, raised the Walther with both hands, and fired straight at its head. But the gull dipped at the last possible moment and the shot sailed just under its beak, splashing down thirty yards beyond into the bay.

Okay, okay. Still a chance for another shot. This time I took aim at its midsection, squinting into the sun. There it was. I had it in my sights. I had it.

My arms straight, eyes razor sharp, I sucked in a deep breath and fired. The shot seemed to take a long time to make its way to the gull. Clouds crawled across the sky. The sun sank inches. The bullet was headed dead into the gull's chest when out of nowhere another gull, a mottled one, flew in front, breaking the shot's trajectory and taking the round in the neck. A string of blood flew from its mouth and it spun out, crashing into the churning waves.

I watched as the white gull pulled up, turned its head toward me defiantly, and glided out over Penobscot Bay.

40

That evening David was at the head of a long line of forest dwellers who were bringing food and supplies from his truck back to their village. Most of them, David included, bore their loads on their heads. Immediately behind him, Nara looked every bit the Third World mother, nestling Von on her hip with one hand and a package of disposable diapers on the other. Small children followed alongside, chirping with excitement.

The forest was growing dark, and a cold front was moving in. David felt as if he were leading some sort of ancient procession, like that of a Dionysian wheat cult. Or a Nabatean caravan plying its way through an oasis along the Euphrates. Or a Cro-Magnon hunting party returning with the kill.

Nara and he had spent the better part of the day cleaning out their house of things they couldn't take with them on their trip to New Brunswick. The forest dwellers had great need for baby items, winter clothes, blankets and medicine. David and Nara took care of those and a lot more. After packing out their own considerable supplies for the forest dwellers, they began buying up the Sparks general store before moving on to the grocery store near the mall.

The group came upon the line of trees that sheltered the village. Moe broke ranks and ran ahead with his load of thermal blankets. David heard Nara's gasp as the sprawling tangle of huts and lean-to's came into view. They slowly made their way down the slope leading to the village.

David first spotted Moe stoking a large bonfire in a clearing. The few villagers who had not accompanied the supp party were beginning to gather there, and David waved at the man who had served him coffee that morning: Murat Bey. David took a bag from Laszlo's pack and handed it to Murat Bey, who beamed when he looked inside and found copies of the last three months of *Millyet* newspapers from Turkey, and copies of every other Turkish newspaper and magazine David could get on a chartered plane from New York earlier today.

Then a figure materialized from the shadows at the edge of the fire, making David's blood run cold. David's eyes moved over the canary baseball cap, clownish oversized coat, and multiple layers of clothing. Moe came toward David, took his hand, and led him over toward the fire. Nara watched it all, not understanding.

"David McAdam," Moe said, taking David's hand and pulling him gently toward the ghost, "I want to introduce Tien-yu Chang—T.Y., for short."

David brought his trembling hand up to shake T.Y.'s, which was disconcertingly solid and real.

"Pleased to meet you," David said hoarsely.

As the fire popped and crackled, sending sparks into the cold night sky, David and Nara snuggled under a thermal blanket with a sleeping Von and listened to the forest dwellers' stories of coming to the United States. They each had their own tales—roller-coaster rides of pain, exhilaration, and, finally, fearful frustration—as they made their way over one obstacle after another until arriving in Sparks.

Moe's father, Rajinder, who called himself Roger, told about the "snake," a labyrinth of smugglers, agents, and other petty criminals who, for a price, had accompanied the illegals through the various stages of their journey.

"I was an industrial engineer in New Delhi," Roger said quietly, his voice barely audible above the fire, "running a big semiconductor factory, but was not part of the company's 'master plan.' We are Sikhs and you never know sometimes if there's room for us in any master plan. But I knew they would eventually sack me for whatever reason, so Piara, my wife, and I agreed that our only hope for our kids' future was to come to America. We tried to get work visas through professional associates and family friends, but nothing panned out. Apparently you have too many industrial engineers here already.

"So, we have to make some big decisions. We sold our flat and Piara's jewelry, withdrew all our money from the bank, and agreed to pay some chaps we met who said they could get us all to America. Their fee was very dear, and it took just about everything we had to engage them.

"We began a long, difficult trip with Mohan and his sisters—they're sleeping now. We went by rail to the Indian–Burmese border and then stowed away in the back of a truck that took us all the way to Rangoon. We stayed in a house there, very dirty, for several weeks and were taken by car, rail, foot, and finally small aircraft over the border into Thailand. We stayed in Bangkok for months, rotting in an old abandoned slaughterhouse with Chinese, Vietnamese, Laotians, everybody. One day the slaughterhouse was raided by police and we slipped out. I'm still not sure if they were really police or if the whole thing was staged by the snake heads."

Shadows moved out beyond the fire. David kept his eyes on them until he recognized the outlines of Moe, Pia, and Laszlo slinking into the shantytown. What're they up to? David wondered. He was tempted to follow them, but Roger Singh's voice pulled him back.

"Anyway," he went on, "we wandered the streets of Bangkok, nearly penniless, hungry, the children sick. Then we heard about another snake, one that cost nothing but required a promise to work for seven years for a company in America. Well, we were desperate and this sounded too good to be true.

"The men running this snake were different from others we had seen before. These were very hard men, gangsters. I saw one of them actually shoot a man in the head because he would not give him a ring he was wearing. They took us through the jungles of Thailand until we reached water. A boat was there, waiting for us, and it took us to another boat, which took us to another, and we sailed for what seemed like weeks until someone told us we were in Mexico. It was late at night. We were herded into lorries with false bottoms and hidden there for two days, hot as hell, as the lorry passed over the border and headed east. I didn't know this until later; at the time I had no idea where we were.

"We had to change lorries for the last leg of the trip, and I remember my first glimpse of America was of an old petrol station in Texas, I think, that actually had a machine selling birth-control devices in the bathroom. Amazing, I thought to myself, and I remember chattering about it with Piara all the way through the country. We arrived here approximately eleven months and nineteen days since leaving India.

"We had no idea that the worst part of the trip was still before us. The men operating the snake from this end were very tough and wouldn't hesitate to beat you if they thought you might mean trouble for them. They told us that we would be separated for a while, that Piara and the girls would be sent to train in quilt making for a couple weeks and Moe and I would stay in Sparks to make furniture. Okay, I thought, we can live with that.

"That was until I met other people in the furniture shop who told me they hadn't seen their families in over a year. They had no idea where they were or when they would be released. They lived and worked in constant fear, worried that if they did something wrong, their families would suffer.

"Moe and I decided that we could not go on like this. Stupidly, I asked one of the guards when I would see my wife and children again, and he beat me senseless. I still have a numbness in my left arm. So, Moe and I joined with T.Y., who was breaking out to see his wife, who had been in a tin-punching center for almost a year.

"We escaped from our minibus one morning while the driver was using the loo in our house. He forgot to lock the bus door. We ran and ran, first to the tin-punching center, where a woman there told T.Y. that his wife had died six months earlier. We took T.Y. with us to the quilt-making place, where they let the women take unsupervised breaks outside. During one of their breaks we snuck out of the woods and spotted Piara and the girls, grabbed their arms while they were sitting, and led them away until we found others like us hiding out in the woods. We formed this little community and do what we can to help others escape.

"Roman Grabaukus sitting over there," he said, nodding toward a man whose tinted glasses could not hide the dark circles under his eyes, "was a Communist Party functionary in Lithuania and had to run away or be imprisoned or shot, so he and his son hid in trains bound for the Ukraine and hopped aboard a freighter in Odessa. He says that a Country Customs boat picked them up off the Rhode Island coast and brought them straight here.

"The de la Cruz family came through the snake over the Rio Grande one night where a Country Customs lorry was waiting for them. They say that some immigrants were helping the Country Customs people, doing the driving and standing guard.

"And then there is T.Y. He was the first of us here, having left China after lying in front of the tanks in Tiananmen Square. He was a foreign language professor at Beijing University, and traveled with his wife by foot through Honduras, Guatemala, and then Mexico, where his Country Customs coyote slipped him through the border patrol and into America. Tonight is a big occasion for him, the beginning of the Chinese New Year."

T.Y., eating something from a plate, nodded at David. "It's the year of the dog," he said, smiling. "Lucky year for me."

David looked covetously at the food, a pile of barbecue, until T.Y. offered him some. "This is great," David said, stuffing his face. "What is it?"

"Armadillo," T.Y. said, and David almost gagged. "It's my New Year feast. I've been trying to get it fat for a couple of months now. Would have had more if other one hadn't gotten away."

David looked at him. "You wouldn't happen to own a rooster too?"

"Or an alligator?" Nara said.

T.Y. nodded his head happily. "You seen them, huh?"

"A few weeks ago, the Tran family celebrated Tet," Roger said. "And in April is our big festival—the first of Baisakh, commemorating the birth of Khalsa, the holy fraternity of the Sikhs, almost three hundred years ago. Seems like every week we have a major holiday around here."

David nodded, trying to take it all in, and recalled something Ron Lindblad had said: "I sure could use some cash." Obviously, Ron had a huge operation to finance before the profits would start coming in from the work of all these unpaid workers.

"There's enough material here for a year of magazine stories," Nara said to David. "What was it like for you in the Country Customs sweatshops?" she said to Roger and Piara and pulling a notebook out of her bag.

David felt a tug on his arm. It was Moe, who wanted David to follow him. With Pia and Laszlo tagging along, they slipped away to Moe's "office"—the A-frame with the computer.

"I should have known this was yours," David said to Moe. "So this is where you hacked into my system."

The three cyberpunks laughed together. "How did you get all this stuff?" David asked. "I mean, how could you afford it?"

Moe shrugged, as if he never had given much thought to the question. "Picking blueberries, working at car washes, collecting returnable bottles," he said. "Anything that comes along and doesn't require a Social Security number, even though I've assigned each of us one in case we need it."

"You *assigned* it?" David said, incredulous.

"Yeah," Moe said, waving his hand dismissively at the triteness of the whole matter. "Look, I want to show you something." He pulled back an old castoff carpet to reveal an even older chest, which he opened and carefully withdrew a hand-sized instrument. David studied the instrument, realizing he had seen one twice before.

"This," Moe said, pointing the instrument at David, "is a Gauss meter, named after Karl Gauss, the nineteenth-century German mathematician. It measures magnetic flux density, the intensity of electromagnetic fields."

"Yeah," David said sourly, "they seem to be popular items in Sparks lately."

"Pudden?"

"Nothing. What were you going to show me?"

"Let's step outside."

Moe left the door to his hut open and pushed a button on the Gauss meter. As he did so, a dial on the instrument swung sharply to the left. "See that?" he said and held it out to Pia, who took a reading.

"Seventy four point eight hertz," she announced. "Up about one unit since this morning."

"Tsk, tsk," Moe said, concerned. "The usual exposure level from power-transmission lines is fifty to sixty hertz. We're high around here. Very high. Unfortunately, I don't have baseline data, having just started taking these measurements in the past five weeks."

"So, you're saying the power lines, those new ones out on the highway, are responsible for these readings?" David said.

"Oh, certainly," Pia said. "We've taken readings all over this area. The closer we get to the power lines, and to that new power station, the higher the readings."

David thought this through, remembering his trip to the doctor's with Von, the increase in illness—especially among children—in Sparks. He thought about his son's and his own ill health. Could electrical energy be the cause? Was that even possible? And if it was, who could be behind it all? Who could be so utterly malicious?

"Ron Lindblad," Moe said, reading David's mind. "Remember, David, you saw on the computer that he's the chairman of the local electrical utility board."

"But why would he do this? What does he have to gain?"

"We've talked about that," Laszlo said, "many times.

We always come to same conclusion: he need power for sweatshops. And he want to make place unbearable, to push up electromagnetic field above even sixty hertz level so no one can stand it anymore."

"Yeah," David said skeptically, "but that EMF business is pretty shaky. No one's conclusively proved a link between cancer and exposure to extremely low-frequency fields."

"The literature is pretty grim on the subject," Moe said quietly. "Studies have linked ELF field exposure to leukemia, pineal gland dysfunction, breast cancer, abnormal fetal development. The jury's still out on the subject.

"But think about it, David. The basis of the physical world, including our bodies, is electrical. We evolved from electrical energy. It zapped the great primordial chemical soup, creating amino acids—the building blocks of life—and nearly a billion years later our ancestors crawled out of the tidal pools. How can prolonged exposure to these fields *not* affect us? Didn't you tell me you and your family felt better once you were out of Sparks and on your island?"

"Okay," David said, "even if ELF fields are that bad and Lindblad is upping them around here to drive everyone out, what's he hope to gain? A two-by-four town? Why not just kill everyone off and be done with—" David stopped when he realized that that could be exactly what was going on.

"Yes, he seems to want everyone out," Moe said. "That is, everyone but his slaves. Where would they go anyway?"

"He must be paying everyone off," David said. "The police, the electrical people."

"What do we do?" Pia asked him.

"We're going in there," David said. "I am, anyway."

"Where?" all three of them said at once.

"Country Customs."

"What for?" Moe said. "We got into their computer system, but that gave us nothing."

"I don't know," David said, rubbing the scar on his chin,

"but there might be something—paper files—anything we can use."

"We'll help you," Moe said, making a fist. "You'll never cover that place by yourself, it's too big. And we have a stake in this."

David frowned at Moe, knowing he was right but wishing he wasn't. "We'll see," he said solemnly.

"When do we go?" Laszlo piped up, getting excited.

"Tonight," David answered. "But first there're a couple of things I need to get." He looked up the winding main street of the shantytown, past the fragile houses, to the campfire, which was now burning down. "Remember, not a word of this to anyone."

"Right," Moe said. Suddenly the light in his hut, and the lights all over the village, began to flicker and grow dimmer. Moe ducked in the hut to switch off the light. In the distance they heard what sounded like a siren.

"Another brownout," Pia said. "The power around here is crazy, just like in Addis Ababa."

"Why the siren?" David asked.

"Car alarm," Moe answered. "EMF fluctuations can set them off."

Something occurred to David. "Hey, answer me this question," he said. "How do you get electricity way back in here? Through the forest, I mean."

Laszlo snickered into his hand, and Pia shot him a disapproving look. Moe cast his eyes down at his shoes. "I know how to get into the lines," Moe mumbled. "We just pulled some power in here."

David laughed heartily, appreciating the prank. "So, who's the asshole whose power you're ripping off?"

"You are," Moe said innocently.

41

A few miles from the forest dwellers' village, along the dark edge of Penobscot Bay, K. K. Thorner finally settled down after a long night with her daughter. She rewound the videotape of *All My Children* she had recorded that day, wondering, as she had for the past nine years she'd been watching the show, who the "my" was in *All My Children*. It could have been Mona Kane, Ericka's mother, poor woman, or Ruth Martin, or Phoebe Wallingford, still stuck with the professor. God, K. K. thought, if she had children who turned out like the people on that show, she'd have been dead of a heart attack years ago.

As the tape rewound, K. K. dropped down on the couch with her marketing textbook, the script of *Mother Courage,* and the telephone book for Fort Myers and vicinity. Ray had made some noises about coming over tonight, but K. K. wasn't holding her breath.

Viveca had been crying ever since K. K. picked her up earlier that evening. Her teachers at day-care said she'd been moody and aggressive all day, completely out of character.

"Are there any problems at home?" one of them asked K. K., who just about laughed in the woman's face.

No problems here, K. K. thought to herself. Just your average white trash single mother with a joke of a job, an at-best questionable future, and a boyfriend about as dependable as Maine weather. On top of all that, Estelle Grout—one of the few good things in Viveca's life—suddenly disappears without a trace.

Thinking about Estelle, K. K. put aside her textbook and

script and began to thumb through the phone book liberated from the reference room at the university library. As she did so, she trained her memory on Estelle, recalling conversations with her, snippets of dialogue, details. K. K. focused on a conversation of a few weeks ago in which Estelle had talked about her sister, mentioning her by name. Estelle also had mentioned the name of the town in which her sister lived.

What had Estelle said? She was thinking of visiting her sister, and would K. K. and Viveca mind if she disappeared for a few days? "Disappeared," that was the word she used. What if Estelle just decided on a whim to visit her sister, tried to call K. K. and couldn't find her, or just forgot to tell her? Hope bubbled up in K. K., and she concentrated hard on reconstructing that conversation.

The tide was going out and the waves churned beneath the old lobster house. A chill seemed to pass through the house, and K. K. drew the two blankets on her lap up to her neck. What was the name of the town? Bonita something.

K. K. flipped to the front of the phone book, to the part that listed towns with their exchanges. She found listings for three communities with Bonita in their names: Bonita Beach, Bonita Shores, and Bonita Springs. Bonita Shores, K. K. thought, that's the one. She wrote down its three-number exchange.

K. K. closed her eyes and let the memories fill her head. Estelle had been in her pantry, putting away flour and other ingredients for the home-made sculptor's clay that Viveca loved to play with. Estelle had been telling K. K. a story about her sister, how they used to play piano together as girls, even performing duets at recitals. Estelle's sister used to practice long hours on the piano, but Estelle was too busy chasing boys, or so she said. As a result, her sister became too fast on the keyboard for Estelle, and they eventually had to break up the duet.

Estelle said her sister still played piano at her retirement home. K. K. flipped to the yellow pages and found the listings for retirement homes in Bonita Shores. There were four of them.

But the name. What was the sister's name? K. K. bore down, her eyes shut tight. The *name,* she commanded herself, what is the name?

Estelle had mentioned the name once, K. K. remembered. There was something special about it. What was it? K. K. pressed her eyes with her fingers. The name was from a song, the first song the girls had played together as a duet. K. K. recalled that at the time of the conversation, she had noted how similar the name was to Estelle's and wondered why some parents gave their children rhyming or alliterative names.

Alliterative, that was what was similar. K. K. concentrated on names beginning with *E,* and they came rushing into her head in a jumble.

"Slow it down," she told herself, "get it organized." In reverse alphabetical order, beginning, appropriately enough, with Eve, K. K. slowly whispered: "Eve . . . Ethel . . . Esther . . . Ericka . . . Emily . . . Elaine . . . Ellen . . . Elise."

Elise. That was it! And the song was . . . "For Elise" by Beethoven.

"Yes," she said, pumping her arm. She jumped up from the couch, forgetting the cold, and dashed to the phone with the directory. She began to call the first retirement home on the list, but stopped herself. What time was it anyway? It was almost eleven. What the hell, K. K. thought, a call late at night might bring better results anyway.

As K. K. dialed the number, she was unaware of the dark eyes peering in through the window. A slight crack in the curtains provided a limited view into the house. K. K. was visible for a brief second as she paced, waiting for someone to pick up.

A second was all I needed to know she was alone.

I swung around the house in a crouch, sizing up the place and looking for an opening. The old pine wharf creaked lightly. It was a small house, not much room to maneuver in. On the other hand, it presented certain advantages: it was off by itself—at least one hundred yards from the next house—and the churning of the ocean would drown out just about any sound, including screams. And my truck could get right up here.

I had learned an important lesson at the Haslems'. With people already inside a house, things had to be done differently. There was no way to simply break in, find a hiding place, and wait for an opening to strike. Timing and speed were more important than patience. One had to come in fast and move aggressively, precisely, if possible.

For those reasons it was good to have the gun along. Perhaps it would be necessary for this one. It was tucked in the front of my pants, loaded, next to the Wüsthof.

At the rear of the house, I found a storm door leading to what looked like a small storage cuddy off the kitchen. I checked the door. It was only a sheet of glass surrounded by a steel frame with a pneumatic closer and one of those cheap latch locks. No dead bolt, chain fastener, or even a hook and eye to slow things down.

With the tide going out, I decided that now was as good a time as any to go in. Taking the handle of the latch lock firmly in hand, I gave it a short, hard twist. The door opened easily. The next part was getting into the main house.

As I examined the door to the house, I had to keep myself from laughing out loud. The lock was nothing more than the kind found on any interior door. A simple push-button lock. Kids open them with credit cards. I needed only the Wüsthof, which slid readily from its case. In minutes it would all be over.

Crouching next to the interior door, I could hear K. K. Thorner's voice, speaking into the telephone. Mr. Lindblad had said that she had been calling the police, asking questions and causing trouble. Maybe she was talking to the police now. Best to wait until she hung up. When she did, I would strike, using the gun with silencer. One shot at the head. And then the little girl.

I was ready to collect the garbage.

* * *

Inside the house, on the phone with the night shift concierge at the retirement home, K. K. counted slowly to ten one more time. "I don't know the last name," she said, restraining her anger, "that's what I've been trying to tell you. All I have is the first name and the maiden name. Don't you have a file or a computer or something? Yes, I'll wait."

A minute later, the tired, bored voice came back on. K. K. couldn't tell if it was a man or woman. "All's I show in the directory is an Ellie G. Townshend," the voice droned. "Nothing else."

"That could be her," K. K. said excitedly, "can you connect me?"

"It's awfully late," the voice said.

"It's an emergency," K. K. said. "A matter of life or death."

"Mmm, are you family?"

That question again. "Yes," she said with as much righteous indignation as she could muster.

A long pause. "If you're family, how come you don't know the last name?"

"It's my husband's family," K. K. insisted. "He's—he's been in a car wreck, a really terrible one, and I'm supposed to call all the relatives to give them a chance to come up here before he passes." K. K. was cooking now, getting into the vernacular. "Ellie is his favorite aunt and he's her favorite nephew. But I've never met her."

Another pause. "Okay, seeing how's you're family." The line went dead and K. K. thought, shit, she lost the connection. And then a voice came on: old, tired, but sweet. K. K. was certain it was Elise.

"Is this Ms. Ellie Townshend?" K. K. said.

"It's *Mrs.* Townshend. Who is this?"

"Ma'am, my name is K. K. Thorner and I'm calling from Sparks, Maine. I know it's late, but I—"

"It's Estelle, is she all right? You know, I've been trying to reach her for days."

"You have? Then she's not with you?"

"Certainly not. What did you say your name was?"

K. K. felt her heart sink. "When did you last speak with her, Mrs. Townshend?"

"Oh, dear, it must've been two weeks ago. We talk every Sunday. It was Estelle's turn to call last weekend, and I didn't hear from her. So I called her but got one of those messages, the one that said her phone had been disconnected."

Disconnected, K. K. thought. She hadn't realize she had said it aloud.

"What was that?" Ellie said.

"Mrs. Townshend, did Estelle say anything to you about selling her house and moving down with you?"

"For heaven's sake, no. That is, nothing that meant anything by it. We talked about it now and again, but Estelle was quite happy where she was. I think she would never leave Maine. She just loves it there too much."

K. K. was pacing hard now, thinking.

"You know," Ellie said, "I did call someone up there, a sheriff in Rockland. Can't remember his name at the moment. What did you say *your* name was again?"

"Thorner, K. K. Thorner."

"Are you the one with the little girl?"

"Yes, ma'am."

"Estelle loves that child. She's the granddaughter she never had."

"I know," K. K. mumbled, a pain stabbing in her chest. "What did the sheriff tell you?"

"He told me not to worry, that he'd look into it. That was last Monday."

"He hasn't called you back?"

"Not that I know of."

"Shit," K. K. whispered.

"What was that?" Ellie said.

"Nothing," K. K. said, embarrassed. "Listen, I'm going to visit that sheriff and call you back tomorrow. Okay?"

"That's fine, dear. But I'm sure that it's nothing more than a—"

K. K.'s head jerked away from the phone as the lights in the house flickered wildly. Then an alarm went off in her neighbor's truck, an obnoxious high-pitched squeal that echoed over the water, audible for miles. The smoke detector on the kitchen ceiling began to buzz noisily just after K. K. heard another sound, something thumping at the back of the house. When the hell is this? she wondered.

"I've got to go," she said into the phone. "Call you back."

In three steps she was in the kitchen cuddy, where she found the storm door flapping in the bitter night wind. The smoke detector stopped as suddenly as it had begun. Another brownout, she realized.

K. K. looked through the door and into the dark night. "I'm going to have to get that door fixed," she said to no one at all.

42

"It's easy," David was saying to Moe, Pia, and Laszlo, who were squeezed into the cab of his truck. They were parked in the shadows stretching from the back of the Country Customs plant. Other than an occasional guard who strolled by on the plant grounds, the place was deserted.

The four of them were transfixed by the screen of the sub-notebook computer on Pia's lap. The computer was powered by a small portable power pack that was plugged into the cigarette lighter on the dashboard.

"Laszlo," David said, "reach under the seat there and give me the cellular phone, will you? Thanks. Now, what we're going to do is get into Country Customs' system by way of Sid Bromley's computer, which we know is linked into the company. Let me just call his number here," which David did with great difficulty, Moe mashed up against him.

He placed the phone onto the portable modem attached to the sub-notebpook. "There," he said. "We're in. Now, we run this little program here and, *voilà,* welcome to the dirty little world of Country Customs."

Pia and Laszlo oohed and aahed at the sudden rush of data onto the little screen. Moe was quiet, having seen it all before.

David spoke as he ran through the command protocol of the Country Customs database. "Okay, like I said, it's real easy. Let's call up the physical plant directory and, there, now we go into the power grid. I found out by studying the system that the Country Customs plant is a fully computerized facility—they call them intelligent buildings—in which the heat, air conditioning, and power are controlled electronically."

"Def," Laszlo said.

"If you liked *that,* just wait." The cyberpunks watched carefully as David entered a series of commands on the miniaturized keyboard. "I just stumbled onto this last night when I was poking around in the system. Country Customs has a direct link to the local power supply—a Windows-operated system from which they can control the amount of power flowing from the substation out on the highway, gauging the power to the individual needs of the company. If Ron Lindblad wants to up his power to meet a deadline, all he has to do is do it. Isn't that wild? So what we're going to do—"

"Is shut down the company's power so we can get into the building," Pia finished for him.

"Precisely," said David.

"Def," Laszlo said.

"And they'll just think it's another brownout, like the one we had earlier," Moe said and looked up admiringly at his hero.

"Exactly," David said. "So, are we ready?"

"Who's going in?" Moe asked.

"Mmmm, someone needs to stay here with the computer, to make sure no one in the company overrides our commands when we need to get out." David looked at Moe. "Can you do it? You know the system better than Pia and Laszlo."

Moe cast his eyes down and said stoically, "Fine." It was clear to everyone in the truck that he wanted to go inside.

David passed out wire clippers to Pia and Laszlo. "Let's go," he said, and then quietly swung open the truck door.

David was staring at the luminous dial of his digital watch, flat on his belly on the cold ground at the edge of Country Customs' fence. In about fifteen seconds Moe would kill the electrical power in Country Customs, at which point David, Pia, and Laszlo would dash in through a side door.

"Remember," David whispered to the others, lying on either side of him, "the power will come back up in two minutes. By then we have to be through the fence and in the building. Then we'll have twenty minutes of low power to go through the building. Got your maps?"

"Yes," Pia and Laszlo whispered.

The lights around the building suddenly went out, and dogs began to bark near the guard posts. The three drew out their wire clippers and went to work on the fence. They made three small holes, through which they wriggled and then bolted across the lawn and to the building. David held his breath as he was about to open the door, praying it was unlocked.

Swinging open the door, he whispered, "Good job," to Moe, who could not hear him. Inside, they waited until their eyes adjusted to darkness. With David in the lead, they slunk along the wall toward an intersection in the corridor where they would split up.

They found the intersection and the lights came blazing back on, blinding them even at low power. David blinked back incandescent afterimages swimming across his field of vision.

"Wow," Laszlo said, rubbing his eyes, "that was intense."

"Everybody okay?" David asked, able to see again. Pia and Laszlo nodded their heads. "All right. I programmed the computer to keep the cameras from working. You won't see any guards, they stay outside and at the front security console.

"Remember, you're looking for file rooms, storage closets, any place where we might find evidence on paper. If you find something, we can always come back again for it. We meet back here no later than 9:50—that's twenty-one minutes from now. Don't be late and be careful."

As David jogged down his appointed hallway, he glanced over his shoulder as Laszlo and Pia disappeared into the bowels of the building. A chill went down his spine at the thought that he might never see them again.

* * *

After he had wandered fifteen long minutes through the maze of corridors and rooms in Country Customs' ground floor, exhaustion began to catch up with David. He realized that he hadn't slept for almost forty-eight hours. As best as he could determine from the map, he had done almost a complete circle around the building, and he still hadn't found a thing, not a scrap of evidence. He'd seen storage rooms for just about everything Country Customs sold: furniture, dried flower wreaths, candles, Christmas ornaments, knickknacks. He had peeked in a few offices, scanning desks and checking out the custom-made computer hardware.

He also had seen assembly rooms, cavernous halls crowded with engines and generators with no light and barely any room for Ron Lindblad's slaves to stand. No wonder Lindblad needed so much electricity, David thought. Something was definitely wrong here: Country Customs' products were supposed to be hand-made.

According to the map, David was just a corridor away from the door through which the three of them had come in. He decided to set an example and be the first to return. Rounding a corner into the last hallway, he heard a familiar sound coming from behind a door. Putting his ear to the door, he realized what it was: the beep of a mainframe storing data.

It was a computer room, maybe the one Sid was going to show David when he was last here. David studied the digital lock on the door and then remembered that Moe had disabled all electronic locks in the building. He pushed open the door and entered.

"Good Lord," David muttered as he took in the vast expanse of the computer room, reminding him of an operations center at AT&T. A single custom-built console for operating the mainframe swept across the room. Orange and yellow light winked in the darkness. The beeps were loud now. David flipped on a switch and the room was showered in harsh fluorescent light.

This was the guts, the nerve center, of Country Customs'

system, the same system that he had broken into and Moe was manipulating out in the truck.

"Shit," he muttered and checked his watch. He had one minute to get back before the electricity would go out. He quickly scoured the room, checking drawers and filing cabinets for printouts. In a closet, usually locked by electronic control, he found something that struck him as odd: an old PanTech model, nothing like the high-end hardware David had been seeing all over the place. What would this be doing here?

And then an image came into his head, of a yellow box floating in darkness. Zooming into the box, he saw the blue screen of a computer monitor. A PanTech computer, an old 286 David himself had designed years ago, lifetimes ago. The yellow box was the Haslems' window at night.

And he knew: this was it. Doug Haslem's computer.

David quickly pulled out jacks from the central processing unit. All he needed was that CPU's hard disk. The monitor and printer could stay behind. As soon as he pulled the last plug, the lights went out. Moe killed the power right on schedule.

David lifted the CPU, a heavy old thing, and began to head for the door. He cursed as he became entangled in a web of wires and cables and kicked them away. The hallways were completely dark, and he had feel his way along the wall, hoping he was stumbling in the right direction. Seconds ticked by until he ran head-first into someone in the darkness, almost scaring the water out of him.

"Who's there?" he said.

"David?" It was Pia. "Where've you been?"

"I found something. But let's get out of here. Where's Laszlo?"

"Over here," came a voice from a far corner of the corridor.

"We don't have much time," David said, breaking for the door. They all ran into each other in the darkness, and David barely saved the CPU from crashing to the floor.

"Pia, you go first, then Laszlo," David said. He heard feet shuffling ahead of him as Pia and Laszlo moved alon the wall. The door swung open and David caught a glimpse of them going through, and then the door slammed shut.

Struggling to keep a firm hold on the CPU, David worked his way to the door and tried to push it open. But it was jammed somehow. He checked his watch, which glowed in the dark. He had less than thirty seconds before the lights came on again.

Finally, the door gave just as light flooded the sides of the building. Pia and Laszlo were nowhere in sight. David made his way in the shadows along the walls toward the holes in the fence. Strange, he thought as he began to crawl through the fence on his belly, the CPU cradled in his arms. Why were no guards around?

Having made it through, David was relieved to see the truck still parked in the shadows, with Moe in the cab. But Pia and Laszlo were nowhere in sight. David climbed in the driver's side and said anxiously, "Where're the others?"

But Moe was too absorbed with something on the sub-notebook to answer. "This is great," he said, using the computer's keyboard mouse to guide an arrow around the multicolored window screens. "I've been going through the design for the electrical substation, that sub-file of Country Customs' system. Did you know that this one substation distributes enough power to light up a small city?"

"Moe, look at me," David said. Moe's head shot up immediately. "Have you seen Pia or Laszlo?"

"I thought they were with you," Moe said.

"They went on ahead of me. Didn't you see them?"

"I haven't seen anyone," Moe said. "What is that?" he asked, pointing at the CPU in David's hands.

David thumped the machine on Moe's lap. "I'll explain later," he said and released the brake, letting the truck roll a few yards before starting it up and heading off into the darkness.

43

Garbage. It's all around us, haunting us like ghosts and revealing our true selves like a taped confession. Garbage is as human as sin and almost as plentiful. Why, we produce more garbage than corn in this country. Much of what we know about our forebears was revealed to us through their garbage. No doubt our great legacy to the future will be our own waste. It is ironic that no matter what it is—our trash, our leftovers, our own excrement—we want our waste out of sight immediately.

The reason we want it gone so quickly is that it reminds us of our own mortality. Oh, we might say that it is unhygienic to keep garbage around, that it will offend us with its smell if we don't remove it quickly. But the real reason—lurking just below the surface of our consciousness—is that we ourselves are no more than garbage, walking symbols of death. Take a look at someone and what do you see? Probably the first thing is skin, the top, visible layers of which is dead matter. You won't find living, reproducing tissue until you dig down several layers more. What else is there? Hair, fingernails, toenails—things so many of us work hard to adorn—are also dead tissue, garbage.

They're doing amazing things with garbage these days. Even if you leave out recycling, trash has spawned an industry unto itself. All over the country—the world, really—people are finding constructive ways to use their waste.

The other day I was reading about a company in California that uses trash to generate energy. Just one plant converts enough energy from garbage to heat a school district. And those Germans, they use processed garbage as construction material. They just fill up building blocks with garbage and then seal them tight. Trash is a great insulator, they found.

I have also heard about landscapers and developers who use landfill garbage in their work. One enterprising developer in Florida built a golf course over an enormous landfill. Somewhere else, another piled the garbage up high, covered it with plastic and dirt, and made a ski slope. Imagine, skiing down a mountain of trash! Someday someone will come up with a creative use for those enormous landfills we call cemeteries.

I was trying myself to come up with some uses for the garbage I was creating. They say the human body is worth no more than a dollar or so in chemicals, so that use was out. There was always the food industry—fast food seemed promising—or pet food. Then there was medical potential: cadavers for study or organs for transplantation. But the risks were too great, and I didn't need to be dealing with any more people than I had to now.

Besides, right now I needed to concentrate on the task at hand. The woman was moving around in her house, I had been watching her for some time. She didn't appear tired, even at this late hour. I had found a way into the house and I was ready to go in after her. I was resigned to using the gun.

The back door was nothing, a cobweb I only had to poke my hand through. The floors were a mix of hardwood and carpeting. I stayed on the rugs that muffled the sound of my footsteps. The woman was in the dining room, at the table with her back to me. I would get as close as I could without disturbing her.

Approaching the dining room, I passed a wall mirror. I looked at myself, well covered in my parka and black ski mask. But there was no one around to see me except for someone who would be dead very soon.

I went through the house quickly, silently. And there she was, directly in the line of fire, hunched over writing at the dining room table. She couldn't have given me an easier shot.

I drew out the pistol with silencer and leveled it at her, using the two-handed grip, a slight bend in my knees. I squeezed the trigger and the bullet spat from the muzzle and hit her hard at the base of the neck. Her head landed on the table with a sharp crack.

I stood a moment in the position, ready for another shot. But it wasn't necessary. That was the end of her.

I returned the gun to my belt and slipped through the house back to the rear door. The night air felt strong and bracing as I stepped outside.

I thought: this killing should make them happy. A bonus. Wasn't that what they had given me? I was just giving them one back. No need to trouble them, I would call the cleaning people myself and have them come over.

And I thought: that gun wasn't so bad after all.

44

Back at home after a wild ride through the night, David quietly brought the central processing unit he had taken from Country Customs through the front door so as not to wake Nara and Von. He had just dropped off Moe up the road near his village, asking him to keep an eye out for Pia and Laszlo. Moe shook his head dismissively and told David that Pia and Laszlo knew the woods like the back of their hand and that there was nothing to worry about.

Inside, David checked in on Nara and Von, asleep in bed together, and padded back downstairs. He started a pot of Kona in the kitchen and then went into the living room to work on the CPU, plugging a monitor into it and running a quick diagnostic. Everything looked fine. He took in a breath and booted it up.

Well, he thought, not much to see here: your basic DOS software. An old version of Word Perfect, Lotus, a couple of pedestrian games, and a personal financial-management package. David wasn't sure what he'd been expecting, perhaps blood to ooze off the screen.

He went first into Word Perfect, just to confirm that this was Haslem's computer. David found a letter, dated last October, in which Douglas Haslem had accepted Ron Lindblad's offer to join the Country Customs family. Big mistake there, on hindsight. David flipped through the rest of the word processing directory, but most of it was pretty innocuous.

He then went into Lotus, checking the directory. He saw quite a bit there. The Lotus package has a nice feature, in which the user can examine records through a key words index. David went through about twenty or so records before he came up on a locked file named D, the only locked record in the system. David had to think for a minute or two about the commands for overriding a record lock on Lotus. Damn, nothing was easy, he thought. He tried a couple of commands before he managed to get through to the document.

David hungrily scrolled down through the spread sheet, looking for a clue, a piece of dirt on Country Customs, but all he arrived at was the conclusion that life is one big anticlimax. What he found were two small directories, one called Active, the other Terminated. He tried Terminated, which turned out to be nothing more than a list of names, each followed by a series of notations. He shook his head and began to log off before the last name on the list caught his eye: Robert Kellum.

Robert Kellum. Bob, the engineer from the mall. Bob, who had stopped coming to the mall one day.

David went back to the list and began at the top:

ALAN LOGUE	$12	11/17/93	no NOK
IRENE MCNAMARA	9	12/12/93	no NOK
GUY NEEDLEMAN	11	12/19/93	no NOK
ROXANNE WARD	18	1/12/94	no NOK
GUNTHER KRIEBEL	4	1/26/94	no NOK
ROBERT KELLUM	14		no NOK

Very strange, David thought. He had the eerie feeling he had seen this list, or some variation of it, somewhere before. He thought for a couple of minutes and then went upstairs to the room where Nara and Von were sleeping, crept inside to Nara's side of the bed, and lifted something off her nightstand—the papers Simon Globus had sent her from New York. In them was a list of recent home sales in the Sparks area.

Back in front of the computer, David shuffled through the papers. Nara had shown them to him a few days ago, and he hadn't thought much of them at the time. But there on page three, after the foreclosures and commercial real estate transactions, was the following information:

Transaction	Sale Price	Sale Date
Alan Logue to Busy B's, Inc.	$12,000	November 18, 1993
Irene McNamara to Busy B's, Inc.	$9,700	December 13, 1993
Guy Needleman to Busy B's, Inc.	$11,000	December 20, 1993
Roxanne Ward to Busy B's, Inc.	$18,000	January 13, 1994
Gunther Kriebel to Busy B's, Inc.	$4,450	January 27, 1994
Robert Kellum to Busy B's, Inc.	$14,000	February 2, 1994

What *was* this? David wondered. What had Haslem been up to? Had he been keeping nothing more than a list of home sales in the area?

David studied both lists. The first thing he noticed was that the sale prices were identical. The buyer of each house was the same—Busy B's, Inc.—Barb Bromley's company. But the sale dates on Haslem's lists usually fell a day before those on Simon's list. And what was the notation "no NOK" on Haslem's list?

David sat for long minutes in front of the screen, studying the lists. The key here was Barb Bromley, or Busy B's, which, as David knew, was some kind of front for Country Customs. He recalled the first time he'd encountered the name, during his visit to the county courthouse in Rockland after the Haslems disappeared. What he found most startling was the fact that the sale had been transacted and entered within the country records only one day after he heard the screams on the baby monitor.

A day. *Exactly the difference between the dates on Haslem's and Globus's list.*

And then David rang up three cherries: these were two

different lists. Simon's was a straight list of homes sales. Haslem's was a record of when these people had been murdered. Evidence.

David looked at Haslem's list with new eyes. "NOK," he realized, was "Next of Kin." Why was that important?

Because next of kin could dispute the sale of their relative's property, that's why.

Ron Lindblad was knocking off people with no next of kin so he could easily appropriate their property. Those sale prices were ridiculously low. David guessed that Barb Bromley paid nothing for the houses and inserted a low purchase price into a fake contract to avoid paying tax on the properties. She might even have been underreporting the prices of Lindblad, ripping him off of his take of the profits.

The name of the record—D—must have meant "disappeared." Or "dead."

David sat back, crossed his arms, and tried to reconstruct the events leading to this list. Douglas Haslem had come to Sparks last year to work for Country Customs as an accountant. At first he had been a diligent little drone for Ron Lindblad until he somehow discovered that Country Customs was bringing in illegal aliens to help the company grow while Ron was having the locals killed off so he could grab their houses. Or maybe Ron tried to rope Haslem in, giving him some seemingly innocuous task that was, in reality, illegal. Something to be used later, as blackmail. But somehow Ron found out that Haslem, his new golden boy, was spying on him and collecting evidence, so Ron had his family and him killed.

David guessed that there was no date on Doug Haslem's list for Bob Kellum because Kellum had been targeted for murder at the time Haslem was doing the list, but Lindblad got to Haslem first. And Estelle Grout had been killed after Haslem. David remembered his last fleeting glimpse of Haslem furtively loading a steamer trunk into his station wagon. The poor schmuck was probably planning on cutting out the day Lindblad got him.

David rose from his chair and began to prowl around

house, his thumb working vigorously at the scar on his chin. Something was nagging him, a piece of the puzzle not yet fitting in. He could not imagine Ron Lindblad doing these killings. He probably had a polyurethene-sealed alibi for each one. And David did not quite see Sid Bromley—the next logical suspect—as a killer. But who knows, maybe Sid was a different guy on crystal meth.

In the kitchen, David poured a cup of Kona and was drawn by some inexplicable magnetism to the picture window in the rear dining room. On the way, the motion-activated video camera on the ceiling squealed annoyingly as it swiveled to follow him through the living room. At first David was inclined to pull the damn thing off the ceiling, but left it alone.

In the dining room, David gazed out the window at the Haslem's house, shrouded in darkness. What had gone on in there, what unspeakable violence? How many times had it been repeated? Was it happening somewhere tonight, perhaps at this moment? His face was so close to the windowpane he could feel the sharp cold from outside tingling his skin. A question seemed to float out of the darkness, haunting him.

If the killer wasn't Ron or Sid, who was it?

Then something else tugged at him, something he had just seen. He scurried back to the computer, exited out of the Terminated directory, and went into the Active one. He hadn't looked at that one yet. This directory was formatted the same as the other one, but it had only one listing in it.

As David gazed at the screen, he felt Douglas Haslem's hand reaching out from his grave—wherever that was—and tap him on the shoulder. David almost turned to look but he couldn't take his eyes from the bright orange letters in front of him:

ACTIVE

DAVID, NARA, VON MURATA

45

Driving up the access road to his home, Ron Lindblad was surprised to see the lights still on in the house. Norma was usually in bed by now, conking out around nine after killing off a pitcher of martinis. He glanced down at the backlit digital clock display on his dashboard. It was 10:49.

Ron smiled grimly when he realized why Norma was still awake: she wanted him to sign her new will. He'd already decided he just wouldn't do it. The hell with her. Let her try to divorce him, he'd rake her over the coals. And so what if she kicked off and the estate was tied up in probate, sucked down by lawyers? A little was better than nothing at all, and she wouldn't get the satisfaction of his signing.

Norma and her reptilian lawyer probably had thrown some pocket change for him into the will, an inducement to sign it. But he wouldn't bite. Ron knew there would be a scene when he got inside. That was okay, let it come.

He was feeling pretty good, having just come from one of his new plants, this one farther up the bay near Searsport. A new group had come in tonight from Mexico, Sid having cleared up the little problem they were having at the border. According to Sid's calculations, as of tonight's load, Country Customs now had 227 unsalaried, unbenefitted people working from 7:00 A.M. to 8:00 P.M. six days a week, 313 days a year. Ron gave them Sundays off or he'd have had riots on his hands.

His plans were falling into place. Pretty soon he could start scaling back on his shipments and just concentrate on the people he had, maybe bringing in a few loads aroun

Christmas and Mother's Day, the peak times. Maybe he could start selling them—to restaurants, car wash chains, or any place that needed cheap labor—if his cash got low. It wouldn't be long before he could begin pulling people out of the houses they occupied in Sparks and putting them in the Quonset huts he was building.

Then he could start creating Outlet City by converting the houses into retail areas—upscale discount stores specializing in New England crafts. Each store would be owned by Country Customs, but tourists would think they were shopping in authentic craft shops. As governor, Ron would get the Sparks city council to change the name of the town. All he had to do was get them by their balls and squeeze until they played along. Outlet City would gradually become an even bigger tourist stop than Freeport. Ron lived to see the day when he would put L.L. Bean out of business, the whole damn company thrown into Chapter Eleven.

Ron skipped up the front walk and unlocked the door, fully expecting to find Norma standing there, pen and paper in hand. But no one was around. He ducked into the study and fixed himself a TNT. He noticed the red light blinking on the answering machine. Before drinking, he needed something to eat. He'd had a craving for red meat all day and decided to do something about it in the kitchen.

On his way, through the corner of his eye, he spotted Norma at the dining room table. She appeared to have fallen asleep right on the table. Curious, he moved closer. Papers were spread out around her. So he was right, she *was* planning to nail him on the will. Ron decided to let her stay there and wake up with a sore neck.

It was then that he noticed that her metallic blue eyes were open, staring vacantly at him. Next he saw the red spreading over the table, seeping into the papers, dripping onto the floor, and spotting the Tabriz. Ron felt his own blood freeze and the ice cubes in his drink began to rattle. He came up behind Norma to check her pulse and backed away quickly as he saw the red-black spot the size of a half dollar on the back of her neck.

How often had he dreamed of this moment, to see Norma dead? But finding her like this only made him fearful and slightly sick to his stomach. A thought pierced him: what if the killer was still here?

Ron hustled back to his study and drew his Beretta from a locked drawer and made a sweep of the house, checking every room and closet, but no one was there. It gave him a chance to assimilate what had happened, devise a plan. Who had done this? A burglar? Someone she knew? No matter, he had to get the hell out of there, establish an alibi. Maybe get over to Sid's.

Ron had the presence of mind to wipe the house clean of prints he had made since coming in. He wasn't sure if the police could determine the time prints were left, but he didn't want to take the chance. What he'd do was get out of there and come back later after he'd been with Sid awhile. Maybe they'd go out somewhere, be seen having a couple of drinks. As Ron dumped his TNT into the sink, the phone rang. He let it ring until he heard Sid's voice on the answering machine intercom.

"This is Sid Bromley calling for Ron at, uh, 11:20—"

Ron picked it up. "Yeah, Sid?"

As he listened to Sid, Ron had trouble concentrating. He couldn't shake the memory of Norma's dead eyes staring accusingly at him. He wanted to escape from the house but forced himself to hear what Sid had to say. As he did so, his eyes grew narrow, his face and neck reddened, and his mouth began to twitch. He furiously scratched the back of his neck. Sid finished and Ron nodded his head.

"I'll be right there," he said.

Ron had to pass by the dining room to put the highball glass in the dishwasher, but he fought the temptation to look at the papers on the table, lest he leave prints or some other evidence. Using his handkerchief to place the glass in the dishwasher, he tried to assess his situation.

The worst that could happen was that he would be a suspect in the shooting and the resulting scandal could rob him of the governorship. Yet maybe Norma's death would work to his advantage, generate sympathy for him and strengthen his get-tough-on-crime platform. Ron was sure he would get off, maybe not even be charged for the murder. But it wouldn't hurt to take precautions.

What a night, he thought as he left the house. What else could go wrong?

Speeding through the dark secondary roads toward Country Customs, Ron noticed the Jiffy Cleaning Service truck passing him from the opposite direction. He watched the truck in his rearview mirror until it was out of sight. He could not see the truck as it pulled into the driveway to his house.

"What are *they* doing out here at this hour?" he said to himself. "Did Sid call for them?"

Ron reached the plant in record time, glowering at the security guard at the station. "What the hell's going on here?" he barked at the guard. "You people getting too comfortable in your jobs?"

"No, sir, Mr. Lindblad," the guard stammered, quickly opening the gate.

"Well, you'd better start looking for another one," he said and left the man standing there with a faceful of diesel exhaust.

Inside the building, Ron took the elevator to the sixth floor and stomped into his office. Sid greeted him, gun in hand, and led Ron to a small conference room where Pia and Laszlo were seated in chairs, their hands and feet tied, electrical tape across their mouths. Blood trickled down the side of Laszlo's face where Sid had pistol-whipped him. Pia was slouched over, her midsection bruised by Sid's punches.

"Who are they?" Ron asked impatiently, looking at them, his eyes lingering on Pia.

"I don't know," Sid answered. "They won't talk."

"Any ID on them?"

Sid held up a little plastic brontosaurus that Von had hidden in Pia's pocket as a gift. "Just this," Sid said.

Ron, in no mood to fool around with these punks,

stepped up in front of Laszlo and roughly pulled the tape from across his mouth. "I'll give you one chance," Ron said softly. "Maybe you won't do it for yourself, but you can at least save your girlfriend here. I spent almost two million on security for this place and you two waltz in through it. Who are you and how did you get in here?"

Pia sat up, shaking her head and making muffled noises from behind the tape.

"You motherfucker," Laszlo spat out. "We know all about you. The cops will be on you like fly on—"

Ron slapped him hard with the back of his hand, and Laszlo's head snapped back. "You hear that accent?" Ron said to Sid. "I'll bet you he's one of our runaways. Her too. We've had too many of them. I wonder if they know where the others are.

"We have to take care of them," Ron said, "just like we did with Doug Haslem and his family."

Sid thought for a moment about Doug Haslem, remembering him as someone he had distrusted the minute he met him. Sid never mentioned to Ron that he considered Haslem a rival, someone who could potentially come between Ron and him. Sid had had Haslem bugged—his office, his home, even his car. It was Sid who had discovered Haslem was on to their plans and collecting evidence on his computer. And it was Sid who had put the killer on to Haslem.

For his part, Ron, always practical, was trying to come up with a way of dealing with the two intruders. He thought of separating them, giving the big guy to Sid to dispose of and taking the girl somewhere quiet, spend some time alone with her before killing her. She looked pretty good to him, even with her outrageous haircut. Then Ron thought of Norma and knew he had to concentrate on business tonight. No time for pleasure.

Suddenly an idea came to Ron, something so exquisitely perfect that even he could barely believe he thought of it. "Who else knows they're here?" he said.

"Just one guard," Sid answered, "someone I trust."

"All right. Here's what we do. Get one of the cleaning

trucks. We're taking them back to my place. You drive the truck, I'll take the Mercedes."

"What're we doing?" Sid asked, stuffing the gun into his belt.

"Killing two birds with one stone," Ron said.

46

"I don't believe this," K. K. said over the phone to Sheriff Donner of the Knox County Police Department up in Rockland. "You mean the best I can do is file *another* missing-person's report that will end up lining your trash can? That'd be the third one this week."

She held the phone away from her ear as Sheriff Donner reminded her in the voice he reserved for particularly difficult citizens that it was now almost half past midnight and he'd been asleep in bed and she was about one inch away from being charged with telephone harassment. She rolled her eyes and looked around the tiny house. Viveca was asleep in her room, having woken up screaming twice already. K. K. was at her wit's end trying to figure out what was wrong with her.

Donner stopped his speech to take in a breath, and K. K. put in: "Yeah, well, let me tell you something. I just spoke to Estelle Grout's sister, and she says she hasn't seen or talked with her sister in two weeks. But she has spoken with you, hasn't she, Sheriff? Yeah, sure. I might just go ahead and call the FBI. See what *they* turn up."

She hung up on him. What could she do now? Who was there left to call? Maybe Nara and David had some ideas, she thought. But it was too late to be calling them. She dialed Ray's number, but no one answered. Wonder where he is, K. K. thought, but resisted the urge to call the diner. They were probably locking up now anyway.

K. K. began thumbing through the greater Augusta telephone book for the number of the FBI. Where would it be? She turned to the blue pages in the back under U.S.

GOVERNMENT. Nothing there. Where was the FBI when you needed it?

Then she realized she still had the Fort Myers directory and hunted around for it, finding it under a pile of newspapers. Its blue pages section was much longer than the other book's, and she moved her finger down the column until she found a series of numbers for the FBI, and one in Miami that was open twenty-four hours. She could call this number and explain the situation, maybe get them to send someone up here first thing in the morning.

K. K. looked up as she heard a noise, the creaking of the wharf buckling from the push of the cold, relentless sea. She started to dial, her head swiveling from the phone book to the telephone. Suddenly she heard a sound and, looking up, saw a blur of black and felt hot pain searing her forearm.

She dropped the phone and fell back across the couch, holding her arm, blood leaking through her fingers. The black figure fell over her, its arm pumping like a piston, the knife missing her but shredding the couch. K. K. jumped back in spasms, avoiding the knife as it plunged toward her. Ignoring the pain, she drew in her legs and found a place for her feet on the intruder's chest. Her legs sprang out, sending the intruder backward, crashing into the room.

K. K. scanned the room quickly for a weapon, anything, and groped blindly for the telephone. The pain in her arm was almost unbearable. The intruder rose and approached slowly, menacingly. K. K. looked the intruder over, taking in the dark green parka she'd thought was black, the black ski mask, and the long, razor-sharp knife. K. K. drew in air in quick, shallow gulps, her lungs locked with fear. Her hand found the telephone and she gripped it.

What could she do? Where could she go? Where was Viveca?

The attacker changed grips, holding the knife down in a power-stab position. K. K. bolted for the back door with the phone in hand, but the intruder charged forward, the knife raised. K. K. screamed and swung the telephone wildly, smashing the intruder squarely in the face. Stunned, the killer fell backward, dropping the knife.

K. K. streaked into Viv's room, scooped the sleeping child out of bed with her good arm and rested her bottom on the stab wound, direct pressure to quell the bleeding. Was the intruder still there? K. K. wondered, thinking quickly, calculating. Had she killed him? Or was he lying in wait, preparing for when she'd come back through the living room?

K. K. took in a breath and, with her good hand, opened the window in Viveca's room, and somehow—in a way she would never figure out later—managed to squirm through with Viveca still in the other hand. She raced over the frozen ground out of sight from the house, and into the woods.

But the killer was already gone from the house, having staggered out to the truck and passed out in the front seat.

47

On his fourth cup of coffee, having abandoned all hope of getting to sleep tonight, David contemplated the moves open to him. The more he thought about it, the less he believed in the credibility of his evidence against Ron Lindblad. Oh, sure, he could call the state's attorney general, or even the feds, but after a big investigation all Ron would get is a suspended sentence for hiring illegal aliens. (He'd claim he hadn't brought them in.) More likely, he'd get off scot free, then move to another state and start the whole sordid business all over again.

Spread out on the couch, David rolled to his side and set the cup on the floor. He needed something more to nail Ron Lindblad. He needed—as the Watergate prosecutors sought—a smoking gun.

David was brought to his feet by a light rapping on his front door. He glanced at the digital clock on top of a computer: 12:21. Looking at those numbers, a thought occurred to him and he turned the clock upside down; it still read the same time. He picked up a stout modem to defend himself with and checked the security monitors.

"Wow," he said to himself. Lined up outside his door was a sizable contingent of forest dwellers, led by Moe. David moved to the door and opened it.

"Hi, Moe," David said. "Evening, everybody." There was a murmuring of "good evenings" in maybe a dozen different languages.

"Can we come in a moment?" Moe said, shivering in the night air.

"Well, I think so," David said, trying to estimate the size

of the crowd. It looked like a good twenty or so. "Nara and Von are asleep."

"Not anymore," said Nara from behind. She was holding a groggy Von in her arms.

"Join the party," David said to her. The group filed in quietly, respectfully. David recognized several of them from the campfire: Mr. and Mrs. Singh, Mr. Grabaukus, Mrs. Meharatab, and T.Y. David was amused at the gasps of surprise from some of them, reactions to the stockpile of equipment littering the living room.

"So, what brings you here?" David said cordially. He wanted to offer them something but realized that if he did, he could be serving people all night.

Moe spoke for them. "It's Pia and Laszlo, David. They haven't come home yet. We've been waiting up anxiously, but there's been no sign of them. I had to explain everything to Pia's and Laszlo's parents. They understand why we broke into Country Customs, but they're very worried."

David felt his cheeks burn, guilty with a twenty-four-point G.

"I understand," he said, trying to collect his thoughts. What was the worst that could have happened? Pia and Laszlo had been caught at Country Customs and killed, that's what. Possible they might have been caught, but unlikely they would have been killed. Where would they be? He thought of Ron Lindblad.

"All right," David said. "Listen. If they were caught, there's two places they're likely to be: still at Country Customs or out at Ron Lindblad's house. I say we split up; one group goes to the plant, the other to the house."

David waited for a hurrah or some other sign of assent, but the group was silent. They're afraid, he thought, fearful of being out and exposed. "All right," he said, "I'll take the group to the plant. Mr. Singh, how about you leading the other group to Lindblad's house?"

"Very good," he sid quietly. "How do we get there?"

"Uh, you take Nara's Range Rover. I'll drive the truck. Anything else?"

The doorbell rang. What now? David wondered. When

he opened it, he muttered, "Shit" in disbelief as he found K. K. Thorner, covered with blood and slumped against the wall, holding her weeping daughter.

As David helped her into the house, everyone rushed forward to help. He waved them back. "K. K., what happened?" he said.

"She's going into shock," Nara said. "She's lost of a lot of blood. I'll take her to the hospital. Her car's outside."

"She *drove* here?" David said incredulously.

"David, shouldn't we call the police?" Moe asked.

"No," K. K. shouted. "Don't call them. They don't know—"

Nara caught K. K. before she fell, and David grabbed Viveca.

"Get going," he said to Nara, and she and Mrs. Singh helped K. K. to her car and put her in the backseat. Mrs. Singh climbed in next to K. K., Nara slid behind the wheel, and they took off.

David tried to think. He had to get going to find Pia and Laszlo, but who would stay with the kids?

"Anybody here up for some baby-sitting?" he said, but his plea was met with averted eyes.

David went to the phone and dialed Jean Burke's number. He waited five, six rings until Jean's thick voice came on, sounding very confused. David imagined he had got her out of bed.

"Jean," David said. "It's David. David Murata. We've got an emergency here. Can you come over right away?"

Jean was still groggy. "Emergency?" she croaked.

"Yes," David said, anxious to get moving. "I can explain when you get here. Can you do it?"

There was a pause of twenty long seconds. "Yes," she said finally, a bit unsteady, and hung up.

David looked down at Viveca, dozing soundly on his chest, her face sticky with her mother's blood. Mr. Singh was holding Von, who was also asleep. David gave Mr. Singh the keys to the Range Rover and took Von in his free arm.

"Why don't you take off?" David suggested. "I'll be on my way to the plant shortly."

Thankful to get moving, Mr. Singh took the keys and was followed out the door by eight or nine of the forest dwellers. The rest waited patiently on the living room floor.

Upstairs, David put Von in his crib. In the bathroom he took awhile to wash all the blood off Viveca's face and arms, and then tucked her into his bed.

When he got downstairs, Jean was already there. She looked terrible, as some people do when they're awakened in the middle of the night. Her face was puffy and she had a frowzy, browbeaten look that was unusual for her.

"Jean, you're a life saver," David said. "Listen, we need someone to stay with the kids. They're both upstairs asleep."

"Both?" Jean said feebly, still confused.

"Yeah," David said, forgetting or choosing not to explain the events of the evening. "Shove some of that junk off the couch and take a nap." Jean nodded her head, seeming not to comprehend what David was saying. "C'mon, everybody," he said and left.

David jumped in the truck, followed by the dozen or so remaining forest dwellers, who piled in the back. In the shotgun seat was Moe, who had been there for a while, studying the schematics for the electrical substation on the notebook David had forgotten to remove from the truck.

David looked back at the house and waved at Jean, silhouetted in the vertical bar of light at the door's edge. She nodded her head once at David and slowly shut the door.

48

Heading up his driveway for the second time that night, his house coming into view, Ron sensed something was not quite right. He looked at the displays on his dashboard and then into the darkness all around him. Nothing there. Then he glanced in the rearview mirror and saw the headlights of the Jiffy cleaning truck Sid was driving with the two punks tied up in the back. What could be wrong? he wondered. Suddenly it occurred to him: the lights in his house were all out. He distinctly recalled leaving them on when he had left.

Could the police have come already? No, that was impossible, no one came out this way, unless whoever killed Norma had called them. But that would be crazy. Another thought, even more frightening, dawned on him: what if Norma wasn't dead? Could she have called an ambulance or crawled out of there and gone for help? Then he realized: it was just another blackout, there had already been two of them this evening.

Ron parked the Mercedes, hopped out, and waited for Sid, who pulled up right behind him. Unbeknownst to Ron, Sid had snorted a couple of spoonfuls of Power on the way and was ready for action.

"What's the drill?" Sid asked eagerly, hopping from one foot to the other in nervous anticipation.

"The 'drill,' " Ron said with more than the usual edge in his voice, "is to do exactly what I tell you to do. Norma is inside, dead, shot in the back of the neck. I found her when I came home just as you called. I don't know who did it, probably a burglar.

"We're going to take these kids in and shoot them with my gun. Then we're going to shoot Norma in the head and neck a few times with your gun, enough to blow away the evidence from the first shooting. We put your gun in the big guy's hand. Then you get out of here and I'll call the police, tell them the kids had broken in and there was a shoot-out. You had been at the plant all evening and don't know a thing about it. Just make sure your guard friend—the one who knows about the kids—is taken care of. Kill him if you have to."

"Jesus Christ, Ron," was all Sid could say.

"No need for profanity," Ron said angrily. "Okay, ready?"

"But—"

"Is there a problem?" Ron said.

"No," Sid mumbled, and he slid open the back door of the truck and pulled Laszlo up from the floor. Ron grabbed Pia by her *kuncho* braids and led her to the front door.

"You're going to wait here until the police come," Ron said to them, pushing Pia inside. "Let's go."

Out of habit, Ron hit the foyer light and he was shocked when it came on. "Someone *was* here," he said aloud. Or Norma was still alive.

He led Pia past the dining room toward the kitchen. He stopped in his tracks when he saw the dining room table clean—free of papers, blood, and Norma's body.

"What the—" he muttered.

"Hey, Ron," Sid said loudly, coming up behind him with Laszlo in tow, "where's Norma? I thought you said—"

"Shut up, you asshole," Ron hissed. "It was here, there, on the table. I saw it myself. Someone moved it. Or she called an ambulance."

"Jesus—" Sid began to say, but stopped himself. He looked at Ron, trying to determine if he was drunk or had gone off the deep end. "I don't know, Ron, but I've never heard of anyone taking a shot to the back of the head and walking away from it."

Ron was looking around for signs of Norma. He got down on all fours and scoured the Tabriz. There wasn't a trace of blood to be found. "Who said anything about walking away?" he said, standing up and shaking his head. "Someone's obviously taken her. C'mon, let's get out of here. We still have these two to deal with."

"So where're we going now?" Sid asked, his doubts about Ron growing by the second.

"To execute Plan B," Ron said ominously and pulled Pia toward the door.

49

As he raced through the night toward the Country Customs building, thousands of thoughts flew in and out of David's head. He tried to anticipate what he would encounter when he got there. Even if he could shut down the power again, the villagers and he were likely to face armed guards. He reluctantly concluded that they would need some heat.

"Anybody back there packing?" David said, pointing with his thumb at the back of the truck, stuffed with illegal immigrants.

"Pudden?" Moe said. "Can't you turn the radio down?" The big band station was doing its Monday night cavalcade of vocal hits. "Or at least put on a good station."

"Guns. Does anyone back there have one?"

"Are you kidding?" Moe said. "Well, actually, I think Mr. Grabaukus has one, but he went with the other group."

"Great," David said. They were passing though town, about to hit the highway toward Country Customs, when David swung the truck around. "I think I know where we can get one," he shouted above the squealing of the tires.

"David," Moe said, "do you really think they would keep Pia and Laszlo at Country Customs?"

David was trying to pick up street names from the signs. "What?" he said.

"I was thinking," Moe said, folding his hands and touching his fingertips to his lips. "Ron Lindblad is no fool. If he plans to do something with them, like kill them, he wouldn't do it there. It could draw attention to his operation, putting the whole thing in jeopardy. It's too risky."

"First of all," David said, "nobody is going to kill anyone. And besides, where else would he take them, other than his house?" He found the street he was looking for and searched desperately for the house.

"He would want it to look like an accident," Moe said, staring out the window. "For instance, he could—"

"There it is," David shouted and yanked the truck into a U-turn and parked in front of the house, almost losing a couple of people in the back. He snapped the transmission into neutral and pulled back the emergency brake. "Wait here," he said and hopped out, leaving the motor running.

While flying through town, David had remembered something Jean once had told him, that she kept a gun in her house. He couldn't recall what kind of gun or where she kept it, but it was the only gun he was going to get as they made their run on Country Customs. Maybe he could call Jean at his house from inside and ask her where the gun was.

The front and back doors were locked. He decided to try the garage, and if that was locked, he could break in through the back. Lucky for him, the garage door was unlocked. He was surprised to find a truck parked in there. He didn't know Jean owned one; she always drove her Buick to his place. He found a cord dangling from the ceiling and snapped on a bare bulb at the end of it.

The garage was musty, with a faint foul odor he couldn't quite place coming from the truck. David spied the door to the house and headed for it. It was locked.

"Damn," he said, realizing he'd have to break in. He snapped off the light and turned to leave. Looking down for the first time, something caught his eye, something luminous on the dark garage floor. It was red.

Curious, he squatted down and examined it but couldn't quite figure out what it was. He stood and turned on the light again. He studied the spots on the floor. It was Day-Glo paint. What would Jean be doing with Day-Glo paint? he wondered. David noticed other drops of the paint on the floor and followed them to a can of it on a shelf.

Suddenly an image flashed in his mind, that of the obscene message scrawled across the front of his house. A boiling noise rose in his ears, the sound of blood rushing through his veins. Then a thought almost too terrible for his mind to hold: Jean was the killer.

"Bloody hell," he gasped, trying to steady himself. "Von. Oh, no."

David quickly looked inside Jean's truck and saw the keys in the ignition. He streaked out to his truck to tell Moe and the others to go on ahead to Country Customs.

"David, what's the matter?" Moe said.

"Can't explain now," David said frantically, fighting back panic. "Do what you can out there. Gotta go." Back in the garage, into the truck, praying it would start. It did, and he backed out and roared up the street past Moe, who was clumsily trying to change gears to David's truck.

Moe finally got it into gear and started down the street, only not in the direction of Country Customs. If David had heard Moe out, he would have known where he was headed. Moe thought of something his father used to say as his family made its way to the United States through one blind alley after another:

"Sometimes," his father would say, "you have to risk it all or it's just not worth it."

50

Ron was a few minutes ahead of Sid and the cleaning truck arriving at the electrical substation. It was nearly two in the morning, and Ron thought it very unlikely that anyone would be happening by to spoil his plans. He unlocked the gates and surveyed the place.

The air around the substation buzzed with the power that rippled through the transmission lines and swelled in the transformers. The place was a dynamo, a juggernaut of sheer electrical energy that could take down anything in its path. Ron grunted in pleasure at the sight of it, a true testimony to his greatness.

Amazing he hadn't thought before tonight of using the substation as a direct means of disposing of those in his way. The substation and power lines did help serve that purpose by emitting a great deal of radiation that he hoped would sicken and drive out the people of Sparks. It had begun to work, he knew from the long lines at the doctors' offices. But that would not quite do the job for him, so he had taken more aggressive action.

But, like any good manager, Ron had to think ahead, anticipate events. He knew that things had a way of unraveling just when you thought they were coming together. He had been thinking hard, assessing his situation, and had come to the conclusion that his plans would have to change soon. Major adjustments would have to be made—personnel adjustments. Sid would have to go, he was getting too erratic. And his confederate, the killer, would have to go too. They had served their purpose, but that would soon be fulfilled.

Ron had an idea how to get rid of them. As usual, his solution to his problem was practical and clean. He would pit each one against the other by setting up a situation where they would kill each other without implicating him or his plans. Oh, there would be some temporary unpleasantness with the police and the press, but he could overcome that.

But to more immediate problems, this strange business with Norma had unnerved him a bit, causing him to doubt his grip on events that had been absolute up to now. He still hadn't figured out what could have happened to her body. He suspected a blackmailer might be at work, perhaps some acquaintance of Norma's who had happened by after the murder and decided to take advantage of the situation by removing the body and later approaching him for a payoff. Well, let them. They didn't know whom they were dealing with.

A pair of headlights appeared on the dark highway. Ron watched the lights grow brighter as they approached on the service road and were almost upon him, shining on him like stage lights. He stood large at the end of the road, his arms folded at his chest and his feet planted on the ground, seeing himself as a Wagnerian figure, something out of the "Twilight of the Gods." He knew that his shadow behind him loomed wide, blanketing the substation.

Sid killed the lights and climbed out of the truck. He stood there for several moments studying Ron, and walked over to him. "You okay there, Ron?" he said.

Ron stood still as a statue and spoke toward the sky. "What is the name of that character from 'The Twilight of the Gods,' " he said softly, "the one who kills Siegfried as Valhalla burns, the last remaining god?"

"Huh?" Sid said, almost having to shout above the electrical hum. He squinted at Ron. The guy was going weird on him, all right. Best to keep things moving. "So, what do you want done with the two in the truck?"

Ron turned to look at Sid. "Did you blindfold them as I instructed?"

Sid nodded his head.

"First," Ron said, "you'll use the wire cutters to make a hole in the fence over in the corner there. Next we'll lead them out of the truck to the circuit breakers. You take the boy, I'll take the girl. I have two cans of oil we'll dump on them at the last minute that'll help conduct the electricity.

"Then we'll push them into the circuit breakers and they will be electrocuted. This should do no harm to the circuitry. If they give us any trouble, we'll tap them on the head with the sap, just enough to render them unconscious but not to leave any suspicious marks on their skulls."

"What about the ropes on their hands and legs? And the tape?"

"The tape we can remove just before we push them. The ropes will be incinerated by the electricity. Don't forget to put the wire cutters in the boy's rear pocket *before* you push him."

"Right," Sid said.

"One thing first," Ron said, turning to look at his substation. "After this is over, I want you to get rid of your killer once those last two remaining troublemakers are dispatched. Do whatever is necessary, but we won't be needing that kind of assistance any longer."

Ron paused for a moment and, not getting a response, said, "Understand?"

Sid blinked twice, trying to comprehend what he was hearing while riding out the tidal waves of crystal meth crashing into him. Christ, what was next? Where was all this going?

"Understand?" Ron said again, looking straight at him now.

"Er, yeah," Sid managed to say.

"All right," Ron said, heading to the truck, brushing past him. "Let's get going."

Moe's biggest struggle on the way to the substation was coming to terms with David's radio. The thing was stuck—both the tuner and the volume control—assaulting Moe's ears and affecting his ability to concentrate. As the truck plowed through the night, Smilin' Jack, the DJ, introduced Count Basie and his orchestra doing "Blues for the Barbecue."

"Great," Moe said, his eyes on road rushing up at him as the music flew out into the night.

Moe wanted to come up on the substation quietly, as quietly as he could with the radio on. He switched off the headlights as the lights around the substation came into view. He hadn't anticipated just how dark it would be on the highway, and he gripped the wheel, holding it steady.

Moe glanced in the rearview mirror at the people in the back. They still had the same stoic expressions on their faces as they had when they started out on this trip. T.Y., sitting near the cab, noticed Moe's look and nodded to him. Moe knew it was cold back there, but these people had already suffered much worse.

Moe downshifted as he came up on the substation, took his foot off the accelerator, and let the truck roll quietly to the entrance of the service road before gently braking. Down the road he saw a car and a van, behind the trees. He took the truck out of gear and let it roll a bit more until he could get a good view of the entire substation. He heard a tapping on the back window just as he saw Pia and Laszlo—blindfolded and off to the side of the station—a heavy man behind them holding something in his hand. It looked like a gun.

Moe was glad that neither Mr. Grabaukus nor Mr. and Mrs. Meharatab were in the truck or they might have done something precipitous, like go after their kids. Moe rolled down his window and watched as another man, a bald one, cut away a section of the fence at the far corner of the substation.

Moe turned around and put his finger to his lips, a gesture for the people in the back to keep quiet. They nodded their heads, and it was then that Moe saw the knives and machetes in the hands of some of them. He rolled his eyes and drew the sub-notebook onto his lap, switched it on, and called a number on David's cellular phone, which he then inserted into the modem's port. A couple of commands later, Moe was in the Country Customs database and then into the schematics for the substation. He had to leave the truck running so that the power from the cigarette lighter could feed into the computer.

When Moe had studied the schematics earlier, he had figured out the principal components of the substation and how to operate them through the computer. Since the entire substation was computerized, it was relatively easy for him to use the keyboard mouse to move the arrow to the window for, say, their air circuit breakers and then to shut them down. The only problem was that he wasn't exactly sure what the air circuit breakers did, or any other component, for that matter.

Another tap on the window and Moe looked up to see the man who was cutting the fence, the bald one, now walking toward Pia, Laszlo, and the gunman. Moe squinted at the man, recognizing him from his appearances in the Country Customs furniture shop where Moe once worked. Normally he wore a wig. The man's name was Sid Bromley. If he was Bromley, then the other man was probably Ron Lindblad. Biting his lower lip, Moe knew he had to make a decision fast. What to do? What to shut down?

Moe watched as Bromley stuffed something into Laszlo's pocket. Uh-oh, Moe thought. This was it. He gritted his teeth and moved the arrow to the window for General Shutdown. He clicked the mouse and held his breath.

Bromley and Lindblad were behind Pia and Laszlo now, talking between themselves. Moe noticed that the electrical buzz of the substation was diminishing. The men noticed it too and were looking around, trying to figure out what was going on. Then they picked up cans from the ground, dumped their contents over Pia's and Laszlo's heads, ripped the tape from their mouths, and shoved them into a panel mounted on cement slabs below steel-reinforced support pylons.

Moe shut his eyes, waiting for the horrible sound of sputtering electricity. But it never came. The computer had worked! He opened his eyes and saw the men shouting at each other in panic, both of them brandishing guns. Then he looked in the back of the truck and muttered, "Bloody hell," when he saw that it was empty.

51

After speeding through Sparks, flying up the road to his house, and hiding Jean's truck behind the blackberry bushes on the edge of his property, David paused a moment before sliding the key into the door. He had to fight down terrible images flooding his mind, of Jean—the woman whom he had trusted with his child—as a psychotic killer. How could she have done this? Why? How deep in it was she? And how could he have been so blind?

His hands were trembling, and sweat oozed down the sides of his face.

Relax, he told himself, you're not even sure she is the killer. Even so, he did not want to confront Jean on his own, especially with the children in there. He had to appear normal and let her leave, walk out. David wiped his face with his sleeve, sucked in lungfuls of air, and slowly opened the door.

Sitting in the middle of the living room floor, playing with Tinker Toys, were Von, Viveca, and Jean. They all looked up as David entered, and Von ran to him. David lifted him up and held him close, suppressing the urge to flee out the door.

"How is everybody?" David said with all the good cheer he could muster. His words sounded hollow to him, and he told himself to move with all the care of a lion tamer in a cage with an angry, hungry lion.

"Oh, just fine," Jean said with the same spacey voice she'd had on the phone.

"Sure looks like you're having fun," he said.

"Oh, yes, we like the old-fashioned toys the best, don't we?" she said, snuggling Viveca.

David cleared his throat. "Well, it's way past bedtime for you little people. Jean, thanks so much for coming over."

She waved her hand dismissively. "What was all the commotion about?" she said, rising.

"Oh, some friends of Nara's needed help. I'm not really sure myself what the story was."

Jean nodded sympathetically. "No need to explain," she said. "Need any help he-ah?"

"Oh, no, no," David said. "It's under control."

"I'll just see myself out, then," she said, drawing on her parka. "Night, kids."

David's cheeks burned as he smiled, watching her leave. He locked the door, bolted it, and went to the window and felt sweet relief as she started the Buick and rolled down the driveway. If she found her truck missing when she got home, David thought, she would have no idea where it had gone. Just let her call the police to report it.

"Is my mommy coming back soon?" Viveca asked David quietly.

"Of course, sweetheart," David said, lifting her up with his free arm. "But she asked me to put you to bed. Are you ready?"

Viveca nodded her head and then planted it on David's shoulder. Von was already asleep. He carried them upstairs and laid them down on his bed. Just to be safe, he would take the children into town and spend the night at the bed and breakfast there. First he would gather up a few things and leave Nara a note.

David found the baby bag in a downstairs closet and began collecting toys and diapers. In the kitchen he dug the milk out of the refrigerator and filled a bottle. He wondered how everyone was doing: K. K., Pia, Laszlo, and everyone else. As he tightened a nipple on the bottle, he felt a bizarre kinship with Albert Einstein, who, like David but on a much grander scale, had unlocked a great secret and lived to regret it.

David stopped what he was doing when he heard a light

sound outside. He cocked his ear to the air and then heard a horrible sound, the one he would have least wanted to hear in the world.

It was Jean's voice.

He turned quickly and drew in a breath when he saw her standing there in her parka and black ski mask. In her hand was a gun, a semi-automatic with a fat barrel, pointed at his heart. David recognized it as a silencer. He realized that this was probably the last thing that everyone on Douglas Haslem's morbid list had seen in their lives.

"I didn't want to have to do this," Jean said. "I tried to warn you."

"Wh-what?" David stammered.

"The message, the dog. They wanted me to kill you, but I did my best just to scare you away. I even tried to get them to let me stop."

"Jean," David said, his mind racing feverishly. "Why did you do it?"

"You don't know what it's like," she said, stepping closer, "being alone, no money, dumped out on the street like so much garbage."

"I do know, Jean," David said, buying time.

"Delbert, my husband, died without leaving me so much as a penny. His pension from working at the lighthouse was only good as long as he lived. I was at wit's end, eating dog food and selling what little I had to stay alive. You don't know what I went through growing up, David. I did without all my life and wasn't going to let it happen again. No, sir.

"Then Mr. Lindblad came into my life, found me destitute and trying to borrow money with no collateral whatsoever at the S&L he owns up in Searsport. He put me in charge of the Lobster Museum. He was on the board, and gave me money through it. I felt like somebody, David, for the first time in my life."

David felt his heart beating out of control, his legs and arms shaking. Where can I go? he wondered. How do I get out of this?

"Then he asked me to do things for him," Jean droned

on, "small things like what I did to your house, the dog. I went along. But then he asked me to do . . . bigger things. I said one time, just once, but then, after, he threatened to turn me in. He made me go on. And he paid me, David."

"It's over, Jean," David said. "The police are after Lindblad and Bromley and the whole crew. Give it up before anyone else is hurt."

"I found my truck, outside," Jean said, her voice trailing off. "It took me a little while, but I found it. When I left, I didn't see yours. And I knew you knew. It was all over your face anyway when you walked through the door."

David's eyes darted around the kitchen, looking for knives, serving forks, heavy objects. The closest thing to him was the coffee maker. He couldn't very well throw *that* at her. He wondered if any hot coffee was left in the pot.

Jean took another step toward him. He knew that a silencer reduced the velocity of a bullet as well as its accuracy. If he stayed away, maybe a few yards, she might miss or just make a superficial wound. He took two steps back, testing her.

"Don't make it harder than it has to be," Jean said. "I can't let you go. If they lock me up, I'll die in prison."

"Jean," David said, starting to feel panicky. "Why don't you just turn around and go? Tie me up if you want to, but just get in the truck and drive all night to Canada. You could make it."

"What is there for me in Canada?" she said, her voice slow and unearthly.

David wondered if she had suffered some cranial damage from her run-in with K. K. Maybe it had slowed her down. Maybe he could get away from her.

"No sir," she said, "I'm going to live out my days right he-ah in Sparks—"

Suddenly the lights went out and David saw a flash in the darkness just after he dropped to the floor. The coffeepot exploded as a bullet pierced it. And yes, there was hot coffee in it, showering David's back.

He crawled through the kitchen on the slick floor and around the center island. Up on his knees, he felt around the island for a knife but couldn't find one. Damn! He knew would have to do something; the power could come back on any second.

David found what was left of the coffeepot and threw it into the living room, shattering somewhere in there. The pistol fired again, a snapping sound in the darkness. David ran in a crouch through the other kitchen entrance into the dining room and living room, and up the stairs.

In the bedroom, he scooped the sleeping children into his arms and headed back toward the stairs. Jean was somewhere down there, waiting for him with her gun. There was no way out from the second floor, other than jumping through a window.

He thought of calling someone on the telephone. But who?

He thought of looking for a weapon of some kind, but he had nothing to match a gun.

He thought of the closest window and wondered if two little children in his arms could survive a jump. He wasn't sure.

His options were narrowing. He had to think fast. The lights could come any time now, and a madwoman desperately wanted him dead.

52

At the substation, perched on the front seat of the truck, Moe concentrated hard, trying to decide what to do. The electrical power was still down in the substation, but he didn't know how long it would hold. Also, he didn't know if the men who had been holding Pia and Laszlo prisoner could reactivate the substation manually.

Moe watched as Ron Lindblad and Sid Bromley scrambled around, shouting at each other. He wondered what was going on. Suddenly Bromley reached for his head and fell over to the ground. Moe saw the people from his village, led by T.Y., moving along the fence, hurling rocks over and through the fence at the men. The man who was still standing, Ron Lindblad, fired his gun and everyone—Pia, Laszlo, and the others—dropped to the ground.

Lindblad roughly pulled Pia to her feet and pushed her into the substation, where the pylons, transformer coils, and power lines reticulated toward the middle, forming a huge steel spiderweb that shielded them from the rocks. One of the villagers tried to move toward Laszlo but dropped down when Lindblad fired again.

Pia and Lindblad were barely visible in the web of the wires and circuitry. Moe studied the substation schematics on the computer screen, matching what he saw on the screen to the actual components. The pylons were nothing more than supports for the transmission lines feeding in and out of the station. The lines on the north side of the station brought power into the substation from the power plant, and the ones on the south side sent it out to smaller transformers throughout the area.

At the periphery of the substation, near the fence, were vertical poles with iron coils at the top, connected to the substation and main lines by overhead wires with disconnect switches. According to the schematic, these were also transformers. But really important to Moe's purposes were the circuit breakers, most of which were housed in the panels and cabinets close in to the substation. The circuit breakers were the on-off switches for the system that worked to balance the level of electrical current entering and leaving the substation. They also maintained the system's overall current level.

Moe looked up as shots rang out, ricocheting off a cabinet and sending a spray of sparks into the air. The villagers had crawled closer and were peppering the area around the substation with rocks, keeping them away from Pia but clearly unnerving Lindblad. Laszlo was still on the ground near a circuit breaker, huddled in the fetal position, and Bromley was out cold.

The villagers began shouting among themselves, ordering each other to stop throwing, as Lindblad slowly emerged from the middle of the substation with Pia in front of him, his gun pointed at her head. Her blindfold was off. Sid Bromley began to stir and got up on his knees, shaking the cobwebs from his head.

Lindblad, still holding the gun at Pia, said something to Bromley, and Pia took the cue. She ducked her head and, with the heel of her boot, kicked Lindblad hard in the shin. He staggered away in pain, and she bolted toward Laszlo. The villagers began firing again. Rocks rained down on both men, who retreated into the middle of the substation, Lindblad limping and Bromley crawling.

But they still had their guns and they began shooting again. Moe gasped as he saw one of the villagers go down, taking a shot to the chest. Blinking back tears, he studied the schematic again. The problem: how to activate the power in the middle transformers where the gunmen were hiding while keeping the power off in the circuit breakers near Pia and Laszlo, pinned down at the edge of the substation. Another problem: how to concentrate while Johnny Mercer began to croon "Glow Worm."

> Shine, little glow worm, glimmer.
> Shine, little glow worm, glimmer.

Moe was sure there was a proper way to do it by using the mouse, but, in the interest of time, he typed in a command to the computer to keep off power at the outer circuits while activating the middle transformers. He had no idea if it would work. Suddenly the power started up with a roar as circuits—compensating for the sudden burst of electricity—snapped, sending a shower of sparks out from transformers around the inner core.

> Glow, little glow worm, fly afire.
> Glow like an incandescent wire.

Desperately trying to harness the power surge, Moe cut the power flowing into the inner core. Suddenly there was a tremendous explosion as a transformer blew out on the far side of the substation. Villagers screamed and beat it out of there, followed by more gunshots.

> This night could use a little brightenin'.
> Light up, you li'l old bug of lightnin'.

"Surrender!" Moe screamed at the gunmen. "Throw down your guns and come out."

Then he saw one of them—Ron Lindblad—climbing up a steel support pylon, gun in hand. What in the hell? Moe thought, trying to guess Lindblad's intentions. Was he trying to surrender? Reaching the top of the pylon, Lindblad took aim at Pia and Laszlo, who were cowering near a circuit breaker. Sid Bromley began to climb but was clearly having trouble. Moe could see blood streaming down his bald head.

Lindblad fired at Pia and Laszlo but missed. He secured his good leg—the one Pia hadn't kicked—around a steel cross-beam in the pylon and reached over the side of the pylon to help Bromley up.

"Enough is enough," Moe said, feeling cold, detached. He moved the arrow to the window labeled General Activation. Stealing a quick look at Pia and Laszlo, Moe saw that they were close to the circuit breaker but maybe far enough away to be out of danger. If they stayed where they were, they would be potted like ducks by the men on the pylon.

Little glow worm, turn the key on,
You are equipped with tail like neon.

Ron Lindblad, at the top of the support pylon, stretched out his hand for Sid Bromley, who was struggling up the pylon webbing, blood flowing freely from the gash in his head. Ron trained his Beretta at the kids hunkered down by the circuit breaker. If he couldn't get the others, he could at least get them. He felt Sid's fingers fluttering in his palm, and then Sid's hand grasping his.

Ron gripped Sid's hand just as Moe clicked the keyboard mouse for General Activation. In a sudden burst, 139,000 volts of electric current raged through the power lines and slammed into the transformers with tidal wave force. Electricity crackled around the substation, exploding circuit breakers and snapping power lines. Luminous electrical arcs—formed between the open breakers—rainbowed over the substation. Showers of sparks plumed and cascaded into the night sky.

When you gotta glow, you gotta glow,
Glow, little glow worm, glow.

Trapped at the top of the steel pylon, his hand clamped on Sid's, Ron watched in horror as Sid's mouth stretched wide and his eyes bulged and the thin hair around his temples burst into flames just before the current shuddered through his own body, twisting it around the pylon and igniting it in a sudden apocalyptic flash.

53

David had to strain over the sound of the pistons of his heart to listen for Jean Burke, lying in wait somewhere downstairs. He was on the floor near the top of the stairs, behind a clothes hamper ripe with the smell of perspiration and baby vomit. He had removed his shoes and socks so he could move quietly and surely on the hardwood floors. Von and Viveca, both deeply asleep, snored lightly under his chin.

David thought of hiding the kids somewhere upstairs, but decided against it. As a last resort, he could order them to run out the door and into the woods as he charged at Jean. Jean knew this house as well as her own. David enjoyed no advantages, other than that she didn't know where he was. Not yet, anyway.

The front door was on the opposite side of the long living room from the staircase. It was locked, he remembered, and it would take him maybe five seconds to get it open. The distance would work for him if Jean shot from the kitchen, the darkness protecting them and her fire attenuated by the silencer on her gun. He would keep his back to Jean, with the kids in front shielded by his body.

David's head shot up as he heard Jean walking in the kitchen, her feet crunching glass from the broken coffeepot. This was his chance to break for the door. He moved Viveca to his right arm with Von, giving him full use of his left hand. He rose to his feet and raced down the stairs, his chin tucked over the children's heads.

Darting through the blackness around computers, TVs, digital displays, David was almost halfway through the living room when he screamed in disbelief as the lights flared back on, blinding him momentarily. Blinking hard, he stumbled toward the door over his virtual-reality headset.

He heard Jean coming up behind him. "Stop!" she shrieked, but he kept moving to the door, loose silicon chips and circuit boards digging into his bare feet. At the door, the kids waking up, David fumbled with the lock. He snapped back the dead bolt and threw open the door, forgetting he had chained it.

"Shit," he yelled and then moved his hand up to the chain as part of the door exploded near his face, splinters flying as a bullet rocketed through it. Another shot split the middle of the door, barely missing him. David dropped to the floor and the room again went black.

On his knees, the children crying now, David crawled to the far wall behind a row of computer terminals, trying to keep his head together, calculating, anticipating. Curling up behind a CPU and monitor, he came face to face with the spike suppressor unit, its master switch controlling the house's legion of electronic devices. David stared for three long seconds at the switch, an idea forming in his fevered mind.

"What the hell?" he thought, and flipped the switch.

Just as suddenly as it had gone out, the electricity came back on, this time activating the twenty-two computers in the living room, as well as the eight televisions, the stereo and assorted CD players, lava lights, digital display panel, and illuminated speakers. Curled in a ball around the children, David kept his head down, marshaling his concentration on one goal: getting out of the house.

Jean stood in a crouch in the middle of the room, both hands on the Walther, searching desperately for David. The din and confusion were overwhelming, an electronic carnival coming at her from everywhere at once. She swept th gun over the room, keying on one distraction after anothe

On one TV was an old movie, *The Maltese Falcon,* co peting with loud rock music on MTV on another, wh was next to one with a beeping test pattern on top of one with the sports channel featuring luge racing

Switzerland. The computer screens bloomed with their own test patterns: fireworks displays, oscillating webs of color, shooting stars. Red digital letters raced past on a display bearing the message: TRASH COLLECTION DAY . . . REMEMBER TO RECYCLE!

The worst thing was the music—about eight or nine different tracks, all at high volume. Depending on what Jean concentrated on, she could hear rock 'n' roll, classical, big band, a weather report, and some strange late-night cult interview show.

As she prepared to fire at something, a new stimulus—a face from a screen, an exploding test pattern—would catch her attention. She opened her mouth wide to keep out the deafening noise.

"Where are you?" she screamed.

Jean whipped her head around as a voice behind her said, "Give them Cairo." It was Humphrey Bogart on TV, grinning maniacally at a nervous, sweating Peter Lorre. She aimed the Walther and fired it at Bogart, who seemed to implode at the bullet's impact. Then she fired another one at Chris Shenkel interviewing an Austrian luge racer, and at another one full of snowy static, leaving their screens shattered and black.

That was better.

She took aim at the stereo, snapping off rounds and silencing Artie Shaw doing "Smoke Gets in Your Eyes." With the children cradled in his arms, David crawled away from behind the computers just as Jean began firing at the machines. He tried to count her shots but gave up, channeling all his energy into figuring out a means of escape.

He slithered into the dining room, knees and elbows digging at the floor, trying to angle his way through the series of rooms and into the kitchen. He would try for the kitchen door, hoping that the confusion in the living room would continue to distract Jean. David crawled across a large square of the picture window illuminated on the floor. He kept wondering: What was causing these power fluctuations?

Back in the living room, Jean had destroyed a good number of the annoying machines before she had to load a new clip into the gun. She realized that David was not in there and began to move toward the dining room when the electricity went down and then up again, the music louder, the remaining TVs more distracting than ever.

"Stop it!" she screamed and began firing indiscriminately at anything with light on it, machinery ripped apart and left smoking by the gunshots. The living room grew quiet. Jean reloaded and moved on, determined to finish David now.

He was almost out of the dining room when he heard a sound he knew too well, the squeal of the motion-activated video camera mounted on the ceiling. It meant that Jean was coming his way.

He knew he'd never make it to the kitchen. She'd cut them all down before he got the door open. He looked around quickly, spying a cluster of computer equipment in the corner, stacked around his large disk array file server. David nestled the children behind two vertical steel monster cases that housed his redundant power backup system. Maybe the kids would make it, David thought. To the best of his knowledge, Jean didn't know he had them.

The massive file server—over two feet high, a foot and a half deep, and seventy pounds of boards, circuits, and disk drives in a steel case—loomed next to him. Damn thing was as heavy as a small car. Or a shield. *A shield.* David began desperately pulling jacks from the back of it, unhooking it from the networked computers and backup system.

Then a fuse blew and everything went off. Jean stood still for nearly a minute, waiting for the power to come back on. But it didn't. Good, she thought. She worked better in the dark. In a corner of the dining room, she spotted David flat on his belly like an animal, pulling plugs from computer equipment.

A curious thing to do just before he would die, Jean thought. She approached slowly, raising the Walther, taking aim.

David heard her footfall behind him. That was it. He knew she had him.

"Okay," he whispered, "you want me, you got me." Gr

ting his teeth, he took the file server in his hands and gathered his legs under him. He rose into a crouch, his legs tucked underneath him, his head and chest behind the file server, and began his charge straight at a startled Jean.

He heard the snap of the gun. "Unnh," he groaned as a bullet ricocheted off the edge of the server past his ear and into the plaster wall with a sucking sound. Jean, her trigger finger working, peeled off two more fast shots, each hitting the server dead center with a shudder. But David kept coming, blindly aiming the front edge of the steel case at her throat.

He caught her a little lower than he wanted, square in the chest, forcing the air from her lungs and driving her backward over a chair. They crashed through the picture window, David tumbling end over end, shards of glass showering his face. A high-pitched scream went through his ear like a spike and trailed off behind him. He saw the black sky for a half second before landing face first on the hard ground. A dull throb pulsed across his face and up his nose.

David lay still, fully expecting Jean to come for him. When she didn't, he stood up slowly, holding his head in his hands. Then he felt the blood leave his face as he looked up and saw Jean sprawled across the window ledge, a leg caught in the chair, and a shard of glass the shape of an icicle impaled in her throat. The gun was still in her hand, which dangled from her lifeless body.

David pulled the body off the ledge and climbed over it into the house. He found Von and Viveca weeping quietly behind the power backups where he had left them. He took them in his arms and huddled with them until Nara arrived at daybreak.

54

"Here," Nara said to David, "let me straighten that for you." She stood up on her toes and adjusted his tie, the first one he had willingly worn in, oh, maybe twelve years. He let his arms fall helplessly at his side as Nara tightened the tie, a ratty gray woolen one.

"There," she said, stepping back and looking at him. "That's better."

David turned toward the bathroom mirror and looked at himself. The tie was fine, as they go, but he couldn't help but notice his nose, still a bit red and bulbous after breaking it while wrestling with Jean Burke nearly a month ago. Nara said it made him look sexy. Moe said it made him look tough. David thought it looked broken, that's all.

Nara, now digging in her purse, wore a simple velvet floor-length hunter green gown and green suede pumps—a very subdued look for her. To David, she looked wonderfully elegant. He checked the alarm clock on the nightstand. It was nearly seven-thirty and the curtain was at eight. They were heading up to Augusta to see K. K. in the opening night of *Mother Courage*.

"So what is K. K. doing in this play?" David said, absently fondling his nose.

Nara looked up from her purse at him. "Do you mean, what role does she have?"

"Yeah, I guess."

"She's playing a character named Yvette Pottier, a young peasant woman who works as a prostitute during the Thirty Years' War."

"A prostitute?" David said, his voice rising half an octave.

Nara gave him a look. "So when did you become a Puritan? This is a key role in a distinguished play. K. K. was thrilled to get it. You should have been here when she ran over after getting the news. When I opened the door, she was yelling: 'I got the whore, I got the whore.' It was hysterical."

David shrugged, either not getting the joke or expressing displeasure with his tie, or both. "So how's she doing?" he asked, remembering the scene on his front porch, K. K. bleeding from knife wounds, her daughter's face smeared with blood.

Nara's voice was low, little more than a murmur. "Good. She looked good. She told me she's back at work, catching up with her classes, and can leave Viveca with a sitter. I think that was the hardest thing for her, leaving Viveca."

"And Viveca's okay?"

"Yeah. K. K. said she suffered from nightmares for a couple of weeks, but they went away."

David's gaze drifted over the bedroom and out a window at the gathering dark. He was still dealing with his own nightmares, which he claimed were converting him into a neophyte insomniac. They were essentially the same each time: a faceless intruder attacking him in his sleep. There were minor variations. Sometimes the attacker had a gun, other times a knife, or on one night the attack would take place at his old home in the Florida Keys and the next in Maine. But each time the sensations, the fears, were the same: claustrophobic darkness, swarming hands reaching for him, the metallic gleam of a knife or gun.

His eyes came to rest on the diaper hamper near the door. A long gush of air issued from his mouth as a memory flashed in his mind of Jean stalking him in her ski mask. He carried with him odd, vivid details of those moments of terror: the sting of carpet burn on his elbows and knees as he struggled to escape, the smell of K. K.'s blood in Viveca's hair, Von's runny nose. At least Von appeared to suffer no ill effects from that night, he thought. As terrible as that night was, David knew how much worse it could have been. He shut the thought down before it went any further.

"Are we ready?" Nara asked, checking something in her purse.

"I guess," David said, unsteady in hard leather shoes.

She took his arm as he led her down the steps. Stretched out on the living room floor were Moe, Pia, and Laszlo, the baby-sitters for the evening, punning with each other.

"I'd say you almost lost the family joules out there at that substation," Moe said. They all laughed.

"That would be shocking," Laszlo said in a falsetto voice, grabbing his crotch.

"You're revolting," Pia said, and they laughed again.

"Yeah," Moe said, "you should learn to conduct yourself."

They looked up as David and Nara descended the staircase, quietly respectful for a moment, and then broke into cheers and whistles.

Nara shushed them, reminding them that Von and Viveca were asleep upstairs. They settled down. "I've written down the number of the restaurant in Rockland we're taking K. K. to after the performance," she said. "And there's plenty of food in the refrigerator if you get hungry."

"What?" Laszlo said, cupping his hand to his ear. He still hadn't recovered his full hearing ever since his beating by Sid Bromley. David had brought in specialists who assured him that the hearing would come back on its own over time. Pia had suffered a couple of cracked ribs and, young and tough like Laszlo, she was bouncing back quickly.

"Food," Nara said directly to Laszlo. "In the refrigerator."

"Def," he said happily.

Pia looked up at David and Nara. "Do you mind if I stay over tonight?" she said. "I promised Viveca I'd do her hair like mine tomorrow."

David winced as he took in Pia's *kuncho*—shaved head and tangle of braids in the back.

Pia caught the look. "Oh, don't worry," she said reproachfully, "I'm just going to braid it."

"Why do you want to stay here?" David said. "You don't like your new place?" He was, of course, kidding her. Pia, her family, and some of the other forest dwellers were now living in the Lindblad house, which David had bought from Norma Lindblad's next of kin—a second cousin—and had it converted in to a luxury bed and breakfast. Pia's parents were the resident managers. She'd never had it so good.

"Oh, it's all right, I guess," she said, deadpan. "The tennis courts do need to be resurfaced, and the riding trails are terribly overgrown."

"Brave of you to suffer through it," David said. "Well, we're off," he announced.

"Hey, I heard Barb Bromley's trial ended today," Moe said.

Nara's journalist's ears pricked up immediately. "So what happened?" she asked. David frowned and made a show of looking at his watch.

"Guilty," Moe answered. "On all counts of conspiracy and fraud."

Laszlo and Pia smiled and nodded, quietly satisfied at the news.

"Sentencing is tomorrow," Moe said. "They say she's looking at four to eight years in South Windham. She'll probably be out in two."

It occurred to David that one bit of luck coming out of the whole mess was that all the media attention following the killings and the scandals focused on Ron Lindblad and Moe, the latter of whom emerged as the big hero following his pyrotechnics at the substation. David and Nara had come away unscathed, out of the public eye, just the way David wanted it. At least they didn't have to move.

David tapped Nara on the shoulder. "If we leave now, we'll just make—"

"South Windham," Nara said. "That's where they sent Al Cheseldine, the former president of the electrical utility. And some of the Jiffy Cleaners folks are there, the ones who weren't convicted of federal crimes and sent out of state. They should all have a good time there, keeping each other company."

"I can't believe that some of our own were helping Lindblad, even cleaning up the carnage for him," Pia said.

"He gave them special privileges," David said, pulling on his tie. "They probably got free Country Customs calendars." He clapped his hands. "Okay, time to hit the road."

"Did the police find all the bodies?" Pia asked.

"No," Moe said, shaking his head gravely. "There are still a few unaccounted for. They think Jean Burke dumped them somewhere like Penobscot Bay or up in the bog country. They found a lot of mud all over her lorry."

"I hear they found bones in an incinerator behind Country Customs," Laszlo contributed. "That's where Jiffy Cleaners got rid of bodies. Police matched some teeth with Norma Lindblad's dental records. Others they haven't yet identified."

"You know," Nara said, "I wonder what will happen to all the houses Barb Bromley stole in Sparks. She couldn't just keep them, could she? I'll bet we could pick them up for a song and rent them to the people we're keeping in motels, the rest of the forest people."

David nodded his head enthusiastically. "Yeah. Or we could sell them at low interest rates, just like Jimmy Stewart did in *It's a Wonderful Life*. What was the name of that neighborhood where he built the houses?"

"Don't get started," Nara said, pushing him toward the door. "We have to get going."

"Great idea," David said dryly.

"If you're staying here tonight," Moe said to Pia, "will you make it in to work tomorrow? That new demographic software you ordered is supposed to come in."

Pia, who was now assistant vice-president of marketing for the new Country Customs Company, curled down a corner of her lower lip. "Don't worry, Mr. Bill Gates," she retorted. "I'll be there."

"Good," said David, who now owned the company and had hired the forest dwellers to run it for him. Rajinder Singh, Moe's father and an industrial engineer, was president.

"Besides," she added, "I'm not sure I can stay here."

Nara bumped David with her hip. "Of course you can stay, Pia," she said. "Anytime."

"David," Moe said meekly, "would you mind if we used your disk array file server and a couple of computers to beta-test a new network software I wrote?"

David gave him his hardest look, using his broken nose to great effect. "This is the deal," David said. "You can use the file server if you agree to . . . repair five of the computers stored in the basement." These were some of the computers Jean had destroyed on her rampage. Miraculously, the file server still worked perfectly despite taking a couple of rounds from Jean's gun. David's counter-offer to Moe was ridiculously one-sided, but David hated to repair things.

Moe paused a minute, considering. "If I can use the file server for three more beta-tests, you have a deal."

"Done," David said.

"Well, we're off," Nara said. Passing one of the floor speakers, she switched on the baby monitor on top of it. David stood for a long minute looking at the monitor. He smiled at her, walked over, and turned it off. He had refused to use the monitor ever since hearing the Haslem family on it.

"I don't think we need this anymore," he said.

Nara frowned, paused a moment, and said, "Let's go outside."

David and Nara stepped out onto the front porch and closed the door. Moe, Pia, and Laszlo looked at each other and then scrambled merrily to the window, anticipating a fight. They first heard Nara and then David and then Nara again through the door. Even with their ears trained toward the window, they could hear only the voices and not the words.

"What's going on?" Laszlo said, a little loudly.

"Sssh!" Pia and Moe said at once.

They jumped back into their chairs as the door swung open. Nara came in smiling, switched on the baby monitor, and walked out.